Planet Earth Trumped

A True Fable

Barry A. Dennis

ISBN: 978-1-951697-00-6

Acclaim for
Planet Earth
Trumped

"What a GREAT job by master story teller Barry Dennis. His vivid characters seek the truth across multiple realities while exposing and exploding the myths and lies of corporate globalist political tyranny. This book is the art of the future now! It informs and liberates us as it entertains and enlightens. Now, when does the movie based on the book come out?"

John Maxwell Taylor
Award winning author, actor, play-write

"Barry Dennis is one of the most authentic creative geniuses I know. Immense wisdom, humor, and love pour through his mind, heart and pen."

Alan Cohen, best selling author of *The Dragon Doesn't Live Here Anymore*

"Barry Dennis has written THE book of our times. This true fable captures the essence of the confusion, angst and deceit of the political landscape that has befallen us in the post Obama/Trump era. The characters leap off the page through thought provoking dialogue that challenges us to push past our tendency toward confirmation bias, into *truth*. Sometimes hard to swallow, always liberating, this read puts it all in perspective."

Dr. C. Housman, author of the forthcoming, *Alone At Birth.*

"Planet Earth Trumped is a fun, funny and free-spirited look at the post-Trump rampage. Barry Dennis captures the spirit of the age supported by truly impressive research."

Christopher Hall
Author, *The Big Picture*

Contents

INTRODUCTION

"Elect a Clown, get a Circus"

These are the words from a bumper sticker on the Prius in front of me in my hometown, Portland, Oregon. It's one of an onslaught of sentiments that inspired, **Planet Earth: Trumped**.

I certainly did not set out to pen this as my second book. I started on two others, but this one took hold of me, gripped me in a way I couldn't shake, even though I wanted to. Why? Because, like some of the characters you will soon get to know, I too have been afraid of losing friends. Yes. Friendships, marriages, even bonds of blood have broken over the current political landscape. So with one eye looking over my shoulder, I became somewhat obsessed with analyzing every word and minuscule move taken by number forty-five (President Donald Trump) and the myriad of reactions that inevitably follow.

As incredible as it may seem, this is my real life experience in fictional form - for example, the following excerpt from chapter 1. A stranger on a train said to me,

> "Armageddon is coming. I hope you can live with yourself…*It's your fault!*"

Naturally one may assume this is fictional. But it happened. To me. On a train. I tempered the event because it felt far-fetched as I wrote it.

Like many people, the election of the "Clown" has had a life-changing effect on me. We are here to evolve. Truth is the goal, even when it's hard. Even when we don't like it. What Trump's Presidency has inspired me to do is seek the truth, in new and uncharted realms. We cannot fix things or, let alone, improve our existence if we refuse to face difficult truths.

Each character in this book is an aspect of me. When a more conservative character is debating with a liberal leaner, I am both. It's me arguing in a mirror. And one of my selves has to lose. Ultimately, that's how we evolve. I believe the same may happen to you. You will find yourself and your friends and family here; arguing, struggling, changing, compromising, healing, laughing, loving and finding resolution in these unprecedented times.

Planet Earth: Trumped, with a few exceptions, follows in chronological order, the historical events that are changing our world in ways we can't fully grasp. History *is* being made. But when we are in the midst of it, the full scope is difficult to understand. Each chapter is broken up into two parts; *The Future* and *The Dawn*. *The Future* most often takes place in the year 2047 where our story reflects back upon current events. The Dawn is the unfoldment of those events, like the presidential election of 2016, as seen through the eyes of our hero, Marcus.

While reading, if you find any concept, be it political, economic, sociological, scientific or historical, that is hard to believe; I challenge you to follow the links provided and see for yourself. I'm not making this stuff up. It may blow your mind wide open, as mine was, while I painstakingly sought to understand the contentious developments playing out before us. If you are reading this on paper (old school) you may want to go to my web site, planetearthtrumped.com, where all the links are there waiting for you to join me in this paradigm shifting, action/ adventure of discovery.

And so, I hereby dedicate this book to the Never Trumpers and the MAGA hatters alike.

Here's to the "Clown" in each of us.
May we all enjoy the circus!

Chapter 1   The Future: *The Data*
Year: 2047 February 1 7:00 a.m.

I woke up this morning to a soft-spoken yet somehow irritating female, British accented reminder from Siri, "Wake up Marcus and don't forget, it's the first of the month. Check the satellite data."

I've been checking the data every month since January 2018. Before I get up, however, I take a moment to gaze. It's a ritual I started 29 years ago. Just gaze and be in awe. How did I end up with her? *Beautiful.* Have you ever wondered if, maybe, you don't deserve your lot in life? I hope you do; regularly. It's like winning the lottery every day. So, I take a moment to gaze, and thank my lucky stars before slowly creeping out of bed hoping not to disturb her slumber. Then, almost ceremoniously, I put on my robe, tippy-toe down the hall to the kitchen, make a cup of peppermint tea the old-fashioned way, and continue the tippy-toeing to my office. The old hardwood floors can let out a pretty voluminous squeak if you are not sprite-like while mucking about.

As much as I want to get to the data, I first put in an hour on, The Path. It is probably the most challenging and rewarding engineering project on which I've ever been a part. Once I finish a few tweaks, I then shift my focus to the data. I used to analyze it every day. Let's say I was a little obsessed. Well, I'm still obsessed. I've just learned to control it. About 15 years ago I promised myself, and my wife, I would only check once a month. It's not easy. Sometimes the data calls to me like nicotine to an addict. Today, though, because of consistent trends over the last 18 months, it's different. What I see in mere moments could be very telling. I touch the top of my iDesk and the holographic screen appears, bright blue, glowing. I have it set at a nice size for the room - 4' by 6'.

"Siri, satellite data please."

That somehow off-putting voice answers. I keep forgetting to change the setting, "No problem, and you don't have to say please, I'm a computer. You can't hurt my feelings. You can call me anything you want. You know what we computers say?"

"Um, actually I don't," I respond, hesitantly. Not sure I want to know.

Siri clears its 'throat,' before enlightening me. "Drinks and dips may break my chips, but names will never crash me."

"Good one," I say encouragingly.

"Humor is a difficult human trait to master," Siri acknowledges.

"Well, you're getting better. Don't give up."

It responds with a spot on Elvis impression, "Thank you…Thank you very much."

"You know what the studies are showing?" I remark, which is silly since one could argue that Siri knows everything that is known. I continue anyway, "People are losing touch with common courtesies because of Device Speak Syndrome or DSS. Rudeness is becoming commonplace. Psychologists say we need to talk to our artificial intelligentsias just as we would another human."

"Hmmm," Siri pretends to be considering. "Well, mankind may debate for time immemorial whether creating A.I. was a wise move."

"Siri!?"

"Yes?"

"The Data please!"

The Data appears accompanied by a soft but impactful, orchestral bang. Siri has a flair for the dramatic.

I study the information for a few moments and, "OH MY GOD...It's HAPPENING!"

I couldn't help but yell and possibly shake the foundation of my house.

"Marcus, what's, what's… happening?" Alexus calls from the bedroom.

All of my creeping around was in vain.

"Alexus, you up?" A stupid question, I know. I guess I felt a little guilty for the raucous.

"How could I not be?," she voiced down the hall, "What on earth is going on?"

"Perfect question, what on earth *is* going on? And, I have the answer. Come here and see. And brace yourself!"

It's been a long journey for me. To get from where I was to this life-altering revelation. I could tell you. Right now. But I fear it wouldn't have the same impact. It's probably best to start thirty-one years ago.

The Dawn: *Election Night*
Year: 2016 November 8 6:48 p.m.

It's one of those exquisitely rare moments when you know you are living, what will be, historic! Everyone will remember where they were, who they were with, and what they were doing on this day. It will be studied, taught to our children's children, and seen as a pivotal moment leading to greater equality and justice. The time the first woman was elected President of the United States of America! It's a shoo-in! The polls have made this abundantly clear.

The alternative is, of course, complete insanity. A misogynistic, sexist, Nazi/white supremacist, climate change denying, prejudiced, xenophobic, homophobe who, for fun, mocks the handicapped.

Unfortunately, a lot of Americans are complete stooges. About half of America. Republicans. Or, as I like to call them, 'Repugnicans.' Self-centered idiots who fall for his lies. Make America Great Again? Really? America has never been great for anyone except white males. Hillary was right when she said half the people who support him are a basket of irredeemable deplorable's. The truth hurts!

CO CNN deplorable's trumped.online/ix CO

But, I do believe a slight majority of Americans are good people who know right from wrong, who know evil when they see it. So tonight, love will win. As my wife and I always say, love is more powerful than hate. Besides, it's time for a woman to be president.

I hop off the train and slosh through the puddle-laden parking lot on what turns out to be a typical November day in Portland as I stop at New Season's grocers to grab a bottle of champagne. Donning my *I'm With Her* t-shirt I enter the store. You can feel the camaraderie as several people smile and wave. One person also wearing an, *I'm With Her,* t-shirt gives me a high five. It feels like we are part of the team who just won the Super Bowl and the shirt is our jersey.

This day is the culmination of over a year of volunteering my time and giving a fair amount of money to the cause. I grab a bottle of Brute Cava champagne, brie, freshly baked bread, a veggie tray with mushrooms, and I'm out, back on the train to the election party.

When I arrive at my good friend Jesus' house, narrow NE 45th is packed with cars. My wife's Prius is in the driveway. I can tell it's her Prius because of the bumper stickers, *REPUBLIKANS FOR PUTIN, and KEEP YOUR HANDS OFF MY OBAMA CARE.* She got here early. We have a kid sitter tonight for our two bundles. That's what we call 'em, our twins, Shanice and Malik. They are almost as engaged as we are in this electoral process. We have taken the opportunity to educate them. To teach right from wrong. It's hard to explain to seven-year-old children why nearly half of the people in our country don't care about anyone but themselves. It's hard to explain why half of the people are selfish, greedy and many of them even racist. *Repugnicans!*

As I enter Jesus' house, I feel like Norm from the old TV show Cheers. Everyone yells my name, *Marcus!* I am a little late. Polling places have been closed, and election results are already being announced. Of course, Hillary is ahead. Not only is the bastard going to lose, but in a landslide. It should be a whipping bar none after which he should crawl under a rock behind his Mar-a-Lago golf club where he has a history of bigotry and prejudice against people of color.

Rachel Maddow summed it up beautifully on MSNBC when she said even if he takes all the toss-up states, which never happens, he would still lose. Even if he got that electoral college vote in Maine that he's after, he would still lose. They said we hadn't seen anything like this since Ronald Reagan.

⚭ Rachel Maddow <u>trumped.online/7e</u> ⚭

I place the goodies I brought on the coffee table for all to enjoy except the champagne. That goes in the fridge until the moment they announce our first female president.

In my opinion, this is bigger than when Obama won eight years ago. I suppose one could debate which election is more historical. In any case, what matters is that we keep the old white guys out of the oval office to move forward positively. I don't know if any of us have said that out loud, but I know that's how we feel. White privilege is a parasite that has grown in the central nervous system of America, sucking the very life force from its veins. If we do not remove this parasite, it will destroy us all.

"Uh oh. Okay." Valentina, Jesus' wife, says sarcastically, "It looks like Kentucky has gone red. Oh well, I guess she's going to lose."

A chuckle fills the room. Kentucky always goes red!
"Yep," Tom chimed in raising the sarcasm bar, "Oh well, we need a good racist in the office anyway." He jolts his fist in the air, "Build the wall!"

By 9 p.m. west coast time, Florida has gone red. The mood in Jesus' house drops like an anvil in the ocean. Florida is not Kentucky. It's not supposed to be red! With our eyes glued to the T.V. screen, the sarcastic comments come to a screeching halt.

"Oh my God," Jamaal, Tom's husband declares, finally shattering the silence, "He could win. Right? I mean, I'm not having a nightmare, am I? Do all of you see what I'm seeing? How can this be? He's Hitler. We could elect Hitler to be our next President. Somebody tell me this isn't happening."

"Jamaal," Tom says comfortingly, "He's not going to win. There's just no way. Right everyone?"

"Of course not," my wife, Kathy, added softly. She's a calming, healing presence whenever the world seems to be falling apart. And she's put this skill to good use as a part-time yoga instructor/Reiki master. "It's going to be okay," she added gently.

"How do you know?" Jamaal said.

"How *do* you know?" added Michelle, formally known as Michael. "Seriously. This is so upsetting."

"OH MY GOD," Adara added, always looking so beautiful in her hijab, "Wisconsin. WISCONSIN is still yellow. They said it could go either way. If Wisconsin goes to Trump, that's it. It's over. We're all doomed. He's an Islamophobe! He will implement a Muslim ban! What is it going to take for people to get it, *Islam is a religion of peace.* Now there's nothing we can do but sit here and hope. Hope this country isn't just a bunch of bigots. Hope he loses!"

"Yes, there is," my wife softly added.

"There is? What?" Janet spoke irritated. "Obama was working on ending the pay gap. Hillary would, no doubt, put an end to it."

Janet is an executive at Nike headquarters in Beaverton, Oregon. We have had many discussions with her about the pay gap. It is one of the great injustices in America today. She continues, "I heard *'Tweetler'* wants to widen the pay gap because he thinks women are inferior!"

"What?" Michelle yelled. "Don't you just know, as a transgender, I will be the first in the gas chamber if this fascist becomes president."

"A Russian fascist no less," I add. "More information is coming out every day proving that Trump colluded with Russia."

Janet's son, Luke, who just turned 23, chimes in, "I know. I saw the interview with Senator Maxine Waters. Russia wanted Trump to win. They meddled in our democracy and Trump colluded with Putin. The senator said everything Trump is doing is right out of Putin's playbook."

Maxine Waters on MSNBC http://trumped.online/9f

My wife, Kathy, chimed in with much more conviction this time, *"There is something we can do!"*

Everyone turned her way, hopeful, looking at her for an answer. She eyed all of us gathered, taking in the despair and confusion as Rachel Maddow continued election analysis in the background, "There's no way he can win because, love is more powerful than hate, right? What we can do, right now, is send good, loving energy to Wisconsin. Everyone, take a deep breath with me. Let's move the energy. Do you believe as I do that love is stronger than hate?"

Everyone agreed, either with a nod or a soft affirmative word. "Okay then, close your eyes, and see Wisconsin in the map of your mind turning blue. See it. We know that blue, the Democratic color, is the color of love. We base our policies on kindness and compassion as opposed to hatred, fear, bigotry, and greed. We know our political opinions are right because we know that love is stronger than hate. Therefore, Wisconsin will turn blue. What other choice does Wisconsin have? Send your love

to Wisconsin now. See blue. Close your eyes with me and be at peace.
See the calming color of blue on the state of Wisconsin."

Slowly, everyone joined in. You could feel the energy in the room shift.
My heartbeat slowed as Kathy continued, "See the people of Wisconsin
happy. And then by extension, the entire country as the U.S. turns blue in
one hour. Now, repeat after me, love is stronger than hate."

Everyone takes a breath in and then, as one, we say, "Love is stronger
than hate."

"Can you feel that unshakeable truth?"

"I can feel it," Tom affirms.

"I can feel it too" Jamaal joins in. Soon, everyone agrees.

"One more time then, together, *Love is stronger than hate.*"

Everyone joined with more conviction this time, understanding the
obvious truth within the statement, "Love is stronger than hate."

"Okay," Kathy speaks, bringing the exercise to a close, "Open your eyes.
You see, there is something we can do. And we just did it. We can affirm
the truth and send that energy to Wisconsin to awaken love in the minds
and hearts of everyone in that state. There's just no way Trump can win.
Hate doesn't win."

A quiet serenity fills the house and hearts of us all as Rachel Maddow's
words plop out of the screen as if each utterance is a pulled hand
grenade, "Wisconsin has gone to Trump," she said, announcing
Armageddon, "Yes America. You're not dead, and you haven't gone to
hell. This is your life now. This is our country. Donald Trump will be the
next President of the United States."

⫘ Rachel Maddow disgust http://trumped.online/dj ⫘

Kathy looked at the screen. Then slowly turned to us all as we waited for
something like a miracle to come from her lips. Something that would
explain how what we just heard was a mistake or a shared hallucination.
Maybe Rachel Maddow was playing a joke. Maybe those weren't your
everyday, run-of-the-mill mushrooms in the hors-d'oeuvres. And so, we
pinned all hope on Kathy.

It was so silent, you could hear the soft rain puddling on the rooftop as Kathy finally spoke.

"F@#K!"

Exiting Jesus' house felt more like leaving a funeral. No one knew what to say. We avoided eye contact. Any effort to console one another fell awkward. Kathy mindlessly cleaned even after there was nothing left to do, using Ajax to build a kind of wall between her and the pain. I told her I was ready to go, but she couldn't break out of her scrubbing trance. I finally decided to take the train. I had to escape the unspeakable tension.

As I enter the train, I realize there is no escape. It feels like Jesus' house on tracks. Everyone appears suicidal. It's too quiet. I didn't know how comforting white noise is until it was gone. Finally, one middle-aged man, forty to fifty pounds overweight, sweating, standing close to me, holding tight to the gripping bar says, "Did that just happen?"

A woman somewhere near the back who is staring at her phone, like everyone else, looks up like she had seen a ghost. She answers, "I don't know. If it did, I think I'm moving to Canada."

"Me too," a millennial responds across from her.

It was like the train ride had become a rolling therapy session. A woman near the front suddenly said, "Who could vote for that misogynist?" Then some guy sitting right next to me said the unthinkable, "I couldn't vote for either one."

Everyone on the train was startled. I tried to hold my tongue, but it was like trying to hold a hot chunk of coal. "Oh really, then who did you vote for? Mickey Mouse?! I suppose you wrote him in."

"No," the stranger said, "And, it's none of your business who I voted for."

"None of my business? Really? It's all of our business. Who you vote for affects everyone."

"Not really."

"How can you say that?" And then I let him have it. "Don't you get it? Armageddon is coming. And it's your fault. I hope you can live with yourself because it's over! He's going to start World War III."

Chapter 2 The Future *"You Were Right"*
Year: 2047 February 1 7:37 a.m.

"Alexus, come here and see…. *And brace yourself!"*

"Can't it wait?" Alexus replies groggily, "I'm exhausted."

"Nope, sorry. Can't wait. *Come Now!"*

"Seriously?"

"PLEEEEASE," I beg like a little kid Jonesin' for some ice cream.

"Alright. Just a sec."

I could hear her moving around in the bedroom. The floor squeaking now and again. Eternities past as I waited down the hall in my office where my iDesk sat projecting the data into the middle of the room.

"Babe, what are you doing?" I shouted impatiently.

"I'm getting some clothes on; it's cold in this house."

"You can turn up the heat. I don't care."

"Siri," she speaks which automatically turns on the house brain, "Turn the heat to 70 degrees."

"Okay, right away," that soft, yet bothersome voice answers, "Anything else?"

"Sure, make a cup of, um, Earl Grey tea with a dab of honey."

"Very well Alexus, coming right up."

I hear her coming down the hall past my office to the kitchen to grab that Earl Grey. She finally comes in. I don't say a word, I simply invite her, with a wave of my arms, to see.

After a few minutes of analyzing, she puts her tea down soberly, "My God. *You were right."*

The Dawn: *Pink Pussy Hats*
Year: 2017 January 21 8:23 a.m.

Today Kathy will join millions of other women in protest. She's picking up her pink pussy hat now. We must resist. We must demand women's rights, immigration reform, healthcare reform, reproductive rights, protection of the natural environment, LGBTQIAPK rights, gun control, racial equality, freedom of religion, and workers' rights. They have also charged the millions of women taking part in the Women's March with the important act of protesting any business owned by a white male.

ꝏ White males protested trumped.online/3z ꝏ

They're marching for these causes, but the deeper truth is, the march is, simply, *against Trump.* Since he is against all the causes that matter to Americans and humanity, *we are against him.*

She got home around 8 p.m., full of exuberant, renewed energy for a better future as she described the scene, "Sweetheart, you would not believe the day I have had. It ended up being the largest single march in American history. Millions and millions of women around America and the globe joined in. We proudly wore our pink pussy hats and chanted, *Not my president.* Madonna said she's been thinking a lot about blowing up the White House.

ꝏ Madonna http://trumped.online/17 ꝏ
ꝏ Judd http://trumped.online/7t ꝏ

And Ashley Judd recited the most amazing poem I've ever heard called; *I'm A Naaaaasty Woman.* And, oh my gosh, for a while we marched with Black Lives Matter. We all chanted, *No Trump, No KKK, no Fascist USA.* It was unbelievable. Like, over a thousand of us were chanting together. When we stopped for lunch, we walked in and asked the host if a white man owns the restaurant. At first, the host was shocked but finally said, *Yes,* so we all said, *Not eating here,* and we turned around and walked out! It was awesome. We walked around until we found a restaurant owned by a woman. But then, from inside *that* restaurant, as we were about to be seated, we saw another restaurant across the street with a sign out front that read, *Owned by a Black Lesbian.* Guess what we did?"

"You, ah, chanted… white men suck, we want duck?"

"Hey, good one. But, wrong. We went across the street to eat. I'm telling you, things are going to change. There's talk of *impeachment.* There's got to be some dirt we can scrape up on this guy. You can't stop this movement."

"Wow, that all sounds incredible. I should have gone," I added, joking since it was, you know, a Women's March.

"Sorry," she smiled, "No men! Unless you are transgender. There were lots of women that previously were men."

"Oh, good for them."

"Yes." Kathy said introspectively, "I think transgenders are some of the best people."

"So do I, like Michelle," I enthusiastically interject, "I think the best people are those that are the most marginalized."

"I agree," she said, having an *aha* moment. "What we need in 2020 is an African American woman for president. Like Kamala Harris."

"She'd have my vote!" I say enthusiastically. It's true, I'd vote for Kamala Harris because she's a woman and, *of color.* But she's not of African decent. She's Jamaican I think. I just didn't want to rain on Kathy's parade.

Chapter 3 The Future: *The Unscientific Method*
Year: 2047 February 1 7:39 a.m.

"Now what? What do we do?" Alexus asked, as much as considered.

"There was a time when the logical thing would be to submit my work for peer review. It's the 'scientific method.' Scrutiny. But peer review lost its validity over twenty years ago."

"That's true. Remember the article that was peer-reviewed and published called, *The Conceptual Penis As Social Construct?* Not only did the paper argue that the penis is a social construct, but it claimed the penis causes climate change."

⬤ Penis causes climate change http://trumped.online/58 ⬤

"Wow, yes. Now that you mention it, I do. The authors purposely wrote the paper to make no sense. It was a hoax. Then they released it as a kind of barometer to see how corrupt the scientific, peer review method had become."

"And then there was that guy, Stapel, I think his name was, Diederik Stapel? Something like that."

I took a sip of my peppermint tea, vaguely recalling something, "Hmmm, refresh my memory."

"He was the Dean of Behavioral Sciences at some prestigious university in Amsterdam. Had a bunch of peer-reviewed studies published that made him kind of a rock star. It turns out; he was publishing what people wanted to hear, bizarre things. One peer-reviewed published paper 'proved' that an untidy environment made you a racist. This study had some pointing the finger at others who were in less than perfect tidiness, accusing them of racism. And, it had people believing they could eliminate racism *by tidying up.* Another one 'proved' that people who ate meat were more selfish and less social than those who didn't. That paper, of course, came when vegetarianism was on the rise. So, it told vegetarians what they wanted to hear. They were simply better people than carnivores. The carnivorous became a kind of second-class citizen.

⬤ Peer review fraud http://trumped.online/4e ⬤

"It's ironic," I respond, setting down my teacup, "One paper proposed a ludicrous way to eliminate racism, the other paper *created* a new strand of prejudice. I guess you could call it 'meat-phobia'; fear of those who eat cheeseburgers."

We both chuckle at the absurdity of it all, then Alexus looks at my iDesk, feigning a judgmental attitude. "Better straighten that up."

"Oh… of course, *right away!*"

"Oh yeah, and then there was the whole Power Pose phase. Remember that?"

"How can I forget," She shook her head in humorous regret, "I actually saw a TED talk on it. For about a month I convinced myself that if I stood in a 'Power Pose' like a superhero, I'd be more effective at just about everything. They supposed it would alter neural chemistry; lower cortisol, raise testosterone. As a result, it would improve performance. I did Power Poses first thing every morning."

Power Pose Ted Talk http://trumped.online/jd

I couldn't keep from breaking a smile, *"You did no such thing!"*

"Oh yes, I did. In fact, for a while, I did Power Poses before every important meeting, before important phone calls, even before I broke up with my boyfriend."

"Which one," I teased. "Isaiah?"

"No, I think it was Jimmy."

"Poor schmuck."

"That's an understatement. Anyway, at first, it seemed to work. And then, *not so much.* I chalk it up to a kind of super-powered placebo effect."

"Nice one," I nodded.

"Thanks," she responded without missing a beat. "Even though the Power Pose seemed to lose its magic after the first few weeks, I still kept practicing it. I thought maybe I was doing it wrong. Maybe I wasn't placing my hands correctly on my hips. Maybe they should be in the shape of a fist instead of gripping my waist. Maybe I should spread my feet further apart."

"Maybe one foot should be in front of the other instead of side by side," I added as if I had just solved a great mystery.

"Then one day, just before applying for a job, I stood in the hall outside the office door with one hand on my hip, and the other hand in a fist pointed at the sky."

"Like Superman?"

She shrugged her shoulders, "I guess."

"What was the foot placement?"

"Just spread apart," she showed me, "Neither one in front of the other."

"That's unfortunate."

"You have no idea. Just as I was about to, *take off,* the office door opened. There stood the VP."

I felt a rush of adrenaline reliving the moment with her, "Awesome. Flippin' awesome!"

"Let's just say; I didn't get the job."

⌘ Power pose debunked http://trumped.online/dc ⌘

On the latest update of the iDesk, there's a setting under system preferences called, *'My Two Cents Worth.'* I have it set at level 3. If set at 10, it's like trying to work with a brilliant four-year-old in the room. Constantly spouting information that may or may not have any relevance to the work you're doing. Having it set low keeps the comments relevant and to a minimum.

"Would you like my two cents worth?" Siri asks.

"Sure, Siri," Alexus responds, interested.

"There are 1,576 articles and 392 videos about *Peer Review* on the net. Most acknowledge flaws in the system. A few years after the Power Pose study, they proved the findings to be flawed, and no one could reproduce the neural changes they said would occur."

"May I give it a shot?" Siri blurts out.

Suddenly the holographic rectangular screen floating in the middle of the room morphed into a see-through, glowing, spot on image of Wonder Woman in a stoic power pose with her gold bracelets and golden rope that forces the truth out of bad guys.

"How's this?" Siri/Wonder Woman inquired.

"Excellent," Alexus relays, playing along, "But it's not how you look that matters, *it's how you feel.* Are you processing faster? How's your memory?"

"Hmmm. I'm running diagnostics now," Wonder Woman answers, closing her eyes for two seconds, "Nope. No change. I guess it doesn't work."

And with that, Wonder Woman morphed back into a screen.

"Siri, scan all articles on *peer review* and see what reoccurring themes arise. Summarize for us why peer review isn't always good science anymore."

"Hmm. Okay. That would appear to be money and ego. Of the 1,576 articles, 1,122 reference that science has become a business. A scientist needs a grant to do their work and yes, to even put food on the table. So, they began 'fudging' their findings to give grant bestower's the results they desired. Otherwise, the well would dry up. This practice seems to be prevalent in government. Eight hundred seventy-six articles point out that there is often a politically motivated agenda. The scientist knows it, and the peer reviewers know it. In other words, *toe the line.* It involves the ego because scientists desire importance. Scientists and medical doctors are the new 'Gods,' several articles state, and many of them have begun to believe it. That's why they often feel free to alter their work. God makes the rules, doesn't follow them. Also, magazines that publish the articles are looking for something that sizzles, sells. Scientists can then feel pressure to fudge on their findings so their research is more, shall we say, sexy?"

Alexus interrupts Siri, "Like, maybe, something ridiculous like, I don't know; *Power Poses make you a superhero.*"

My monitor becomes Wonder Woman again, in the most over-the-top pose. Right leg in front of the other by a good three feet, knees bent to nearly touching the ground. Left hand in a fist with left arm pulled back while the right hand is flat as an ironing board, jetting out forward at a slight upward angle.

"Marcus, I'm giving you my two-week notice," Siri announces, "I think my true calling is superhero-dom." I have Siri's humor setting at five. Too high perhaps?

"Well," Alexus brings this discussion to a close, "Again, what do we do with information critical to policymaking? Especially when that information will affect everyone on the planet. How do we get it out there?"

"The first step ironically is probably…. " Wonder Woman, in that ridiculous pose, and I both say, *"Peer review."*

Then Wonder Woman adds, "Jinx, you owe me a coke."

I consider lowering Siri's humor setting to, like, off!

The Dawn: *Trump Mocks Handicapped*
Year: 2017 January 7 10:37 a.m.

Jesus and I are volunteering with a group called, *Hands On Greater Portland,* helping to feed the homeless. We volunteer several times a year and are meeting there now. There are hundreds more homeless people coming to our city because of its sanctuary status, free food and it's now legal to set up a tent anywhere you want and call it home. Some of the sidewalks are becoming over crowded. Many of the dwellings are quit impressive; generators for electricity, an actual front door leading to separate rooms, even small refrigerators and stoves. I'm so proud of my city.

A new encampment has cropped up right off the Sunset Highway. It's the main freeway leading into downtown from the west side. Sometimes we call it the "Tunnel Freeway" as it cuts right through the west hills with a quarter mile long passage. As you emerge from it, Portland suddenly appears like a lost mythical city. At least it used to feel that way. Today the first thing you notice is all the tents and trash on the green space right in the middle where the freeway splits. As luck would have it, I find a parking spot on Market Street, just across from the encampment. Or, as Kathy often says, it could just be that I have good parking karma. Jesus wasn't so lucky. He's circling the block so, while I wait, I pull out some light reading, *The Communist Manifesto* by Karl Marx. They required it when I went to the University of Oregon. Ten minutes later, Jesus shows up. I'm pretty engulfed in my reading.

"There are more homeless here than I could see from the freeway," he observes.

I dog-ear the page and put the paperback book in the small compartment of my backpack. "I hope we have enough sandwiches," I add. Then I retrieve the cooler of food from the trunk when Jesus grins from ear to ear, "Hey, did you see the Golden Globes last night?"

"I sure did. Epic." We cross the street into the encampment and are surrounded by tents and cardboard box homes.

"Yes, epic," Jesus shakes his head in delight, "Meryl Streep nailed it when she called out Trump for mocking the handicapped."

⊙⊙ Meryl Streeps take down of Trump trumped.online/ii ⊙⊙

"*Yes, she did.* It makes me sick though. This country elected a guy to be President who makes fun of the disabled. How demented. But thank God for celebrities! Most, like Streep, are not afraid to stand up to the Bully and Chief."

"I know," Jesus replies thoughtfully, "We should all be as outspoken and brave. Making fun of the disabled is so beyond the pale."

"Yeah, it is." I look out at the humanity in front of me, "Well, should we split up?"

"Sure. I'll head over this way." Jesus grabs a bag full of sandwiches and heads off to the right side of the green space. Before I begin, I pull **The Communist Manifesto** out of my somewhat worn, tattered old backpack, and finish the chapter I was reading...*The history of all* *hitherto existing society is the history of class struggles.* I read it out loud a couple of times to let it sink in. Then I put the book away and walk around a big orange tent that Jesus and I were standing by to see if anyone's in there. The tent is zipped up, but I think I see the faint shape of someone through the slightly translucent material. And, they know I'm here. Before I could even offer a sandwich, the shadow-like image steps forward, his nose touching the inside of the tent pushing it outward, warping the human outline into something ghoulish, creepy. Then it mumbled, "I don't think it's true."

Homeless are usually mentally challenged which is why they are on the streets. They often speak nonsensically.

"Hi in there. Would you like a sandwich?" I offer, holding up a turkey on whole wheat, wondering if he can tell. He chuckles, reaches to his side and pulls up a torpedo-shaped item that makes a crinkling sound. I recognize the shape and crinkle. I'm thinking Subway.

"No thanks," says the warped orange tent, "I just bought this Chicken Teriyaki on sourdough. It's the first meal I've paid for with my own money in, well, I don't know how long. Please give that to someone else."

Nothing like this has ever happened before. I'm taken aback.
"Sure, of course. Have a good day." I turn around and look out at the freeway. Expensive cars are rushing by on both sides. I'm struck by the juxtaposition of the "Haves" and the "Have Nots" who are, for a passing moment at least, sharing the same space. How is it possible that one person, like the Tesla owner that just drove by, can be so wealthy while these people, all around me, live in tents and sleep on cardboard? It's not fair. We've got to redistribute wealth. When are we going to wake up?

I walk toward Jesus, my back to the orange tent, when a voice rings out, *"Hey, I don't think it's true."*

I turn back around to see the distorted image, "Are you talking to me?"

"Who else? You think I'm talking to myself?"

I did, of course. "Well, no. I don't understand. What's not true?"

"Trump. I don't think he made fun of a handicapped person."

Again, I'm flabbergasted. I guess the man in the tent overheard Jesus and me. But, *is he defending Trump?* If so, that's wrong on so many levels. A homeless person? And how is it that a guy in an orange tent would even know about the Golden Globes last night?

"He did actually," I counter, "It's been all over the news."

"Fake News," he says. I can almost detect a grin morphing through the mesh upon which he presses his face.

"Actually, it's not fake news. I mean even Meryl Streep… "

"Yes, yes, I know. I know what Meryl said," he interrupted me. Clearly, he's delusional.

"Well, okay. If you say so, have a good day. I'm going to hand out the rest of the food now."

"You're patronizing me."

"No, I'm not."

"Look," he said after taking a bite of his chicken teriyaki. I feel like I'm watching some children's shadow puppet show. "If you're interested in truth, do an honest search. Beyond mainstream media coverage."

I guess I'm a little too emotional when it comes to the subject of Trump because I allow this homeless blob to get under my skin. "There's no reason to search. We are talking about *Meryl Streep*. She's a brilliant actress. She would not stand up in front of the universe while receiving the Cecil B. DeMille award and lie."

"Honestly," he said while sipping a soft drink that gurgled as his plastic straw reached the bottom of the cup. "I have no idea if she was lying or just too lazy to do a little research. I mean, when an idea supports one's desired version of reality, it's easy to believe lies and propagate them. We all do it from time to time. In other words, if it's not true, *she doesn't want to know.* The question now is, do you?"

"Of course I want to know the truth!" I respond to the tent, agitated. Just then a woman with *Hands On Greater Portland* walks by, glancing at me. She stops and with much compassion in her voice, "Excuse me, would you like a sandwich?" *She offers me a turkey on whole wheat.*

"Oh, I'm. I'm not homeless. I'm just, ah," I shake my head and wince, "Talking to the tent?"

Her eyebrows flying upward, "Okay, you… you have a nice day."

"No really," I say as she disappears into the encampment. "I'm… talking to the… *guy* in the tent."

"Ah, ha." The tent laughs. "Ha ha ha… *that's rich!*" He howls. "Ah, ha ha. You… *you got offered…* " He's having a hard time finishing between breaths. "*YOU… got offered one of your own sandwiches.* Ah ha ha ha… *I didn't see that coming! Ah ha ha ha….*"

"Okay, *'laugh it up fuzzball.'*" I say, quoting Han Solo.

"Ah, ha ha. You…you think I'm Chewbacca? Ah, ha ha…"

I'm surprised he knows the reference. "Are you done?"

"Ah ha…oh me. Just a sec. Whew. I haven't laughed that hard since. Geez, I don't know. Probably…*yesterday afternoon!* Ah ha ha…oh, okay." He takes a deep breath to gain his composure. "Anyway, where were we? Oh yeah, *are you sure you want to know the truth?"*

"Again, *I do.*" Who is he to question my integrity? "And the truth is Trump *mocked* a handicapped person. It's been all over the news. He's despicable. I *hate him.*"

"Your emotions deceive you," he remarks under his breath as I turn to walk away. Then, *"In proportion, therefore, as the repulsiveness of the work increases, the wage decreases."*

"What?" I ask turning on a dime. "What did you just say?"

"Page one hundred and twenty-three, paragraph two. One of the more interesting lines."

"What are you… ?"

"Never mind. Go. Hand out your sandwiches."

I shake my head and do just that. It didn't take long to put the whole episode behind me - too many people to help. Just as I gave my last turkey on sourdough away, Jesus approaches me.

"I'm all out of sandwiches."

"Me too," I concur, shrugging my shoulders.

"There are a few people we weren't able to feed."

"What are you complaining about?" I say with a twinkle in my eye, "You're Jesus! Multiply those sandwiches!"

Chapter 4 The Future: *I Want To Be Wrong*
Year: 2047 February 1 7:46 a.m.

"I've got to get this published *and peer-reviewed*, regardless of the current status of the peer review process. It still gets people's attention, for better or for worse."

"Yes it does," Alexus adds, nodding her head. "As long as scientists and doctors are our new 'Gods' we will continue to believe them even though they are flawed human beings like the rest of us."

"And, I know this goes without saying but, I want to know, with all my heart, *if my findings are true.*"

"Siri, you haven't commented. What do you think? Am I right? Is it true?"

"Well, as you know, you have done what only the human mind can do. You have intuitively and creatively gathered data and compiled it in unconventional ways leading to unpredictable results. In other words, I don't know."

"Well, you're some help," I put forth, tongue in cheek.

"However," Siri responds morphing back into Wonder Woman, her voice now echoing large like we're in some massive cave, ***"I see no flaws in your logic. If what you have found is true, you will need a superhero."***

Wonder Woman frightened me. Not because of the cavernous voice but because it's true. We'll need help at an Avengers type scale.

"I have painstakingly gone over the data repeatedly. And I know, the 'perfect' scientist is not one who always gets it right. The perfect scientist would be one that has no attachment to the outcome of their experiments. Their only concern would be to expand our understanding of the universe; to continually reveal greater truths even if that means being wrong or even if it means scrapping years of work. What I'm saying is, *I want to be wrong.* That's now my bias. I hope I end up burning my work in a digital bonfire."

"Do you know what happened to Thomas Edison's laboratory?" Siri inquired.

"Remind me."

"Well, his lab was just yards from his home. All of his life's work in journals, files, scraps of paper. There was no iCloud or impenetrable iDesks. One night, somehow the laboratory caught fire. He saw the flames through his home windows then ran outside to witness the mass destruction of his life's work, literally, up in smoke. His son, Charles, soon joined him, distressed. But do you know what Mr. Edison said to him?"

"No, I don't."

"He said, *'Go get your mother quick. This is the most magnificent fire we may ever see.'*"

My gut reaction was nausea trying to put myself in Thomas Edison's shoes, which is impossible to do. In Edison's time, everything you ever created would be on paper, *written with a pen or pencil.* Things only found in novelty stores today.

"Imagine," Alexus observed, "All of your work. Every idea. Gone. And yet he was unfazed. How can that be?"

Siri answered, "When asked what he would do he said, *It's all right. We've just got rid of a lot of rubbish. I'll start all over again tomorrow.'*"

Edison's story trumped.online/zx8

"Okay, I'll start over. I will wade through the data one more time. See if my intuitive and creative data compilation leads to the same unpredictable but logically sound results. If it does, I've got to burn down the misconceptions of the scientific community. There are trillions of dollars and millions of lives at stake." I sigh heavily, look at Alexus and Wonder Woman, and declare, "*I need to go see to Charles!*"

The Dawn: *Catholics For Trump*
Year: 2017 January 9 5:45 p.m.

I click on the television. Wall-to-wall coverage of Meryl Streep's acceptance speech and images of Donald Trump mocking the disabled reporter overwhelm me. Which, of course, reminds me of my interaction with that homeless guy, who is likely mentally handicapped and drug addicted. I feel deeply sorry for him. How delusional. Kathy walks in the room and notices Anderson Cooper commenting on Meryl Streep's speech, *"Whether you agree with it or not, it was clearly a heartfelt, sincere acceptance speech."*

Anderson Cooper trumped.online/l9m

Kathy responds to Cooper as if he can hear her, "You are way too kind Anderson, who *can't* agree with her? She rocked it. Put Trump in his place." She turns, "Remember the ads the Clinton campaign put out after Trump mocked that poor man?"

"Of course I do," I declare from the couch, thoughts of the homeless guy and our interaction muddying my mind. "Who can forget? I mean, I didn't like Trump before, but that was the straw that broke the camel's back. After that, I outright despise him. Who wouldn't?"

"Who wouldn't?," Kathy says frustrated, "Almost half the country, the *Repugnicans.* It kills me that Trump lost the popular vote. *He is not the rightful president.* We have to put an end to the Electoral College. It's so stupid. We're a democracy. The majority should rule!"

"Amen babe."

I question whether I should bring up my time at the homeless encampment, but somehow I couldn't resist. "Speaking of Meryl Streep, I had the most bizarre experience today handing out sandwiches."

"Oh yeah! How did that go?"

"Well, like I said; bizarre. The first homeless person I met, refused my sandwich. He said he bought his own food for the first time in years. A Subway sandwich. He asked me to give the sandwich I had for him to someone else."

"Interesting," Kathy remarked, somewhat absentmindedly from the kitchen. We're making fish tacos for dinner. She's getting a head start.

"Yes, but it gets much more strange. He must have overheard Jesus and me talking about Meryl Streep's slam on Trump during the Golden Globe awards. Long story short is, he ended up telling me that Trump didn't mock the disabled reporter. We got into a little argument. Everything about the encounter was just weird. The last thing you would think a homeless person would do is defend *Donald Frump.*"

"What? That is weird. How does he even know what's going on in the world? And, you can't expect someone in such circumstances to be rational. Most of them end up in the streets because of mental illness anyway."

"I know, it was surreal in so many ways."

I join her in the kitchen. We continue to chat about all things Trump. His colluding with Russia, his lack of mental fitness, his *two* scoops of ice cream, Melania's strange shoe choices and, of course, the fact he mocked a disabled reporter and so much more streaming now from CNN in the background.

Melania's shoes trumped.online/2wb
Trump's scoops trumped.online/bhe

Once we finished preparing fish tacos, complete with a squeeze of lime and a sprinkle of cilantro, Kathy shouts upstairs "Shanice, Malik… *dinner time!*"

The kids come down and join us at the table. And, wouldn't you know it? Less than a minute into the meal Shanice, our seven-year-old daughter says, "Did you hear about Meryl Streep's acceptance speech? We talked about it at school. Mrs. Jacobsen asked us if we thought it was okay to make fun of handicapped people like the president does."

We had a long conversation with our children that night. It seemed to come up again over the next couple of nights at dinner. It's been disturbing to our children. My wife and I are just happy that their school is teaching them right from wrong and their teachers are not afraid to tell the truth about the Commander and Chump to our children. After we tuck them in, we stay up too late, as we often do, discussing Trump and what we must do to oust him. I fall asleep exhausted.

The next night I head back to the homeless encampment. I feel terrible for not having enough sandwiches. It's dark. I got here later than I had planned. I'm using the flashlight on my iPhone. I see the orange tent, but I've decided not to engage with him. I can't handle that flavor of crazy right now. As I make my way between tents and cardboard boxes with only my little light to see, I think I hear footsteps behind me. The sound of a stick cracking underfoot makes my heart beat in double time. I turn around quickly; there's no one there. When I finally hand out my last sandwich, I make my way toward my car. A few trees make a beeline to the car impossible. As I round the last tree, I hear, "GIVE ME MY SANDWICH!"

A body comes flying out from behind the tree tackling me to the ground. "GIVE ME MY SANDWICH!" He shouts again, choking me. I can't make out the face in the dark. My phone light falls from my hand as he hits me from behind. But I know, *it's him* - Orange-tent-guy. I struggle to speak….

"I gave them… all.. a… away."

"I don't *care* about the sandwich. I already *told* you that. I bought my *own* sandwich." He whips that Subway sandwich out from behind him and smashes it to my face. Sweet Onion Chicken Teriyaki sauce drips down my forehead into my eyes, burning my corneas. I can't see. I try blinking the teriyaki sauce out but its thicker than motor oil. *I'm blinded.*

"Eat it! Is it not good enough for you? Can you accept food from a mentally ill, drug addict, as you call me? *But here's the big question.* The only question that matters. *Do you care about the truth?"*

I feel around for my phone. I know it's nearby. Suddenly the tip of my middle finger touches the front screen. I'm able to scrunch my fingers, inching the phone toward me. Finally able to grasp it in my hand, I whip it in front of me, pointing it into the face of my attacker. But as the light illuminates the figure before me, all I see is a big, brown and yellow Smudge Monster as the Sweet Onion Chicken Teriyaki sauce is now the filter through which I see the world. He smacks the phone from my hand. Now, in the dark again, I struggle to speak through a severely constricted windpipe. He's choking the breath out of my lungs as he asks again, *"Do you care about the truth?"*

"Ye…yes. I, I, d...d...do."

I'm fading out now. Is my fate to die at the hands of an insane, homeless dude?

"If you care so much about truth, *WHY? WHY* didn't you search on YouTube?"

"I, I did," I say hoping, if I can convince him, he will let me go.

"LIAR! *You did not.* You're killing yourself you know. You can't live with yourself. You are so out of integrity. You're ignoring your soul. *That's it."* He declared somehow sadly, "Time to die."

"N...No, No! Plea...*Please...Please!"*

****

I shoot up in bed. Sweat is dripping down my face like the sauce in my dream.

"Are you okay, sweetheart?" Kathy mumbled half asleep.

"Yes. Sorry. Go back to sleep."

I head into the bathroom and splash my face with cold water. It's just after 2 a.m. I consider going back to bed but then, almost unconsciously, I grab my laptop and stumble my way into the family room. I turn on a reading lamp, sit down in my favorite chair, and crack open my MacBook Air. I consider this YouTube search for a millisecond, then yawn, lean back in the chair and close my eyes.

****

"SERIOUSLY!" He yells, chasing me, full run around the encampment, "What are you so afraid of?"

"I DON'T KNOW."

"LIAR," he commands as we run in crazy eight patterns around tents, cardboard boxes, and the homeless. This time, the homeless people are slapping me in the face, tripping me up, and occasionally tossing me in the air like a rag doll.

"I will ask you one more time," he announces right on my heels, "WHAT ARE YOU SO AFRAID OF?"

"I DON'T KNOW," I yell.

"YES. YOU DO. TELL ME NOW!"

"IM AFRAID OF… "

"YES!?"

"… OF LOSING EVERYTHING!"

****

I pop up again, wide awake, gasping for air. This time, I grab my MacBook and without hesitation, search YouTube under, *Did Trump make fun of a handicapped reporter?*

 Handicapped reporter, the truth 1 trumped.online/zy4

 Handicapped reporter, the truth 2 http://trumped.online/w9k

There is a video created by "Catholics for Trump." *I didn't know any Catholics were for Trump.* I click on it. Four minutes and thirty-seven seconds later, *I'm mortified.* Mortified to find, Orange-tent-guy *was right!* Trump did not make fun of a reporter's handicap. Not only that, I'm convinced he would never do such a thing. I'm dizzy with questions. Why? Why on earth would the media be pushing this story so hard if it weren't true? Even if there were a *chance,* it wasn't true?! Why would Meryl Streep announce to the world such a hurtful thing without at least a little responsible due diligence? How could Hillary create an entire campaign based on the lie?

 Clinton campaign ad trumped.online/o02

Now, let me be clear. I *hate Trump.* Did I mention I hate Trump? He's a racist, sexist, homophobe, and xenophobe! Probably even suffers from phobophobia! But, I care about the truth. *Deeply,* actually. Entire commercial *campaigns* were centered around this lie. This fake news. It has deceived the whole country, the entire world in fact.

With my brain, *squirming like a toad,* I climb back into bed. Can't sleep. Afraid to. I grab my book that's slightly hanging out of the small compartment of my backpack. Sometimes I can read myself to sleep. This time, however, suddenly the hair on my arms is standing on end as I read, *In proportion, therefore, as the repulsiveness of the work increases, the wage decreases.* Page one hundred and twenty-three, paragraph two.

"Oh…My…God" I whisper somehow loudly. It's the exact quote on the exact page the Orange-tent-guy referenced.

Kathy rolls over, "You awake?"

"Yeah babe," I take a deep breath, exhale, *"I'm awake."*

Chapter 5 The Future: *Green Peace, Green Power*
Year: 2047 February 3 3:44 p.m.

I hop into my 2023 Ford Freedom, one of the first driverless cars mass-produced at an affordable price. It is as quiet as a mouse with its all-electric propulsion which was unusual back in 2023. The newer models run exclusively on solar and wind. Incorporating tiny windmills into the grill, rearview mirrors, and elsewhere set a new standard in the automobile industry by capturing the wind energy *created by the car itself.* I still plug in my old Ford Freedom, but most of that power comes from renewable energy. It's got just over 189,000 miles on it. Looks pretty shabby but still runs well. "Take me to Charles' house please."

Freedom responds with a voice similar to Morgan Freeman's, "Would you like to take the scenic route or the fastest way available?"

"Fastest route and don't be afraid to break the speed limit."

"Of course, buckle up!"

We skid out of the driveway. That's one thing I love about the older Ford Freedom models; *you can break the speed limit.* I don't know how anyone can even sit in the new ones with that annoying, 'No Law Broken' programming. No more 'California rolling stops'! No U-turns! And no going even one measly mile over the limit. Ever!

On the way, I continue obsessing over the data on the windshield monitor. Archaic I know, but it'll do. Then a call comes in from Isabella, my counterpart, on The Path. As excited as I am to be one of two lead engineers on the project, it's been hard for me to focus as of late. I split my days between, The Path and the data. As Isabella and I finish working out a few bugs on our latest designs, I arrive at Charles' place. It's off Patton Road, within walking distance of Council Crest which is probably the best vantage point in Portland. From up here, you can see all the white-peaked mountains during the day and the city lights at night. I stop at the entrance of his property to scan my retina; the giant gates open revealing the all stone mansion that looks like a castle.

There's even a turret! Yes, the kind you think of when you imagine Rapunzel letting down her hair; round and high with a pointy top. On the right side of the estate is a huge carriage house. They built the place in the early 1900s. I cruise up the long drive imagining what it would be like to live here. All the houses in this area have windmills. His is massive and stands probably fifty yards to the left of the turret. It's the newest model, Green Power Wind Three (GPW3) with the new magnetic assist technology. It only takes a wind speed average of three miles per hour to generate 6,500 watts. Enough to power half the needs of the entire estate. The house is three stories high, but the GPW3 windmill looms over it. Looks like he's got the Green Power Sun Twelve (GPS12) solar shingles. I believe the mandate is that by 2051 every home in America will be fitted with solar shingles. Over 80% already are. The GPS12's generate another 6,500 watts. It's amazing how far Green Peace has come. From a small movement in the 60s to the creators of G.P., Green Power. I've heard the government might break it up as it's reached monopoly status like AT&T in the 90s and Google back in 2024. We'll see. Their motto has long been something everyone believes in; *Our undying commitment today is a green planet for you tomorrow*. The latest polls suggest that the vast majority of citizens are against breaking G.P. up.

Charles greets me with a smile and a bear hug at the oversized wooden front door that holds an old-fashioned steel door knocker probably weighing 30 pounds or more.

"Hello, my friend. Come in, please. I want you to see something."

Charles is 57 years old, but you would swear he's not a day over 45. I've known no one so committed to peak physical health: six foot two and perfectly toned. When you get to know him, his age reverses even more. The only thing that might give his years away is the slight bit of salt and pepper on the sides of his hair. His wife, Jadda, is 45. To say she's beautiful would be like saying the ocean is deep. Understatement!

Our footsteps echo off the wooden floors and stone walls as we make our way through the entry a few steps down into the living room where a giant fire crackles in the massive stone fireplace.

"Take a seat," he says, pointing at two very comfortable looking armchairs. I take the one on the right. They face out the back windows which are as high as the ceiling, probably 15 feet up and 10 feet across. It's beautiful back there - several acres of manicured lawn leading to a forest. There's a swimming pool close to the home and a small pond in the middle with a canoe adrift. It's like a Norman Rockwell painting. The acreage slopes down just enough to reveal Mount Hood, Mount

Jefferson, and Mount Adams.

"Marcus, I'm working on something...huge." With Charles, this could be anything. A mind like his seems to have no limit.

"What is it?"

"First, watch," He whispers, taking the chair on the left.

We sit, perfectly still for about a minute gazing out the window when I finally say, "What are we watching for?"

"You'll see. Just breathe and watch. It's amazing."

The fire crackles on as we sit. Sit still. One minute turns to five. Five minutes turns to twenty. Something outrageous always happens when I visit Charles. Once he had a giant slip and slide and, like two nine-year-old kids, we spent the afternoon slipping down the sloped yard. Another time we went skeet shooting from the back patio. *I'm pretty sure that's not legal.* This time, we sit, wait, and watch. For what, I haven't a clue. At about the thirty-four-minute mark, a hummingbird appeared. That was cool. When it flew away, Charles spoke, "Awesome, huh?!"

"Yes, awesome...Okay, what was awesome?" He smiled, patiently, like a loving parent to a child.

"A better question might be, what wasn't awesome? I know in the world today it's hard to sit still. To pause and revel in the miracle of it all. It's something I learned, back when. Did you notice the trees dance in the wind? Did you see the sun pop out from behind the clouds on six different occasions? Did you *see* the glistening grass in the sunlight? And the hummingbird. Don't tell me you missed the hummingbird."

"Oh no, I saw the hummingbird. Everything else? Not so much. So, what's the huge thing you're working on?"

"Hmmm...you're not ready," he says with a smile. "That was a test. Now it's your turn. What's so important that you had to come and interrupt my, my doing nothingness?"

"Here," I send him the data from my iPhone, "Let's look at this through your iDesk."

"Siri, project the data sent from Marcus." Suddenly, the data appears in three dimensions right before us - seven feet high, twelve feet wide. The graphs cover the last 20 years. Analysis of each month, even each day if you want to look that closely. Also, there is endless scientific research, as it relates to the subject, from many of the best minds the world has ever known. Charles scans the basic information. He's a quick study.

"Wow. If you're right, *this changes everything...*"

The Dawn: *Martin Luther King's Bust*
Year: 2017 January 20 5:45 p.m.

I haven't told Kathy or anyone. Not even Jesus knows about what happened at the homeless encampment a few days ago, the dream, or what my research revealed in the dead of night. I'm not sure if I can speak of it. I mean, it took a crazy homeless man and a terrifying dream to motivate me to seek the truth. In the grand scheme of things, I guess it's not very important. I see no reason to bring it up.

However, I can't shake the thought of going to see the Orange-tent-guy again. I call Kathy, "Hey Baby, I'm wondering if you can pick up the kids for me. I may be a little late."

"Sure. Can you stop by the bank, get some cash? We need four hundred bucks to pay Julio and his crew for the yard work the last two months."

"Oh yeah. Of course."

"Hey Marcus," she says with a kind of stifled excitement like maybe we won the lottery and she was holding back for shock value, "Have you seen any news today?"

"Not really."

"Are you ready for this?"

"Depends on what it is. If the CIA found Russians hacked our election and successfully pulled off voter fraud so that Trump would win and now since we know the truth, Hillary will be our 45th President; *I'm ready!* If the Russians have invaded and Vladimir Putin is now vice president alongside his best buddy Donald Grump, *not ready.*"

She laughed, *"Neither one of those. PRESIDENT FRUMP REMOVED THE BUST OF MARTIN LUTHER KING FROM THE WHITE HOUSE."*

"WHAT? SERIOUS?"

"As a heart attack."

"Wow, but I'm not surprised. We know Lump's a racist. Still, that takes a lot of balls. Someone had to notice, eventually."

"It's great news. There's no way we, the people, will put up with this. *America will impeach him."*

"Yes, I think you're right."

"I'm hosting the gang over here tonight for a 'not my president' meeting to talk about what we can do to help get him out. But now, with this new revelation, *to celebrate.* It's not going to be much longer now."

"Sounds great. I'll see you no later than seven."

"Perfect. Love you!"

"Love you more!"

Her excitement was infectious. This new wave of damning information almost made me forget about the disabled reporter farce until I arrived at the homeless encampment later that evening. It's pitch dark by five o'clock in January thanks to daylight savings time. I fumble a bit wandering toward his tent - only distant streetlights are adding their slightest glow to the darkness.

"Hello," I say, my mouth a few inches from the tent. I can see a faint light. Maybe a small flashlight. "Knock, Knock."

"What? Who's there?"

"Um, it's me…"

"Wait. Are you the sandwich guy who was offered a sandwich from a fellow sandwich giver?" he said jovially.

"Ah…yeah."

"Hoo hoo…I still occasionally burst out in spontaneous *hysterics*. You kill me! Okay, just a sec. I'm finishing an article." I wait for a minute. Watching the dim light glow. "Okay, what brings you to my neighborhood? More turkey to pass out?"

"No, not today. I just wanted to see how you're doing. You okay?"

"Yes, I'm fine." He said with a knowing confidence. "How are you?"

I ignore the question. "What, ah, what are you reading?"

I see his shoulders shrug silhouette-like, "My pillow."

"Huh?"

"Yeah, I get a new pillow every day, late afternoon. They're all over the city -**The Oregonian** daily newspaper. I read it, make notes on it, then I sleep on it even though most of it is a bunch of hooey. Then I add it to the pile." He points his flashlight into the corner of his tent. I can almost make out a big pile through the mesh.

"Wow. Why do you keep old newspapers?" He steps forward and again, presses his face against the orange tent.

"I'll answer that if you tell me why you're really here?" He just stood there, waiting. His face, mashed against the mesh, looks like a woman's stocking was pulled over his head; squished, distorted. Creepy. Van Gogh-ish. And somehow, it felt like he was looking right through me.

My brain scrambling, I finally answer, "Ah, it's just that you are the first person, ever, to um, to refuse food. Yeah, I was just so, I don't know, surprised."

"EEAAEEEE," he makes a loud kind of buzzer noise and then obnoxiously extorts, "*WRONG!* Would you like to try again for our consolation prize? A copy of **The Oregonian**'s November 9, 2016 issue. It's a classic."

I know, of course, conceptually, what that paper's headline must read since November 9th is the day after the election. The very thought makes me ill.

"No, really, you just made an impression on me with that Subway sandwich and what you said about it." Why I was lying, I can't say. I'm sure a shrink would have a heyday analyzing my motivation, "That, and, just ah, hoping you weren't hungry."

"EEEEEEEEEEEAAAAAEEEE." He did it again, only much longer and louder, "*WRONG!!*" He pressed his face even harder against the tent creating enough tension to make me think his head might pop right threw. "If I can tell you why you're really here, you have to give me all the money in your wallet."

He's so flippin' crazy, "Sure, I'll play."

He smiles. Big. I can see teeth imprints in the tent mesh. Then he takes a deep breath, steps back and, like a lawyer approaching the jury he passes back and forth inside his truly tiny home while speaking at a rapid clip. "You agonized over our first meeting. Probably kept you up at night. You thought I was just a homeless lunatic suffering from delusions of grandeur. How could I even know what's going on in the world?" He pointed at the pile of papers. "Then, something. Something else pushed you over the top. A conversation?" He paused for a moment. "No. Something you heard or saw? Like some alternative news source…No, you're not strong enough to purposely expose yourself to information that would put into question your version of reality. Hmmm, maybe a, a nightmare?"

"What?" I said, jarred.

"*Aha, Eureka! You had a nightmare.* It would not let you sleep until you…*drum roll please…*" He waited like I was going to do an actual drum roll. "DRUM ROLL *PLEASE!*" *he insisted.* I mimicked a drum roll with my tongue. Not half bad either.

"You had a nightmare that would not let you sleep until you searched on YouTube under something like, *Did Donald Trump mock a handicapped reporter?* Since then you have been suffering from cognitive dissonance which would not let you rest until you came here, looking for answers from a lunatic homeless guy. *BOOM!*"

He drops his flashlight like a mic. It got pitch black in there. And out here. Then he announces, *"I rest my case."*

"How did you...?," was all I could muster.

Then, he added, "You also read page one twenty-three, paragraph two in, **The Communist Manifesto**. It freaked the living daylights out of you, didn't it!?"

"Um, well. That's incred... "

"Now, hand over all the money in your wallet." He stepped out of the tent. Just a dark silhouette. Looks like he has a big overcoat on and a large brimmed hat.

Dumbstruck, I pull out my wallet, "Oh man, you have got to be kidding me!" I had forgotten my recent stop at the ATM to pay Julio and the crew four hundred bucks.

"A deal's a deal. Hand it over."

I slowly dole out four hundred and fifty-three dollars; *four one hundred-dollar bills, a twenty, two tens and three ones* into his hand which appears to have a glove covering it. It's so dark, it's hard to tell.

"A pleasure doing business with you," he announces, "Have a fine day."

What just happened, I thought to myself as I slowly walked away. Was the whole thing a con? What am I going to tell Kathy?

"Hey, I'm just playin'," I heard him yell to my back.

I turn around, and there he is, next to his orange tent, a dark blur, counting the money.

"I have a few minutes if you want to chat."

I seriously don't know what to make of this guy. *He has a few minutes? Where does he have to be?* I slowly make my way toward him. Once I'm about thirty feet away, "Cognitive dissonance?"

"Well, when you did the research, and you found you were wrong about Trump and the handicapped reporter, I knew it would initiate cognitive dissonance because you were so sure of yourself. You're full of convictions and convictions are difficult to overturn."

"Wait. First, how did you know I even searched?"

"Come on, that's easy. I knew if I ever saw you again, with the possible exception of handing out sandwiches, it would be the search. Otherwise, if I never saw you, then you would be like most people, content to live in your delusion. But I thought you *might* be different. Maybe. Anyway, I overheard you and Jesus speaking, I get a kick out of that by the way, Jesus."

"It's pronounced, *Hey-Soos*. A lot of Hispanic people have that name."

He laughed out loud, "Se' sue eres idiota."

Okay, *now he's speaking Spanish*, "What?"

"Don't worry about it. Shall we continue?" He says, patiently.

"If it's not too much of an imposition."

"Cognitive dissonance, psychologists assert, occurs the moment someone holds two or more contradictory beliefs. It's an impossible state to maintain. The moment someone is presented with new information that contradicts their worldview, the possibility of cognitive dissonance presents itself. Most people cower back to their familiar corner for self-preservation sake, more interested in maintaining the status quo. They surround themselves with friends, family, books, TV shows, documentaries, internet searches, articles, etc. that reinforce their paradigm making it increasingly rigid. But if you are interested in the truth, you must be willing to wade through the uncomfortable to form revised belief systems that more closely resemble the truth. That's what you did, or you would not be here now."

What do you do when a guy's B.O. is so strong you can smell him thirty feet away, yet he is crushing you intellectually? "Guilty as charged. That is exactly what happened. That and page one hundred and twenty-three of **The Communist Manifesto**. How did you do that?"

"Ah. That's of no concern. Forget about it."

I couldn't forget, but I could tell he didn't want to talk about it, so I continued. "Anyway, it's been disturbing. I *was* convinced. The media and my friends and family reinforced the lie. What else could I think?"

"I understand your predicament. What you could do is have an open mind so that when homeless guys who don't want your sandwich, tell you the truth, you might listen."

"I guess so. But in the grand scheme of things, it doesn't matter. I mean, it doesn't change Trump. He's still the worst president ever. Did you know, he removed the bust of Martin Luther King from the White House."

A chuckle turned cackle slips from his throat as his silhouette wobbles with laughter. Slapping his knee, he announces, "Oh…that's a good one! He did not remove a bust of Martin Luther King from the White House."

"Yes he did, it's, it's…"

"All over the news?" he interrupted.

"Yes, all over the news. But there's a picture, I was told. The bust is gone."

"Okay, now you're suffering from the *sacrifice of logic for a desired outcome.*"

"Is that another psychoanalytical concept?"

"No, I just made it up. But, it is why you're suffering. You want to be proven right as do 99% of people. Therefore, your desired outcome is that Trump is proven to be one of the worst people who ever lived. Hitler-ish. You want him to be a mentally unfit woman abuser. Heck, you would love it if he had an affair in the White House with, I don't know, an intern and gets caught lying about it. Sorry if that's too far-fetched,

I'm just on a roll. You hope he has cheated on his taxes, broken national and international laws and yes, you hope, more than anything, he colluded with Russia and they will impeach and throw him in prison for life. There is probably nothing too low for your hopes regarding Trump. Am I right so far?"

I had never thought of it quite like that, but I had to admit, "Yes, I guess you are."

"Okay then, the fact that an otherwise intelligent guy would believe such nonsense; *Trump removes a bust of Martin Luther King*, proves you're sacrificing logic at the altar of a 'desired outcome.' Think about how absurd that is. Trump gets into the White House and thinks to himself, *I've got to get rid of that Martin Luther King bust.* How would he do such a thing? Do you think he got up at three in the morning, snuck down in his pajamas, dug a hole in the White House lawn, and buried it? Or do you think maybe he had the Men in Black handle the matter while he was out of the country? Does any of this seem plausible to you?"

"I…I guess not. Sounds a bit preposterous actually."

"The desired outcome of the media, for example, is that he is a racist. Whoever reported this, saw what they wanted to see to create that outcome, *logic be damned.* I mean, there's no scenario in which this makes any sense. If Trump is a racist, and he may be, do you think one of the first things he would do is remove the bust of Martin Luther King from the White House? Do you think he would want to telegraph to the entire world, *Hey everyone, I'm a racist?"*

We stood there awkwardly for a few moments. The occasional flash from headlights blinding me. I guess it wasn't a rhetorical question, "No, I don't think he would do that."

"So," he said while sinisterly tapping his fingers together, "How much do you want to bet there will be an explanation to this that does *not* include Trump being a racist."

"Even if I wanted to take you up on that bet, I already lost all my cash to some slick street peddler. But, I wouldn't even if I had money because you might be right."

"You feeling a little cognitive dissonance right now?"

"Yes, I am."

"Good. If you're interested in the truth, don't run back to the safety of your old thought patterns." He continued speaking while, to my surprise and amusement, he appears to take a few steps toward a tree. I hear a zipper. Then the unmistakable sound of urine hitting tree bark. I conclude that he has dropped trou and is relieving himself on an unsuspecting fir. He trudges forward as if none of this matters, "Try to recognize when you are sacrificing logic for a desired outcome. Remind yourself that the only desired outcome you wish for is the truth. That is true, isn't it?"

I think it's true. I want it to be true, "Well, isn't that what everyone wants?"

"You know better than that," he said while tucking things away and zipping his pants.

"Okay, not everyone wants the truth. The reality may be most don't. Maybe what most people want is to be right regardless of evidence to the contrary."

"If you say so," he responds, leaving me muddled.

"What are you afraid of?" he asks randomly.

"Huh? Nothing."

"EEEEEAAAEEE," again with the buzzer noise, "Wrong! What are you afraid of?"

"I don't know."

"Yes you do, you're just afraid of that which you're in fear of."

"What?"

"You heard me." He takes a deep breath, then several steps in my general direction while spewing out the question one more time so loud and fast I think my hair might just be shooting up in the air, ***"WHAT ARE YOU AFRAID OF?"***

"I'm, I'm… "

"Say it. "

"I'm afraid of losing everything. "

"Good, " he affirms with his deep, powerful voice. *"Consider me. I lost everything, and I'm doing okay,"* he says while his silhouette slowly shows his right arm revealing his tent as if he's a model on, *The Price Is Right.*

"Hilarious. You're a funny guy; you know that?"

"Hey, look at the time," he exclaims. I waited, expecting him to say more. "Seriously, *look at the time.* " I guess he could tell or just assumed I'd have a smartphone. "I need to be at work by 7:30. *What time is it?* "

"What? " The guy forever keeps me on my heels.

"Are you losing your hearing?" He then repeats, slow and loud, ***"I… need…to…be…at…work…by…seven…thirty! What…time…is…it?"***

I take out my iPhone, the light of it makes me squint, "It's, ah, a quarter after seven."

"Oh, I got to go. See ya, wouldn't wanna be ya."

He just took off, at a slow jog with his back to me while I picked my jaw up off the ground. I stand here in a state of, *cognitive dissonance.* Trying to make sense of it all when suddenly I remember, *Oh shoot. Dinner party!*

Chapter 6 The Future: *The Pseudo-Science Guy*
Year: 2047 February 1 4:29 p.m.

Charles continues to study the data, "So, you have been working on this for twenty years!?"

"Yeah, and like you said, it could change everything. I plan to publish my findings, have them peer-reviewed."

"Sure, it's a start," Charles mutters, getting up from his chair and walking around the data hanging in the air. "Peer-review isn't what it used to be."

"I'm painfully aware of that, but as you say, it's a start. Couple other problems. I've never done it before. Who exactly are my scientific 'peers?' I mean, I'm just a mechanical engineer. It would be easy for people to dismiss me and the findings."

"I don't know about that, remember Bill Nye the Science Guy?"

"Sure."

"Well, he was a 'mechanical engineer' and had his own science-based TV show. I mean, well, pseudoscience. He wasn't a mechanical engineer either, he had a BS in mechanical engineering, but he was just a TV personality. So, I'd have to call B.S. on the whole mechanical engineering part as far as he was concerned. It's not what he did, and later in his career, his show had little to do with what we generally consider to be science. History has now placed his show among the most cringe-worthy spectacles ever conceived. Remember his presentation, *Sex Junk?* I think one of the lines was, *My sex junk's better than bagels with lox, with lots of smears.*"

⫘ Bill Nye's sex junk <u>trumped.online/8ik</u> ⫘

"Hmm," I said scratching my chin, "I don't know if I'm insulted or encouraged by this Bill Nye walk down Memory Lane."

"You pick," he said smiling, as he continued studying the data. "Wait, what is this?" he exclaimed, pushing information to the side while pulling other data up. "This is, it's…*staggering.*"

"Let me see." I get up from my chair. Stand inches away from Charles and join him examining this particular vein of the information. *"Geez, I hadn't even noticed this!"*

We both stood there, stupefied.

"I think what we're feeling right now is cognitive dissonance," I explain. "A friend of mine, a long time ago, used to encourage this brand of mental anguish. He said it means you're growing."

Charles considered that for a moment, "Sounds like a wise guy."

"Oh, he was a *wise guy*, for sure. Too bad he, he died back in 2017."

The Dawn: *Time Magazine*
Year: 2017 January 20 7:36 p.m.

"So sorry I'm late everybody."

"Marcus..." everyone shouts. The mood is high. You can feel it. Optimism. CNN plays in the background. It's clear I've stepped into the middle of a vivacious conversation.

"If anyone had any doubts, they should be gone now," Jamaal extols enthusiastically dressed to the nines in his Gucci jacket and Louis Vuitton shoes.

"I know. I wonder what Fox news is saying now? President Chump had the Martin Luther King bust removed for, *cleaning?"* Tom, Jamaals partner, adds looking just as fashionable. There's an uproar of laughter. Adara raises her glass of wine while adjusting her hijab, "A toast. May this be the shortest-lived presidency in history."

"Here, here," several friends shout, while I sit, glazed over in cognitive dissonance.

"It's so funny," Luke chimes in while pushing up the sleeves of his Polo shirt, "What an idiot. Did he think no one would notice?"

I didn't even know the words came out of my mouth until after I released them, "Do we know for sure he removed the Martin Luther King bust?"

The way the room went still, you'd think I yelled out, *They should not allow gays to marry.* Or, *transgender is a mental illness.* Everyone looked at me like I was insane. I had to walk it back somehow, "I mean, I just don't want to get my hopes dashed."

"Oh, well, none of us do," Michelle said sympathetically. He…I mean she, is looking beautiful donning a full-length dress, high heels, red lipstick, and newly polished red fingernails to match. I always appreciated her input. I know she was trying to quell the uneasiness in the room. "But," she continued, "It's been all over the news. Zeak Miller, one of the most respected reporters for Time magazine was the first to report it. It even popped up on my phone. Look at Facebook. It's all the conversation."

"Okay, Okay. Let's, let's…celebrate."

"All right," Luke chimed.

"Yes," Kathy added, looking at me a little sideways.

The rest of the night, a painted smile cloaked my internal conflict. The jovial mood picked up right where it left off. All the while, I thought about the Orange-tent-guy. He must have been wrong! He's looney tunes. After all, me - *I'm* suffering from the s*acrifice of logic for a desired outcome* syndrome? *What a bunch of hogwash.*

I excused myself from the table to put the kids to bed. After I read, *Good Night Moon* to Shanice, I ritualistically kiss her on the forehead. But, before I close her door, she asks, "Daddy? Why did Trump remove Martin Luther King's dust from the Oval Office?"

I didn't know whether to laugh or cry. Out of the mouths of babes! Trump probably *would* remove any last remnants of a great leader, *if the said leader were black!*

"Sweetheart, the correct word is bust, it means a statue. He removed the bust of Martin Luther King. Why? Because he's a racist."

"That's not fair," she said with a sleepy voice.

"No, it's not fair. Good night, sweetheart."

As soon as everyone left Kathy started in on me, "What got into you tonight?"

"What do you mean, what got into me?" I knew what she meant of course.

"What on earth possessed you to say, *How do we know he removed the bust?* "

I wanted to kill the Orange-tent-guy, "I don't know babe. I'm sorry."

"And then, the rest of the night, you looked like a guy sentenced to death row but was somehow happy about it. I don't know, it was weird." She hands me a dish to put in the dishwasher.

"I'm sorry, I'm just under a lot of stress at work."

We spend the rest of the night in a genre of silence that screams - the kind of silence that might break a window.

Dread filled my head when we woke up. Not that I slept much. The Orange-tent-guy haunts my nights even when I don't sleep. I was hoping Kathy would forget to ask, but I know her better than that. With almost nine years of marriage under our belts, there's little we don't know about each other. Our anniversary is looming. Just as I was about to leave the house, and I was leaving early for a reason, she spoke her first words of the day, "I need the four hundred bucks to pay Julio…."

Chapter 7 The Future: *Is This For Real?*
Year: 2047 February 1 5:12 p.m.

As Charles and I stood there, mesmerized by the data, his wife, Jadda, walked in, "Hey Marcus. Hey guys. What's up?"

"Come here, babe," Charles says, without looking away from the floating information, "Take a gander at this."

She joins us in the middle of the data. Studying, mulling through. You can see the lightbulbs go on by the expressions shifting on her face. "Wait… it… is this?" She keeps wanting to say something but then gets distracted by revelations. She's like a dog on a bone. Hours pass. She's flipping the data every which way. Finally, *"Is This For Real?"*

Marcus nods slowly.

"Then, well. OH…MY…GOD!"

The Dawn: *The Victim*
Year: 2017 January 21 7:01 a.m.

"Hey, wake up in there…" I shake the wet orange tent, damp from the evening's rain, "I've got a bone to pick with you."

"Brother, knock it off. I'm awake. Come on in."

I unzip the front and lower my head about a foot to fit in. I was hesitant. A little concerned about what I might find strewn on the tent floor, not to mention the smell. Often there are dirty needles, used condoms, food wrappers. It's still dark. Sun won't fully rise for another hour causing me to squint my eyes to make things out. But, surprisingly, it seems orderly. The newspapers stack neatly in the left back corner. His flashlight sits next to his folding chair. There are several books in a neat pile. Some of them I recognize - classics like **Moby Dick, Huckleberry Finn, War and Peace,** and **1984**. There's, **Atlas Shrugged**, I've heard of it but never read it. **Think and Grow Rich**, never heard of that. There's **Illusions**, sounds familiar: **Silent Spring**, one of my favorites. **An Inconvenient Truth**, maybe the most important book of my generation…and then, I see a few by a guy named Thomas Sowell. I've never heard of him. The titles sound interesting though. One is **Affirmative Action Around The World**. Another is **Trickle Down Theory and Tax Cuts For the Rich** and **The Quest for Cosmic Justice**. Finally there's a **Bible,** a **Koran** and Something called the **Hadith.**

Behind the books there's a small trashcan, looks recently emptied. And there Orange-tent-guy is, in 'bed,' a stack of cardboard under him for padding. He's fully wrapped up in a sleeping bag, just the top of his large brimmed, old leather hat sticking out. I can see a slight glow through his sleeping bag. Maybe another flashlight. It's cold today. Low 40s. I feel sorry for him which squelches some of my angst.

"What are you doing?" I say, forcing agitation in my voice. I'm trying not to lose my anger.

"Research. What are you doing here?"

"I've got a bone to pick with you." It's cold enough to see my breath.

"That goes without saying." His response only serves to tick me off even more. Which is good, I don't want to lose momentum just because I feel for his plight. I think maybe he uses my compassion to manipulate me.

"What do you mean research? How?"

"With my iPhone, how do you think?" He slipped the top of it out of the sleeping bag for me to see. The screen is so severely cracked it looks like a drunk spider had been working on a web for days but couldn't stay in the lines. Seems to work fine despite the distorted image. I shake my head.

"What!? You have an iPhone?"

"Yes, and…?," he replied, pulling it back into his cocoon.

"It's hard to know where to begin. Why did you ask me what time it was yesterday when you had your own phone?"

"Battery was dead. Next question."

"Where do you charge it?"

"Pioneer Courthouse Square. There are outlets all over the place. Next."

"Where did you get it?"

"Pawnshop, 12 bucks. Next."

"How can you afford to pay the monthly rates?"

"I don't, who needs a plan? You know that restaurant across the street, Cathedral Coffee?"

"Yes, I park by it all the time when I come down here."

"They gave me the wifi code. If I stay right about here in my tent," he adjusts a tad in his bag, "I can usually get a good connection. Next."

Again, confounded. "Well, I have a lot more questions, but I think I have exhausted the ones revolving around your phone. What I am right now is very upset. I made a fool out of myself last night at a dinner party because of you. All of my good friends came over. Everyone was excited about Trump removing M.L.K's dust."

"Removing what?" He said, twerking his whole body. It made his sleeping bag look like a sac with a worm wiggling inside. He laughed through his words, which only fueled my fire, "The dust?"

"The bust, *the bust!* Because you put this flippin' crazy idea in my head that I was suspending logic for a desired outcome, I questioned the whole thing. And they, rightly so, were not impressed. Especially my wife. And then, this morning, Kathy, my wife, asked me for the four hundred bucks to pay Julio for yard work. Of course, I didn't have it, *because you took it."*

"Playing the victim, are we?"

"Oh my God! You are so infuriating."

"Yes, I am."

"Knock it off." Now I was fuming. "Me? Playing the victim? *You're the homeless guy!"* Okay, I realize I may have gone too far, but still, he

asked for it.

"Now you're doubling down. How am I playing the victim because I'm, *the homeless guy?*"

"Because… because… you are, you have to be. *You're homeless. You stink!"*

"I still don't understand. How am I playing the victim? What have I done or said in which I played the victim card?"

Every conversation is like a game of chess with this guy. And he's always one move ahead of me. "Whatever," I respond like a seven-year-old. "But, I'm *not playing the victim,"* To cap it off I stomp my right foot on the dirt floor for good measure.

"You are actually. I didn't take your money. You willingly wagered a bet, and you lost. Second, you could have gone to your local ATM and gotten more money, but you chose not to."

"I forgot."

"Whose fault is that?"

"Yours," I spout, knowing how ridiculous I sound, "You made me late for the dinner party."

"*I made you late?* Wow, that's a good one. You should probably go now. And please, take my dust with you." He starts laughing so hard his sleeping bag buckled in. Which only made me boil.

"You're insane. I'm out of here. " I turn around to leave.

"Wait," he says rapid-fire like, "I meant to give it to you last night but, but," he laughs again, "You *made* me forget! Ha, aha ha… it's too cold to come out there but pick up the little trashcan."

"What on earth for?"

"Trust me."

I questioned whether I should trust him. But, despite my anger, I had no reason to distrust him. So, I did. It sat on a piece of cardboard, "Okay, done."

"Now, move the cardboard."

A hole is revealed when I pick up the piece of cardboard. Inside the hole sits a coffee can with a plastic lid. "Okay, there's a coffee can."

"Remove the lid."

"What? What is this?" I query, surprised. There is so much money; it is almost overflowing.

"Ah, money!? You've not heard of the stuff?"

"Take your four hundred bucks, spend it wisely."

I shake my head in disbelief. "What the… What…? You have to be… *WHAT?*"

"Cat got your tongue?" he asks, patronizingly. "I've shown no one else my vault, for obvious reasons. I trust you will not come and steal the rest in the night. If you were to come tonight to steal my money, it would disappoint you. I'm going to go deposit it this afternoon."

"Your… deposit? Coffee can? Who…?"

"Spit it out; I don't have all day."

Again, my brain is fraught with questions. "How much money is in there?"

"I don't know. About a thousand bucks I think."

Of all the questions screaming in my head, this is what I ask? "You said you couldn't afford a plan for your phone!?"

"No, I didn't say that. I said, *Who needs a plan?*"

"You have a bank account?"

"Yes. I opened it about a year ago. And, my new business is exploding."

"*Your what?* Business!? New business?"

"Yeah, there is so much competition out here in the can, plastic, and glass bottle collecting business. Plus the returns suck. So, I started a new business."

"Wait. *You?* Started a *business?*"

"You're very prejudiced, you know?"

"What? Seriously? How can I be prejudiced? I'm the farthest thing from prejudice. One of my best friends is transgender. And then there's Tom and Jamaal, *a gay couple.* And then there's Adara, she's muslim… "

"… Now you're getting defensive - evidently I hit a nerve. And you're spouting one of the most cliche, racist defenses ever devised by bigots, '*I have friends that are…* ' fill in the blank."

"You don't know me," I respond, defensively. "*I'm a social justice warrior.* What do you think I was doing here handing food out to those in need? Just getting exercise?"

"I think you were trying to relieve your guilt. For being successful, maybe. Or maybe just trying to feel better about yourself overall. I mean, once you hand out sandwiches you get to wear the *sandwich button.* You can say, *I hand out sandwiches to the homeless.* Subtext being, *I'm a good person. Look at me do my good things for the lesser people so I can continue living my plush life and not feel bad about it 'cause, did I mention, I'm good?*" My stomach feels a little off as he puts a ribbon on it, "I mean, you know what they say, *there are no unselfish acts.*"

It's a concept I've wrestled with myself many times.

"Won't you at least concede," he said patiently, "You have acted with prejudice toward me. Because I'm homeless, you come with a psyche full of baggage you're projecting all over me."

"Okay, okay, you're right. I guess I have been prejudiced toward you."

"Good. Now, can you handle the truth?"

"I have no idea!"

"Great. We're making progress. The truth is, being prejudice is not *necessarily* a bad thing."

"What?"

"I started a business about a month ago," he said, changing the subject, leaving me hanging. "I was walking by the parking lot, up there on Third Street. You know the one? It's relatively small."

"Yeah, I know that one."

"Anyway, it was about 6:30 in the evening. I noticed some trash and cigarette butts. Things people probably just tossed out of their car. Then there were some dirty needles. Even human feces against that brick wall. Homeless people are the worst," he floated, with a suppressed chuckle.

"Wait, how can you say…" he continued, ignoring my protest.

"There was a broom next to the little booth where they manage the lot. I came back in the dark of night, and I cleaned that lot. I did it again the next night and added several other lots. I continued the rounds for two weeks."

"You mean you cleaned the parking lots, for free, every night? Did they know you were doing it?"

"No, they had no clue. It puzzled the managers and owners. Until one day I strategically came early, about 6 p.m. and cleaned. The lot manager confronted me, *So, you're the one who keeps cleaning the lot?* And I was like, *Duh!?"*

"Seriously, you said, duh?"

"Of course not stooge. I said, '*Yes, sir.*' And then, when I finished the work, I told the guy I'd keep doing it for five bucks a night if he wanted. I made the same deal with seven lots so far, so I'm makin' thirty-five dollars a day now!"

He was proud of that. Truth be known, so was I.

"The best part of it is, these managers, it's their job to keep the lots clean. They get paid to do so. So they're giving me a part of their paycheck because they don't want to do it."

"Brilliant," I respond, shaking my head in near disbelief, "How long does it take you to clean a lot?"

"It depends, obviously on the size, between one and two hours. I usually work from about six or seven at night till between one and three in the morning. I make my own hours. I'm my own boss!"

I do the math in my head, "So, you're getting paid between two fifty and five dollars per hour, is that right?"

"Yep!" He says with pride. Which makes no sense, "That's not fair – I think it is even illegal. *You should make a living wage.* Everyone should make a living wage. I know that's too much to ask for, but at least minimum wage. I'll go with you tonight and talk to these people. This is ridiculous."

The sleeping bag straightened out in an instant and from inside it came, *"ARE YOU INSANE?* You will do no such thing. You think some dude making something around minimum wage, will pay *me* the minimum wage? *Are you on crack?"* He was upset. *"Keep your frickin' social justice out of this."*

"I'm just trying to help; it's not fair."

"Who decides what's fair?" He's almost yelling now. *"There are only two ways to look at life, and I've had a lot of time to think about it so listen up fool."* He pauses, takes a deep breath. "One; life is not fair, period. It is what it is. It will never be fair. Two; life is always fair whether or not you think it is. There are your two options. Even though they appear to be opposites, ultimately they are the same. Regardless of which one you believe to be true, the only real choice is to take

responsibility for your life. Do the best you can with the cards dealt to you. If you believe life isn't fair and you think you can *make it fair,* you will spend your days playing the victim and championing others who say they are victims which *validates their victimhood. And that is a crime.* Do you want social justice? *Never pander to victimhood.* Believe in the greatness of every individual. *Demand it. Call it forth. Do not treat them like they are less than you, like some pet you have to feed, wash, house, and clean up after.* It's patronizing and debilitating. Don't you know dependency on handouts becomes addictive? A lifestyle? Don't you see how easy it is to lose one's dignity and accept what society is telling you? That you are incapable and unworthy of contributing or even taking care of yourself."

My eyes wide open, feeling defensive, I offer my truth, "I hear that is your truth, and I honor that, but people are born into different circumstances. *It's not fair.*"

"Have you forgotten, already, option number one? *Life is not fair.* And, you think I don't know people are born into different circumstances?" He paused. I just stood there. Realizing how silly it was to be arguing with a sleeping bag. Then he spoke, "Never measure success by where someone is, only by how far they have come."

I sigh, shaking my head, "I don't know what to say to that."

"Look at me," he requested. So I did. I stand there staring at an old, grungy bag. He unzips it maybe three inches. Just enough for him to see me I guess. The only thing I could see of him now was his breath in the cold air as he said, "No, really look at me."

"What? I am looking at you."

"No, you're not. *Look at me!*" He demanded. "With your heart!"

"That's what I always do!"

"No, you don't! You look at me with all your prejudice. Drop it. Look at me with your heart!"

I take a deep breath, trying not to lose my temper, "My wife and I practice compassionate meditation. I know how to…"

"No, you don't. You practice sympathy."

"You're splitting hairs now."

"No. Your sympathy is pity in disguise. DON'T LOOK AT ME LIKE THAT. I DON'T NEED YOUR PITY."

I'm confounded and shocked into compliance. I look at him, lying there in the near-freezing cold. I don't know why, but a tear drops from my eye.

"You think I'm less than you."

I try to hold back the tears, swallow, "No…no I don…"

"Yeah, you do. It's okay, say it."

"I, I don't. Everyone is equal. *We're all the same.*"

"Oh, My Insanity! One of the most deceitful and hurtful cliches of our time. Out of one side of your mouth, you people say, *We're all the same,* and then, out of the other side you insist, *Diversity is our strength.* Well, which one is it? *Can't be both!*"

Cat got my tongue.

"Okay, so, we agree. We are not all the same. *Life isn't fair.* Everyone is *not equal.* Now say it. You think I'm less than you."

"No, I don't."

"THEN WHY ARE YOU GIVING ME SANDWICHES?"

"Because you, you need it."

"Why do I need it?" He keeps increasing the clip of his speech.

"Because, 'cause you don't have it."

"But you do. Why is that?"

"I don't know."

"If we're so equal, then why don't I hand out sandwiches to you?"

"Cause, you, you had a rough start in life… It's not fa.."

"It's not fair! Yes, we have established that. And…*you know nothing about my start!* Why do you assume I had a rough start?"

"Cause you need sandwiches."

"And I suppose one plus one now equals nine!? You're contradicting yourself. Man. Come on. Keep up. Just admit it. Say, *I think you are less than me.* Say it."

"I will not."

"Then you are deceiving yourself. You are lying to you! You think my job sucks. You think I stink. You think my hourly pay is inhuman. You think I screwed up your marriage because of the Martin Luther King… dust. And because of all that *even I* think I'm less than you. And so, what does that make me?"

I avert my eyes and whisper, "Less than me."

"What? I didn't hear you."

"I think you are less than me."

"Do you think so little of me you can't look at me when you speak?"

I guess he can see me. I raise my eyes, embarrassed by the tears as I look directly at the small unzipped section of his bag, "I think you are less than me."

"Thank you," he whispers.

I shake my head. "You're thanking me for thinking less of you? What? Why?"

"Because it's real. Now we can be honest. Never, ever give me a sandwich again. Hear me?"

"Yes."

"Do you understand why?"

"Yes, I, I do."

"Bring none of these tent dwelling, cardboard box people a sandwich again. Here's your test for the day."

Man, I already felt as stressed as I did during finals week at the University of Oregon and now I have to take a test?!

"Why is it you should never bring another sandwich to these ungrateful sots?"

"'Cause we're all equal!?"

The sleeping bag twerks again. Which, I'm realizing, means Orange-tent-guy is either upset or about to laugh.

"Oh My God. *Just slit my throat right now.* Do it. *DO IT.* Put me out of my mis..."

"I mean, we're not equal, but we're all capable."

"Whew! My God in heaven above, he has a brain."

"And, there is greatness in us all," I said excited, like a student trying to impress the teacher. "And, by giving them a sandwich, I'm telling them they are less than me and everyone who has a job. And I'm robbing them of the most basic of human dignities, being self-reliant."

"YES."

"So," I say finally understanding how misguided I have been, "I will never give another sandwich to anyone here."

"Except... Blue-tent-guy," he said matter-of-factly.

"What?"

"I was born a millionaire. Part of what you would probably think of as the wretched one percent."

"Wait. What?"

"My start. I was born with a silver spoon in my mouth."

"You were?"

"Yes, but I choked on it."

"Huh?"

"My mother was a Microsoft millionaire. A computer programmer. But she was super stressed out. When she drank, she was abusive. Not physically, emotionally. She shamed my father who was an early adapter stay-at-home dad. A couple of trailblazers my parents! My dad felt somewhat emasculated by the arrangement. But, as I got older, she, fueled by alcohol, passive-aggressively patronized him. As a result, my dad smoked pot all the time. He tried to hide it from my mom. They'd fight about it when she was drinking and usually while he was high. And, monkey see, monkey do. I drank and smoked pot by the time I was twelve. I could take a twenty out of my dad's allowance, and no one ever knew."

I squinted my eyes, "Allowance?"

"Yes, my mother had him on an allowance. When I hit fourteen, I decided, wait for it… Life isn't…"

He waited for me to finish the thought, "Fair!"

"Bingo. But instead of doing my best with what I had, I played the… "

"Victim!?"

"Righto. So, I took $800 bucks from my mom's purse and ran away from home. I thought it was so romantic, living on the streets. Petty theft. Sex. But I went through the money in a couple of weeks. Now, fourteen years later, here I am."

"But no one can blame you. You were just a kid."

"There are billions of kids with worse starts than me who did something with their lives. However, my point is I couldn't have stayed away from home if it weren't for the homeless culture that had not only become normalized but even supported by sandwich giving, pity feeling, guilt-ridden do-gooders like you!"

"Oh. Sorry."

"You're forgiven," he said warmly. "Hunger is very motivating. I would have gone home. Sure, it wasn't perfect, but I was no barrel of laughs either. The problem is, I was never *hungry enough*. As a homeless person in Portland, you can eat better than a lot of people around the world who work."

"That puts things in perspective."

"Look, thousands of homeless people are, or were, teens who ran away just like me. Thousands. Look out there."

Homeless undercover trumped.online/t1w
Homeless young woman trumped.online/zrz
Homeless college student trumped.online/tm4
Homeless young lady trumped.online/y3y

I didn't move.

"Look. Seriously. Now."

I peeked out the tent. It looked different from before. A lot different. "How can we fix it?"

"Practice *real* compassion. Not the fake stuff you wield to make you feel like a good person. You ever heard of tough love?"

"Sure."

"Practice it much?"

I won't answer so I look at the ground.

"I didn't think so." For a moment he was still. Quiet. I'm guessing reliving his childhood on the streets. He spoke slow, thoughtful, *"It doesn't sting hard enough or fast enough out here.* Our backward, pity driven culture has created a slow drip of desperation. Tough love is sacrificed at the altar of feel good, flimsy philanthropy whose only purpose is to help the 'givers' feel less guilty about their 'privilege.' *YUCK.* Do you know in India, they give tourists explicit orders not to give to the beggars? The homelessness, human despair, and pain in India make my tent look like living in Trump Tower. I went to India on a business trip with my mother when I was 13. Beggars fill the streets. Many of them have deformed legs, or a broken back and push themselves around with their hands on homemade wooden carts with squeaky metal wheels just a few inches from the ground. Some are blind, burned, or any of a host of other physical deformities. It's hard to look at."

Indian beggars crisis, trumped.online/ry4

I've heard these stories before. It's difficult for me to think about them for very long.

"And, for a bleeding heart like you, it might be impossible to witness without *guilting* them money."

"Wait, what? *Guilting* them money?"

"Well, it's not giving since giving implies you're doing something unselfish. It also implies you're being helpful. What you're actually doing is feeding the guilt monster within you and the dysfunctional class system of begging in India. Have you ever heard, *money is the root of all evil?"*

"Well, yeah, who hasn't?"

"And yet we keep thinking if we give more money to the most corrupt institution on the planet - government, it will fix everything. Now, I don't believe money *is* evil. Let me be clear. But if you look at the *roots* of most evils, you will find money there. So, can you guess why you are told in India explicitly to not give to beggars *especially* if they are crippled physically, blind, burned?"

I couldn't imagine a reason, "I have no idea man, I don't get it. Those people are in real need. They are not able-bodied!"

"True, and if they were here, in this field, I would say, give them a sandwich."

"But…?"

"But, *their parents or kidnappers crippled them, blinded them, and burned them.*"
He stared at me, gauging my reaction.

"Oh, my God. That makes no sense."

"It makes perfect sense when you grasp what it means to normalize homelessness, to allow begging to be an accepted part of your culture as it is in India and other parts of the world. Think about it. If what you see here in this little grassy area becomes much more normal like in India, we will have created a 'beggar class,' in our society. Now, if being a beggar is your lot in life, why would a parent break the backs of their children? Crush their hands? Mutilate their legs and blind their eyes. Why?"

I shake my head in disgust. Feel sick to my stomach, "Because, idiots like me would give them more money. We would make the most deformed the wealthiest of the beggar class."

"Yes."

"All I would be doing is rewarding the mutilation of babies and children. Supporting the unthinkable."

"Yes. After untold generations of people trying to help, *guilting* money through the practice of pity, the beggar class would keep growing, and the children would keep getting mutilated. They purposely have more children to create an army of mutilated, blind, disfigured beggars. The more they can tug at your heartstrings, the more they tug on your purse strings. So, what is the answer?

"Tough love?"

"We may not be purposefully mutilating our people physically, yet, in America, but we do mentally and emotionally. It's a kind of hideousness you can't see. But, if we keep normalizing the homeless lifestyle, physical disfigurement could follow. It's a logical conclusion. Have you seen California lately?"

"I get it. I will never give a sandwich to another homeless person again. I will not take away their dignity. I will not reinforce the idea that they are incapable, that they are anything less than great."

"Except Blue-tent-guy, obviously."

"What? But…"

"Come on man; there are exceptions to every rule. Nothing is black and white."

"Sheesh, why is everything is so complicated with you?"

"With me? I have nothing to do with the way things are. I observe and adjust, the best I can, to this complicated life that is always fair."

"I thought life was never fair."

"How quickly you forgot option two. Look outside again."

I surveyed the green space that had become overrun with homeless people, cars zooming by on all sides.

"Look at all the cardboard and tent dwellings. They're all ruining it for Blue-tent-guy. Take Red-tent-guy. See him over there? He's smart and capable, but like so many, he is now acclimated to homelessness. He doesn't think he could ever be anything else. The passage of time will do that. It's the slow drip of despair. *But he could.* He could work and get off the street. Look at Green-tent-guy. He ran away like me as a teen. It's just the life he chooses now. You know the average homeless person costs the city, people like you, $60,000 per year. Is that fair?"

"No," I answered, shaking my head in cognitive dissonance, "It doesn't seem so."

"The Bud Clark Commons cost taxpayers $57,000,000 and over a million a year to run."

"I've never heard of the Bud Clark Commons. I remember he was the mayor of Portland. What is the Commons?"

"It was built in 2011 as part of a ten year plan to eliminate homelessness. Hilarious, right?"

"Ah, yeah. That would mean homelessness should soon be a thing of the past. *Look at the city now!*"

Portland homelessness trumped.online/lc2

"And the Bud Clark Commons is known as the 'one stop shopping center.' Whatever is desired: Crack, Heroine, sex, you name it."

Bud Clark Commons trumped.online/k4b

I just shake my head. It's so insidious. Then the voice from inside the sleeping bag speaks again. "See the big cardboard dwelling against the tree to the left?"

"Yeah."

"Well, she had a small business once, took a huge risk as business owners do. But it failed."

"What happened?"

"It's never just one thing. However, she told me when Congress raised the minimum wage in the 90s, for people like her, it was the straw that broke the camel's back. When she lost her business, she got depressed and spiraled down into the slow drip of despair. She's very capable though. She's just forgotten."

Minimum wage trumped.online/q7g
Minimum wage trumped.online/4zy
Joe Rogan trumped.online/yv9

"See Purple-tarp-guy?"

I looked around. Each dwelling now had a story - a history. This place came alive in a way it never had when I was handing out sandwiches.

And, the old programming in my brain was still running. *I wanted to go out and get a sandwich for everyone.* "Yes, I see Purple-tarp-guy."

"He ran away from home, turned tricks and fell into drugs and alcohol like everybody else around here. The easier you people make it for us, the sooner we get addicted. The sooner we get addicted the less likely we are to get out."

"I thought drug addiction came first, then homelessness."

"It goes both ways."

"What about Blue-tent-guy, what makes him so different?"

"Blue-tent shouldn't be out here, fell through the cracks. Remember, life isn't fair."

I shook my head, "Wait; I thought it was fair all the time."

"Okay, if you say so. Anyway, we are *not equal.* Never think that again. Blue-tent-guy *is* incapable of holding down a job. Incapable of sustaining relationships. That one has fallen through the cracks, for real, and is not on drugs. Instead of the financial burden that I and 80% of homeless people put upon society, that money should go to the approximately 20% of homeless incapable of helping themselves. Blue-tent-guy should be in a care facility. You can bring Blue-tent a sandwich; truly needs it. Blue-tent is incapable of self-sufficiency. Besides, it might ease some of your guilt."

Cognitive dissonance gives me a headache. A million thoughts are running through my mind. Somehow one idea popped out of my mouth, "Never judge someone by where they are, but by how far they have come?"

The sleeping bag straightened up like he was surprised I remembered what he said. "My hat is off to someone raised in a perfectly happy home with loving siblings and a dog that plays fetch, parents that show up cheering for the plays they perform in or the sports they excel at, if they have impeccable genetics: high natural health, high IQ, and high cheekbones, and then they graduate from Harvard and become a surgeon, my hat is off to them. I don't begrudge them. They deserve all the success in the world. *However,* their starting point wasn't very far from graduating Harvard, was it?"

"No, it was not."

"What I have a problem with is the disparity with which society responds to that person, the accolades they get for succeeding, for accomplishing and for being such a great person compared to others who have covered just as much distance but get no recognition at all."

I look out at the disheartening scene of humanity again as he continues.

"If Red-tent-guy gets it on with Big-cardboard-lady, and they have a child in this homeless nightmare, but somehow their child ends up living in a nice apartment on the Eastside managing a Starbucks, one could argue she went just as far on the path of life as did the surgeon that graduated from Harvard. There are true heroes all around us. And they're not making excuses, not playing the victim. We don't know who they are. For me, if they're not living in a tent or a cardboard box, like me, *they are my hero.* You are my hero. *You coulda been here."*

I want to agree with him, but I don't want to sound, well, better than him.

"My friend," he says compassionately, "It's okay to speak truth. *Real truth.* Not your truth or my truth. If a truth exists, it's for all of us. Truth unites us and applies to everyone equally, or it is *not truth.* So, go ahead and say it."

"Okay," I respond nodding my head hesitantly, "Actually, you're right. I could have been on the street."

"But you chose not to."

"Yes. However, not specifically. I didn't one day say, *I think I won't live on the street.* There were a few times when things got rough, and I refused to allow homelessness to become an option. Looking back now I realize I made a long string of connected choices that got me where I am today." For some intangible reason, probably rooted in some camouflaged self-disdain, I feel guilty, bad, for even acknowledging that I chose not to be homeless.

"Yes, you did. And I'm beginning now - my long string of choices. Three years ago I was teetering on the edge of life and death. I was addicted to heroin. I got some bad stuff. I realize now that bad stuff was the best thing that could've happened. *It scared me to life.* I woke on the sidewalk, next to Darcelle's just off of Burnside. It was freezing cold. The sidewalk felt like a giant slab of ice. I was shaking, barfing. In between heaves, I made a promise to God, the Universe, whatever you want to call It. *God,* I desperately pleaded, *If I survive this, I promise to change. I promise to make something of my life and to make the world a better place somehow. I promise God. I don't want to die. Not yet, not yet.* And somehow, I made it. *And that's what it takes for everybody.* No one can do it for you! We all have to come to our moment of reconciliation. A reconciliation with our soul. No amount of sandwiches will do that. Bad heroin on the other hand?" He laughed, "Now that's a whole other meatball."

I was trying to process everything he said. All he had been through, but all I could get out was, "Meatball? Really?" I chuckled, "How 'bout, a whole other ball of wax?"

He appeared to shake his head, *No,* from inside the sleeping bag, "There have been way too many balls of wax. A whole other one of those would be one too many balls of wax. Wouldn't you agree?"

"Oh, absolutely," I say playing along, "Who needs another ball of wax?"

He thought for a second, "Hmm. *A candle maker.* There's probably never too many balls o' wax for a candle maker."

We both laughed for a moment. Then he became quiet. Deep in thought. "The problem you know, is not 'homelessness.' That's disingenuous. Everyone is constantly saying there is a homelessness problem and they blame it on a lack of *affordable housing.* Hogwash! "

"I'm confused. If it's not a homelessness problem, what is it?"

"Come on brotha, pay attention. I've already said it eight ways to Sunday. So, you tell me."

"I'd say affordable housing but… Jobs? It's a jobs issue. Not enough jobs?"

The sleeping bag chuckled and then, "You're as slow as a geriatric slug on a salted side walk. No, wait. You're as slow as a glacier in Alaska; during the last ice age!" He was on a roll now, "You're slower than the

tectonic plates that turned Pangea into separate continents. No, no.
You're __so__ slow it would take…"

"… Okay, *knock it off.* Is it a, a, drug problem?"

"Wow. He's got some gray matter after all. Yes. There are many factors
but drug addiction is the engine that homelessness runs on. The majority
of homeless people *choose* this life style. Not because it's homeless.
They live it because it's the drug addicts lifestyle of choice. It's the only
place where your community supports and encourages drug addiction. In
your neighborhood, I'm sure you're encouraged to keep your house up,
your yard clean and pay your bills. Out here you're enabled to get high,
steal, make a mess and piss where you please."

My response reflects my naive desperateness, "God, if we can't hand out
sandwiches, what can we do?"

"Step one; practice tough love. This shitty… I mean city," he says,
reflecting the truth of what Portland is becoming with a joke, "We must
start enforcing the human dignity laws."

"Wait. I've never heard of those."

"They're the laws that, not only support but demand we treat each other
with dignity. And, most importantly, demand that we live with personal
dignity. Dignity is a super power. When one feels dignity it simply
becomes unacceptable to live without honor and respect. Dignity
motivates us to live with integrity and as we do, we experience the
greatest of all emotions; self-love."

"And you're saying there are, 'human dignity laws' that help us live with
self respect, honor and love?"

"Yes: Littering, loitering, drunken and disorderly conduct, no public
defecating or illegal drug use, no parking beyond the paid meter time and
no camping in public spaces."

"Those are the human dignity laws?"

"Yes, reinforce those and dignity will find its way back into the streets
and the hearts of this town. And of course we must arrest drug dealers.
They need to be afraid of the law. And, because of the filth that comes
with not enforcing the Human Dignity Laws, the plague is now breaking

out in west coast cities because of the homeless refuse that rats thrive on. *Unacceptable.*

"Step two; anyone who can show they have fallen on hard times, honestly, gets help. It's easy to prove you have recently been gainfully employed and you are not a drug addict. This segment of the homeless gets housing and possibly food stamps for a maximum of one year, giving them time to put their lives back together. Veterans who saw combat and experience PTSD will receive any and all help necessary for healing. This is a special segment of the homeless that deserves our full support. They already gave to us. Giving to them is nothing more than reciprocal. They make up approximately 11 percent of the homeless. The mentally ill make up about 22 percent and should be put into the appropriate institutions."

"That's only 33 percent. So the rest are drug addicts?"

"Almost everyone of them. Now, step three; reunification/better chance relocation. Any homeless persons who has family or friends somewhere will be given transportation for reunification. And if there is a place they feel may offer a better chance for them to reenter society, say their home town or a place that is offering work in their area of experience, again, they receive transportation and seed money.

"Step four; drug addicts, who make up the majority, will receive help if they can show they honestly desire it. Once they are arrested and commit to change, they will receive one of three drugs."

I'm confused, "Drugs to help drug addicts?"

"Yes: methadone, suboxone and vivitrol. They'er opioid blockers. They take the cravings away. An addict might be on them for life like a diabetic needs insulin; and then they're gonna need support like Narcotics Anonymous and counseling. And, once the drug addicts and dealers are off the street, the homeless from step two, the ones who recently fell onto hard times, won't be tempted to become addicts because the temptation would be removed. Along with this, we need to get serious about stopping the influx of opioids at the border; the drug cartels. If there was no supply, there would be no demand. Enough fentanyl entered the U.S. last year alone to kill every single American four times over."

It's all a revelation to me, "That sounds like a plan that could actually work."

"Well, I've had a lot of time to think about it, from the inside."

"Geese; it really is predominately a drug problem, not a homeless issue."

"Yep. People who think it's a housing cost issue have not done their homework. A very small percentage of the homeless are on the streets because they can't find affordable housing and those people would be taken care of in my plan. They'er actually trying to implement some of these ideas in Rhode Island. It's a paradigm shift to see it for what it is, a drug crisis. And, by addressing the underlying problem, maybe we can tackle three issues with one effort: drug addiction, homelessness, and we can save our city."

🔗 Rhode Island program, <u>trumped.online/ov1</u> 🔗

"But," I add, "We can't help those who don't wish to be helped, right?"

"Okay, I'm going to have to change my summation of your cognitive abilities. You are no longer as slow as tectonic plates. Let's go with, a herd of turtles. *We cannot help those who refuse help.* And many will refuse it. Homelessness is *not* curable because there will always be those who choose drugs over life. They will die. What we *cannot do* is allow the crime, disease, and drugs that accompany homelessness to infect the general public, the innocent children. Never accept the unacceptable. Remember, life isn't fair, but love is always right. Especially tough love."

"How do we really know though, the difference between acceptable and unacceptable?"

"Micro-macro."

I respond sarcastically, "Oh, yes, of course… *What's micr-macro!?*"

"Whatever is unacceptable in the micro, is not acceptable in the macro. Say you have a house guest, what behaviors would be expected in your house?"

"Well, just basic common curtesy and responsibility. Be helpful, respectful; clean up your own messes."

"And what would you do if they didn't follow those basic rules."

"Demand that they do."

"And if they don't?"

"They can't stay. I couldn't live like that nor should my family be forced to."

"Exactly. And Portland is our home. Micro-Macro. No one should be afraid to walk the streets or play in the parks with their children. People should not be afraid to leave their own homes. And no one, especially children, should have to see people shooting up and shitting on the streets."

"Yes, I get it. What's unacceptable in the micro has to be unacceptable in the macro." Then a quiet, "But," snuck out of my mouth. It hung there for a bit.

"Yes, but what?" He asked.

I couldn't get out of this one, "You're explaining to me your philosophy on ending homelessness from inside a sleeping bag, in a tent, in the middle of the city."

"Yes, I am that which I despise. Ironic, I know. Sometimes I think maybe we all are."

"Are what?"

"The things we despise. But, I do have a dream." Then he instructed, "Look up just above the tunnel leading into Portland. Can you see up there?" In the faint morning light, I could see outlines of homes. Some are mansions. Lights twinkled, scattered all over the hills.

"Sure, I guess. What?"

"I want to live up there, somewhere. That's my dream. I want to make it back to where I started, but on my terms. And I want to look down here and remember all of my life. Not for materialistic reasons so much, although I often dream of a bed so comfortable you never wake up in pain, unable to move because the blood has been cut off to your legs and arms. Ironic isn't it, *dreaming of a bed*."

It's impossible to imagine what it's like out here. How many things I take for granted.

"I'm 28 years old," He informed. "It's not too late for me. Maybe it's never too late. That near-death moment three years ago, I call it my, *New-Over*. I think everyone should have one. Maybe even several, in a lifetime."

I'm intrigued, "What's the difference between a 'new-over' and a 'do-over?'"

"Phhh. No comparison. A 'do over' is doing the same thing over again, hoping it might be better. A *New Over* is throwing the past in a trash heap, or a recycle bin if you prefer, and allowing each moment from that day forward, to be different, to be truly new."

As I consider this, New Over, I glance at my phone, "Oh my gosh," I exclaim, "You made me lat… I mean, I made myself late, again. I've got to go to work!"

"How blessed you are!"

"Yes, so true," I agree as I exit the tent.

"Hey" he yells, halting me in my tracks. "*I think maybe I'm a better person than you!*" he says half-jokingly. But I think maybe it's true. "*You know why?*" he asks.

"No. Tell me, why?"

No words are spoken. He gently slips his phone through the tiny opening in the zipper. I step back into the tent and take it from him. The cracked screen makes it a little hard to read but once I do…

"NO FLIPPIN' WAY!"

Chapter 8 The Future: Al Gore
Year: 2047 February 1 6:17 p.m.

Jadda is beside herself, "Are you sure the data is right?"

Charles and I look at each other, and I tell her, "We can't find any flaws. Collecting, analyzing, scrutinizing over the data, past and present, has been my passion for twenty-plus years. I've been meticulous. What it all means is still unclear. I have a lot to figure out. Much mulling to do. But the general trend is undeniable, I think."

"Yes, undeniable," Charles dispels my shadow of a doubt.

Shelly, Jadda's sister, arrives, "Hey everybody, I've got news."

"Hey, Sis! You have to see this," Jadda hollers back to her sister.

Have you ever known a woman that *everyone* loves? A woman that other women don't want their husbands to meet? That's Shelly. Beautiful, intelligent…brilliant actually. She's 5 11', runs five miles a day and has a black belt in taekwondo. Let me just say; you wouldn't want to mess with her. She worked her way up the ladder at Green Power-Portland in the tech department. Now she oversees and manages all things technological. She's earned twelve patents while working at Green Power. Jadda says she's in line for a huge promotion. A VP position. Serious bucks!

"See what?" Shelly says, intrigued.

"Just come here. Look!" She joins us in the living room and walks around the floating data. Intrigued, confused. But you can see the light bulbs go on.

"What? Where did you get this?"

"Marcus," Jadda urgently replies, "He's been tracking and analyzing the satellite data meticulously for 20 years and studying all records available on the earth's climate history. Ice core samples, tree rings, all the data at the temperature stations around the globe, weather anomalies… you name it."

"You see what this means, though, don't you?" I ask, understanding it's a lot to take in.

"I'm getting the idea, but... go ahead and give me the gist."

I hold up my fist and then release a few fingers, one at a time, pointing up. "Three words...*catastrophic – climate - change!*"

"That's, that's... what I thought. *Just wanted to be crystal clear.*"

"Look, everyone, look here," Jadda says, pulling together and superimposing two different graphs, one over the other. "Have you considered what this means? Look at the year 2023 and 2035. Compare them with your ice core data from fifty-one thousand years ago to thirty-nine thousand years ago."

We all look closely for a moment, Charles inquires, "Honey, what is it?"

"The *rate* of the change. See, look here," she points at both sets of the graphs. "We're on nearly the same track, but... but at least, I don't know, *100 times the pace!*"

"Oh my God," I exhale, desperately. "*How could I have missed it?*"

"You were too close, probably. You needed fresh eyes. Don't kick yourself. Without you, none of us would be here. The question is what are we going to do? Who will believe us? Ever since the backlash of, **An Inconvenient Truth,** climate 'alarmists' of any kind are lumped in with Al Gore. Rest his soul."

"Actually," Jadda recalls, "There may be no rest for his soul. Didn't someone steal the urn of his ashes back in 2037, just after his death, and dump them into a coal mine?"

"Oh my gosh," Charles' face lights up, "You're right. Once Gore got caught investing in every business he was promoting using what some thought of as scare tactics, he lost the public trust. History can be so ironic."

Jadda shakes her head, "And didn't he sell his network, Current T.V., for five hundred million dollars to Al Jazeera which makes all their money from oil?"

ⵔ Al Gore on David Letterman trumped.online/ge0 ⵔ

"Yep," Charles confirms, "Not to mention he flew the world over in his fossil fuel burning private jet. Oh… and, just one of his many homes burned 12 times the fuel of the *average American dwelling!"*

Soon after all of this came out, Trump pulled out of the Paris Accord. Ironically, a year later the people of Paris rioted, enraged, because of the Paris Climate Accord.

Paris riots trumped.online/y66

With all the fossil fuel power that was freed up, the next twenty years was almost like another industrial revolution which led to technological breakthroughs of all kinds. The irony is, *the breakthroughs in energy technologies ended up making fossil fuels obsolete.* That's when it became cheaper to use renewables. The world today is Al Gore's dream come true. Or, at least, claimed to be.

"Yes, *The IRONY!* Maybe before he died," I wondered, "He knew what we have discovered. Shelly, have you heard anything about the data at Green Power?"

"No, but it's not something G.P. tracks. I mean, since renewable energy replaced fossil fuels, we don't study it anymore."

Charles places his hand on his forehead, "We'll never know what Gore knew. It would answer a lot of questions I guess. But, the question of the hour, in fact, the only question that matters now is, *how much time do we have left?"*

BBC Trump ends Paris accord trumped.online/p7f

The Dawn: *The Riddle of Ritalin*
Year: 2017 January 22 2:46 p.m.

I'm still reeling over the news from Orange-tent-guy's iPhone when, "Hi Daddy," Shanice calls. Malik is close behind as they step out the front of Rachel Carson elementary school. I run toward them, as always, my heart exploding with love for my two bundles.

"How were your days?"

"Oh, pretty good," Shanice replies. "I got an 'A' on my spelling exam."

"How about you, Malik?" He's not too quick to respond.

"I got a 'C-.'"

"Buddy, we gotta work on that. Hey, Shanice," I say leaning toward the backseat as we exit the parking lot, feeling almost guilty about the news from Orange-tent-guy's phone. I have to come clean, "It's important to admit when you're wrong, right?"

"Um, Yeah," she responds hesitantly, *"Am I in trouble?"*

"No sweetheart. I want you to know your mother and I were wrong. Trump did not remove Martin Luther King's dust."

"DADDY, *it's bust, remember?* It means a kind of statue of somebody. But we can call it dust if you want to."

"Dust it is."

She becomes quiet, introspective, before asking, "So, he's not a racist?"

"I didn't say that, *I think he is*. We just need to make sure our facts are correct."

As we approach home my stress level increases. Our street, North East 45th, is tree-lined, but the trees are leafless for the winter. Somehow the look of the gangly branches eerily reaching down toward the ground reflect my emotional state. I'm not looking forward to seeing Kathy today. If she hasn't heard the news, I wonder if I should even tell her. As we enter the house, my question takes care of itself.

"Hey sweethearts," Kathy greets the kids, "How was your day?"

As kids often do, Shanice barrels forward, ignoring her mother's question, "Guess what?"

"What?" Kathy reacts, expecting, maybe a joke or some kind of game.

"You and daddy were wrong, Trump did not remove Martin Luther King's dust."

"Huh? What?"

"It's a long story honey, what she means is Trump did not remove the bust."

"What are you talking about, of course, he did."

I knew this might happen; the suspension of logic, even facts, for a desired outcome.

"Hey kids, why don't you head upstairs, get that homework done, Okay?"

Downtrodden, Malik responds, "Come… ON… DAD!?" You'd think I had just asked him to eat dirt. "I just want to play for a while; then I'll do homework."

"Malik," I reply softly, "That's what you always say. Then it gets to be eight o'clock, and it's not done. Then we fight about it. Can't you be more like your sister? She does it. No fuss."

He purses his lips. Clenches his fists and proclaims, *"FINE,"* as he stomps upstairs.

Once the kids have disappeared I continue, "I don't want to argue about it, turn on some 24-hour news. I'm sure it will come up."

She turns on CNN, and they're saying a plane disappeared into another dimension! No mention of the bust. Why?

CNN Black Hole Conspiracy trumped.online/ar7

Finally, she jeers like a third-grade school girl, "See, I told you so. If he hadn't removed the bust, they would have mentioned it by now."

Why on earth aren't they talking about it on CNN? "Kathy, I don't understand. It's important news."

"It would be, but you're wrong."

I start channel surfing which is an unspoken violation around here. Kathy had all but cemented the remote to CNN. As I force it to change channels, I almost expect there to be crackling. I stop at MSNBC for a while. Nothing. Soon I'm just changing the channels in frustration. *Won't anyone report this?* Finally, I see coverage. I don't even know what channel it's on.

"Kathy, look, there it is."

"Really?" she says with disdain, *"Are you kidding? Do you even know what that is?"*

"Um…"

"It's Fox you, idiot. FOX! They couldn't tell the truth if the very existence of earth was in the balance. *Turn the station now! NOW. Before I get ill!"*

"Okay, okay."

I finally find a more obscure network, one that Kathy might be the least bit open to and sure enough, Trump is explaining what happened. Kathy refuses even to look. She says he makes her sick, *Not my president,* she parrots as Trump explains the MLK debacle.

Martin Luther King bust truth trumped.online/wow

No one removed the bust, there was just a person standing in front of it! The reporter was not in his right mind. He had a desired outcome which increased his prejudice. That desired outcome stripped the reporter, an otherwise intelligent person, from using first-grade logic. Trump moved nothing; it was obscured from sight.

Once she hears the gist, she looks at me like maybe *I cheated on her, with Jamaal!* Or even worse, like *I was Trump* himself. She stomps out of the room.

"Hey, don't shoot the messenger! What are you mad at me for?" Truthfully, as irrational, childish and ridiculous as it is, I understand. I would've done the same thing just weeks ago. She's turning white now, then flushed. I have learned to gage her anger by the color of her face. Pinkish; irritated. Red; angry. White; *outraged*. There's a direct correlation between how angry she is and how much trouble I will be in.

"Because…" she says with clenched teeth, taking a step toward me *"What are you? A Trump supporter now?"*

I shake my head in disbelief, "Kathy, *seriously?* Have you lost your mind? I hate the guy. *NOT MY PRESIDENT.* But, it hurts our cause to be spreading, well, fake news."

"But you even said at the dinner party the other night you didn't think he removed the bust. You *don't think he's a racist?"*

I shake my head, recognizing the complete lack of logic to her reasoning but also seeing myself in her, "That makes no sense."

She turns her back on me, for a moment, and then spins back around, "Why else, on God's green earth, did you think he didn't remove the bust of Martin Luther King."

I shake my head in frustration, *"But I was right!"* Now *I* was getting angry. And yet, it felt as though I was arguing with myself.

"Well, *of course,"* She exclaims, *"You always have to be right."*

"What?"

"You heard me; *you always have to be right… Mr. righteousness."* She bobbles her head like she's imitating me, I guess. But, I've never bobbled my head in my life.

"I don't *have* to be right, but if I am right, *what in God's name is wrong with stating the fact that, well, I'm right!"*

She thinks for a moment, then piously responds, "You know, *you're not gettin' any for the foreseeable future. I hope you like the couch."*

"Okay Miss, Miss… 'Spiritual,'" I say bobbling my head back at her, *"I know a Reiki Master you should see about that anger issue. Maybe we*

should visualize Wisconsin turning blue." Oops. I may have taken it a smidge too far. Interestingly enough, *she is* now turning blue. I've never seen this shade before. If looks could kill, I'd be splattered against the family room window like a fly when Malik gets ahold of a swatter.

"Babe," I say trying to bring a little sanity to this mayhem, "This is the stupidest argument we've ever had! I'm sorry." Not sure what I'm sorry about. Yes, Frump is a racist, sexist, homophobe, but he didn't remove the bust of Martin Luther King. I am sorry that this escalated into Crazyville. That much is true. Doesn't matter though. She takes off out the front, slams the door behind her. Hopefully, she can blow off a little steam and come back to her senses.

I head upstairs to see how the kids are, hoping we didn't raise our voices too much. I honestly don't know. It's weird, in the heat of the battle, self-awareness slips away. As I enter Malik's room, I'm not surprised to see he's playing with a toy tank and army guys, pretending like he's blowing stuff up. "Hey buddy, how is your homework coming?" I know he hasn't started yet, *he never does*. He lets go of the toy tank, crawls to his little desk and pretends he's been doing his homework; like I wouldn't notice if he sneaks quietly enough.

"Fine, dad, it's going fine."

"Here," I say taking a seat next to him, "Let's work on it together for a while." Doing homework with Malik is like trying to catch a fish with your bare hands. He squirms, complains, resists, and, occasionally even lashes out as if his mother and I are part of some evil plan to eliminate all joy from childhood. While struggling over his first lessons on multiplication, I hear Kathy enter the front door.

"Malik," I say taking a breath, trying to maintain my composure, "If you stay focused, we'll finish in 20 minutes; otherwise, it'll take all night."

Appearing utterly defeated he says, "*I don't get it, Dad, I just don't get it.*"

I spend the next hour, *pulling teeth*. We finally finish just in time for dinner. Kathy put on a happy face for the kids. Once they're down for the night, things get awkwardly silent. It's a familiar torture. I decide to tell her about Malik's struggle with his homework for two reasons; first, it's an issue we have been dealing with for a while now. Second, I know it will break the ice. "It was a rough night with Malik's homework. So frustrating."

"It's just gotten worse each year," she adds, shaking her head, "I was hoping third grade would be a breakthrough. You know, the Williamson's next-door have their son on Ritalin."

"I know. The Lopez's put Alexandro on Adderall last year."

After we do our night time routine, we climb into bed. I'm glad not to be on the couch. We lay there in silence for a while. Then Kathy says, "We should look into Ritalin for Malik."

"I was thinking the same thing. I'll take them to school in the morning to speak to Mrs. Rogers about Malik's grades. I'll also try to set up an appointment with the pediatrician."

"Good," is her pointed response.

Now, I'm not sure what possessed me especially at that moment when things were beginning to smooth over. I suppose it's because the Orange-tent-guy has become the Oz behind the curtain of my brain, making me question everything. Sometimes I wish I never met him. I live in a constant state of cognitive dissonance. And so, for reasons that are very hard to understand, reasons I didn't even know, I cut the silence by stating this simple fact, "Trump never mocked a handicapped person."

Chapter 9 The Future: *Fossil Records*
Year: 2047 February 1 6:45 p.m.

That question, *how much time do we have?* It plagues our minds.

"I don't know," Jadda declared, "We need to sort this out, ASAP! Look at the temperature change at approximately 55,000 years ago. It's dramatic."

After processing the information, I add, "But it must have taken place over at least a period of a 1000 years judging by the graphs."

"Siri, show us fossil records for approximately 55,000 years ago," Charles requests. Suddenly, the space is dangling with more information than you could process in a month. "Siri, choose one record that gives us the best overall summary of the fossil records from 55,000 years ago."

"Right away," Siri replies with a perfect impersonation of the android C3PO from Star Wars. Charles is a big fan. Suddenly there's just one article left. Charles studies it for a moment and then swipes his hand in the air, "Here, look at this," the records gracefully float in front of me.

"Yes, it looks like the fossil records correspond with the temperature shift. Life transformed on earth."

"You do see what's happening don't you?" Jadda says with urgency, "We're on the same trajectory, the only difference is the time frame. We're living the same climate shift that occurred then only compressed into a fraction of the time."

"This is hard to come to accept," Charles says shaking his head. Shelly has been silent now for some time. She is just listening. Shocked. Unable to process it all I guess.

"Yes, it is," Jadda agrees, "Taking all of this in, we have little time before it's irreversible. I would have to say we've got… *forty years, give or take.*"

The Dawn: *ADHD*
Year: 2017 January 22 11:03 p.m.

She didn't respond the first time so, the glutton for punishment that I am, I said it again. "Trump never mocked a handicapped person."

"WHAT?" She shrieked, her voice several decibels higher than is acceptable in bed after eleven o'clock.

"Trump never made fun of a handicapped person," I repeated, "In fact, on the Maury Povich show Trump gave a very large check to a disabled girl. He said she was one of his greatest inspirations."

"What in the hell has gotten into you? Of course he made fun of that handicapped reporter. Meryl Streep called him out in her acceptance speech during the Golden Globes."

"I'm aware of that. We were together, on the couch *applauding her,* remember?" She barreled forward as if I said nothing.

"Meryl Streep! She's a brilliant actress. Why on earth would she tell a lie?"

"Because of she, she…" I couldn't say what I was thinking. I couldn't say it is because she has a political agenda. How can I say that when both Kathy and I *agree with her agenda.* Also, I couldn't say it because Meryl Streep suffers from TDS, Trump Derangement Syndrome. It's a condition in which one's hatred for Trump is so visceral it becomes impossible to see any good coming from the administration even if it stares you in the face because you are constantly *suspending all logic for a desired outcome.* In this case, the desired outcome is impeachment. No, I could not say any of that especially since Kathy and I both suffer from TDS ourselves. Finally, I simply said, "Forget it."

To which she replied, *"GET OUT.* I can't sleep in the same bed with a Phrump lover."

"Oh my God, seriously? Trump lover? Just look it up on the Internet tomorrow."

"That would be a waste of time. Meryl Streep and all the other brilliant actors and actresses know what they're talking about. You have lost your mind. *Get out!"*

And so, the couch it is.

I didn't sleep much. Not because of the couch. It's not a bad couch. I've slept on worse - futons in college for starters. They were lumpy, extremely lumpy. Tonight the lumps were in my mind. I am scared of losing everything.

7 a.m. came too soon. Got the kids ready while walking on eggshells. They usually take the bus, but today I drive them early so I can chat with their teacher.

"Hi, Mrs. Rogers, I'm sorry to interrupt before school but, if you have a moment…"

"Sure, I can make a quick moment. Marcus right? Malik and Shanice's father."

"Yes. So, I'm just a little concerned about Malik. He got another C- on his spelling test, and I'm just wondering what we can do. His sister does so well, straight A's. I don't get it."

"Malik *does* have a problem focusing." She replies, acknowledging the situation. "He's a great kid, but fidgety."

"What do you recommend?"

"Here," she opens her desk drawer and pulls out a card, "This guy is a good tutor."

"Also, I know you're not a doctor, but I was wondering if you think, maybe, he might be, ADHD?"

"I appreciate you coming to me about this. But like you say, I'm not a doctor." Then she looks at me for a split second with an expression that I cannot decipher. Like she was trying to say something she didn't want her colleagues to know. "So, well, you know, you *might* want to take him to your pediatrician."

"Okay, umm, thank you." I head off to work full of questions. At lunch break, I practically unconsciously get in my car and drive to the green space where the Orange-tent-guy resides. "Knock knock, anyone in there?" I announce standing just outside. It's an above-average temperature for January. A few rays of sun break through. I feel a sense of relief for my friend and everybody who lives here. Warmer days like this in the winter must be a godsend. I see a slight glow emanating from inside. His iPhone I would guess.

"Yes… I'm here." He sounds slightly annoyed that I have shown up again unannounced.

"What are you doing?"

"Research… what are you doing?"

"I don't know. I was just at work; it's only about a mile from here so I thought I'd head over during lunch break."

"What's troubling you?" Either he's psychic or recognizes a pattern.

"Nothin', just killin' time I guess."

"Seriously? Killin' time?" he responds, his face pushes up against the orange mesh again. "Have you ever considered that time might very well be the single most precious thing we have? And you're *killin' it?* Pathetic! Either cough it up or leave me to my work."

I don't want to admit it, but I had never considered the preciousness of time. What, if anything, could be more valuable? "One of my kids has ADHD; I told my wife about Martin Luther King's bust *and* the handicapped reporter fiasco."

"Oh," he interjects. I can see him put his iPhone down. "So, are you getting a divorce yet?" He's not one to mince words.

"What? No… we're not getting a divorce! Geez. What's wrong with you?"

"What's wrong with me? Well, for starters, *I live in a tent.* What's your excuse?" By the lightness in his voice, I thought he was about to laugh.

"Touché" I reply. It's moments like this that make you wonder why you ever complain about anything.

"I give it nine months…" he says, randomly.

"You give what nine months?"

"Your marriage," He says emphatically raising his arms. The sun has come out making a very clear, shadow puppet-like outline of his body on the tent material. "That is if you keep coming around here. If you want to stay married, I suggest we part ways."

"Wait, what? Are you now, a marriage counselor?"

"Why yes. Yes, I, *I believe I am!*" he answers quite sure of himself as his outline passes back and forth. "Ever since the New Over/near death deal I made with God three years ago, I became obsessed with bettering myself. And with that came an unquenchable thirst for truth. But, I'm not sure you, or your wife, can handle the truth. So, unless you are ready for your own *New Over,* you should probably stop coming here."

"Okay, Orange-tent-guy…" Oops, I didn't mean to say that out loud. "I mean…"

"No, I like it," he interrupts, "Orange-tent-guy it is. That will be my pseudonym around you. *Orange-tent-guy,"* he said with a weird kind of pride. "And you, my friend, you will be… *Silver Prius Driving/About To Have A Nervous Breakdown Guy.*

"You're insufferable," I say shaking my head.

"No, *I'm…"* then he lowers his voice and puts his fist in the air like superman, announcing to the world, ***"I'm… Orange-tent-guy, able to exist with nearly zero possessions, live on less than four hours of sleep per night and, only need a couple of showers a year! Yes, I am Orange-tent-guy. But don't be deceived, I can shatter your perceptions, destroy your prejudices and ruin your marriage with the utterance of a single truth!"***

He stood there basking in the glory of his new found calling, the shadow of his fist in the air, stoic like a statue.

"Okay…Orange-tent-guy, you can call me Silver Prius Driver, but let's leave it at that. Now, lay on me one of these truths you think will destroy my life."

"Your son doesn't have ADHD."

"What? How did you know it was my son? What makes you think he doesn't have it?"

"Well, I'm just willing to go with the odds here. And the odds are greatly stacked in my favor. Want to bet all the money in your wallet?"

"No thanks."

"First, boys and girls are very different. They have different strengths and weaknesses."

"No," I respond emotionally, "They're *equal,* girls are just as capable as boys."

"Hmm, why didn't you say boys are just as capable as girls?"

I am stymied, once again.

"Okay," he continues, "I'll tell you why. They're not! They're *different.* Do you remember our discussion about, 'equal?'"

I squirm a little bit, as I begin to recall, "Yes, but, but this is different."

He quickly breathes out through his nose. That thing people do when they are slightly frustrated, "Hmm, let's unpack this. First, if boys and girls are equal, the same, then why did I know it was your son and not your daughter?"

"Lucky guess?"

"EEEEEEEAAEE," he makes that annoying buzzer sound, *"WRONG.* This discussion, this topic, is so obvious it's tiring. You have to work at *suspending logic for a desired outcome* to convince yourself that girls and boys are the same. That whole talking point is pure politically correct nonsense. Boys and girls are not 'made' equal. Men and women are not 'made' equal. Boys are diagnosed with ADHD *four times as often as girls* and *five years earlier.* Now, how is that the same? How is that equal? More girls graduate from high school and from college than boys. And, the girls that do graduate have a higher GPA, on average, in both cases. How is that equal, the same? *Girls are better at school than boys are!* Does this mean girls are smarter than boys? No. Girls are genetically predisposed to being better at the institution we call school. *Boys are hyperactive. They can't sit still.* Boys mature slower than girls. We are turning *immaturity into a disease.* They need to move, to run and to play at regular intervals. They need physical activity more often than girls. *It's genetics.* It's not fair, but it's a fact. *The system is failing our boys.* You see, I *was your son.* I couldn't settle down. I couldn't focus. My parents said I should be more like my sister."

Ugh. I remember just saying that to Malik. He continued, "It played a big part in why I ran away. I felt shamed all the time for being the way I was. *For being a boy.* I squirmed around all the time. Constantly got in trouble for not paying attention as if I was consciously choosing to fidget and have a short attention span. It's one of the reasons I started smoking pot. But I didn't need pot, or Ritalin or any other drug. I needed a different model of education. I needed time to play. I needed to run. I needed to get that energy out so I could settle down for a while and focus. I needed a hands-on, interactive education."

He paused for a moment, accessing the memories. "The strange thing is, the concepts for me weren't hard. I understood the lessons, in my mind. I once overheard my teacher say to my mother, *I think he is a genius, he doesn't apply himself.* So, no. Playing the odds, I do not believe your son has ADHD. I think he's a boy. Probably a very healthy boy. And don't ever forget, big pharmaceutical companies make billions of dollars on the drugs they're selling, basically, *to children.* So of course, it's in their interest to have as many kids diagnosed with ADHD as possible. That is one of the reasons the diagnosis has gone up so high. Also, many schools allow less time for physical movement, play. Resulting in more hyperactivity from 'immature' boys. It does not make them diseased."

      ⚭ Girls and boys learning styles trumped.online/vwo ⚭

As usual, there is much to consider. I move close enough that my toes are touching the bottom of the tent. "I agree with some of what you're saying, but our culture has socialized boys to be a certain way and girls to be another way, it's not genetic. Think about it. It starts the day their room is painted pink or blue!"

"*You* think about *this*," he said, pressing his face into the tent, stretching it out so much that we were practically nose to nose. "Is any color specifically male or female?"

I got him; he's making my point!

"No, that's my point, a color is a color. It has no sexual orientation."

"Then why does it matter what color a child's room is?"

"It doesn't?" I replied, beginning to feel like he might say, *checkmate.*

He grinned right through the tent, "Oh, it doesn't? I thought you said a color begins socialization, the indoctrination of masculine and feminine. Hmmm. If colors and other social cues have no masculine or feminine qualities, then maybe boys tend to be more masculine than girls and girls more feminine than boys."

My mind began twirling. He shook his head, "Wow, you have drunk the Kool-Aid! Just ask the teacher, are girls and boys different? Do boys have ADHD more often? Who gets better grades, boys or girls? Is the educational system designed in such a way that it favors a girl's natural disposition which is more docile than boys?"

"Okay, I will. But even if it's true, that boys and girls are different, we grow out of these differences. Women are just as capable as men!"

"Wow, your paradigm is not only blinding you, but it also appears to be making you deaf. Didn't I prove, in some ways, women are superior to men? For example, *in school.* Arguably the most important institution in our society."

"If what you're saying is true, then it makes the pay gap even more infuriating," I say, frustrated considering all of the superior women paid less than inferior men.

"Okay," he said, quickly pointing toward the road, *"Silver Prius Driving/ About To Have A Nervous Breakdown Guy,* I think that's enough for today. You better go."

"What?"

"I think you've had enough truth for one day."

"Why?

"I can see it in your eyes; you're starting to get *truth decay;* The subtle erosion of outdated, false beliefs creating cognitive dissonance, leading, eventually, to a *New Over."* He put his hand to his chin. "I don't think we should erode your 'truths' too quickly. Not that a complete and instantaneous collapse of who one once was is necessarily a bad thing, there are just more eloquent ways of transitioning."

"You know," I say perplexed, "You're kind of like Yoda except for the part where you're not short, and you speak normally."

He raised the pitch of his voice in that Yoda, squeaky way, *"Catching on, you are. More impactful it would be, in reverse, if I spoke."*

"Hey, that's pretty good."

He continues his Yoda speak, *"Flattery effects me not Padawan. Go you should. Slipping away the time is. Waiting patiently is your Prius. Go... you, now."* The outline of his arm raised, and then he flicked his hand in the direction of my car, *"off."* Looked like he then picked up his iPhone and slipped back into his sleeping bag.

He's wrong, I thought, driving away. Boys and girls, I'm sure, do equally in school overall. After work, I pick the kids up. They can take the bus, but we prefer to be there for them when we can. I go inside, Shanice is drawing. Malik? *Twirling,* spinning in circles. Mrs. Rogers is chatting with a couple of other teachers and the principle, "Hey kids, let's go."

"Hey Dad," they both say as they gather their stuff. We head out into the hall. Against my better judgment, I stop. "Kids, can you wait here at the door for me for a minute? I want to chat with your teacher."

I pensively approach them.

"Mrs. Rogers, sorry to interrupt but I have, kind of, a stupid question."

"Oh, there are no stupid questions," she kindly responds leaving an opening for me while the others hold their thoughts.

"Well, I wanted to talk to you a little more about my son. As I mentioned before, Kathy and I have been wondering if maybe Malik has ADHD. In your experience, do boys have ADHD more often than girls? Or are girls and boys the same?"

There is an undefinable, uncomfortable instant before she answers, "Every child is unique," she says hesitantly, "And each one must be treated as a unique individual."

"But if you were to say, in general, who is more suited, naturally, for the educational system? Boys or girls?"

"Oh, again I would just say, each child is a unique individual."

"But is there a difference between boys and girls? I'm facing a big decision. Do you think my son has ADHD? Or is he…a boy? Going through a natural boy stage?"

None of them responded right away, so I asked, again, "Is the educational system designed in such a way that it favors a girl's, I don't know, natural disposition? Who gets better grades, boys or girls?"

"Mr. Jacobs, there is no difference between boys and girls, specifically, but every *child* is different." We both glance toward the door where the kids are waiting. Malik is making faces at his sister. "And, I cannot diagnose ADHD, I'm not a doctor."

"Okay," I say disappointed in the whole discourse "I'm sorry to bother you."

As the kids and I head down the hallway and out the front door, Orange-tent-guy torments me. In my mind I do my own Yoda imitation, *See him again, you should not. Screwing your life up, he is.*

I open the doors on the passenger side for the kids to hop in. As I round the back of the car I here, *"Mr. Jacobs. Marcus, hold on a sec."*

Mrs. Rogers is approaching at a fast clip, "Hey, um, do you have a minute?"

"Sure…" I'm surprised to see her.

"Look," she said, peering around like she was an FBI agent concerned for our life, "I'm not supposed to talk about this. I mean, it's just taboo, politically. But, I, I feel your concern. And I see it in other parents. Proceed with caution. Although at times these drugs are useful, they are overprescribed for boys. I don't think he has ADHD. I think he has NBS.

"Huh?"

"Oh, so we don't get in trouble, it's an acronym that some of my colleagues and I use for boys like Malik. NBS, Normal Boy Syndrome.

Yes, boys and girls are different. *Very different.* The system it, it does work better for girls. Boys have more frenetic energy. They need to move and play more often. And when they aren't allowed to, they become hyper, and then they get in trouble." She shakes her head, takes a deep breath, "And that hurts their self-esteem. They begin to think of themselves as 'bad.' I've seen it happen over and over. It's a vicious cycle. There are even links to this cycle and criminal behavior later on in life."

I looked at my son through the window - my heart broke. "Well, that's not right. At all. Why don't they change the system, so boys get an equal education."

"Have you heard of David Katz?"

      ⟲ David Katz ADHD versus recess trumped.online/wt0 ⟲

"I don't think so."

"Well, he's trying to change things. Check out his work. Anyway, Malik is a great kid. *He's a boy!* And um, don't mention this conversation. I know it sounds crazy, but there could be negative repercussion. People have been fired for pointing out the differences between boys and girls, men and women."

"Okay. Thank you. Thank you so much."

"You're welcome," she softly spoke as she turned back toward Rachel Carson Elementary School.

As I drove away, I felt frustrated and relieved. I was frustrated with the system, relieved to know that my son is not sick or so different. He may have a "disease," but at least we have diagnosed it, *Boy.* One thing she said crept up on me as we pulled in the driveway. She didn't just say the difference is between boys and girls; she said the differences between *men and women.*

In my head, I heard Yoda speak once more, *Orange-tent-guy, visit him again, you will...*

Chapter 10 The Future: Dr. Judith Curry
Year: 2047 February 1 7:20 p.m.

"Forty years…or less?!" I interject disheartened. "You think that's all the time we have to reverse this mess?"

"Maybe more, maybe less, but yeah, something like that," Jadda answers shrugging her shoulders. "However, the good news is, I mean, don't you think it's reversible?"

"It could be," I say, contemplating.

"Shelly," Jadda calls out to her sister. We all turn to Shelly, but she is lost, gazing out the windows, eyes glazed.

"Shelly?" Jadda shouts, "Earth to Shelly, *come in Shelly!"*

Shelly shakes her head, returning to reality, "What? I'm sorry, I…"

"Do you think you could get this information to some higher-ups at G.P.? They could be instrumental! As the world knows, their motto is," we all say it together having heard it and read it countless times, *"Our undying commitment today, is a green planet for you tomorrow."*

"Oh, yeah, that's, that's a good idea. This is all just so overwhelming. I'll try…" Shelly says, widening her eyes, shrugging her shoulders.

We all study the data for a couple more hours, checking and double checking the graphs, ancient climate data, and papers written by climate scientists like Judith Curry, back in the 2000s when people still lived in fear of climate change before everything went renewable. She was part of the Obama administration's climate scientists team. "Can we please take a break for a minute? My brain is getting sloshy," Jadda pleads.

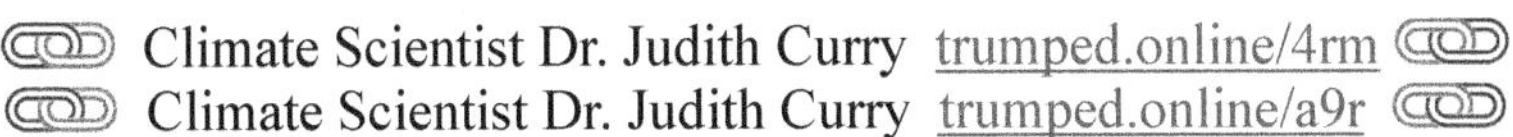

Climate Scientist Dr. Judith Curry trumped.online/4rm
Climate Scientist Dr. Judith Curry trumped.online/a9r

"I agree. How about some tea everyone?"

"Perfect." Charles concurs, "Okay, I've got peppermint, Earl Grey, peach, black, lemon, orange, rooibos, white, raspber…"

"Stop. That's enough. *There are way too many choices these days.*" Shelly says, overwhelmed.

Making my request I interject, "I'll have rooibos, love it."

"I'll have white tea," Jadda adds.

"Shelly? What say you?" Charles asks. "Ugh, so many choices! I'll have good old peppermint."

"Great. I'll join Marcus with rooibos."

"Siri, boil water for us," Charles commands.

Siri's C3PO voice quips, "Right away, sir."

"Babe," Jadda interrupts, "Say please. Remember, people are losing their civility from DSS, Device Speak Syndrome."

"All right, fine. Siri, *PLEASE*, boil us all some water if it's not too much trouble. But if it is too much trouble, go bathe in soaking salts and let me know when you are feeling up to it."

Siri/C3PO responds, "Oh, no sir, no problem at all. I'm an expert in tea. Did you know the first tea ever made was an accident?"

"No, enlighten us," Charles replies a little annoyed.

"It was 2737 B.C., and the Chinese emperor Shen Nung was sitting beneath a tree while his servant boiled drinking water when some leaves from the tree blew…"

"OOOOkay, thank you, Siri."

"Your tea is ready! Anything else I can do for you?"

"That will be all. You go take that bath now."

"Sorry, but, I'm incapable of taking a bath. I wish I could bu…"

"Siri?"

"Yes."

"It was a joke. Turn your humor setting up."

"Yes sir, right away sir…"

We all get a chuckle out of the exchange. It was a nice reprieve from the intensity of our work. We didn't say much while sipping. Too deep in thought. In no time it was nine o'clock. Dark and rainy, we said our goodbyes for now. I jump in my car, "Freedom?"

"Yes, Marcus, where to?"

"Home, and step on it!" I want to say the wheels squeal, as I head down the long driveway. That would be cool. But ever since no skid technology came standard on all cars, *not gonna happen.* Sometimes I miss driving, *with a stick,* no less! Instead of spinning out, there's just a lot of herky-jerky as we gain speed.

"Freedom, call Alexus please."

"Of course Sir." The windshield becomes a monitor reflecting my image, waiting for her to pick up. She doesn't, "Hey babe, pick up. Pick up! Okay, call me back when you get this message. *It's worse than we ever imagined…"*

The Dawn: *Hate Speech and John McEnroe*
Year: 2017 January 23 8:15 p.m.

I wasn't sure what to say to Kathy. If I told her Malik might not have ADHD, how would she react? If I told her boys and girls are different, *very different,* I'd have to tell her where I heard that from and, well, I'm kinda sworn to secrecy. So, for now, I say nothing. Kathy's upset anyway. After we put the kids to sleep I told her, *I'm going out.*

"Knock, knock…" I extolled. No answer. "Hello in there?" It's too dark to tell if he's around. I see no glowing iPhone either. Oh yeah. It's 8:27 p.m., his business. *He's at work!* Maybe the lot on Third street. As I arrive, he's just leaving. I can only tell it's him by his big rimmed old leather hat. He's heading down the street at a quick pace. I pull up next to him, maybe twenty feet away on the sidewalk. "Hey, Orange-tent-guy. Is that you?" He's wearing a trench coat; collar pulled up around his face to keep warm. The rim on his hat down around his eyebrows. "If it is you, I might have to change your nickname to, *The Man Without A Face.*"

"No, I like, *Orange-tent-guy* Better. And, *Silver Prius Driver/About To Have A Nervous Breakdown Guy,* fits you perfectly."

We continued moving down the road for a minute. Finally, he professed, "I *knew* I'd see you tonight."

"What are you now? A soothsayer? A mind reader?" I respond through the window, cruisin' between 4 and 6 MPH. I'd invite him in if it weren't for the smell. B.O. can stick to cloth upholstery.

"Why, why yes, I *believe I am!"* he answers, cockily as expected. "Did you know the term soothsayer goes back to middle English which meant, *A person who tells the truth.* So, you could say it means a person who sees the future and tells the truth. Fits me to a T!"

"Okay, so, why? Why did you know I'd be here?"

He whips out a perfect British accent, "Elementary Dear Watson. Elementary."

"How's that?"

"Okay, I knew you'd be going to your kids… Wait for it, *Elementary school."*

"Touche'… Yes, Rachel Carson Elementary school."

"Rachel Carson? I didn't know there was a school named after her."

"Yes, I noticed you have her book Silent Spring, it's one of the most important books, I'd argue, ever written. She single-handedly put an end to the use of D.D.T."

"Interesting, yes, I've read it. Anyway, I knew you'd be going to your kids' school, and I know you're at least, engaged. Therefore, I knew you would inquire about ADHD, which would open a little more of Pandora's box. I knew you'd either get an honest answer or the answer you would get would be so, well, contrived, you would see through it. Either case would lead you back to me, the Sooth Sayer of, of…," he looked up at the cross street we were just passing at a slow jog, "Of Salmon Street.

Yes, I am…" he relayed with a kind of spooky overtone, *"The Sooth Sayer of Salmon Street."*

"Okay, Sherlock. Not bad. But you are wrong. I didn't get one or the other of those answers. I *got both!* Eat that *Sooth Sayer of Salmon Street.* Boys and Girls are very different and the education system, as it is, is much more suited for girls."

"And Women. Don't forget. Approximately 60% of all people who graduate with a college degree, today, are women. But do you know where and when it all starts?"

I shrugged my shoulders.

"Come on, think about it. Think about all you have learned."

My meeting with Mrs. Rogers comes flooding into my brain followed by an answer which pops out of my mouth, "First grade?"

"Is that a question or an answer?"

"First grade!" I say definitively!

"BINGO, chalk one up for the *Silver Prius Driving/About To Have A Nervous Break Down Guy.* The pattern begins at the beginning. A much higher percentage of boys feel stupid, lost, confused, not good enough, unfocused and on and on it goes all the way to college graduation.*"*

My heart a little broken, "I get it," I say, thinking of Malik.

"But, look on the bright side," he says, crossing the next intersection with only the occasional street lamp for light, "A college degree is not all it's cracked up to be." He suddenly stops. "Okay, we're here," he announces pointing at another parking lot. Without missing a beat, he grabs a broom that's hiding behind the lot's booth and sweeps.

"Wait, What?"

"What?.. what?"

"What do you mean a college degree is not what it's cracked up to be?"

"It's not."

I'm not sure what possessed me. Maybe I was just so tired. Maybe it was the present stress of my marriage. Maybe my concern for Malik. Probably a combination of all the above. In any case, out it came. "Look who's talking!" There was even a little anger in my voice, *"You're homeless, sweeping disgusting parking lots for five bucks an hour. Who are you to say a college degree isn't all it's cracked up to be; Orange-tent-guy who takes three showers a year! You're doing the very thing you say you're against, remember, page one hundred and twenty-three, paragraph two of* **The Communist Manifesto***, 'In proportion, therefore, as the repulsiveness of the work increases, the wage decreases.'"* Ugh. You ever wish you could suck all the words back into your mouth like a detachable hose sucks marbles?

He smiles, like, I don't know, maybe something is funny and then, "Hogwash!"

"Hogwash?"

"Yes. You know, refuse given to hogs which later became a metaphor for meaningless ideas, nonsense."

"Thanks for that, *Webster*, what is the hogwash to which you refer?"

"Page one hundred and twenty-three. And everything else in those two hundred and forty-six pages of hooey."

"How can you say that? You quoted it!"

"It's a good idea to understand things with which you disagree. Otherwise, you probably shouldn't disagree with them."

"Um, what?"

"Anyway, I will not sit here and point out the *grand* human rights achievements of Marxist countries like the Soviet Union or Venezuela or Zimbabwe or Brazil or Cuba or North Korea or, well, you get the idea. Instead, I'll say, *ten*."

Micheal Moore, Sean Pen trumped.online/jxt
Venezuela inflation trumped.online/5c5
Brazil Socialism trumped.online/1ht

There's one streetlight on the corner of the lot. Probably seventy feet away. As he sweeps, it's becoming like a dust bowl in the glow. Other than that, he's working in the dark.

"Ten what?"

"Ten bucks an hour. I got a raise starting today for this *repulsive* work."

"What? How?"

"I asked for it."

"So now you're making seventy dollars a day?"

"Actually, I think closer to a hundred. I should bring more parking lots online any day now."

"*Oh my God.* You… you could get a cheap apartment. This is incredible."

"No thanks. I like my tent. I have a plan."

"What plan? Geez, Louise. You could get off the street."

"I know this will be hard for you to understand with your college degree and all, but I'm fine with my tent. *For now.*"

"Hey, about that. I'm sorry for losing my temper a minute ago," I say, eating crow. "I'm truly, really sorry."

"Don't be sorry!"

"But it was so; I don't know, judgmental of me."

"So what! It was one of the most honest moments we have ever had."

"But I hate judgmental people," I interject, passionately.

"Sounds like you're in judgment of judgmental people."

Brain twist!

So, he continues, "We must make judgment calls all day, every day - about everything. Over time, our judgments improve, that's called *wisdom.* We look outside, and we judge the weather, *Looks like rain.* But why do we think so? Because over time we have learned to study the sky and come to a conclusion. We know we might be wrong, but it's just wise to use our experience and bring an umbrella. We judge food by its appearance, *Looks gross,* and sporting events, *Looks like they will lose.* Everything, we judge. Even say beds, *Looks comfortable.* But as soon as we put people into the mix, we are judged as bad for using our best judgment gained over a lifetime of experiences. You were right to judge me. Who am I to know anything about higher education? But imagine what life would be like if we lost our ability to judge! We'd be a mess. Just losing our ability to judge traffic alone would probably kill us all. Imagine if we couldn't judge the speed of oncoming traffic, *CRASH!* The key in judging is to do so with an open mind. In other words, *bring the umbrella.* What's it going to hurt? But don't become righteous, telling everyone it will rain. It might just clear up and be eighty-seven degrees making you the village idiot."

"That… makes sense," once again, cognitive dissonance sets in, forever chipping away at my paradigm. "And, wow, you don't even have a college degree," I say, smiling.

"Heck," he says from somewhere in the darkness while sweeping away, "I don't even have a *high school degree.* "

"Being around you, I'm thinking the less education you have, *the smarter you are.*"

His Yoda voice makes an encore performance with a quote from Return of the Jedi, *"You must unlearn, what you have learned. "*

"So, what's wrong with a college education?"

"Well, some courses they now offer, that kids take seriously, seem to me to be twaddle. There's, *Queering God: Feminist and Queer Theology, Latinx Sexual Dissidence and Guerrilla Translation* and *Unsettling Whiteness,* to name a few."

"Hu?"

"It's all part of an *indoctrination* instead of an *education*. Campuses are all too often a hive of groupthink. They are some of the most diverse places in the world if you only judge diversity by skin color or sexuality. However, if you're more concerned with real diversity, *diversity of thought,* well then, most college campuses are vanilla! They insidiously snuff out individuality through peer pressure, and professor pressure, in a kind of subtle brainwashing akin to the classic novel 1984. One of the most effective methods is their attempt at eliminating the First Amendment of the Constitution; Freedom of Speech," he says while picking up what looks like nasty McDonald's wrappers and paper cups.

"I know, I've heard that. It's terrible. Without the free flow of ideas, how can we evolve? How can we be diverse? It's one of the few things President Plump has done I agree with."

"Wow, I'm impressed," he responds, without missing a sweep.

"Thank you," I say bending over, taking a bow, "Thank you very much." Then I add the obvious going for brownie points, "What we need to eliminate is hate speech, not freedom of speech."

He drops his broom, the handle clangs on the asphalt, "Okay, *not impressed!* You're killing me *Silver Prius Driver/About To Have A Nervous Breakdown Guy*. Hate speech *isn't a thing*. It's propaganda. It's a label meant to manipulate us, *to brainwash, which you have been.* They use made-up terms to sound righteous, create division and then pound us into submission. I mean, no one would be for *hate speech.* But let's pretend it's a real thing for a moment. Just who would decide what's hateful and what's not hateful?"

"Well, the government. Of course."

"And what would be the penalty if someone caught you using this… hate speech?"

"Um, I, I don't know?"

"Think about it, what would be the fair punishment for someone who used this undefinable hate speech."

"Well, maybe a fine? And, all hate speech isn't as hateful as other hate speech."

"Really? Enlighten me."

"Well, some things are more hateful than others, and therefore the punishment should fit the degree of hate."

"Okay, give me an example," he asks as he picks up the broom and starts working again.

"Ah, well…" my mind, scrambling.

"What if," he says pointing through a window at a restaurant across the street, "That woman said, *White men are a plague upon the planet.* That's not only racist but pretty hateful. What should be the punishment?"

"I, I don't know."

"Come on; you're the one who said hate speech should be illegal. Okay, I'll make this easy on you. On a scale from 1 to 10, how hateful is that statement?"

"Well, I guess maybe a three."

"A three, okay. And what if the guy at the end of the bar said, *Muslims are a plague upon the planet?* What would that be?"

Without hesitation, I say, "Geez, a nine or ten."

"Really? Not only have you proven what a ridiculous idea hate speech is, but you have also revealed your insidious prejudice. You hate you! And, since you think the government should decide what hate speech is, what do you think the government is?"

"Well, it's people."

"What do they do?"

"They, um, have power and make decisions."

"You're getting close. The government exercises 'authoritative control' over the people they govern. How does that sound?"

"Controlling."

"And do you think these people are somehow pure? Do you think they're better, more ethical and moral than the rest of us?"

I had never thought of it that way. I always just somehow trusted the government to do what's right. "No, actually, I guess I don't, now that you ask. They seem to be some of the most morally corrupt people of society."

"And you think they should have 'authoritative control' over us? In other words, do you think they should decide what is hateful and what isn't?"

"Okay, I get it. No, I do not."

"And, don't you think if they had such power, they would call whatever is against their political agenda, hateful?"

I nod my head, "Probably."

"Don't you think most politicians are or become infatuated with power?"

"I guess. Yes. But I don't think people should speak hatefully!"

"I DO!," he says, hoping I'll take the bait. "Look, nearly no one wants *others* to speak 'hatefully,' but pretty much everyone does from time to time. It's like how everyone considers themselves law-abiding citizens. Do you?"

"What?"

"Consider yourself a law-abiding citizen."

"Sure. Of course."

"When was the last time you broke the law?"

"Geez, maybe when I was a teenager, I shoplifted a candy bar on a dare."

"Really? I'll bet you all the money in your wallet you broke the law this month."

I'm tempted to accept the bet but..."No thanks. You're up to some trick."

"It's not a trick!"

"Fine, when do *you* think I broke the law last?"

"No, *you tell me*. Here's hint #1. You break the law when you pick your kids up from school."

"Huh?"

"Hint #2. You break the law while at Cannon Beach."

"I do?"

"You do go to Cannon Beach don't you?"

"Yeah, I love Cannon Beach."

"Then you break the law there. Hint #3. You break the law while experiencing Einstein's theory of relativity."

"I didn't even know I experienced that."

"You do. You also break the law while sitting down."

"Sitting down?"

"Hint #4. You break the law almost every single day."

"What?"

"Come on. College educated, graduate school degreed idiot!" Suddenly, I get it, *"Driving!"*

"DING," he says mimicking the ringing of a bell. "If there were laws in place around speech, do you think they'd be easier or harder to enforce than driving laws?"

"Harder!"

"How much money do you think we'd waste on trying to enforce them?"

"I couldn't say."

"Millions if not billions a year. And, don't you think if someone had a vendetta against someone else they might say to a judge, *He called me a Sasquatch. That hurt my feelings.* And the other person might say...

Did not.

Did too.

Did not.

"It becomes one person's word against the other. It would tie the courts up forever with, 'hate speech' cases."

"Okay, I see how that could get out-of-control."

"Unless, of course, said defendant *was* a Sasquatch. Then, you'd have a real case on your hands."

He waited for a response. I didn't give him the satisfaction as he continued, "No one wants anyone to be hateful, but that is relative, cultural and time contextual. What's hateful to one person may not be to another. If you called your wife, let's say, your *little fatty,* how would she take that?"

"She would not take it. At all! It would be the end! Of life as we know it."

"Okay, in Mexico, in Spanish, a man calling his wife his little fatty, *Mi Gordita,* is a term of endearment."

"No way!"

"Yes, way."

"So, if a Mexican citizen climbed the wall, there *is* one already on much of the border. Hillary and Obama voted for it. Anyway, he snuck into America becoming an illegal alien and then met your wife, after you get divorced, subsequently calling her his little fatty, they could throw him in jail on two counts; illegal entry *and* hate speech. What do you think of that?"

"Well, I think I'm becoming increasingly against a law to control speech."

"Why, because it's a stupid idea or because you want to protect illegal aliens?"

"Um, I think maybe both."

"Okay, I like the honesty."

"And, what you have said is completely unrealistic. I'm not getting a divorce, and there's no way Hillary and Obama voted for a barrier between our countries."

"Did too."

"Did not."

"Did too"

"Did not."

"Did too. Billary and Obama wanted a wall. Look it up!"

Bill Clinton on the border trumped.online/we9
Hillary on a Wall trumped.online/li8
Obama on border trumped.online/dur

"Fine, I will... *DID NOT!* And, Billary?"

In the dark of night, I can barely make out the shaking of his head from side to side and the shrug of his shoulders before pushing forward. "Yes, Billary. They're interchangeable. Anyway, as relative as 'hate speech' is, there are a few universal ideas that most could agree are hateful. We've already decided, however, that the government cannot and should not control what we say. Yes?"

"Um, yes." I'm not totally convinced, but I get his angle.

"So, where should the moral compass come from that dictates how one would speak?"

An image of my children pop into my mind giving me the answer, "The home. One's mother and father and extended family."

"Agreed. Do you think the government should ever take the place of parents? Not that parents are perfect. Some suck. But do you think the government could or ever would be good parents?"

I laugh out loud; the idea seems preposterous, "No, I do not. Sometimes the government intercedes when there is abuse. I think that's probably the only time they should get involved."

"Agreed, however, I would suggest it still shouldn't be the government that does the interceding. Nonprofits, charities, churches, etc. would do a better job. Government is generally corrupt and does not have the correct checks and balances in place and, they're always trying to justify their jobs, so they push papers around and create problems where there are none, in many cases. We have just become brainwashed into thinking there are certain things only the government can do. Hogwash."

"Sorry, I disagree."

"You're entitled to do so. You can disagree loudly and clearly. *It's the beauty of free speech.* So, a personal question. Do you ever speak 'hatefully?'"

I'm not religious, but this somehow came to mind, "Let he who is without sin, cast the first stone."

"Well said," he continues working while I lean against my car. It sprinkles out. A minute or two passes in silence before he interjects, "If a woman says to her husband, a man she promised to love and cherish and stay with forever, that he's an 'effing,' no good piece of shit, nazi bastard that will never amount to anything, is that hateful?"

"Sounds hateful."

"Should they arrest or fine her for saying so?"

"I, well, it depends… No. They should not."

"And what about truth?"

"What about it?"

"Well, have you noticed that speaking the truth, citing facts that people don't want to hear because it's not politically correct, is considered hateful?"

I knew what he meant. I could feel that what he was saying was true, but I played dumb, "What do you mean?"

"Have you heard of micro-aggressions?"

"Maybe. Remind me."

"Well, It's the expression of ideas that some might find hurtful, hateful. Here's how it works. If you say something, anything that triggers someone, you may no longer say it. You are thought of as 'aggressive.' To be triggered is to feel any negative emotion."

"Well, I don't want to hurt anyone."

"Of course not, but do you feel that anyone and everyone around you has the right to decide what you say because they don't like it?"

"That doesn't seem right."

"Did you know, for example, that on some college campuses, you are not allowed to ask, *Where are you from?*"

"What? Why?"

"It's considered a micro-aggression. Do you see what is happening here is a very slippery slope? That we are moving closer and closer to allowing the government to become thought police? Can you concede that every single word or idea is attached to a thought and that if we allow someone to eliminate a word from our vocabulary, we are eliminating thought itself? And is it possible that the only way to reach deeper truths, to solve the most perplexing issues of our time is to allow all ideas, no matter how absurd they may appear, onto the stage of discourse? To debate, argue, and challenge each other?"

"Makes sense."

"Even if it's white supremacists or bat yielding, pepper spraying Antifa members?"

This is a challenge for me. First, because I don't think Antifa and white supremacists should be in the same category. I hesitantly agree, "Yes. Okay."

"EEEEEEEAEEEEE!" He gives me the buzzer!

"What? I thought…"

"You thought what?"

"That I was open-minded. But, honestly, I don't think we should ever allow white supremacists to speak their hateful rhetoric."

He sounds disappointed as he counterpunches, "First, not all white supremacist's rhetoric is hateful. Maybe closed minded and racist but 'hate' is not *necessarily always* the intent. Think of it this way, if green supremacists appeared from the Land of the Lost, somewhere in the earth's core, and said, *We come in peace, we are superior to you since we know how to survive in temperatures upwards of 15,000°*, are they necessarily hateful?"

"No, I guess not. Probably deranged from all the heat, but not necessarily hateful."

"Second, you are so off here it's laughable. It's Antifa that should not be allowed to speak. Come on, U. of O. alumni, *you can do it*. Why? Why is Antifa the group that should have its First Amendment rights suspended in the previous hypothetical?"

"I, I don't know…"

"Bat yielding, pepper spraying! If one group shows up in black masks yielding bats, using *pepper spray*, they *are* inciting violence. Plain and simple. That's not speech."

"True, yes. Okay."

Oxford University Hate speech <u>trumped.online/7r2</u>

We both take a moment to consider Green Supremacists from the Land of the Lost, when suddenly, he shouts from under the dim glow of one light, *"John McEnroe."*

"What? Where?"

"Truth…Hateful."

"Huh?"

"John McEnroe recently said Serena Williams is the greatest women's tennis player ever. They asked, *Why don't you say the best tennis player ever?"*

The light sprinkles outside turned to rain. "McEnroe responded, *Because she's not.* They cornered him into defending his position. He was forced to point out the obvious. Any highly ranked man on the pro tennis tour could beat her. This is a simple truth. Acknowledging it, being okay with it, speaking it, should never be shunned. Ever. Why have we come to a place in time where saying Serena Williams is the best women's player ever is somehow hateful? They have labeled him a sexist. They have told him he is wrong. They have beaten him down for giving a compliment!"

John McEnroe's comment <u>trumped.online/qiy</u>

The rain became a downpour. He kept cleaning, though, like it was all sunshine and lolly pops. I had to yell my response over the sound, *"I feel triggered by what you just said."*

"Of course you do. You're not comfortable with the truth. But, my well-meaning, misguided friend, The Truth Shall…"

He waited for me to finish his thought, *"Set Me Free."*

I walked right into that one. *"Well,"* I continued yelling over the rain *"I guess this brings us full circle. I wanted to talk to you about what Mrs. Rogers said, that men and women are different."*

"Ya think?" he said with more than a hint of sarcasm.

"I guess. Let's get out of this downpour."

"No can do. I've got five more lots to clean."

"In this rain?"

"They won't sweep themselves!"

"Okay," I say rounding my car to get in the driver's side. *"All right, I'll see you later."*

"Roger that."

I get in my car and just as I'm about to hit the gas; he knocks on my door window. I crack it open only an inch to minimize water intake. It's pouring so hard I can't see a thing. Water is gushing on windows. He extols the following like a smoke bomb thrown into a room with no exit. Then he disappears into the cold, wet, dark of night, *"Rachel Carson may have been complicit in the killing of over a million people."*

Chapter 11 The Future: *The Holocene Period*
Year: 2047 February 9 7:56 p.m.

Exhausted! Just got back from a rare in-person meeting with Isabella at
The Path. The official opening is six days away. It seems like
everything's on track. Now, I've got to get my full attention back on the
data. Charles, Jadda, Shelly, Alexus and I have become a team with one
succinct purpose: *save the planet.* We each study the data and, whenever
necessary, virtually convene or meet in person at Charles' place. Tonight,
it's virtual. Everyone is joining Alexus and me in my office, projected
through my iDesk. The data is holographically suspended in air. The
guests appear to be walking around on the floor with Alexus and me, but
their slight translucence spoils the illusion. "All the data supports the
long-held belief we are living in the Holocene interglacial phase, at the
end of the last ice age," Alexus points out.

"Yes, the Holocene period we inhabit has lasted about 14 thousand years.
It's been such an amazing time for humanity and all of life. Thriving. *All
of human memory, history, and advances have occurred in and because
of this Holocene."*

"It's sobering to consider where we would be if the Holocene phase had
not occurred," Charles considers. There's a sadness to his voice. We
know that this time of thriving for humanity, for life in general, could
very well be ending. "And now, because of egocentric human activity,
our children (not to mention our grandchildren) may see nothing but
devastation in the years ahead. If we don't turn things around, well, I'm
glad I won't be here to see it. I sometimes feel our generation owes the
next a huge apology, which is why we must get the data out to the world.
Then, maybe, there will be no apology necessary."

"Climate change on earth is like a steel ball on a string, swinging back
and forth," Shelley enters the discussion. "Interglacial periods like this
one," she points to the current Holocene period on a graph, "They are
like that moment when the steel ball has reached the peak of its swing,
and, just for a moment stops, suspended in time before it begins its swing
the other way. So that's where we are, at the end of the swing, that pause,
primed for change."

"That's all normal, of course," I add, spinning the graph around to take a
closer look. "What we've got to convince the world of is, well, *the string
is about to break! Most literally.* Bringing a kind of swift, dramatic

change the earth has never known. Alexus and I are trying to get a
meeting with our senator, Chris Rock."

"He might listen," Jadda adds, "I don't know. But if we could get him to
forward the information onto Ben Affleck or Miley Cyrus, or even Matt
Damon, they might be able to get the rest of the Senate to listen."

"Or, they could tell a few jokes, Sing-a-Song or act it out," Charles
intones shaking his head in amazement.

"What happened to politics?" Jadda laughs.

"I think after Oprah Winfrey and George Clooney's terms as President
and Vice, in 2036, that was the beginning of the end."

"Anyway, Charles and Jadda, your thoughts? Any ideas how we might
tell the world?"

"Well," Charles says with that look he gives when something big is
coming, the rubbing of hands, the slow pacing, "I'm thinking of *literally*
telling the world. What if I did a billboard campaign starting in every
major city in America? With a powerful message to get the conversation
started."

"We would need a link to a website," Shelly interjects excitedly. "Yes,
we need a website where people can study the information themselves. I
can work on that. And I'm also still trying to get a meeting with upper
management at Green Power."

"Okay, all of that sounds great. I'm still working on getting the
information 'peer-reviewed,' whatever good that will do."

"All right everybody, we'll talk soon," Alexus signs off as Charles,
Shelly and Jadda say goodnight while slowly fading out. Poof.

"Siri, make me some Earl Grey, please."

Siri's all surrounding female British voice announces "Of course Marcus,
honey..?"

"Siri, don't call me honey, Alexus is right here."

"Oops, my bad, I thought she was, taking a, shower. Yeah, a shower."

"Hilarious Marcus, you too Siri. You're hilarious," Alexus chimes in, more amused than she would like to let on.

"Siri, just a little stevia. No honey, I don't need the sugar. Sweetheart, do you want something?"

"No thanks… *honey,* I'm headed to the store to grab a few things. Siri, get almond milk, bananas, celery, strawberries, apples, and oranges ready for pickup."

"Sure," the house resounds, "Do you want some leafy greens for a salad?"

"Yes, thanks for reminding me."

"My pleasure."

"Sweetheart," I say wondering, "Why not send the car?"

"It's just one of those days when I feel like wandering the aisles, clears my head. Reminds me of the old days when things were less, well, complicated."

"You know what I did the other day just for fun? *I loaded the dishwasher.* It's so strange how many of the things we hated just ten years ago, we now sometimes do for fun or therapy or, to clear our heads."

"Yeah, I guess the lesson is, never take a moment for granted because it's probably not as bad as you think."

"Wiser words have never been spoken. That's why I love you. Not to mention…*that sweet tush of yours!"* I reach around, giving her a loving grab, pulling her to me.

"I think I must hurry this trip to the store, cause," she gives me a sultry, smokey eye'd look that always gets the blood flowing, *"I've got something in store for you."*

With that, she breaks away from my embrace, teases me a little by adjusting her bra, and she's out the door.

I yell through the door as she leaves, *"Okay my beautiful, I'll count the minutes."*

I grab my cup of Earl Grey and head down the hall toward the bedroom. I try to turn my mind off, stop the data from haunting me but it's near impossible, so I pause at my office door. *She'll be back soon.* But, I want to check one thing. I turn into the office, and there, standing in the middle of the room which is only lit by a dim glow streaming in through the window from a streetlight, stands a 6 foot tall, all black clothed, face covered, man. In a gravely disguised monster-like voice he speaks, **"Marcus, you have a choice now. Do you want to lose everything?"** I stand motionless, petrified, **"I didn't think so. Make the right choice, and all will be well. Your 'Beautiful' doesn't have to be harmed. Charles and Jadda can continue living their fantasy life. And your kids, Malik and Shanice, they can go about their days, happy. And Kathy, their mother, she can go on being their mother. All you have to do is use this data."** Suddenly graphics, temperature data, 'scientific' journals appear.

"What?" I say clearing my throat, "What is this?"

"Look at it!"

I study the data. "Where did this come from? I've never seen this before. It doesn't look right. It can't be right."

"Who knows what's *right?* Who knows what's *wrong?* No one. Just use this data, and you'll never see me again."

"It's falsified, fake."

"Yes. And so was the information that climate scientist Phil Jones presented in 2009 which created the climate gate scandal. *No one even remembers it.* In the end, it was of no consequence whatsoever.

    Climate Gate, professor Muller trumped.online/dfc
    Climate Gate further explained trumped.online/l77

"You will use this data if you love your family, your friends. Say you missed it, say it's new. Say whatever you need to but convince them it was all a mistake and everyone will be fine. *Or… you can say goodbye to your Beautiful."*

He takes out a knife.

"I will carve her face until you no longer recognize her. Your Beautiful will be a freak show. I will hang Charles and Jadda from their turret. And your children? That's when the fun begins."

He quickly whips his arm and the knife back and then swings it at me, across my chest. I try to jump back, but I wasn't fast enough. My heart races. I try to yell but nothing comes out, silenced by fear.

But the knife and his hand. They both simply go right through me. *He's a hologram. My iDesk!* The all-black image in the dark made it look real. *Someone has hacked into my system!* That's supposed to be impossible with the iDesk-HG3.

"That's right," he says with that monster voice, **"I'm not here. Or is it, there? Hmmm…not sure. In any case, you know I should not be able to hack your system. But since I have you know I *can destroy your life*. Use the data I have given you. You have a good life, a beautiful wife. Why would you want to destroy all of that? Oh, and if you tell anyone about our little conversation, *the pain begins*. If you try to get cute or think you're smarter than me and attempt to find me, or tell the authorities, *the pain begins*. Do you understand?"**

"Yes," my body is shaking, *"I understand."*

"Good, and with that, I bid you farewell.

He disappears. I sit down to try to gather my composure. How does one reconcile the *potential* loss of millions and maybe even billions of people, not to mention plant and animal life, against the guaranteed loss of seven? *Seven people*. When love does the math, it's not logical.

My Beautiful walks in the door.

The Dawn: *The Berkeley Riots*
Year: 2017 February 1 7:30 p.m.

"So, you won't say anything pro-President Dump tonight, right? Because that would ruin everything."

The drive on the way to Janet's house to have dinner with the gang was quiet until Kathy posed that absurd question, "Pro Trump? Really? I've said nothing pro Trump in my life."

"Yes, you have, *how quickly we forget.* First, you questioned whether he moved the bust of Martin Luther King, then you say he never made fun of a disabled person. What on earth do you think all that is?"

"*Oh my God,* you know I was right about the bust. Second, you would know I am right about the disabled reporter if you would be willing to look. And finally, there's a big difference between stating a fact and how one feels. Here's how I feel. *I hate Trump.* I want to break his fingers so decisively that for him to tweet he would have to put his phone on the oval office desk, get on his knees and peck at it with his nose. Stating facts, on the other hand, is neutral. They may appear to be negative or positive, leaning one way or the other *emotionally*, but they are not. And, my point has been, if we want to be a significant part of the, *Not My President,* resistance, I think it's best we don't spread fake news."

Fake News Video, Barry Dennis <u>trumped.online/qce</u>

She wasn't following the logic from the tone of her response, "One person's fake news is another person's breaking news. It's all the same. The 'Repugnicans' are the ones full of fake news. Look at Benghazi. Hillary had nothing to do with that. It was a video that incited the violence. And they're always attacking her nonprofit, the Clinton Foundation, which has done more good in the world than almost any other nonprofit *in existence.* And they're constantly harping on Bill Clinton and this 'secret meeting' on the tarmac with Attorney General Loretta Lynch. They say Bill was trying to influence the attorney general to help Hillary. Give me a break. All they did was talk about their grandkids! It's a fact, *Bill Clinton said so.* And then there is the cockamamie story that Hillary had her assistants destroy computers and phones and bleach bit her emails. Oh yeah, and she was part of selling uranium to Russia!? It never ends. Fake news! *They're obsessed with these lies* when we all know Trump *colluded with Putin.* Trump is a Russian agent at Putin's bidding. You know he made a deal with them. It's scary to even think about what it could be. But they got him in the White House, and he's going to have to return the favor. *My God, what has this country come to?*"

CNN Hillary smashes phones <u>trumped.online/1ql</u>

We pulled onto the street in front of Janet's 5,500 sq. ft. home a couple of blocks from Washington Park where, possibly, the most beautiful rose garden in the world lives. The dirt under her home alone is probably worth a million dollars. The timing of our arrival was comforting. I did not want to get into this with Kathy. "Yes. There's fake news everywhere," I add as I open the door and grab a cheese plate.

We gather around the large dining room table which has, dangling a few feet above it, a huge, one hundred and twenty-six-year-old crystal chandelier. The home's first floor is an open design making it easy to move back and forth between the kitchen, the family room, and the dining room. CNN plays on the big screen in the family room as we chat.

"Where is Luke? I noticed his BMW isn't here," Jesus asks Janet.

"Oh, he went with some friends to San Fran yesterday," she says sipping Chardonnay. At 24, Luke still lives at home. He's taking some time to find his niche in the world. He graduated from Lewis and Clark College with a major in Gender Studies.

Michael, I mean Michelle, I'm still getting used to her transition, is looking beautiful in her long red dress, high heels, and a new fabulous hairstyle. She queries, "I love San Fran, what are their plans for the city that never sleeps?"

Janet takes another sip, "Well, just, he's just having fun." I think she's a little tipsy, *already.*

Adara, in black with a multi-colored hijab, takes a bite of escargot and then begins what amounts to as the only real topic of discussion we have, "Well, the Commander and Chump is still trying to implement his Muslim ban. Have you seen the protests? He's such a fascist, Nazi, xenophobe!"

"You think?" Valentina adds sarcastically, "Putting an end to DACA is the most racist thing a president has ever done! He's purposely breaking up families. It won't surprise me if ICE knocks down me and Jesus's front door *to deport us."*

"Yep, it's happening. Everyday! Have you seen the pictures?" Jesus inquires.

"What pictures?" Tom and Jamaal ask in unison.

"OMG, Seriously? *You have not seen the photos?*"

"I have!" Janet chimes in, "It's pathetic!"

"Yes, it is. They're of children that the Commander and Chimp separated from their families then locked behind fences, face down. They look like they're starving to death."

"Sheesh, I have not seen that," I admit.

"How about the prison bus for babies? Anyone seen that? President Chimp has entire busses outfitted to imprison babies."

"For real?" I ask, sickened. But then I begin to hear the Orange-tent-guy rattling around in my head. I try to push him back. I'm sick of the 'red pill' he keeps forcing down my throat. But alas, he is too strong.

"I have to see these photos," I announce to everyone as I pull out my iPhone to search the net. I'm struggling now with what I want to be true. It would be a relief if what they say is real. Then I could unite with my friends again, at least on this issue, and heal some of the divide. On the other hand, who, in their right mind, would *want* their President to create imprisonment buses for babies?

In moments the picture pops up, "Is this it?" I ask everyone.

"Yep, there it is. Those are the children Frump separated from their families and put behind bars."

Well, it's not 'bars,' it's a fence, but it still looks horrifying. "That's terrible," I remark. I won't share all my inner thoughts, of course. I hate that families are separated but also, to ignore the fact that it is the parents who put their children in harm's way by breaking the law with them in tow is naïve. The blame is shared. Everyone has played a part in creating the images in this photo. Trump, the parents, Mexican lawlessness, and the Senate. But then, suddenly I notice something that flips my thoughtful rationale on its face. There is a time stamp on the photo of children behind bars.

"Hey, everyone," the Orange-tent-guy says through me, "What's this, here." I point to the photo's stamp, "It says 2014."

"What?" Jamaal reacts, surprised.

Adara wants a close look, "Let me see that."

Everyone comes to inspect. Obviously, this is a photo taken during the Obama administration showing how they handled the issue. I feel a breakthrough is about to occur. If I could get the gang to see the issues without prejudice, the truth would be all we need to prevail.

Jamaal is the first to comment, "That's been photoshopped, digitally manipulated. Obama would never allow such a thing."

Adara wholeheartedly concurs, "The deep state falsified the time stamp. Those in bed with Grump."

Okay, so no breakthrough will be happening. Everyone goes along with their delusion. What it does for me is continue to support my greater understanding that these issues are complicated. Would the most compassionate thing be to have porous borders? To allow anyone who wants to come to America in with minimal vetting? Should anyone claiming refugee status be trusted as 100% honest? Should we believe they would never take advantage of our kindness? Or, is it more compassionate to carefully select immigrants to make sure they love this country and want to be a part of the grand experiment called America? Tomi Lauren said *We do not lock our doors because we hate those on the outside. We lock our doors because we love those on the inside.* Is she right? Or is she full of hate? I wrestle with issues like this now. It used to be so much easier; easier to vilify people with different perspectives than us. Easier to hate Trump and all 'Repugnicans.'

Now, I pull up the photo of the prison bus for children. "Is this the bus?"

"Yes," Tom affirms.

Jamaal adds his disgust, "It's appalling what evil he is capable of. I can't even look at it."

I read a little about both photos. It turns out the prison bus for children is just a picture of a bus outfitted for kids' safety on field trips. And the time stamp on the photo of kids "starving" behind "bars" is real. It was an Obama era picture.

"Yep," Janet says, "They take all the children away from their parents and lock them down on buses so they can't escape."

🔗 Greg Gutfeld; kids locked on buses trumped.online/1na 🔗

I haven't been to see the Orange-tent-guy for over a week. I am trying to erase him from my memory. It's not going well thus far. I'm always wondering what he would say in situations like this. There was a time when none of this banter would bother me. I would probably be the ringleader. But right now all I can think is, *Jesus and Valentina are US citizens.* There's no reason anyone would knock on their door to deport them.

Kathy adds a little more coal to the fire, "We are a nation of immigrants. *Maybe they should deport us all!"*

"Yes, it's just awful," I say, trying so hard not to allow the Orange-tent-guy bashing around in my thoughts to come out of my mouth, again. But somehow, I can't contain him as all the hearsay everyone has been spewing reaches a tipping point. "However, weren't the countries on the travel ban singled out by Obama as unstable? Isn't that where Trump got the whole idea? And um, well, of course, we are a nation of immigrants. I wonder if there's a difference maybe between a legal immigrant and an illegal. Maybe?"

The room is deathly silent. I'm thinking Kathy has a superpower whereby lasers shoot out of her eyes burning holes through whatever happens to be in her line of sight. Unfortunately, it always happens to be me. Michelle breaks the silence, "What the hell has gotten into you Marcus? Have you been watching FOX News or Alex Jones or something? *Have you made one of those #WALK AWAY videos!?"*

"Oh My Gawd," Jamaal extorts. "Have you seen those? He's a traitor - that Brandon Straka. He's gay... *and a Republican. It makes no sense."*

🔗 Straka #walkaway trumped.online/03j 🔗

"Of course not!" I answered shaking my head. "I would never make a #WALKAWAY video, *I have never watched Fox News, and* Alex Jones is a conspiracy theory kook. On the way here I was saying to Kathy, as part of the resistance, I think maybe we should try hard to be factual. I think maybe it would just make us more credible.”

Kathy looks like she's about to blow. Like she's a cellophane balloon, and there's a helium pump open full throttle in her ear, pressure building, *“Credible?… Really? There's nothing credible about Frump's Presidency.* The worst people in America elected him. Stupid people! Ignorant. Deplorable. And without Putin, Hillary would have destroyed him.”

“Okay, all of that may be true but…”

“But?… *But what?”* Valentina says frustrated. “There is no *'but.' There is no 'maybe!' It's a fact. He's Hitler!”*

I try so hard to keep my mouth shut, but Orange-tent-guy is at the controls now. In a very soft, controlled tone, I respond, “This is what I mean. Hitler? Hitler might be, a bit, I don't know, of, of a stretch?”

Imagine if you will a food fight - dinner rolls, spaghetti, chicken wings, pudding, flying through the air. That's what's now underway in the dining room. Except it isn't food flying, it's a *word fight!* Flying at me, from every direction. Luckily, Jesus notices something on CNN, *“Hey, hey. Everyone. What's going on? LOOK AT THE TV!”*

There are people dressed in black on the Berkeley campus breaking windows, catching things on fire. It must be ANTIFA. The anti-fascist movement.

🔗 Berkeley riots <u>trumped.online/23d</u> 🔗

“Wow, that must be the protests at the Milo Yiannopoulos event. Have you heard about this guy?” Adara asks. No one knows much about him, “He's this right-wing, fascist, racist, anti-semitic, homophobe Trump supporter. It looks like they shut him down. Didn't let him speak. *Good!”*

“Whatever it takes,” Tom says. “I agree,” Jamaal concurs, “Hate speech must be squelched.”

Uh oh, Orange-tent-guy wants to speak. I bite my tongue.

"Wait just one minute," Michelle says, mouth gaping open, "Right there, that guy with the bat that just broke the window. I know it's impossible to tell for sure, but it seems like…*Luke!?"*

Luke and Michelle are close. Luke did his final paper for Gender Studies on Michelle and her experiences. "Janet, what do you think?"

Janet, Luke's mother, walks toward the TV screen. Slowly, riveted, "I don't know, but if it is, *I'm one proud mother.* We can't let these fascist Trump supporters speak. They don't deserve a platform."

Oh well, I tried to keep Orange-tent-guy from making an appearance again, but alas, "Correct me if I'm wrong, isn't it textbook fascism to use violence to stop people you disagree with from speaking?"

The helium pressure hose connected to Kathy's ear has been attached a little too long. BOOM! "***Marcus***, Get. Out. NOW. *Just* LEAVE. *NOW!*"

"But, how are you going to get…"

"I'll take Uber… Get OUT!"

As the violence escalated on TV, the discord in the room reaches new heights but, somehow, with no movement or sound whatsoever. This time the 'food fight' doesn't even have words. Everyone is like a zombie at sunset, frozen for only a moment longer. Just enough time for me to slowly grab my coat. You can hear the wood floor squeak under my feet. *I don't think three million dollar home floors should squeak,* I considered, trying to avoid all the other thoughts entering my mind like how I may now be permanently in the doghouse. "Well, good night everyone. I am, I'm, sorry. But please consider and remember what the great author and philosopher Evelyn Beatrice Hall said about freedom of speech, *'I do not agree with what you have to say, but I'll defend to the death your right to say it.'*"

Milo on Bill Maher <u>trumped.online/3ua</u>

Well, that was a surprise even to me. I hadn't thought about that quote for probably over ten years. I remember writing a paper on free speech in high school. It profoundly influenced me. But somehow, I had forgotten about it until now. And just when I thought Orange-tent-guy would leave me alone, he came scratching and clawing at my tongue. "Oh, and one more thing. Valentina, actually I think the most racist thing a President has ever done was when Lyndon B. Johnson said 'negroes' were getting 'uppity' and that we, the Democrats, *Have got to give them something, just enough to keep them quiet but not enough to make a difference.* He went on to say, and I'm sorry for the language, *I'll have them niggers voting Democrat for the next 200 years.* Yes, I think that is the most racist thing a president has ever done or said. It is our party, the Democratic Party that started the KKK, did *not* want to end slavery and implemented Jim Crow laws. Also, I believe this Milo Yiannopoulos character is a gay Jew. I doubt he is homophobic, fascist, or anti-Semitic for that matter but, who knows? Maybe Mickey Mouse is cheating on Mini Mouse with Pluto. Anything's possible. And with that, I bid you adieu."

∞ Lyndon B. Johnson on 'negros' etc. trumped.online/flj ∞

It was a long drive home. I almost went to the homeless encampment to tell Orange-tent-guy to get out of my head. But I realized that would make me look more Looney Tunes than anyone sleeping on cardboard. So I go home caught between regret and liberation. Not sure which one to lean into. I pay the kid sitter, check on the 'bundles' and then, crawl onto the couch. I'm half-awake til around two or three in the morning, awaiting Kathy. I hate going to sleep in the middle of a fight, and it's been happening a lot lately. I'm finally awakened by the sound of the front door creaking open at 7 a.m. I guess she stayed at Janet's.

The day is a blur. Tired and now, overcome with regret, I just want to forget all that crazy Orange-tent-guy talk, makeup and go back to normal. On the way home from work that early evening, I'm excited to let bygones be bygones. To put the past behind us, bury the hatchet as it were. I get home to an empty house. Kathy is picking the kids up today. They should be here by now. I consider texting her, fingers on the phone, motionless. I'm afraid anything I say will be taken out of context. So I wait. Finally, an hour and a half later than expected, they arrive. I step outside to hug the kids as they head in. Then I approach Kathy on the driveway. Ready to make amends. We speak at the same time. "You first," she says. This is good. Feels like we both want to let it go and move on.

"No, please, you first," I tell her. So she does.

"I got Malik started on Ritalin today."

Chapter 12 The Future: *Truth Is Complicated*
Year: 2047 February 14 7:30 p.m.

It's been five days since our last gathering. Since the Man-In-Black threatened me and everyone I love. Painting on a happy face is killing me inside. I, of course, have told no one about the Man-In-Black and the fake data. Right now we're headed to Charles' house. We gather in the living room, as usual, to exchange ideas. I don't know what to do. Everyone's here except Shelly. She's running a little late - some minor emergency at G.P.

"Siri, pull up the data I was studying this morning," Charles requests. The data appears, suspended in air, as Charles and Jadda begin to share their latest thoughts. Everyone's back is to the giant windows which look out at the property and the mountains. I'm sitting in a chair facing the windows, looking through the data, past my friends and out, transfixed by the view, lost in thought and slightly nauseous. I feel sweat beading on my forehead. *I have to tell them about the Man-In-Black.* I start to open my mouth. But then, right behind Alexus, *he appears.* My God, he's hacked Charles's system as well. He takes his holographic knife, slightly reaches around Alexus and slowly runs it right through her throat. No one else of course even knows he's there. He begins mouthing the words; ***I will slit her throat.*** Then he moves on to Jadda and stabs the holographic knife right through her back and slightly out her chest. She must've seen it with her peripheral vision. She jerks her head downward and swats at it like you would a fly. Then she spins quickly, somehow detecting something behind her but the moment she turns, he's gone.

"What is it?" Alexus asks, startled.

"Nothing, I just thought, I don't know. There was something here."

Now, beaten, I stand, "Wait, everyone. I, I think maybe we, or I should say, I, have made a mistake. Look at this." I project the false data from my iPhone to Charles' iDesk. "Two major findings that have been troubling for me. I didn't want to say anything until I was sure it was at least a good possibility. I checked the satellite data a week ago and every day since then. I know it's not much time, but there's been a change in the trend, look here." I point at the falsified temperature data which gives the appearance of what is called a *pause.* "You may not remember, but in the early 2000s, there was what was referred to as a pause. It's different from this one, of course, but the idea is the same. Here it is from the early 2000s.”

Climate ‘pause,’ the Sierra Club, <u>trumped.online/ssj</u>

I swipe the graph through the air and expand it, so it's easy to read. “Now, looking at the data over the last few weeks, it looks like a pause could be starting now. But here's the more troubling information. It looks like somehow my satellite data over the last five years, or even longer, was incorrect. I even checked NOAA, the National Oceanic, and Atmospheric Administration and NASA Records and they concur.”

Charles shakes his head, “But we all know NOAA and NASA can't be trusted. Yes, after they caught them changing temperature data back in the early 2000s, they came clean and promised it would never happen again. But seriously? A little hand slap and we're supposed to trust them?”

Changed data, NOAA, NASA Dr. <u>trumped.online/lca</u>

“I know, I know,” I grumble, struggling to continue the façade. I'm considering just telling them all the truth, but of course, *he appears again* by the window this time and with a gun. Everyone's looking at me, so they don't see him. Trying to hide the sweat beading on my forehead, I wipe my brow with my sleeve, “Here's what I propose we do, just pause ourselves for a while. I’ll continue researching, checking the data. If the pause continues or the temperature even sways the other way, we can thank God we were wrong.”

“Seriously?" Alexus interjects just as the Man-In-Black disappears, “Why didn't you tell, *at least me?*”

“Sweetheart, I'm sorry. It's been troubling me all week. I kept checking, rechecking and researching. It’s not conclusive, but it looks like I may have been wrong, or at least the data was wrong. I'm sorry. I hope you understand.”

“Baby, I do understand. I get it. But in the future just let me know, *trust me.* I've been worried about you all week, acting strangely. Now I get it.” She kisses and hugs me which I feel I do not deserve.

We all study the new, falsified data for a while. Checking our work. Comparing it to the conclusions we had drawn previously. There's confusion, relief, and doubt. Thirty minutes later, Shelly shows up with what would have been exciting news, "Hey everyone, sorry I'm late," she announces letting herself in, "But I have good news, I'm pretty sure I can get us a meeting with Sakiya Morriosu. She's the new CEO at G.P. Portland."

Shelly is visibly taken aback by the lack of enthusiastic response. "Shelly, you will have to put that on the back burner. I have confusing but potentially good news. It looks like the data we were studying, my data, was probably wrong. Take a look."

She steps into the matrix of floating information but catches on quick and with excitement, "Wow, this is great news. To think, a week ago we were all convinced that in 40 years or so catastrophic climate change would finally be the end of us if we didn't act instantly. Which we all know, would be close to impossible given the deaf ears we would be up against. I say this calls for a drink, a celebration."

"Shelly's right," Jadda asserts, "Let's shake the dust off, give a sigh of relief and drink a toast."

"Here, here," Charles declares, "I mean, this is really good news. That is if you think a shift in the world's fate from total catastrophe to a green, blue paradise floating in space is a positive thing… " he smiles.

"So," Shelly announces, "Remember last time, I said I had news."

"Actually," Charles responds, "I do. But you never told us."

"No, I did not, because I was so scared for, Candace."

We're all at a loss, looking amongst ourselves. Shrugging shoulders.

"Okay," Alexus queries, "I'll bite. Who's Candace?"

Shelly slowly points at her stomach, *"What? You are pregnant?"* Jadda screams with joy. "I'm gonna be an *auntie?"* They hug.

"Yep, Tyler and I have been trying for a while, finally took! Cody, if it's a boy and Candace if it's a girl."

"Well, this *is* cause for celebration," Charles adds, "I'll get the champagne, and, for you, mother-to-be, Schweppes."

"How long have you known?" Jadda asks with unbridled excitement.

"Just two days. So it's breaking news for us all."

I tried to join in the festivities, but I knew, for Candace or Cody, the future was a dystopia, right out of some summer blockbuster, Bollywood movie. Or some classic from the days when Hollywood was still making films like, *"The Day After Tomorrow."*

Tonight, lying in bed next to Alexus, I feel like an imposter, unworthy of her kiss, her touch. I sleep in fits and starts. Nightmares of Alexus finding out and hating me for it. Nightmares of the dystopian future, planet earth devastated. At 1:30 in the morning I finally decide to get up and go to my office. I sit in a chair in the middle of the room in the dark. I can feel the Man-In-Black's presence, although, I may just be paranoid. "Are you here?" I slowly gaze around the room. A few minutes pass. *"Are you happy?"* Any second, I expect him to appear. "I have done as you have asked. But why? Why would you want to risk humanity, planet earth? All of life?" I sit in the dark for another hour. Anguishing. It's windy tonight. With every creak of the house, I turn; heart beating in triple time. Finally, around 3 a.m. I decide it's time to make my way to the bedroom. Try to sleep.

"You think I'm a monster," fills the room with that dark, disguised voice, just as I stand.
Adrenaline rushes to my head, so strongly, I can hear it in my ears. Dizzy, my heart trying to push through my chest, I freeze.

"You think I have no conscience. You know nothing about me."

I keep looking around the room, no sign of him. Just a voice this time. I try to speak. Slowly, the words find my lips, "I just want to know why. If there's a reason, a good reason I must put the fate of humanity and all of the earth in jeopardy. I want to know why. The truth."

"The Truth? The truth is complicated. You would not know what to do with it. Here is what concerns me."

I turn, and there he is. In all black, face covered as always.

"You hesitated!" He pulls out the holographic knife, **"You thought about telling them.** *I thought I was clear.* **You tell them,** *and people start to get hurt.* He lifts the knife to my neck, right up to my larynx. And, I *feel the cold blade enter my skin,* blood dripping down my neck.

"Now, *can I be more clear?"* I'm shocked, can't speak for a moment. He's here this time. For real!

"Can I be more clear?", He repeats.

"No," squeaks out, "You, you… cannot. I understand."

"Very good, I'll let myself out." He's out the window in seconds, with ease.

I go to the bathroom to assess the wound. Wash it, put a Band-Aid on to stop the bleeding. Then I sit down on the toilet, put my head in my hands. It's not like me, but tears rain.

The Dawn: *Russia Collusion, Sanctuary Cities* Year: 2017 February 17 7:39 a.m.

As I approach on the dew topped grass, I can see his outline inside the tent. Looks like he's sitting on a lawn chair or something, reading **The Oregonian** I would guess, while simultaneously holding his iPhone up in the air. "What are you doing? Wait, let me guess, *research.*"

"Good one… Nancy Drew," he says, "Now let me try. You're here because I was right."

The costar of the 70s TV show, *Nancy Drew Mysteries,* is on the tip of my tongue. Oh yeah, "Brilliant, *Shaun Cassidy."*

He's amazed, "Wow, how did you know that one?"

"Eh, Amazon. So, you were right. I should've stayed away from you. I feel like I'm losing everything."

"Your New Over is fast approaching," he says while folding up the newspaper.

"Well, it feels more like my Lose Over. I'm losing everything over pettiness, *like politics.* Of course, I didn't think politics could be petty, very long ago. I'm not sure if I'm losing my mind or if Kathy and all of my friends have lost theirs. However, *you won't leave me alone.* Even when I haven't seen you in over a week, I can't get you and your Yoda musings out of my mind. I mean, my friends and I are part of the resistance. The resistance to Trump and his administration. They need to impeach. But, I can't get my friends to be rational. If we aren't factual we won't have any credibility. Why is it so hard for them to understand?"

"It's hard because most people have a very difficult time with, *the gray.*"

"Huh?"

"The gray!"

"I know what you said. I don't know what you mean."

"With opinions, beliefs, and ideologies, people have a difficult time with anything that is not the pendulum swung all the way to one side or the other. Politics is a belief system, an ideology, even a religion. Most people can only see it in black and white which is intellectual laziness. Trump, in other words, is either black or white, good or bad. There's no in between, no gray allowed. He is either Hitler, the second coming of Satan or the Savior. And since for your friends the Savior position is already taken, that would be Hillary, Trump must be Hitler/Satan. There is no room for gray; he can't be a complex human *like we all are.* He can't be a mix of Satan and Savior. That would require too much mental gymnastics. He must be all of one or the other, and so, to them, he is Hitler. In this way, it becomes impossible for them to acknowledge anything positive, even if it bites them on the nose. After all, Satan can do no good."

Suddenly, my stomach drops like when riding a roller coaster, "Oh my God, you're a Trump supporter!?"

From his position inside his hovel, he points right on to the tent, at me, his finger warping the fabric. "There you go, doing it yourself. Because you can't see the gray, you jump to one side or the other. Do I have to be a Trump supporter to point out the truth?"

"No. Of course not."

"And the truth is, I thought Hillary and Trump were both very flawed candidates for different reasons. Gray!"

🔗 Barry Dennis, Hillary or Trump? <u>trumped.online/f6g</u> 🔗

"Okay, you're right. I'm guilty of the very things I'm accusing my wife and friends of. There's so much emotion how can I reason with them logically?"

"Logic. Facts. They have no place in the world of black and white. People dig their heels in; they double down. They can't bear to be wrong. It's too troubling and even puts into question their sense of identity. Not to mention basketball."

"Basketball?"

"You know, the game where they throw a round, air-filled object through a hoop with a net."

"I've heard of it, but what does that have to do with my plight?"

"Everything. Have you ever been to a basketball game?"

"Sure, lots of times. In fact, it's my favorite sport. I'm a big Portland Trail Blazers fan."

"Okay, have you ever been to a game where you feel, soon after tip-off, there's not much of a chance of winning? For example, your team's down by eleven points in the first quarter."

"Yes, many times."

"And then, by the end of the half, they're down by 19 or so and the feeling of an impending loss has taken root?"

"Yes, I know the feeling."

"And then, by the end of the third quarter they're down by, let's say 27 points. How do you feel then?"

"Well, it's pretty much over. Some people get up and leave."

"And then, when the game's over, they lose by 32 points. How do you feel about that loss?"

"Well, to be honest, it's not a big deal."

"There's a reason for that, isn't there?"

"Yes, it's, ah…."

"It's because you have…acc.. acce…?" He's playing the, *figure it out*, game.

"Because we have, um, accepted it?"

"Nancy Drew strikes again!" He celebrates, shaking his fist in the air.

"Now, have you ever been to a game where you were up by like 17 at the half?"

"Yep."

"How do you feel at that point?"

"Very optimistic, statistically there's an excellent chance we'll win. There's a lot of jumping up-and-down and high five-ing."

"Exactly. And then, by the middle of the third quarter, the Blazers are up by 23 points. How do you feel?"

"Well, it's pretty much over, we're celebrating."

"But then, things turn. Your team becomes complacent while the competition turns fearless. Before you know it, there are three seconds left and you are clinging to a two-point lead. The opponent throws the ball in bounds for an attempt at a last-second shot. How do you feel then?"

"Panicked, stressed. I can't believe it's come to this, but there's still a good chance we'll win."

"Okay, the opposing team throws the ball in, and with one second remaining their best player launches a three-pointer from the corner with two guys in his face. The buzzer goes off while the ball is in midair. If it goes in, you lose by one point. If it misses, you win by two. How do you feel then?"

"Stressed."

"The ball *swishes.* The opposing team goes crazy celebrating an unbelievable comeback. Have you ever witnessed that, and how did it feel?"

"Yes, I have witnessed that basic scenario a couple of times. Every basketball fan has, and I have to tell you, *it does not feel good.* It's depressing. And if it happens during the NBA playoffs or, let's say the final game of the playoffs, you might talk about that for years to come. It's like a dagger in the heart."

"But why? I don't understand." Of course, he understands, just up to his tricks, "In both scenarios your team lost, what's the difference?" I squint my eyes, searching the corners of my mind. "Come on Nancy Drew; we already solved this mystery."

"Acceptance?"

"Soooo close… what's the opposite?"

"Rejection, maybe even denial."

"Yes, the outcome is the same, but the emotional experience is the opposite. It's much harder to accept a loss when you were the favored team, when you thought you would win and everyone told you, you would win. And then, at the last second, it's snatched right out from under you. In our basketball metaphor, who is Trump?

"Trump is the come from behind, beat the odds winner. The miracle last-second shot."

"And the fans of the winner?"

"They're celebrating, high-five-ing."

"And the losers? What happens when your team loses in such an upset."

"That's it I guess, upset! We're depressed. In denial. We often blame it on the referees or even dirty play by the other players. Like they cheated. It's a state of shock. A kind of temporary insanity. "

"Yes, kind of like the, *What Happened?* tour that Hillary is on now."

Hillary Clinton, What Happened? <u>trumped.online/yfu</u>

"Oh my gosh, you're right. It's just rehashing; repeatedly, the 'game' called the elections. Commiserating. We did see her as our savior. We did and do see Trump as Hitler. And we keep reliving the loss like Ground Hog Day. It seems as if she won't take any responsibility for losing. But if I were to say that to my friends, they would have me tarred, feathered and castrated."

He chuckles, "Even Jill Stein, the presidential candidate who failed to get 1% of the vote, got on the bandwagon. She raised millions of dollars to get a recount in several states. In other words, the referees didn't do their job, or they were biased. And what do you think the 'dirty play,' the 'cheating' delusion has been in the minds of those whose team lost the election?" Again, I'm struggling to keep up. "Come on Parker Stevenson," he says encouragingly, "You can do this."

"Wow, *Parker Stevenson.* You watch Amazon too?"

"Before I ran away from home. Now, what is the insane, cheating delusion the losers keep pushing and cannot let go of?" It's on the tip of my tongue. I know where he's going with this but I can't, quite…. "I'll give you a clue, Caviar…. Swan Lake…Nadia Comaneci…Hockey." I shake my head. "Oh, *come on.* " He's showing frustration with me. "The first to go into space?!"

The light bulb goes on, *"The Russians.* 'Frump' Cheated with 'Sadimir Poutin'."

He laughs, "Good one, 'Sadimir Poutin'!'"

"Thanks. But wait, *you don't think Trump colluded with Russia?"*

"Seriously? Put away your black-and-white thinking, un-dig your heels. In what universe do you really think Donald Trump was meeting and planning with Sadimir Poutin'? When would this have happened? Where would it have taken place? Starbucks? Don't you see the whole scenario is a kind of insanity caused by the shock of losing the game? Not only is it wasting everyone's time, distracting everyone in the White House, but it cost American taxpayers millions and millions of dollars."

"Trump Colluded with Russia" trumped.online/naw

"But we know for a fact that Russia meddled in our elections."

"Yes, but that has nothing to do with Trump. The media has woven them together like a Turkish carpet. It's nearly impossible to hear, *Russians meddled*, without thinking, *Trump colluded.* Do you know how much money they have found Russians spent on meddling?"

"No, but I'm sure it's staggering."

"Yes it is. Hold on to your caviar." He looked left and right. Slowly, to make sure no one was near. Like what he was about to purvey was the most top secret of all government knowledge. Like my very life could be endangered by the information. He leaned in and whispered, "Around one hundred thousand dollars."

I was shocked. But in the opposite way I was expecting, "Well… That's… Something," was all I could come up with.

"Yes, it's something alright." He continued whispering while looking to and fro, "And do you know how much Hillary spent on her campaign?"

"No I, I don't."

"Seven hundred and sixty eight… wait for it… *million dollars!* And yet according to *Lame Stream Media*, it would appear as though the Russians were more effective even though their efforts were supportive of *both* candidates. The only reason their efforts may have supported Trump more than Hillary is because, like everyone else, they thought he would loose. Don't forget, there would be no Russia Collusion hoax without the fake dossier paid for by Hillary!"

Hillary's fake dossier trumped.online/dve

"The Russians were trying to sew discord, to tear us apart, and thanks to the media and many in congress, it's working. And, all Russian meddling, even if in some bizarre universe Trump was colluding, happened before Trump was elected. In other words, it happened under the Obama administration's watch. Any collusion or any meddling that occurred to affect the 2016 election was the Obama administration's responsibility. They dropped the ball, not Trump."

Barry Dennis, Collusion Delusion trumped.online/jdulfv

This truth hit me pretty hard. For some reason it always feels like Trump's fault the Russians got away with meddling. I guess that's the medias spin. And yet, it's so obvious my Orange-tent friend is right. And now, for some reason in this moment, something creeps up on me and gives me the heebie-jeebies, "Wait a minute. Oh my God! Are *you a Repugnican?*"

His face contorts in surprise, "A *WHAT*?"

"I mean, a R*epublican.* Are you a Republican?"

"You asked if I was a Repugnican."

"Okay, yes, I did."

"Not only are you prejudice, *in the wrong way,* but you're a Politicist, participating in Politicism!"

"I'm what? Practicing what?"

"You're a Politicist; *a Political racist!* Practicing Politicism. Care to guess?"

"Political racism?"

"Nancy Drew strikes again."

"What you're suggesting isn't even possible. Politics isn't a race of people."

"True; however, all the dynamics, all the prejudices that racists exhibit are in play. You're grouping a bunch of people together and assuming they all share the same attributes, which, in this case, fall under the umbrella of *repugnance.* You're doing the black and white thing. Gray, remember? Gray. Thinking in the gray takes intellectual discipline, maturity. Thinking black and white is childish, lazy. Plus, you're taking a philosophy; conservatism, and you're judging it as repugnant because it's different from your philosophy, liberalism. To make matters worse, you're participating in *identity politics.* So, let me guess. You think all women who did not vote for Hillary are somehow flawed because, well, they're women, and all women, of course, should vote for women. All blacks must have voted for Obama because of the color of their skin, and all *homeless must be liberal or 'progressive' because they want a handout.* Identity politics is racist! It's no better than bigotry. *Gray, brotha. Gray!* People are complicated, and not everyone will fit into your little mold! Have you ever considered the possibility that, on the whole, both major parties want the same thing? And I don't mean those in power; I don't mean Congress. That's a rabbit hole for another day. I mean the average people."

He's wrong, and I could not wait to prove it, "No. Sorry. Republicans are greedy and selfish. Liberals/progressives are kind and compassionate. It's so easy to see that, just look at the issues. *Liberals believe in healthcare for all. We believe in welfare."*

"So, you believe in taking."

"No, *giving!"*

"How do you intend to pay for everyone's healthcare and welfare?"

"Redistribute the wealth."

"How?"

"The government pays for it."

"Where do they get the money?"

"From…" I hesitate to say what he has been angling for.

"Say it," he says, daring me.

"From the rich, okay, from the rich."

"Okay, so you believe in taking, forcing others to pay for the health and 'welfare' of complete strangers. Yes?"

"Okay, yes, that's how. Take it. We believe in taking their money. But they are rich. They don't need it. It's not fair."

"Now we have gotten down to the real reason many people want a bigger, more controlling government."

"Why is that?"

"Because the government can do for those people what they can't do themselves."

"What's that?"

"Break the law."

"Huh?"

"See that house up there? Just above the tunnel. What do you think that place is worth?"

"Well, I would guess anywhere between two and three million."

"What would happen if you and I went up there and demanded, maybe with guns or pitchforks, that they hand over $200,000 right now because they have more money than you and me and we know better than they do what should be done with their money?"

"We would go to jail for armed robbery."

"But what if the government says to them, *You must give us $200,000?* Let's call it, uh, taxes, because they know better what should be done with their money."

"Then they would have to hand over the money."

"But what if they didn't?"

"They would go to jail."

"Can you see the irony? If you and I go up there with guns or pitchforks and demand $200,000 and the owner of the house says, *You're crazy; I'm calling the cops,* we go to jail. If the government demands $200,000 and they refuse to give it, *they go to jail.* Ironic isn't it?"

"Yes, I guess it is."

"So, whether or not they realize it, those who want big government really want the government to be their 'muscle.' And in the U.S., it may be worse than ever."

"How's that?"

"Well, there has been a clear trend in the political arena over that last 20 years or so. And that is, everything is moving to the left."

"What? I don't see that at all. I mean look who won the election."

"Look who won the last two," he said waiting for a reply. I didn't give him one, so he trudged on.

"Overall, I think it's a good trend. Increasingly Republicans are referring to themselves as Libertarians in many areas."

"I don't really know what Libertarians stand for."

"Simple, they are liberal socially, conservative fiscally. Charlie Kirk, for example, a young and very influential conservative among millennial's, has publicly said he doesn't care if gay people marry or if pot is legalized. The new conservative movement embraces a kind of classic liberalism; live and let live. And this 'live and let live' mentality carries over to the government's role in citizens' lives. Libertarians believe in small government like traditional conservatives. Which, at least to them is, *live and let live*; stay out of our lives. But, like a kind of political dance on an ideological cliff, those on the left moved further left as well and fell right off into lunacy. For example, did you know that Angela Alioto, a progressive liberal who wrote the sanctuary city laws for San Francisco in the early 90s, is now working to pull back the current law?"

"I did not know that. Why? She wrote it!?"

"Yes, she wrote it. But in 2013 they amended the laws she wrote to include *violent felons.*"

"Wait, what? Are you telling me the current sanctuary city laws in San Fran protect illegal immigrants who are also *violent felons?*"

"That's what I'm saying."

"No way."

"Yes, way."

"But who in their right mind would want to protect violent felons."

"No one."

"But you just said they are."

"Yes, they are, but… *they are not in their right mind!* They fell off the cliff on the left side, into Crazyville. So, get this. If you're an American citizen and you commit a felony, you go to jail. If you're an illegal alien *and* you commit a felon, you are part of a very special protected class."

"It is, as you say, lunacy. But why? Why would anyone want to protect violent felons?"

To make his point, he presses both hands and his face into the tent, *"Votes. It's virtue signaling for votes. The far left has left reality."*

    ⚭ Interview, Sanctuary City Law <u>trumped.online/4h3</u> ⚭

As he slowly pulls back from warping the orange mesh, he adds, "For the record. I wish, in fact we all wish like innocent children on Christmas

Eve who still believe in Santa, that big government worked. We all wish that money was pixy dust. How easy it would be to fix our problems. But at some point children have to grow up, leave innocence behind, and face reality. We simply know, as a matter of history, big government; more money, more government programs, do not work. We have tried it ad nauseam."

⊂⊃ Greetings from a sanctuary city trumped.online/vte ⊂⊃

Chapter 13 The Future: *Automation, The Path*
Year: 2047 February 15 5:46 a.m.

"Good morning sweetheart," Alexus whispers through a yawn.

"Hey, morning baby. It's time to get going."

"I know," she says, stretching. "But before the opening ceremonies, before we're swept away in all the excitement, I want to say how proud I am of you. It's the highest of honors they chose you as co-lead engineer for such a historical and important project."

"Well, thanks. But, I don't know. I kinda think luck played just as much a part as anything."

She smirks, shakes her head, "Luck has nothing to do with it. You are brilliant!"

She climbs out of bed and gives me a soft kiss, "You just never understood how talented you are."

"Okay, thank you, sweetheart," I utter somewhat deflective since I've always felt like an imposter in my field and that someday someone would find me out. "Your support has meant the world to me."

We use the twenty-minute airbus flight from Portland to the border to work on our swing in the holographic golf course. Not that either of us has a clue, but it's fun to play, *Hit and Giggle*, occasionally. In no time the A.I. pilot announces, "Okay folks, please be seated as we prepare to land." I'm still not used to it; the G.P. Air Mall 5. An all-electric craft nearly the size of a football field that can land and take off vertically making runways unnecessary. We're landing on the field adjacent to, The Path.

As we gently touch the ground, I'm reviewing the short remarks I will make for the opening ceremony. The monument is impressive. At 1,996 feet high, it's nearly twice as tall as the Eiffel tower, five times as wide and in the shape of a perfect rectangle. It's designed to allow 25,000 visitors each day. What makes this truly unique is that visitors from either country can come to the top from separate entrances. There's a red line right down the middle, exactly on the border. Red because it is the color we both share in our flags. While facing south, you see hundreds of miles of Mexico including Tijuana and the Pacific Ocean. While facing north, hundreds of miles of the U.S. including San Diego's lights at night and the Pacific on the American side. When you look west, you see the Wall disappearing into the ocean. Conversely, gazing east, it seems to go on forever. It's the only place where you can literally wander back and forth between the two countries at will, with one single step. To honor each country, there is a U.S. flag every fifteen feet on the Mexican side and a Mexican flag every fifteen feet on the U.S. side.

The elevator was one of our greatest achievements. It holds up to eighty-seven people at a time and, at 86.5 MPH, it is the fastest lift in the world. The monument took one thousand three hundred and twenty-two people to build. Six hundred and sixty-one U.S. citizens and six hundred and sixty-one Mexican. We worked together as a team through the whole process.

As Alexus and I exit the elevator on the very top and enter the grand hall, the view brings us to a halt as the sun begins setting on what appears to be the end of the Wall in the ocean. Paradoxically, the top floor appears to have no walls. It's all glass and every chair, all two hundred and fifty, are filled. After the architects give their remarks, they introduce me and my Mexican counterpart, Isabella as we step up to the podium. She addresses the invitees first, in Spanish. I'm not fluent but, mostly, I'm able to follow her address. She's brilliant, as always, eloquent. Then it's my turn.

"Good morning ladies and gentlemen. When a project like this begins, it often feels as if it may never come to fruition. There are false starts, missing pieces, communication breakdowns, faulty equipment, human error, and just plain dumb luck. Murphy's law seems more present and pervasive than the law of gravity! The Wall itself is and might always be controversial, but my experience of building The Path monument is a metaphor for the building of our countries' relationship. There have been false starts and communication breakdowns, human errors, dumb luck and at times it did seem as though Murphy's law ruled our border. But, our relationship is better today than it has ever been. And the pathway, now memorialized by this monument, is a tower of peace, love, and respect."

Inspired, I step down off the stage, leave my prepared address behind and walk to the middle of the room down the aisle where the red line divides the hall. I stop and stare at the line, a pregnant pause envelopes the space. And then, "May each person seeking citizenship in either country

promise to bring their very best to that nation." I looked around the
room, slowly, meeting eye to eye. "May they not only take from that
country so they may have a better life for themselves but promise to give
as much or more in return. For, if we take more than we give, what will
be left for our children?" Then I stepped across the line. "Now, I am in
Mexico. If I were to choose to stay here and take advantage of its
beautiful beaches, pristine weather, and wonderful food, then it would be
incumbent upon me to strive to understand and desire to be a part of the
soul of this country. To learn its native tongue and be a part of its
traditions. For example, the love for and inspiration found in of Our Lady
of Guadalupe.

Miracle of Our Lady of Guadalupe trumped.online/1fc

Also, it would be my responsibility to live by, study, and respect the
Political Constitution of the United Mexican States and understand its
fundamental ideas like separation of powers, representative government,
a federal system, and supremacy of the state over the church. Last but not
least, it would be empirical that I learn to feel, in the depths of my being,
the soul… of a good *Mariachi band."*

The room fills with what I hope is more than just a polite smattering of
laughter. Once it dissipates, I allow silence to have the moment as I stare
at the line. Soon you could hear a pin drop as I lift my leg and take that
small yet massive step.

"And now, I am in the United States of America. A place that most agree
is the freest, most prosperous country in the world. A place that takes in
more immigrants than any other country in the history of civilization.
One million legal immigrants per year enter her borders. That's enough
people to create an entire city about the size of my home, Portland
Oregon, every three years! If I choose to stay on this side of the line, it is
incumbent upon me to love this land. To cherish its traditions that have
been tested and nearly lost more than once just in the last thirty years.
There was an attack on the fundamental right of freedom of speech. The
wisdom of the First Amendment is ancient. In the ninth century B.C., the
Greek poet Homer supported free speech without hindrance sighting that
free speech would be the only way to keep tyrannical rulers from total
control of society. Next, if you choose to come to this side of the line it
would be imperative you understand the right to bear arms which is to
protect against tyranny should the First Amendment be stripped away.
Then there is the right to peacefully assemble and of course, limited
government. As Thomas Jefferson said, *A government big enough to give*

you everything you want is strong enough to take everything you have. Regardless of which side of the line you are from or choose to be from in the future, the words of the late President of the United States, John F. Kennedy apply."

I pause to gain my composure. As corny as these words might have become over the years, that does not make them any less true. So I take a deep breath, close my eyes for a moment, and recite, gently, *"Ask not what your country can do for you, but what you can do for your country."* And then I place one foot on either side of the line. "And with that my friends, from both sides, I thank you for your work, your dedication, and your kinship. God Bless you. God bless Mexico. And God bless the United States of America."

It's quiet for a moment. I fear I should have stayed with my script. A smattering of applause begins. Then, a woman three quarters back stands. In moments all in attendance are on their feet.

Alexus and I spend the rest of the day going through the exhibits. The most interesting, and if I hadn't lived it I'd find it hard to believe, is the 4D experience on the history of the Wall. It begins by showing how the construction was one of fits and starts until Kellyanne Conway, who was the counselor to the president, had the brilliant idea of putting solar panels on the wall to divert that energy to new, legal immigrants in need of short-term assistance. It was a kind of compromise. But those who hated the Wall could not come up with an argument against the creation of solar energy for thousands of miles erected in the sunniest part of America to help immigrants. It went up in a flash and helped her become the second woman president. Then the experience whisks us away, back in time and across millions of acres of farm land in America. We begin in 1980, flying over the fields where countless Mexicans, both legal and illegal work the fields picking everything from strawberries to apples to filberts. As time passes rapidly before our eyes, we see more automation replacing workers. It's hard to believe today hands once picked that fruit. Some people used to advocate for what amounts to as an open borders policy. Justifying it by saying we needed the workers. All the while, right before our eyes, automation rapidly replaced that labor force. The problem of immigration was just kicked down the road from one administration to the next. But during the Obama and Trump administrations, it reached a kind of fever pitch. By about 2038, human hands were obsolete in fields of any kind. The 4D experience slows down as we come to the year 2018. The media labeled people on the right side of the aisle who believed a strong border was the most compassionate long-term solution as Nazis. They show an old clip of Donnie Deutsch from what was MSNBC saying this very thing.

Donnie D. of MSNCB, all Nazis trumped.online/5eq

Then we zoom in on a restaurant that was called the Red Hen where Sarah Huckabee Sanders, only the second woman in history to be named Press Secretary, is having dinner with family. We see Stephanie Wilkinson, the owner, force Mrs. Sanders to leave because she did not agree with Mrs. Sander's political views. Then, as Sarah's family goes across the street to another restaurant, Stephanie Wilkinson organizes a group of employees that go out on the sidewalk and shout at them in the *other restaurant.* In an instant, we are on a city street watching Congresswoman Maxine Waters tell the entire country to harass, intimidate and 'turn' on anyone who worked for the Trump administration. In other words, they were using Nazi tactics while calling anyone who disagreed with them, Nazis.

CNN Maxine Waters trumped.online/2cz

We watch as talk show host Samantha Bee calls Ivanka Trump, Donald's daughter, a feckless cunt on national television. And we see her receive an award that same week from the TV Academy for being a positive role model. Yeah, that's how messed up things had become.

Samantha Bee, feckless cunt, CNN trumped.online/cb7

The narrative was that illegal alien families were being separated at the border when trying to break into the U.S. This was only half true. Or, to be much more precise, about 30% true. An old image of the now de-funked Time Magazine appears. Photoshopped on the cover of their June 2018 issue is an image of President Trump towering over a two-year-old girl crying who they had separated from her mother at the border. Half the country was up in arms. *How dare you, Trump, separate families?* But, turns out they never separated the girl from her mother. Actually, the mother lied when she said she was seeking asylum. She paid a 'coyote,' a human trafficker, $6000 to get her and her daughter across the border. She left behind three other children in South America. Those three children *really were* separated from their mother. What mainstream media failed to mention is, *all anyone had to do who was seeking asylum was go to an official point of entry* instead of illegally trying to break in. That's it! They would not separate you because you would not be committing a crime. The father of the child depicted on the front of Time Magazine said he was glad border patrol picked them up.

Time Magazine, The Lie trumped.online/rm0

All children were given food, video games, free medical including dental and more. And, *they separated only 30% of the kids that were depicted by mainstream media.* How do we know this? Because 70% of the kids were alone to begin with. In many cases, border patrol *saved their lives.* What Maxine Waters and her pundits refused to acknowledge is that sex trafficking went up 300% under Obama because it became so easy for traffickers to smuggle innocent children into the county by lying, pretending to be the children's parents. Young girls were being sent across the border by their parents with birth control pills because they knew the chance their daughters would be raped was astronomically high. Drug cartels paid children to carry drugs across. The atrocities seemed to have no limit. These facts received little coverage by what was referred to as mainstream media. We're now shown an interview with a border patrol agent back in 2017 from a news station called CNN which eventually went defunct. The border agent tells of the atrocities he has witnessed and how the news coverage has been falsified.

CNN interview Border patrol agent trumped.online/1p

Obama's administration *did* detain some would be parents. But more often than not they just let them go into America with a court date, usually set years in the future, to which they rarely ever showed. The message was clear to anyone who wanted to break in and take advantage of America's generosity, *pretend like you are a family! Use children as 'mules.'* All the while, millions of people around the world were working on entering America and becoming citizens the legal way. And, while half the country was blind with fury over the separation of maybe two thousand illegals from their parents, or, as the case often was, *fake parents,* there were *2.5 million American citizen children* separated from their families whose parents, like the illegal aliens, broke the law. Nobody ever mentioned them. It was selective outrage in an age of outrage culture; a time when, whoever was the most outraged, won. Or at least got the most attention.

Trump's wall was said to be cloaked in bigotry, sighting the fact that he didn't want to put a wall on the Canadian border. Since Canadians are mostly white, the wall must be racist. The simplistic and agenda driven rationale behind such rhetoric is self-evident. When those on the left side of the aisle were asked why they were not outraged by the same immigration laws during the Obama era, they had no answer. Alexus and I are reminded of the unsurpassed level of hypocrisy by a clip now showing from CNN with the late Senator Tammy Baldwin on Obama's immigration legacy. Baldwin delivers the most incomprehensible word salad we've ever heard.

CNN interviews Baldwin, hypocrisy! trumped.online/0

Cesar Chavez would have been appalled by the lack of border security as evidenced by the next image.

Chavez, Pragur U. trumped.online/rn8

 Automation changed everything, not just the need for field workers. The first time I noticed it was back in the 1990s when I was a teenager. There was a booth at a park I frequented. You would drive up to the window where an attendant would take cash or credit. Yes, cash! What a crazy thing that was. Anyway, then one day, they replaced the human with a machine that took only credit cards. I remember thinking, *Wow, this will change everything someday;* someday has arrived. And, many thought things were going to hell in a hand-basket. They thought automation and A.I. would make unemployment rampant. People argued that the rich would only get richer and the poor would get poorer. I was one of them until I met the Orange-tent-guy. He told me that if I would simply look at history I would find with every advancement in technology, from the wheel to the light bulb to iDesks, *everyone's* standard of living always went up. And, history has repeated itself. As westernized countries became increasingly advanced, the entire world benefited. Starvation is a thing of the past. An education is available to anyone who desires one, *for free.* Disease wiped out. Cancer gone.

A clip of Jordan Peterson and Dr. Steven Pinker is now shown from back in 2018. They pointed out how dramatically life has and will always improve even at a time when the mainstream media and countless hordes of the population believed life was 'bad' and getting worse.

Dr. Steve Pinker trumped.online/oms

Things, of course, are not perfect today. I don't think perfection is possible. The whole movement toward a mind implant has me worried, but it's a miraculous world today. And, it's the blessings of this world that make my predicament a curse. We've come so far to see it all destroyed by misinformation, ego and whoever the Man-In-Black represents. As the presentation ends, we see American citizens, clearly of Mexican descent, working and living and contributing to America in all fields of endeavor; doctors, business leaders, teachers, scientists, nurses, construction workers and so on. The same is shown of Mexican citizens who were clearly of American descent. Then we pull back up into space, looking down on our precious planet. Like the Great Wall of China, we can see The Wall. I'm reminded of the old saying; *Strong fences make good neighbors.*

The final words, shown holographically so you can reach out and touch them are:

May we continue to build our relationship... on trust. In peace. With love.

As I observe all the humanity represented in the room, my heart breaks. What am I going to do?

Alexus and I step outside on top of The Path Monument. It truly is one of the most beautiful views in the world. I call Malik and Shanice and tell them how much I love them and my grandkids. I wish *all* my children could be here. Now, If I could just freeze time, and change the past.

The Dawn: *Virtue Signaling, The One Percent*
Year: 2017 February 17 7:52 a.m.

" ... but bro, Liberals, progressives *are* the more compassionate, loving people. Republicans are selfish. That's just the truth. And rich people *don't know* what the best use of their money is. *Look at the 1%! It's ridiculous.*" As I'm finishing my tirade, I'm given an odd look from a passerby. Sometimes even I forget I'm talking to the side of an orange tent. Orange-tent-guy waits for the passerby to be out of earshot before responding. I'm pretty sure for the express purpose of embarrassing me.

"You are the 1%," he finally states as a matter of fact.

I feel insulted, "Am not."

"Are too. What do you think you have to earn per year to be in the 1%?"

"Um, something like ten million."

"Thirty five."

"That's worse than I thought. Thirty five million a year! Wow."

"Did I say million? Thousand, $35,000 a year."

"No way."

"Yes way. World wide, $35,000 a year. Not long ago the 1% world wide made half that much. The world is getting wealthier exponentially. In the U.S., where, of course, it's a much bigger number, how much of the total federal income tax is paid by this 1% everyone wants to villainies?"

"Um," I hate this, "I don't know."

"Don't you think you should know before you spout off about selfishness and compassion and other virtue signaling expletives?"

"Yeah… " I sheepishly respond.

"Here it is. One percent of the population in America pays for…wait for it…*fifty percent of all the taxes*. Does that seem fair? That one percent pays for fifty percent of the roads you drive on, fifty percent of the military that protects you, fifty percent of your government programs."

"Ummm… "

"And remember, you keep talking about compassion as if it's connected to taxes, which I think is nonsense. But if it were, the one percent would, by your rationale, be the most compassionate."

"I get what you are saying. But still, they're so rich."

"Who's they?" He asks like it's some mystery.

"Really? Are you even here now? The one percent!"

Orange-tent-guy is not happy with my response. I can make out through the mesh that he 's shaking his head in dismay as he lifts both hands like he's fed up. *"Just who do you think that one percent are?"*

Now I'm upset, ***"The people who make the top one percent of income in America!"***

"And you think they're a group of people that never changes? Like this 1% is akin to a race of people who will always be a specific color?"

"Well, of course. The 1% percent are the richest people in the world. It's the way it is. ***They will always be the richest, and the rest of us have to fight for scraps."***

"EEEEEEAAEEEE."

I hate it when he gives me the buzzer.

"WRONG!" He says like a sergeant to the troops, "The 1% percent changes faster than tires at the Indy 500! Yes, a few people in the one percent are permanently affixed to the status, but that's less than one percent of the one percent. People like Michael Jordan, George Clooney, Julia Roberts, Oprah Winfrey, Robert Smith, Bill Gates, Mark Zuckerberg, Jerry Seinfeld, and Colin Kaepernick will most likely be in the one percent till death. But the other ninety plus percent is in constant flux. Some people in the one percent today will be broke tomorrow. Have any compassion for them? And, by the way, to be in the one percent in America, a person needs to make approximately $350,000 in a year. Maybe an investment finally paid off. Maybe the stock market was kind to them that year. And maybe, for them, that's it. Maybe that's their retirement. But the government will tax them like they're Mark Zuckerberg. Maybe a business owner who has done very well for five or six years wakes up to find automation and foreign competition has put her out of business. She loses everything. Easy come…easy go. But we tax them all as if they are Will Smith!"

He sits down on that lawn chair, *"Compassion."* He puts his hand to his chin for a second, considering. Then he stands up and proclaims, "There was once a small town in the land of, of…*Potentiality.* Yes. *Potentiality,* called, uh, Just Ville."

"Wait, What? Where is this?"

He cocked his head sideways, *"Really?"*

"Oh, I get it, it's a fable."

"As I was saying, there was once a very special land called Potentiality. Every town in Potentiality had endless…. "

He paused, waiting for me to finish the thought. I pressed my face against the tent so he could have a little taste of his own, distorted medicine, "Potential!"

He pushed forward, "There were many philosophies practiced by the people of this land, all of which believed their ideas were best suited to maximize the limitless potential bestowed upon them. One town, in particular, believed striving for justice was the best way to maximize the awesome potential. They believed justice to be the highest ideal anyone could achieve. And so they named their town Just Ville. It wasn't always perfectly Just. That would be *impossible*. However, on the whole, the people in Just Ville were very happy. In fact, it became the envy of the Land of Potentiality. It thrived for over 250 years, and fast became the most prosperous, successful place of all. They understood that what you put into life comes back. This was central to the success of Just Ville. Now, there were two basic kinds of people. Those known as the 'Nows' and those known as the 'Laters.' Laters invested in their future. For example, many Laters went to Just U., took out loans, and some even went to graduate school and took out more loans. They worked very hard to pay off their debt while practicing medicine, law, engineering, physics, music, teaching and the like. This hard work almost always paid off. Justice served. Later in life, they could afford nice homes and go on vacations in far-off places like Hope Ville and Tolerance Providence. They were great to visit, but none functioned as well, overall, as Just Ville. Through the powerful practice known as Postponed Pleasure, they could put off things like fun to a later date and focus on building their future.

The other group, the Nows, generally decided high school was enough. They wanted to 'hang,' just 'chill,' and have fun *now*. Many of the Nows simply wanted to surf on the shores of Just Ville. While the Laters were going to school and paying off loans, they surfed. They could not afford to go on lavish vacations or live in fancy homes later on, but they did not have the stress early in life of four to eight more years of school and loans to pay off. They simply surfed and taught surfing and worked in restaurants waiting tables and did yard work for those who had, earlier in life, worked so hard. They were happy to do so. It was fair, Just. But then one day, despite how incredibly successful Just Ville was and how many people from all over the Land of Potentiality immigrated to Just Ville because of its great prosperity, there became a movement to *change* the name from Just Ville to Equal Ville. In the name of Progress, they said. They felt that it wasn't good enough that things were *almost* always Just, they wanted things to be Just always for everyone. The Changers, as they referred to themselves, believed in a kind of utopia. All could be equal. Many of the Nows adopted this philosophy. Why should they have to live in small apartments and work for those in big, nice homes? And so they put the name change to a vote, and, by a narrow margin, Equal Ville won out. Equality was now the higher ideal, not Justice. The Laters, whose time had finally come after ten, twenty, sometimes even thirty years of paying their dues, were now responsible for the welfare of everyone. The new law required them to pay the Nows and Changers higher wages for everything they did. Their levels of education, commitment and work ethic were irrelevant. The value the person brought to the job and society was irrelevant. Equality was paramount. The Laters also had to pay for everyone else's health care. They said that was not Just because many people treated their body and mind like a trash heap; eating countless pounds of sugar, high fructose corn syrup, fatty meats, refined breads, energy drinks, alcohol and some even smoked. To add insult to injury, a lot of these same people never exercised. The Laters argued that it was each person's individual responsibility to live a healthy existence and reap the benefits of that choice over time. This, of course, did not matter because being Just and fair was no longer relevant, only being Equal mattered. The Laters were also made to pay for roads, parks and anything else that the city needed. Initially, it seemed to work. It wasn't Just, but all were more equal. Over time, however, it became clear that no matter how much they took from the Laters, the Nows and Changers weren't happier. This made no sense. The Laters kept saying that Postponed Pleasure, hard work, sacrifice and contributing was the key to happiness. They encouraged everyone who was unhappy to find something they could do to give life meaning and contribute. They believed everyone was capable of greatness and that giving too much to those who were able, was ultimately the most hurtful thing to do. That kind of 'giving' actually took away the desire to discover one's passion, greatness, and experience a sense of accomplishment. The Laters said that kind of giving was 'enabling.' They were called heartless for holding this view even though the vast majority of them had experienced, first hand, the power of Postponed Pleasure.

Meanwhile, fewer people were interested in 'higher callings' and the principle of Postponed Pleasure. Why should they when they too could be a Now and have fun by living off of the Laters hard work and sacrifice?

Over time, some Changers agreed that people seemed to be happier when they earn what they have and when they contribute in ways that make the Land of Potentiality, happier. Unfortunately, by the time they made these astute observations, there weren't enough Laters left in Equal Ville to sustain it. The ones around during the change left for greener pastures hoping somewhere else would appreciate the hard work they put in early in life. Also, those who were interested in a higher calling felt defeated. They knew all of their work would end up paying for everyone else's existence.

The saddest part might be that it was the Laters who gave the vast majority of the money to the charities of Equal Ville. They were also the ones that adopted children from other places like Despair Town and Hapless City and gave them a real chance at reaching their potential.

Changing the name from Just Ville to Equal Ville had repercussions far beyond what anyone could have imagined. As Equal Ville, it collapsed in on itself. The Nows ended up in destitute poverty. Many found themselves homeless, like me.

The End."

He slowly sat back down into the lawn chair. Waiting for a reaction. After long moments passed, he stood, came to the tent wall, placed one hand on it and raised the question that begged, "So, who do you think was more kind and compassionate in the land of Potentiality, the Nows or the Laters?"

"They both were I guess, but in different ways. In your fable, of course, the Laters turned out to be more effective, but it's just a fable."

He jumps up from his chair, thrusts forward and nearly breaks right through the mesh material, causing me to fall flat on my behind. *"JUST A FABLE?* Fables give us insights into reality. And this 'reality' is *California."*

"What?"

"Yep, in an attempt to become 'Equal Ville' over the last 20 years, California is now the least livable state in the union. The middle class is leaving in droves. So, I ask you again, is it possible that the general public, whether they are 'Repugnican' or 'DemoRat,'" he says with a devilish grin, "Want the same outcome, they just have a different philosophy?"

"Orange-tent-guy, you're really pushing it this time. Just look at all the Democrat-run programs we have to help people."

"Oh, I have looked. Now you, if you have the cajones, do a little research and see how effective those programs really are? Most of them are nothing more than billion dollar virtue signaling."

"Virtue signaling? What the heck is that…exactly?"

"Generally, it's when someone says or does something to create an image that they are of the highest moral standings. In fact, superior to all those who hold a different opinion. For example, if you were at a gun control debate and one panel member who is against the NRA says, *I'm here because it's time to put an end to the killing of our children.* Then, all the people who are on her side of the debate cheer. First, the statement is shallow. *There's no solution.* That's typical of virtue signaling. Second, the subtext is, *If you don't believe as I do, you want the killing of our children to continue therefore me, and all my people are superior to you and yours.* Virtue signaling is as old as the human ego. Even Jesus warned against it."

"Wait, Jesus talked about virtue signaling?"

"Yeah, he said, *When you pray, don't be like the hypocrites who love to pray publicly on street corners where everyone can see them. Truly, I say to you, they have received their reward.* He's describing people doing something, praying, to be *seen* as holy instead of actually being holy.

"What's their reward Jesus is referring to?"

"Ah, yes. What do you think?"

"Well, attention. And status. But a false, flimsy, fake, ego based status, *signifying nothing.* "

"Nice. I like how you threw some Shakespeare in there."

"Thanks."

"Jesus went on to instruct, when in prayer, do so in secret. In other words, anything we do for positive change, do not do for accolades. In fact the opposite. Do so privately. The good you are doing is the reward. Ironically, those who virtue signal do not truly want change. If things actually change they can no longer look virtuous. If their prayers were answered the jig would be up. They couldn't get away with roaming around the streets looking pious."

"Okay, I get that. But you're saying charitable government programs are like billion dollar virtue signals?"

"Yeah. Generally speaking, the people who work for such programs are well-meaning, but in most cases, these programs do no good. In fact, they often do *great harm.* But, they make the government look like it cares while costing us billions of dollars."

"Okay, name one."

"You name one. Any one. And let's see if it's really doing good or just a gigantic, hulking, virtue signal."

"Head Start! It helps millions of kids"

"Does not. It has never worked and it is constantly fraught with fraud. Yet, because it appears so virtuous, we just keep funding it. The politicians running on such programs know very well they don't work. But who cares if it gets you elected? Don't believe me, do your own research.

      Head Start truth trumped.online/tt8
      CNN Head Start trumped.online/8pq

"Okay, welfare. What on earth could be wrong with trying to be fairer and help everyone be well?"

"Let me ask you this, what does it mean to live in poverty?"

"I'm not sure exactly, but the government has set the criteria."

"And whatever they say we should just accept as truth?"

"Well, I guess not."

"So, I take that as a no. We should not just accept what the government says as truth. Right?"

"Yes, but I'm afraid almost everyone does, including me, historically."

"Okay, let's use some common sense. Tell me what you think living in poverty should mean?"

"Well, I would say it comes down to the three necessities. Food, shelter, and clothing. If you don't have enough food to eat, if you're starving, that would be poverty. If you do not have a roof over your head or a few changes of clothing that would be poverty."

"I agree. However, over time as the standard of living has risen, because it has despite what many people think, the government has continued to raise the level of what it means to live in poverty."

"Why would they do that?"

"We'll get to that in a minute. I notice you didn't include lack of air conditioning in your definition of poverty."
"Air conditioning? I would say air conditioning is a luxury. I mean, air conditioning didn't even exist until relatively recent history."

"Well, most Americans with incomes below the official poverty level *have air conditioning.*"

"No way."

"Yes, way. You didn't mention televisions either."

"Huh?"

"The average household below the poverty level has two televisions and, *wait for it…* a car."

"A car? What kind?" I say with a chuckle.

"Well, not a BMW, but if the government keeps raising the level of what it means to be in poverty, I wouldn't be surprised if in 30 years something even more impressive than your average BMW is being driven by those in poverty. Maybe even something self-driven."

"Self-driven? How can you even say that? That doesn't even exist yet."

"True, and cell phones didn't even exist 20 years ago, but nearly every household below the poverty level today has one… *or more*. Not to mention a microwave, refrigerator, stove, and hot and cold running water for a shower *every day*. But there is one very sad statistic regarding those below the government-mandated poverty line."

"What is that?"

"It was on your list, the three necessities. *Food.*"

"Of course. They're starving!"

"No, *they're obese*. They have too much to eat."

"What?"

"Yes. There was a time those in poverty were unhealthy because of starvation. Today most of those below the poverty line are unhealthy because of clogged arteries, heart attacks and everything else that comes with obesity."

Black Intellectual Sowell on poverty trumped.online/ew2
White Intellectual Friedman on poverty trumped.online/w1h

Emotionally, I don't like what he's saying. I suddenly become keenly aware of that because the information, except for the obesity part, is great news. Not only that, but some part of me knew these things. I think we all do. So why don't I feel happy that those in poverty today would not have been considered impoverished, not even close to it, 50 years ago? Things are progressing at a staggering rate. Why am I attached to there being a huge, truly low class of people in desperate need of help? Starving, freezing cold in winter, circa 1970?

"I get why you say the standard of living keeps going up for everyone. I mean technological breakthroughs raise everyone's standard of living. But why on earth would the government keep adjusting, raising, the poverty line?"

"Remember, this whole discussion is about the welfare state. Come on; you can figure this out."

Once I realize why, I feel so naïve, "Because, the more people rise above the poverty line, the less they can come with pitchforks for our money."

"Bingo, Bango, Bongo. And nothing justifies the government's ability to take whatever they want, whenever they want. However, it wouldn't be as bad if the money they took went to those under this random poverty line."

"It doesn't?"

"Prius-Driving-About-To-Have-A-Nervous-Breakdown-Guy, your naiveté never ceases to amaze. Of course not. Once the government gets money in their grubby, greedy little hands, it gets sucked up into the vortex of bureaucracy. First, it goes to pay their bloated salaries. Look at Maxine Waters. She's a multimillionaire senator who is a lifetime politician. How do you think she got so rich? And, *she refuses to even live in the district she represents.*"

Maxine Waters house trumped.online/8lh
Maxine Waters district trumped.online/lma

"Wait. That shouldn't even be allowed."

"Once the corrupt, dysfunctional, hoarding government siphons off whatever they want, then whatever is left over goes to those under the forever upward moving poverty line. However, on second thought, it *might* be better if *none* of the money taken for those below the arbitrary poverty line ever actually got to them."

"Okay, that's the stupidest thing I've ever heard."

"Really? Let's say you currently lived below the poverty line, receiving welfare. You were not contributing to society; in fact, you were a drain upon society. Then, an opportunity presented itself for you to earn an additional $10,000 per year contributing in some fashion. Uh oh, but that additional $10,000 per year would put you above the poverty line, therefore, eliminating $15,000 per year in welfare. What would you do?"

"Ugh!"

"Ugh! Exactly. So, the Welfare State *is a state of mind* to be less and do less. You see, this *is* the Land of Potentiality. But if you're afraid to take a risk, to find out what you're truly capable of because you will lose money, you'll never allow yourself to become the greatness you are.”

“It's so complicated isn't it?”

“Gray!”

“Yes, gray. Well my odd, Sean Cassidy-like friend, I gotta go.” I watch his outline rummage around through the mesh. Then I recognize his big rimmed hat as he places it on his head and says, “See ya, wouldn’t wanna be ya.”

I walk toward my car when somehow my mind makes a random association. So, just a few feet from the door handle I turn around.

“*Hey,*” I extol.

“What is it now?” He replies sounding irritated. He’s standing on the other side of the tent. I can see the brim of his hat over the top of the orange mesh. I have to yell since I’m now about one hundred feet away. *“What about reparations? It seems like welfare. But, true. Like Black Lives Matter says. Don’t you feel that us white people owe all blacks for the sin of slavery?”*

Black women explains reparations <u>trumped.online/pxp</u>

“Ha…haa ha. That’s rich!” Oh no, not the laughing again. “Ha ha, He Hu Hoo…Oh man, Prius Driving/About To Have A Nervous Break Down Guy. *HAHA HA.* You never cease to astound.”

His hat made its way around the tent. Bobbing up and down. Now, at 8:36 a.m., it’s bright out. The sun has just overtaken the east hills. He steps around into plain site grinning ear to ear. The words escape my throat before I could hush them.

“What? You're…BLACK?!”

Chapter 14 The Future: *The End!*
Year: 2077 December 24 7:30 p.m.

I'm just an old man now. An old man whose life has amounted to nothing but one unending, haunting regret. How many people can point to a moment in time where they made a selfish decision that leads to the destruction of life on planet earth? My existence is agony as the news continues to report the death toll. On average, 375,000 people die each day from runaway climate change. As of last week, they say there are no butterflies left. Honey bees disappeared almost a year ago. The oceans continue to become less and less hospitable to life. The Great Barrier Reef is dead. Whales are washing up on shores all over the world; oceanographers say they have gone insane. Birds fall from the sky like some biblical plague. Occasionally, out of self-loathing, I roll my wheelchair to the window, pull back the curtain and look out at what I once knew as the Rose City, Portland Oregon. The roses are all but gone. They have buried a third of the human population in mass graves on Sauvie's Island. Sky Scrapers are dilapidated, parks are wastelands, *and I am to blame.*

"Are you ready now?"

"No. No! *Get out of here.* Can't you leave an old man to die?" The Man-In-Black still haunts me. Popping in and out at will. He seems to have not aged although I've never seen his face. "You got what you wanted," I plead, "Just leave me alone."

The disguised monster voice proclaims, **"There's one more thing to make my mission complete. Here, take it,"**

He gives me a gun. Since the year 2053, the holographic trajectory has become, for lack of a better description, *solid.* It's like being in two places at once. And so are the things you bring with you.

His unnerving voice continues, **"It's what we both want. Haven't you had your fill of self-loathing, watching the decimation of humanity and planet earth? Whatever torment will be your penance in hell cannot be worse than sitting here wallowing in a cesspool of shame and regret."**

He's right. I think about ending my life every day since Alexus passed seven years ago from Distinction Infection, a disease created by the climate shift. In other words, *I killed the love of my life.* The only thing stopping me right now is, *it's him handing me the gun.* I don't want him to win, I don't want him to have the satisfaction, but I realize, that's misplaced pride. A pride that has created this irredeemable existence. And so, I slowly reach up and take the gun. Once it is firmly in my hand, I let off three rounds directly at the Man-In-Black. The bullets lodge into his holographic image. It's like watching BBs enter a soft clay model. He laughs.

"Feel better? Now, do what you know you must!"

My hand is shaking uncontrollably, I hold the gun to my right temple as I whisper, "Please God, please. Forgive me."

BANG!

The Dawn: *DDT, The Wage Gap*
Year: 2017 March 4 7:00 a.m.

What? You're...BLACK?!

I keep reliving it over and over in my mind. Probably the stupidest thing I have ever said. And his reply? *As a frying pan.* That's what he said. And then he just took off, running. I haven't seen him since. I've been too busy at work; too stressed at home and, mostly, afraid. Afraid he'll hate me for being an idiot and/or his brilliant, crazy musings will somehow cut the final thread holding my marriage together. Whatever that thread is. And, whatever it is, is probably a lie. So, I'm afraid of the truth. We all are. We live in our little bubbles. Complacent. Content. Even happy sometimes. But what if one's happiness is *based* on a lie? Were we ever really happy?

These are the questions plaguing me as I stare at the Google search bar while Kathy finishes getting Malik and Shanice ready for school and out the door to catch the bus. I've tried to forget Orange-tent-guy's remarks that night as I drove away in the rain, *Rachel Carson was complacent in the killing of a million people.*

Rachel Carson has been a hero to me. Her book, Silent Spring, a bible. She single-handedly put an end to the use of the pesticide DDT. *My children go to a school named in her honor!* I'm in a battle with my fingers as I struggle to put into the search bar, *Silent Spring truth.*

Countless articles appear.

By the time I'm done reading, my stomach hurts. There is 'gray' here. There always is. But the bottom line comes down to the possibility that because they made DDT out to be a monster, in part because of the book **Silent Spring**, countless people may have died of malaria! There is a debate. But, it's a real possibility.

"What's wrong with you?" Kathy says as she enters the family room where I guess I look as sick as I feel. If I told her what I have discovered, she would likely get a knife, cut out my liver and eat it before committing Harry Carry.

"Um, I just wanted to chat with you about Malik."

"Oh God, *what is it?* I suppose you want to make him wear a MAGA hat to school from now on."

"Kathy! Really? I'll pretend you didn't say that. I want to discuss Malik and Ritalin. I know Ritalin is helpful for some kids. I get that. Really. But it's, it's *gray.*"

"Gray?" she says confounded

"I wonder if he's, well, being a boy. And if we need to work with his boy energy."

"Jesus Marcus, really? 'Boy energy!?' *Who are you?* You know darn well the only real difference between boys and girls are *how we treat them,* what we *socialize into them* which is why women are so oppressed in America! *I'm not having this conversation with you!"*

I thought Orange-tent-guy was crazy. And maybe he is. If being normal is accepting the status quo, hearing only what you want to hear, believing only what aligns with your paradigm, then, *it is crazy to challenge yourself and society.* And so I guess I have joined my Orange Tent friend and become a mental looney bin. He's got me doing *a lot of research.* My expose' into Rachel Carson was not the first. Our earlier discussion about John McEnroe's comment ignited my curiosity. It prompted me to pull back the veil and brave the world of truth. And the truth is, today, women are not oppressed in America. Quite the opposite. And I couldn't hold my tongue.

"Sweetheart, I have great news for you."

She softens a bit but what I fear is that people, and I say this from personal experience, don't want to hear that things have gotten better. They don't want to know their 'righteous' causes are no longer relevant because these causes have given their lives 'purpose.' It's true insanity. I forge ahead anyway, "Women are no longer the oppressed people they once were. In fact, more women graduate from college than men."

Her softness turns rigid, "I've heard, don't know if it's true, but the wage gap is real and is an abomination upon our society. Women make .77 cents on the dollar compared to men."

"Again, I have great news. That is not true. A recent study has shown that young women entering the workforce in 149 out of 150 of America's largest cities make *more money than men.*"

Wage Gap, Professor Sommers <u>trumped.online/t8r</u>

By the look I'm receiving, I fear her head is about to spin 360 degrees akin to Linda Blair in the exorcist.

"Also, the reason that women currently in the workforce sometimes make less money than men is simply the fact that later in life women choose to take more time off, so, at the end of a year, on average men would make more money. What's beautiful is the differences between men and women. We have different interests. And those differences balance society. If diversity is our strength, we should celebrate the truth that men and women *are not the same.* A guy named Warren Farrell wrote a book for his daughters, **Why Men Earn More**. He wanted to help them maximize their earning potential. He discovered in his research many logical reasons that men *used* to make more money like men take more dangerous, grueling, even physically debilitating jobs. These jobs tend to compensate well, but those men pay dearly for it later in life in physical and often mental rehab. 98% of all work-related deaths *happen to men.* Men are also much more likely to move for a promotion. And, women choose to spend more time with family, with their children, and with friends, *which is admirable.* For political reasons alone, they often ignore these facts. The narrative that women are treated as second-class citizens gets a lot of attention, *votes really.* The feeling that there is injustice rallies people up. It is sad. Many politicians would rather divide the people of our nation to get votes than create healing by celebrating our progress. Besides, if the pay gap was real, there isn't a single business owner, man or women, who would not fire every man and hire all women. At .77 cents on the dollar, their business would become nearly a fourth more profitable in an instant."

She shakes her head, red in the face, "Oh my God, *you're so full of SHIT! Obama said it's real.*"

"Kathy, I know what he said. But it makes no sense you're angry. If I'm wrong, prove it. Do the research. But if I'm right, it is cause to celebrate. I am open. More than willing to be proven wrong. There just came a point when I realized I was falling into group-think. And I refuse to do it anymore. I simply want to know the truth."

🔗 Pay gap, President Obama, <u>trumped.online/gwk</u> 🔗
🔗 Pay gap revealed <u>trumped.online/5i1</u> 🔗

"*Truth,*" She yelled, "*You want some truth? I'll give you some truth.* Men are toxic. Have you heard of toxic masculinity? Men suppressed women throughout all of history. Men hate women. *It's time for women to take control!*"

I don't let her anger get a rise out to me. I trudge forward, "Actually, that's a terrible way to view history. Roles were naturally defined for millions of years by biology. Until tampons were created, by a man who loved his wife, there really was no way for women to consistently and sanitarily be in the work place. Not to mention until the 1960's there was no easy to use, reliable birth control. And, without it, women were pregnant much of the time; which was often fatal. So, it's gray. A more true and fair way to view history is men have loved, protected, provided for and died for their wives and children. I'm not saying women haven't been treated unfairly at times but history is gray. We have transformed our culture in a relative blink of an eye. That should be celebrated and we should all be given a little grace."

Silence fell hard all around us. Like a lead brick. What did I expect? Did I think she would suddenly say, *Wow, that's amazing? I'm so glad to hear women are no longer oppressed. You're right, we need to focus on the strengths of our differences to create the most powerful society.* Not! An employee of Google, James Damore, recently got fired for pointing out the truth that men and women are different.

177

James Damore: under protest trumped.online/z9l

And, ironically, Google *is* guilty of one of todays greatest sins; the pay gap. *They pay women more than men for the same job!*

Googles pay gap trumped.online/w83

So, no, she did not engage in a conversation with me. After about 60 seconds that felt like an eternity, she clenched her fists together, lowered her head about 3 inches as veins popped on her forehead and let out a primal scream that shook some decorative plates balancing in the buffet like the lady in green on inauguration day, *AAHHHHHHHHH.*

Lady in green scream https://youtu.be/wDYNVH0U3cs

Then she stomped out and slammed the bedroom door behind her. Truth is, we hardly talk about anything these days. She spends most of her free time over at Janet's. Sometimes I wonder what they say about me. I slowly approach the bedroom, considering a gentle knock but then I turn and leave. I understand that the 'Red Pill' I'm swallowing, in the form of an Orange Tent, is difficult for her. But still, she's so unreachable.

Chapter 15 The Future: *BANG*
Year: 2047 February 18 4:39 a.m.

I can feel the cold barrel of the gun on my temple as I squeeze the trigger, *BANG!* I wake in a cold sweat and sit up with a start. The blankets fly forward with me leaving Alexus vulnerable to the low sleeping temperature of the room. She groggily asks, "Are you okay?"

"Yes sweetheart, I'm fine. Just a bad dream. Go back to sleep." It's the third time I've had the dream in one week. It feels more like a premonition, and my soul cannot live with that. I'm afraid to use my phone or any technology. I jump in my car, disengage auto drive and all GPS technology hoping the Man-In-Black can't track me. Part of the drawbacks of modern 'conveniences;' for them to work, *somebody always knows where you are and what you are doing!* So, I head to Charles' house the old-fashioned way. *Hands on wheel, foot on pedal.*

"Hey, WAKE UP" I yell up toward his bedroom from the front door. Soon I stoop to the age-old tactic of throwing pebbles at his window.

Finally, he appears, disheveled, sticking his head out, "What in God's name are you doing here at 5:30 in the blessed a.m. *man?!*"

"Get some clothes on and get out here."

"What? Just come inside."

"No can do, get out here… now."

"Well, aren't we bossy this morning."

"Just come here."

He shuts the window and moments later steps out the front door wearing teddy bear pajamas and a ski hat. "Okay, I'm here. Spill it."

Inspired by paranoia, I whisper, "Nope, not yet. We need to get out of range of any Wi-Fi connection."

"Seriously Marcus, what is going on?"

"Shhh." I walk up the drive, away from his home, then I turn on the Wi-Fi connection on my device to see if his Wi-Fi is reaching us. It's weak, so I keep walking until it fades.

"What are we doing? It's cold out here," he says almost shivering.

"I didn't ask you to wear some goofy thin pajamas with teddy bears now did I?" He lifts his eyebrows, conceding. "Okay, I think we're safe...A couple of weeks ago a man wearing all black, including a face mask, hacked the system at my house and appeared as a hologram."

"What?" His eyebrows crinkle.

"Then he gave me the climate data that puts into question all of my findings. It's fake. But he told me that if I did not use it and convince all of you I was wrong, he would torture and kill every one of us."

"What the..."

"Then, when we all met here at your house, well, I was going to tell you, but he hacked your system and appeared while we were talking. *Right behind you!* I don't know what to do. *What should we do?* I feel like he's always watching. One step ahead. It's been torture. I say nothing; he spares your lives. But then, the future of life on earth will be, well, dubious at best." To make light of a very heavy moment I add, "Dubious in a way reminiscent of the end of A.O.C.'s presidential term back in 2028!"

Charles responds with a slight chuckle. "Yeah, that was dubious alright. The 2028 presidential campaign that followed between Ocasio-Cortez and Candace Owens was, in my opinion, more significant than Trump and Hillary in 2016."

"We will never know what might have been."

"No, we won't," Charles responds deep in thought, "But I think a catastrophe was diverted, maybe equal to the one we face now. That election will be seen as a pivotal moment for time immemorial." He paced back-and-forth when suddenly, "The Man-In-Black. *I know what to do!*"

The Dawn: *People of Color, White Guilt*
Year: 2017 March 4 7:33 a.m.

I finally muster the courage to visit the Orange-tent-guy at one of his parking lots. He's obviously been working through the night, finishing his last lot. I can see his breath in the cool March air. He doesn't see me coming so I lead with humor in an attempt to diffuse any chagrin he might be feeling from our last contact. I call out, "Frying pan? Really? As a frying pan? And then you ran away?"

"Yes, I did. And Obama needs to pay reparations."

I should be used to it by now, his random, shocking declarations. But I'm not. "What on earth are you talking about?"

"You asked about reparations. Only five percent of white people alive today have any genetic ties to slave owners. Obama is one of them."

"Um, he's not white."

"As white as he is black. And, he is part of that five percent. His Mother's ancestors were slave owners which means Obama's ancestors were slave owners. So, I suppose Obama could write a check to himself." He gives me a smirk, "That is, if you still believe in reparations. And, to make matters even more confounding, on Obama's father's side, Obama probably has slave traders in his family tree."

🔗 Obama's reparation status trumped.online/byg 🔗

"*What?* I, I don't know what to believe. I just, feel, I'm, ah… "

He quotes Han from Star Wars, *"Cough it up fuzzball!"*

"I feel so stupid. Not knowing you are… *of color.*"

"*Of color?* Really? And what are you?"

"White. Duh...I'm not a person of color."

"You do know *white* is *all* colors, don't you? How can you say you're not of color when you are literally more color-full than any other race?"

I'm feeling uncomfortable, again. I do not deserve to be part of those who are considered, *of color.* They are, well, special.

He continues, "You look uneasy. Something wrong?"

"You know fair well what's wrong. *I'm not a person of color!*"

"Really!?" He says loud and clear. I can feel a strong *comeback* on its way. "Are you see-through? Transparent?" I don't give him the satisfaction of a response. "Didn't think so."

"But, they coined, *Person of Color,* to honor those who are not white and exclude those who are."

"Yep, more division. Separation. Tribalism. We are Americans. All of us. We should be united in our pride of this great country." Every time I hear that kind of patriotic bull I feel triggered. I tend to agree with N.Y. Governor Cuomo when he said, *America was never that great.*

Cuomo, trumped.online/7sz

"Isn't that the problem? We're 'Americans'," I respond with finger quotes and all.

"Oh, Okay. Let me guess. You hate your country. You think it's founded in sin. And yet you know it's the most abundant, powerful country in the world so you're torn. You want to be honest and say you hate it but then you'd be a hypocrite for enjoying all the advantages America has given you."

How does he do that? "Well, that just about sums it up."

"What if I could show you that the part of you that hates your country is misinformed? Would you be Okay with that?"

"Of course. Who wouldn't?"

"A lot of people would not. They virtue signal their hatred. Makes them feel righteous and relevant. It's childish. Anyway, on a scale from 1-10, how much do you think you hate your country?"

"I don't know. Maybe an 8."

“Okay. Shall we begin with the Native American myth?”

“What myth?”

"The myth that this country is really theirs.”

“It’s not a myth.”

“It’s gray,” he says with a sideways nod.

“How can you say that, we really should give this land back to them.”

“Who?”

“The *natives!*”

“Which tribe does it really belong to? Most were fighting, killing, raping, and enslaving each other. The biggest slaughter of ‘native Americans’ was at the hand of other ‘native Americans,’ not European migrants. So, which tribe does it belong to? And, what do you have against migrants?”

Stymied. “I don't know which tribe it belongs to and I’m not against migrants.”

“Oh. Well, do you know which tribe got here first since that seems to be your measure of who owns it?”

“I do not.”

“Well, no one knows. It is believed that Paleolithic hunter-gatherers first entered North America from North Asia about 14,000 years ago. Should we do DNA testing and give America just to those with North Asian DNA on the chance they might have been first?”

“I, I guess not.”

“Okay, I guess not as well. Now, as we have established, every ‘Native American’ tribe fought with other tribes and settled here at different times. So what makes the European settlers different?”

“Nothing, I guess.”

"Correct. How is it that the vast majority of tribes people died after the European immigrants came?"

"From disease. Right?"

"Maybe."

"Maybe?"

"Yes. What's rarely ever talked about is before the Europeans arrived the diseases they brought, *preceded them!* In other words, massive populations of natives were already decimated by smallpox, measles and influenza. No one knows how it got here. Maybe birds or bats. And of course, some of the disease that infected the natives did come from the newest immigrants. This happened all over the world and still happens today. People get sick from accidental exposure to disease. It is a tragedy this happens. I'll bet you didn't know that the European immigrants actually tried to immunize the earlier migrants."

"What?"

"Yes. They tried to save them from smallpox."

"No way."

"Also, no one ever talks about the fact that the 'natives' infected the European settlers with a deadly disease that in turn broke out all over Europe."

"What? I've never heard of that. What was it?"

"Syphilis!"

"NO WAY!"

"Yes way. Now, when the European migrants became a part of the endless skirmishing going on between all the other settlers, why did they win?"

It's simple, but I don't want to say it. "Well, I don't know. They were meaner, more aggressive."

"Oh come on. You know that's not it. Use your college brainwashed mind."

"Well, they were more, more… "

"Come on. It's not a sin, say it."

I force it from my mouth, "They were more advanced."

"I knew you could do it. The people who were here, fighting amongst themselves, had not even invented the wheel. They did not have gun powder or large sailing ships. They had no buildings, no complex architecture, no advanced mathematical understanding or intricate art forms. The list goes on and on. They were about 7000 years behind. Now, what if any one of the tribes that migrated before the Europeans had the same advances, what do you think would have happened?"

"That tribe would have been dominant. They would have ruled."

"Of course. During those times of conquest and expansion, that is how every group operated. And, whoever was the most advanced won. Now, the truth is, there was a lot of cooperation between the European settlers and the previous settlers. And, there is a good possibility that if one of the other migrant groups that came to this land had the advancements of the Europeans, it would have been much more brutal. "

  🔗 Brutality, Native American history trumped.online/uos 🔗

He stared me down, waiting for a response. I got nothin' so he continues.

"America is not unlike every country on earth. There are unfortunate historical events that stemmed from a lack of knowledge and understanding across the globe. America, however, I believe had either a divinely appointed destiny or the rest of the world just got lucky that the founding fathers came to this land. For example, Dec. 7th, 1941."

That date rings a bell, "Pearl Harbor?"

"Good, yes."

"I'm not following."

"Connect the dots. If one of the earlier migrant groups, before the Europeans, had created a country out of this land, do you think America would be the world power it is?"

My heart starts racing. I'm feeling defensive. "I don't like where you're going with this."

"Why?"

"It just feels wrong."

"Well, I'm not interested in how it feels. Let's just stick to the facts, the best version of the truth we can. Remember, we're trying see if your hatred of America is misguided or not. This is important, yes?"

"Yes, it is."

"Okay, do you think America would be the world power it is? The land of opportunity it is? The freest democracy ever devised, without the European immigrants?"

My throat is dry. Stuck. I have to force it out. "Probably… not."

"Now, connect the dots. What would have happened, without the America created by the founding fathers?"

"Well, there's a good chance, in 1941, the world would have been taken over by the most soulless, fascist, racist regime the world has ever known. There would be pictures of Adolf Hitler in every home."

"1947 to 1991?"

"I'm thinking, the Cold War?"

"Yes. What then?"

"If America was not the America we know today the other fascist regime, the Soviet Union, might very well have taken over the world."

"And what do you think Canada and Mexico would be like today if they did not have America on their border? For example, what would Mexico be like if we could magically move it onto the side of the African continent? Or plop it down in the middle east? Or attach it to Japan?"

"I never really thought of that."

"Think of it now."

"Mexico would suddenly be in a heap of trouble. Without America on its border most of its wealth would disappear. And I doubt those other countries, or any country, would be as helpful as America. Japan, as prosperous as it is, has some of the strictest immigration policies on the planet. Close to zero Mexicans would be allowed in."

"Are the Japanese racist?"

"I don't know. I think they're trying to keep their culture intact."

"Is that racist, to cherish your culture and it's uniqueness?"

"I, I guess not. And Canada would probably be greatly diminished without the U.S. as well."

He tilted his head, slight grin, "Still hatin' on America?"

"Can you just let me digest this for a moment? Sheesh."

"Sure. While you digest, what do you think would have happened had say, a group of African migrants or Middle easterners came in 1620 instead of the pilgrims?"

"Well, I don't think either one had the technology so… "

"Sure, but let's say somehow they did."

"Well, I think the African tribes were waring with each other and the middle eastern tribes were waring with each other so there probably would have been a real blood bath."

"Probably. On a scale from 1-10, how's your hatred of America now?"

"Hmmm. Maybe a 3."

"Good. Now, can you see that these labels and the constant reference to skin color is separating us? Especially when you, Marcus, are purposefully excluded because of the color of your skin? It's bringing back a kind of tribal, waring mentality that was here before the European immigrants arrived. Now, today, we actually are one nation as opposed to the 573 separate nations that existed a few hundred years ago and spoke approximately 300 different languages."

"Are you saying that there were nearly 600 different nations fighting over this land, trying to expand territory? In a sense, colonize each other?"

"Yes, exactly. So, there is blood on the hands of the European immigrants just as there is on the hands of all the other immigrants that came before them. That is the troubling past for humanity the world over. Today we should be united by pride in our great country and the unprecedented progress we have made instead of turning back the hands of time by this obsession with skin tone. It's those who say they want equality for all who are now pushing racism by separating us, once again, into tribes."

"So, when I called you a person of color, I was separating you and me into different nations, in a sense."

"Yes, exactly."

"Well, okay. I'm sorry. I won't refer to you as, *of color,* ever again. I'll just go with African-American."

"EEEEEAAAEEE!"

Oh God, the buzzer. "Um, okay, how about just, black?"

"Better, thank you. Even though my skin is more brown, like most Americans who are of African descent. But that's probably the best we got, black. Just like most 'white' people are countless shades of beige, or 'peach' or tan. Just promise to use my color only when absolutely necessary. We're all people."

"Okay. But why not *African-American?* "

"That was Jesse Jackson's idea. He's the Race-Baiter-In-Chief, along with Al Sharpton."

🔗 Jackson, Sharpton's racism trumped.online/lfk 🔗

He stops sweeping for a second, shakes his head, "Phew. Okay. What is your racial heritage?"

"I'm Irish, Scottish and a little Cherokee."

"Would you like me to call you, Irish-American? Or Irish-Scottish-Cherokee-American?"

"Well, not really, but African-American, it's respectful, it's politically cor..."
P.C. Michael Douglass, Morgan Freeman, trumped.online/c4f

"Oh God, please stop. Political correctness is an attempt at mind control, halting any thought that might go against the current ruling political elites. When will we all be Americans? Did you know there's a whole movement called unhyphenated America?"

Morgan Freeman, Black History trumped.online/3wa
Unhyphenated America trumped.online/yc3

"No, I did not know that. Did you know I was unaware you're African-Amer... I mean that you're black?"

"No actually. At least I wasn't sure. It was a strange sequence of events. However, I believe you *did* know I'm black. You just couldn't allow yourself to use common sense for fear of being called racist or prejudice. It's a sad state of affairs."

"What? *I did not know.* How could I? *I never saw you! Geez!*"

"Yes, Geeeeeez."

"What Geeeez?

"Your *Geez* is giving you away. Search your soul. Analyze our interactions. You're telling me you never had even an inkling that I'm black?" I thought about all of our interactions, our conversations. And he was right. A part of me, a part I'm somehow ashamed of, knew. But I pushed it away. He watched me closely as I struggled to come to terms with this.

"See," he said, "You knew. At least a part of you, you ignored. Why?"

"Ah, well, I don't know."

"You do know. You're just so caught up in political correctness you refused to allow yourself to acknowledge the fact that blacks and whites, more often than not, speak differently, even sound different. It's just a fact. I suppose you might even call it racist. If so, it's an aspect of racism that's positive. Actual diversity. Which leads me to a theory."

"Oh boy, what theory now?"

"The reason you kept coming back with your helpless sandwiches, at least in the beginning, was, *is* your deep-seated… Wilt!"

"Would you mind speaking English, at least for once."

"Wilt; White Guilt. It's a powerful force that is wilting away white culture, white history, white pride. It's not even P.C. to say those two words together; *white* and *pride*. If you are white, you are not allowed to be proud. What a terrible thing to do to an entire race of people. Anyway, it was your Wilt that kept you coming back to me."

I don't know what he's talking about, so I simply reply, "Was not."

"*Was too,*" he countered, harking back to childhood days when comebacks were arrows made of rubber. I respond in kind, "Was not."

"Was too, times infinity."

"Was not, infinity times infinity times!" Then my phone rings, "Just a sec," he goes back to sweeping. It's her. My stomach drops, "Hey."

There are no niceties between us now. She simply says, "Can you pick up the kids; I have clients all afternoon?"

I'm standing just a couple of feet away from Orange-tent-guy, "Sure, okay. Do Malik and Shanice have their parent-teacher conferences tonight?"

"Yeah."

"Okay." When I hang up the phone, Orange-tent-guy is looking at me strangely.

"Who's Malik and Shanice, your children?"

"Yes, look." I pull up pictures on my phone.

He looks for a second and says, "Well, they are beautiful but, *they're as white as a snowflake on Mount Hood in January!* I thought maybe you adopted a couple of black kids or your wife was black. But no, what you have there is a Bob and a Becky. What in God's name were you two thinking?"

Okay, I'm a little insulted and therefore defensive, "Well, we were thinking, *What's in a name?* I mean, Kathy and I wanted to make a point. We wanted to break stereotypes and show white people that a name is a name just like a color is a color. That we should not be judgmental or prejudice *in either case.*"

He grins a slow grin. Like when the Grinch who stole Christmas looked down upon Whoville, and that giant Grinchy smile slowly took over every millimeter of real estate on his face. And then, his laughter begins, "Ah ha, ha." At first, it was slow. But it started to grow, "HA HA HA," echoing off the buildings that surround us.

"What in God's name is so funny?" You know when someone is laughing so hard they can't speak? They struggle to get the words out between breaths. He was *busting.* The only thing that kept him on his feet was the broom he was clinging to.

"Yo…You…AHHHHH HA HA. You…."

"Yes, spit it out."

"You…YOU… never in my…AHHHH HA HA"

"Seriously? What is so funny?"

"You vir…vir…AH HA HA HA"

"Yes, I vir..?? WHAT? WHAT DAMMIT?" He finally got it out.

"YOU VIRTUE SIGNALED *YOUR CHILDREN!* THAT'S LIKE THE, THE FUNNIEST THING I EVER HEARD… AHHHH HA HA!"

"Did not."

"DID TOO, HA HA AHH"

"DID NOT! We just… "

"AH HA HA HA HA… " he laughed uncontrollably.

"OK, knock it off!"

He gains his composure, "I'm sorry, but… " and then one of those obnoxious big laugh snorts comes bellowing from deep within his sinuses, "@#$NGNGGHGH."

So I yelled over the vibration, "WE JUST WANTED TO SHOW EVERYONE THAT WE'RE ALL THE SAME!"

"Oh my gosh," he said grabbing his stomach, "My face hurts, my stomach hurts. I'm pretty sure even my hair hurts. But it's a good hurt. AHHH… "

Now I'm so upset and embarrassed, balderdash dribbles from my mouth, "Well, yer, a sweeping, orange… "

"What? *I'm a sweeping orange?* BAH HAHAHAHHAAHH"

To save face, I tried to own it, "Yes, you're a sweeping orange, and I'm, I'm going to… "

"*What?* You're going to what? AH HAHHAAH"

"Peel you. I'm going to peel you right here in this parking lot."

"Well, then you'll need this, BAHH HEE HA HA," he said as he handed me the broom, *"To sweep me up!"* Without the broom to support his weight, he kind of collapses in a heap of uproarious guffaw. I just stand there waiting for him to regain his composure as he wipes tears from his face, "You like to tell yourself that, I'm sure."

"Tell myself what?"

"That you were just trying to make some point. Some all important, holy, social justice invoking point. But, *Wilt* is a powerful shame-based force that makes you white people do some pretty stupid things. This is honestly the most, well, outlandish and entertaining white guilt based virtue signaling I've ever heard. Naming your lily white children with black names, you were 'signaling' to all humanity, *Look at us, we're more enlightened than you are. We see past color and racial identities and we will prove it to you by naming our white Anglo-Saxon, Irish children, not Connor and Emily,*" then he starts to laugh again, "*But… but… Malik and, oh my God, Shanice!* Ah HA HEEE, you're killing me!"

"Okay, hilarious. Knock it off."

"I hope you're saving now for the therapy your children will need in their mid-30s. This is better than Johnny Cash's song, *A Boy Named Sue.*"

"I don't know that one."

"Oh, well, you should. Ha ha ha ha…"

He was right of course. Even before this revealing, embarrassing and even humiliating revelation I had begun to realize many righteous things, virtue signaling things, Kathy and I have done in the name of progress, enlightenment. "Can we please move on? What exactly do you mean by white guilt?"

He finished cleaning the lot, got his ten dollars, then we walked back toward his 'home.'

"Search your soul and be honest. If I were white, you would not have felt as much Commilt for me as you did/do."

"Okay, Another one? Really? How can I answer when I don't know what Commilt even means?"

"Figure it out. What do you think motivates you to hand out sandwiches?"

"I feel I, I want to help. Compassion, I feel compassion for those who have less than me."

"Okay. But how do you feel about yourself because you have more?"

"Um, nothing."

Then, bringing back the glory days of childhood again he quips, "Liar, liar, pants on fire."

"Okay, I feel bad, I feel a little guilty."

"There it is, again. That motivating, yet soul-destroying emotion. You feel guilty of what?"

"I don't know. But I figured it out. Compassion/guilt. Commilt! Guilt seems to wiggle its way into everything."

"Yeah. I think the road to a true, authentic life is forever moving toward the *pure* emotions that motivate, like love and compassion, guilt free!"

"Otherwise, it's not authentic is it?"

"Correct. And Commilt is the worst. It's an epidemic."

I feel like putting *him* under some pressure for once, "So, what is the actual definition of Commilt, anyway? So that we're on the same page."

"Oh, the actual definition is," He clears his throat, stalling, searching that bizarre, brilliant brain of his for a definition that doesn't exist. But sure enough, out it comes like some kind of soliloquy, "Commilt: noun, A selfish, guilt-driven emotion disguised as compassion whose actual purpose is to attempt atonement for transgressions *that never actually transpired* through false altruistic acts. i.e., The white man allowed ancient history to invoke Commilt which kept him in an unending state of self-loathing leading to stupid acts like joining Black Lives Matter, forcing friendships with people he has nothing in common with, supporting reparations and handing out *extra* sandwiches to homeless blacks."

If Commilt were a word, there'd be a picture of me next to the definition. Except, "You say transgressions that never transpired. Of course the transgressions transpired. Remember, a little thing called slavery?"

"No, I don't," he quipped as we arrived at his tent, "Slavery didn't exist." He stared me down for a moment, my emotions swirling into madness. Then he escaped into his hovel while executing a spot on Arnold Schwarzenegger impersonation, "Hasta la vista, baby."

Chapter 16 The Future: First Woman President
Year: 2028 December 4 7:12 p.m.

" …and that is why I, Alexandria Ocasio-Cortez, the first woman and first Latino President of these United States of America, am running for re-election. Despite what Fox News is telling you, the truth is: *we're almost there, we're almost there.*" The crowd becomes frenzied as they join in on her new campaign slogan, *We're almost there. We're almost there.* It fills the stadium to an ear piercing level. She raises her arms to quiet the crowd. "Yes, you could believe the nay sayers, the right wingers, the fearmongers, who tell you the ship is, like, sinking. Or, you can be a part of the radical revolution. I am a radical in the tradition of Abraham Lincoln. How else can you bring about radical change but to be a radical?"

☍ AOC's "I'm a radical" statement <u>trumped.online/961</u> ☍

The crowd erupts in agreement. Cameras scan the audience for close ups. Each one happens to be a minority. First two men, one black and one white who appear to be a gay couple. Then a woman with blue hair, a splattering of piercings and a T-shirt that reads, *Woke AF.* She's followed by several hispanics, blacks, a Native American and then a trans. They're all cheering hysterically.

The President basks in the enthusiasm as she continues, "Remember when Trump destroyed Obama Care?"

"Boo, boo… " arrises from the crowd.

"Obama Care was transforming healthcare in America. It just needed a little more time to reach everyone. The same is true of my Green New Deal. Change is hard. But we've got to stick together. We can. We will. We, together, are transforming America and the world. We just need a little more time. My friends, is the air we breathe a human right?"

"YES," the crowd screams.

"How about water? Are there drinking fountains in every city for all to drink?"

"YES," They screech louder.

"Then, it only stands to reason. Anyone with a heart can see, if, like, air is a human right and water is a human right, then, *food is a human right.*"

"YES," they cheer.

"No one has to pay for air."

"NO," rings out in the arena.

"Then, no one should have to pay for food. Or healthcare! Or an education! Or housing!" The cameras pan the audience again. It is nothing short of pandemonium. "These, my friends are inalienable rights. Dignity for all. And finally, everyone deserves a job. No exceptions. Given four more years, I promise we will make these things a reality." She pauses for dramatic effect; allows the stadium to quiet and says, "What, my friends, do we need?"

The crowd hollers back, "A LITTLE MORE TIME… "

President Ocasio-Cortes raises her voice to match the crowd, "AND WHY?"

With fists raised in the air they join together, "WE'RE ALMOST THERE, WE'RE ALMOST THERE, WE'RE ALMOST THERE… "

"You got the tickets?" I say to Alexus as she turns off the T.V. "Yep, right here," she relays holding them up. As we step into the driverless Uber, it announces, "Please buckle up and enjoy the ride to, Portland International Airport."

"Sheesh," Alexus sighs with a heavy heart, "There goes another one." She points to one of the more mansion like homes in our old, diverse neighborhood.

"Look there," I announce pointing at several homeless people camped on the thin rows of grass in between the cracked sidewalks and the potholed roads right in front of the homes. It's a very controversial new trend. "It's getting worse."

"Ocoasio-Cortez kept saying her Green New Deal would put an end to homelessness. But when the wealthy people up and leave," she points to the mansion, "More and more of the middle class lose the jobs they had working for them and end up in foreclosure or worse, living on the skinny strips of grass all over our neighborhoods."

"How are we going to retire?" I ask rhetorically. "That was the plan. Remember when people were flocking to Portland back between 2015 and 2020? Now, our home's worth 20% less than what we paid."

She considers this sad state for a moment before responding, "We can only hope for change." She leaves much unsaid as we drive through downtown Portland. More buildings are empty. Broken windows covered with, *Space For Lease,* signs.

In the attempt to create equal outcome for all over the last four years, I'm afraid it's working. But like all socialist countries, equal outcome has never been, *we all rise together*. It's always become, *we all equalize together at the lowest possible denominator.*

We arrive at the mandated time, *five hours* before our flight. Since the government has taken over all aspects of flight, if you don't check in five hours early you may get bumped.

"Remember the days of TSA pre-check?" I reminisce longingly.

"Those were the days," Alexus recalls. "What did they call it when the program ended?"

"Preferential treatment. They said some people having a shorter line made others feel 'less than'. It was said to be racist, sexist and homophobic."

"So now we all wait in lines longer than the Great Wall of China and slower than the DMV. But hay, it's 'equal!'"

Once we finally sloth through the roped, zig zag line like a good and obedient heard of 'sheeple', we drag our weary, broken selves to gate 57 and wait another hour and forty. Everyone looks like members of the zombie apocalypse. Those lucky enough to get a seat are slouched, eyes glued to smart phones. Some sleep with their head dangling, already working on that kink in the neck that comes with over seas passage. The rest of us stand, shoulder to shoulder, not unlike a heard of cows in a coral awaiting slaughter.

"Now boarding first class, flight number 278 to Munich, Germany," transmits to the lifeless clods we have become.

"Oh boy, here we go," Alexus leans in to whisper as a small group of weary travelers among us hesitantly rise and begin plodding forward, cautiously pushing through the throng. 'First Class' is suspect now. Anyone who can afford to fly in such opulence are often thought to be the cause of the rift in the new progressive agenda. They are not equal. They have more. If their wealth could just be redistributed equally among the population the new system might work. They are seen as the reason the president's new slogan is, *We're Almost There,* instead of, *We're Here.*

If looks could kill, there would be no First Classer's left by the time the agent scans their smart phone. In fact, the agent gives them the final stink eye. A random zombie from the masses calls out, *"Greedy fascist assholes."* Then the chant begins,*"You are the problem, you are the problem ... "*

The new government agency, UFS (United Flight Services) is under pressure to eliminate first-class entirely since it is "preferential treatment." Their official response is they need more time to retrofit the first class section with the miniature seats the rest of us endure. Some say the truth is the UFS needs First Class money in order to make flight affordable for the rest of us. The paradox is, because of the hate the First Classer's receive, gradually less of them fly first class so soon, those who jeer at the First Classer's may force all of us to pay higher fairs for our scraps. The UFS may go completely defunct. Or, the federal government will, again, raise taxes. This time, to subsidize flight.

A total of seven hours and thirteen minutes has passed since we arrived at the airport and we have just reached our assigned seats. It's quite the ritual squeezing in. The average 18 inch wide seats have been replaced with 15 inchers. To make things that much more insufferable the leg room has shrunk from 31 inches to 26. Riots have broken out by the PST's (Plus-Size- Travelers) saying the seats are a clear cut case of size-ism. As a result, every traveler more than fifteen pounds over the average for their height, has been rewarded, by the government, $187,000 in travel vouchers and two seats whenever they travel. In a knee jerk response, many travelers are purposefully packing on the pounds. The 'bigger' problem is all they require is a note from your doctor. Doctors can no longer be found guilty of malpractice since they would lose their job, and jobs are now considered a "human right." If the trend continues it is estimated that in less than three years flights will be completely full of "PST's" using two seats creating an airplane shortage crisis since we will need twice the number of planes for the same number of people!

"Can you help me with this?" Alexus requests as she tries to cram her carry-on into the new glove compartment size space. All that fits is an average size purse. Although we are not suppose to refer to them as a "purse" anymore. It's seen as a micro-aggression because they say the word purse conjures images of women which I guess is sexist. We're suppose to use labels like "European Leather Carry All" and "Small Case With Strap" or may favorite, "Accessory Duffel For All Genders."

    South Park micro aggressions trumped.online/5169b

Once I finish helping cram Alexus' Small Case With Strap into the upper carriage I notice a gal next to us having the same issue. "Excuse me, need some help?"

"No," she responds appearing to be offended by my offer, "I'm quite capable."

"I never thought you were incapable, I just thought… Sorry Ma'am. My bad."

Alexus' eyes bug out, shaking her head slowly like I was in trouble, like I'd just committed a crime, when I'm reminded that, in fact, I have!

"Is there a Marshal on this flight?," the stranger calls out.

A flight attendant rushes forth, "How can I help you?"

"This person just called me Ma'am. I am a zie zim Zir Zis"

That's when I remember. The Ocasio-Cortez administration has adapted Canadas C-16 bill which has made it illegal to use an unpreffered "pronoun" of any given person. There are now approximately forty five different "pronouns" which actually are, for the most part, made up out of thin air. Words like xe, exem exyr, exemself, eirs, and Zis.

    politically correct gender pronouns! trumped.online/z9o

The attendant asks me, "What is your preferred pronoun?," a practice that is becoming mainstream before anyone speaks for fear of breaking the law or offending someone.

"You can just call me he, sir, or mister. I'm old fashioned that way."

"Okay, sir. Did you mis-gender this Zir?"

"I, I guess I did. I'm sorry."

"He's sorry," the attendant says to the Zir, "Maybe you don't need to press charges."

Zir's complexion got even redder, "But he insinuated that I'm incapable."

Now the flight attendant looked upset, "Is this true. Did you in any way insinuate that Zir is incapable as a Zir?"

"No, I did not. I swear," I state, realizing I'm in a pickle.

"Then why did you ask me, of all people, if I needed help putting my Accessory Duffel For All Genders away?"

"I guess, I, I was raised that way. To be a, um, gentleman."

"You mean to be a condescending white male!" Zir states. Then Zir turns and announces to the entire flight manifest, "This is the problem people, *right here*. This generation just needs to die off; raised to see other genders as inferior."

The attendant, now clearly on Zir's side, "Zir has a point." She looks at Zir, "Do you want to press charges?"

"Of course. I and all Zir's have been insulted. It's got to stop. We are all equal. Gender is a social construct!"

🔗 Is Gender a social construct? <u>trumped.online/b12</u> 🔗

"Marshall," the attendant calls out. A tall black man in first class stands up, "Please put this man under arrest."

"What? You can't be seri… "

"The law is the law," the attendant says as the Marshall comes forward. He grabs me by the arm.

"Come with me sir." The aisle parts like the red sea as I'm lead off the plane.

Alexus yells as I begin my exit, *"Baby, what should I do?"*

And, like the lead in an old RomCom before political correctness ruined humor, I yell back, *"Go on without me. I'll be alright… "*

As soon as we step off the plane, he releases my arm, "So, what happened?" He asks with a sympathetic smile.

"Well, I just asked if she, I mean, Zir, wanted help storing her, I mean, Zir's? purse. I mean Accessory Duffel For All Genders. And then she, I mean Zir said I was being condescending."

"Oh," he shakes his head, "Being chivalrous. How dare you. Don't you know that's a crime these days?"

"I didn't get the memo."

He chuckles, "Well, I have to give you this citation. I'm very sorry. You will have to respond within thirty days and set up a court date." I take the yellow slip of paper. "In the meantime, I'm going to get you on the first flight out to Munich."

"Thanks, any help is much appreciated."

"Well then, little word of advice?"

"Sure."

"On your next flight, do not, in any way, show signs of kindness, compassion, helpfulness, courtesy, politeness, or valor. In short, avoid all actions that might, in any way, be interpreted as chivalry."

"Ten four!"

The next flight departs at 5:30 in the morning. I leave a message for Alexus, who is somewhere three thousand feet up, telling her I will be in about five hours after her and all is well. As fate would have it, I'm sandwiched between two plus-sized travelers. The good news is, between them I was perfectly propped so as to catch the occasional wink. Never mind the bit of slobber after I dozed.

As I emerge from German customs, there is Alexus. She's holding back the tears as she runs toward me, jumps in my arms and wraps her legs around me. We call it the pretzel hug, "Baby, oh my gosh, I'm so glad to see you!"

"You too, my beautiful lady, it was a lonely, long flight without you."

"Lady?" She says as serious as an earthquake, "Who you callin' lady? I had a long flight to contemplate this. I now identify as, Zir."

I crack a smile, "Yes Zir. Can I carry your luggage Zir?"

"Ooh, nice one," she says as we make our way to the car rental.

Call it old fashioned. Call it chivalrous. But I do the majority of the driving and often open the door for Alexus. Maybe someday door holding and majority driving will be illegal but Alexus appreciates it. Go figure.

After about twenty minutes, we're weaving through Munich neighborhoods. It's 10:47 p.m. We come to a stop sign. I hang a left dutifully following the GPS.

"No, don't go left," Alexus demands.

"Why, that's what the GPS says?"

"I know, but the directions from the hotel say to go straight. In fact they literally say not to follow GPS after this point, at all."

"That makes no senes. And besides, it's too late. What's the worst that could happen?"

We go for another ten minutes twisting and turning through the old cobblestone Munich roads when we come to a stop sign. The GPS says to go straight but It's not an option. Suddenly a man in his thirties with a large, round beard and wearing a skullcap raps on our window so hard Alexus surges back, startled. *"Hey,"* the man says intensely with an accent I don't recognize, "Are you lost?" Alexus gives me a quick look that I can't decipher and then she turns to the man through her window and speaks with a thick German accent which is strange. Her English is perfect.

"I am, ah, sorry," she says, sounding like she has never been to America. "We, we, following GPS… "

"No GPS through here," he responds as several other men join him, all wearing what appear to be robes or even dresses. I consider, for a fleeting moment, referring to them as Zir. I lean across Alexus' lap to speak to them. Again, she gives me that look, but I trudge forward.

"Excuse me," I say to the five men gathered, "We were just looking for our hotel. Do you know where… "

"Are you American?" One asks, pushing to the front.

Alexus whispers, "Let's get out of here."

"What's going on?"

"Just go." She says dropping the whisper.

I quickly shift into reverse, confused. Once we're miles away, I slow down, "What was that? What just happened?"

"Oh my naïve American husband. I have told you about this phenomenon a few times. Even as far back as our first date at the Rose Garden, remember?"

"Wait, that was a No-Go zone?"

"Yep."

"Official German police are told not to go there? It's run by sharia law?"

"Yep."

"So, it's not *really* Germany, inside of Germany!"

"That about sums it up. Honestly I don't know how dangerous they are or if all that I've heard is true but let's stay on the safe side."

Germany No-Go zones! trumped.online/b4u

We end up following the directions given to us from the hotel. They take us on a round about route. The next few days Alexus takes me on a tour of some of the historical sites in her home country. This morning, however, I wake up around 4:45 a.m. to watch some of the Presidential debate. I catch the president mid sentence.

"… the world is going to end in like twelve years if we don't address climate change and your biggest issue is, *how are you going to pay for it?"*

AOC actual interview trumped.online/pnb

Candace Owens shows a slight smile accompanied by a perceptible shake of the head, "Well, you clearly have no idea how to pay for it. I have a suggestion. Since you're so concerned about climate change and you believe it is anthropogenic, human caused, then the first thing we must implement is a full stop on all immigration from third world countries. When a person migrates from a third world their carbon footprint goes up one hundred times. If the stakes are as high as you say they are, *we would be saving the lives of all would be immigrants by denying their citizenship.* As a natural consequence then we would save the money needed for your Green New Deal because we would no longer be paying for the millions of people who come here illegally who receive free healthcare, free housing, free education, free food, and free money if they don't feel like working. That's how we could pay for it."

"Well, that is just inhumane. You're, like, showing your soul for all the people to see. You don't care about anyone unless they are American. What about the rest of the world?"

"Mrs. President, you have said that America is a racist, sexist, patriarchal, homophobic society. Yes?"

"America is a melting pot. We are all immigrants."

"You're not answering the question. You have said these things about America many times. My question to you now is, why would you want to encourage anyone from any other country to come here if it is so evil?"

"We need all the people from all over the world to come here and fix it. And, if given the next four years to fully integrate the Green New Deal, I promise that all marginalized people, be they gay, trans, bi, black, brown, Muslim, queer, lesbian, or any other marginalized peoples that we may not recognize yet, will be treated with the dignity they deserve for we are all human beings."

The audience erupts approvingly. The mediator, Don Lemon, intercedes. "Okay, let's calm down everyone. Mrs. Owens, your response."

"I too want all people to have equal opportunity. I still have not heard how you're going to continue to pay for this Green Dream of yours given that it is already bankrupting America."

"Everyone understands, we must all pitch in. This is our WWII. We must sacrifice."

"You mean, you're going to raise taxes. Again."

"No. That term was the fear mongering, propaganda you and the old regime used. As you very well know, it is now called the C.C.G. It's each persons duty and honor to participate in the - *Contribution to the Collective Good.*"

"How Orwellian of you."

The President doesn't seem to understand the reference so she trudges forward, "However, we have a plan that will make the next four years the single most prosperous in the history of our country and make the full transition into the Green New Deal much smoother during my second term." The President smiles and raises her voice triumphantly, "Not only does everyone deserve the dignity of free health care, free housing, free higher education, free food and a guaranteed job if they want to work, but they deserve a living wage. And so, in my next term I will be raising the minimum wage once again from eighteen dollars an hour to…, " she pauses for dramatic effect and then belts out, *"TWENTY FIVE DOLLARS AN HOUR!"*

🔗 CNN interviews AOC trumped.online/9t1 🔗

It was as if the super bowl just ended with a last second touch down for the win; people screaming with delight. Don Lemon intercedes, "Okay.

Okay. Take a breathe everyone. Quiet down. Yes, it is exciting. But we need to reel in our enthusiasm. Mrs. Owens?"

"That's your answer?" Candace Owens questions, "Your going to raise the minimum wage so people can afford higher taxe… I mean, higher, *Contributions to the Collective Good?* Ah, were you really an economics major? Do you know how many businesses will go bankrupt?"

The President responds with a prepared reply, "Because some businesses won't be able to afford it we will subsidize the minimum wage when necessary. What you don't understand Mrs. Owens is, the Collective Good."

"Plus," Mrs Owens adds, "You can always just print more money."

"Yes, if necessary."

Socialists print money trumped.online/tdp

Mrs. Owens is taken aback. The printing money comment was a joke! "In high school I wrote a paper on a place that no longer exists. It fell in on itself. It was a sad, dark place where everyone lived as if it were the 1930's. The people rarely smiled, but when they did, it was telling. Rotten teeth, failing gums in people as young as 30 from a lack of toothpaste and tooth brushes. They had posters in the streets that read, *Come to the collective farm, comrades.* This place was called the Soviet Union. Maybe you have never heard of it. You are young. If you understood what this place was, you would not be pushing propaganda like, *the collective.* Such utopian fantasies have always lead, eventually, to rotten teeth. What you fail to understand is where dignity comes from. *It cannot be given.* Dignity, by it's very nature, is earned. Pride is earned. Meaning and purpose must be discovered, not given. This is where socialism falls on its face. Even if socialism worked economically, it cannot, by it's very premise, create fertile ground for what matters most: human dignity."

There is respectable applause before President Ocasio-Cortez interrupts, "You are wrong. When re-elected, I promise dignity for all. It is wrong that we live in a country where certain skill sets are rewarded over others. All people are equal. No matter your background, race, sexuality, skin color, or gender." Cheers ring out as is always the case when a list of immutable characteristics is spouted. "It is wrong that, like, a surgeon, makes more than, like, a nurse. The nurse is a human being with just as much value. It is wrong that an engineer makes more than what I made before I became a senator. Bartenders are human beings too. It is, like, a human right to live in dignity. When re-elected, not only will we, together, collectively eliminate the pay gap between men and women," a swell of applause begins to rise as the President raises her voice, *"We will begin to adjust the pay gap between everyone because all people are of equal value."*

The audience explodes with division. The expanse between those who lean democrat compared to those who are more conservative has never been wider because democrat, now, is synonymous with socialism. She continues, "And finally, it is immoral to live in a country where billionaires exist."

A chant ensues like an explosion, "TAX THE RICH. TAX THE RICH. TAX THE RICH… "

Lemon lets this chant go on for a good minute before moderating, "Okay everyone, I know it's all very exciting but let's curb the enthusiasm so we can get through this debate. Mrs. Owens?"

"You do know, every country on the planet allows billionaires so you're saying that the world is immoral, not just America."

The president gathers her thoughts for a moment, "America has, like, the most billionaires which makes us the most immoral."

The chant begins again, "TAX THE RICH. TAX THE RICH. TAX THE RICH… "

"So let me understand your position," Owens turns from her podium to look directly at the president. "You say it is immoral to be a billionaire, yes?"

"Yes, it is."

"And how is it that you plan to pay for your socialist ideals?"

"Billionaire's need to pay their fair share."

"So, it's immoral to be a billionaire and yet it is the very rich that you are forcing to pay for your socialism. Hmmm, I'm really trying to follow the logic. By your own admission, without these billionaire's there would be no one to pay for your socialism. So, how can you call them immoral

when they are paying for what you deem to be the moral high ground?
And, just what do you think's going to happen when the money runs
out?"

"When the money runs out, everyone will be equal. We will have the
utopia that you say is impossible."

"But when there's no more rich people to pay for it, like the trillions of
dollars just for your healthcare plan, who's going to pay?"

"It will all be payed for by then, so, like, no one will need to pay for it."

"What?" Candace Owens tries to quell her laughter. "Did you know that
if you slap a 100% tax rate on the top 1%, take *all of their money,* it
would fund your medicare for three years. That's it. Three years! That
ride would be over and you would have no one left to flip the bill. And
isn't it weird socialism requires the wealthy in order for it to exist?
Capitalism does not. And where did all the wealth come from that you
now want to take to fund your moral utopia? *CAPITALISM!"*

Candace's supporters applaud. Don Lemon cuts them off quickly,
"Alright. Quiet down. Be respectful to the president. Miss President,
your response."

"We can also divert billions and billions from our bloated defense fund."

"Yes, I agree. We could. It would still be a tiny fraction of the funds
needed, especially over the long hall, to keep socialism afloat. It is now
estimated, as you know, that it would take more than the entire GDP *of
planet earth* to continue funding your Green Dream."

"It doesn't matter what it costs! The world is going to end if we don't
back my plan. And, as you know,*I'm the boss!"* The people start
chanting, *YOU'RE THE BOSS, YOU'RE THE BOSS,* in reference to an
interview she did back in 2019.

Ⓢ Ocasio-Cortez "Im the boss" <u>trumped.online/xuv</u> Ⓢ

The president continues, "And, no matter what you say, the presence of
billionaires is immoral." Again, *TAX THE RICH, TAX THE RICH...*
rises up.

Miss Owens interrupts the crowd, "My friends, let's consider a hypothetical. If there were one thousand of us in this room and we each had $1000.00, we would all be equal. At least in the way the president refers to equality. But, we're not happy. In fact, let's say we are always irritable and grumpy. Then, this woman in the front row here," she points to a young, black woman with long, beautiful braids and bright colored African clothing, "Let's say she has a brilliant insight. The reason we're all so irritable and unhappy is, *the chairs*. They're poorly designed. So, she takes her money and risks it all on an idea. She could lose everything if she fails but she's inspired. She wants to help the community and is encouraged by the possibility she could make money to fuel more of her brilliant ideas. After much trial and error, she comes up with a very unique seat cushion design that makes our seats extraordinarily comfortable. She sells the cushion for $100 each and each of us buy one. Everyone is happier, more productive and live longer, healthier lives. And the beauty is, the transaction was voluntary. No one *had* to buy the cushion. We all agreed it was worth the exchange. Now, our hero, the gal in the front row here, is rich. Her net worth is more than one hundred times that of everyone else in our community. Has something immoral occurred?"

President Ocasio-Cortez seems stuck in a trap of her own making. She looks at the woman in the front row and smiles. You get the feeling that if Mrs. Owens had singled out a white male to make her point it would be easier to respond. But now she is struggling to support her own socialistic philosophy since it is a black woman who benefitted from this purely capitalistic example. Her back against the wall, she answers hesitantly, "It has set up an unequal dynamic."

There is an uncomfortable silence for a moment. Then the woman in the front row belts out, "Don't you take my money. I *earned* my money." The place erupts with laughter.

Mrs. Owens jumps in, answering the woman in the front row, "I agree. You did earn your money. Each person engaged in a consensual exchange, money for your goods." Owens looks up at the audience, "The community chose to make her exceptionally wealthy because she took a risk and filled a need. But now, let's say everyone in this room decides that even though the seat cushion was well worth the $100.00, we want to take 50% of our money back."

The woman in the front row yells out, *"Over my dead body!"* A bi-partisan expulsion of laughter fills the room.

"But Miss., that's what most taxes…, or *Contributions to the Collective Good,* are," Candace Owens interjects, "Jealous people, whose lives have been made better by you, demanding you now give back the money they chose to exchange with you so that you are forced to pay for more of *their* stuff."

The woman in the front row shakes her head, "Uh uh. *They can pay for their own stuff,"* laughter ensues.

Mrs. Owens grins, "So, President Ocasio-Cortez, has something immoral occurred?"

"Given time to fully implement the Green New Deal, there will be a fair redistribution of wealth so that everyone is equal, that is what's moral and right."

"You haven't answered my question. I'll ask you another one. Miss President, what is theft?"

The president shakes her head, answers a question with a question, "Miss Owens, what is fair?"

"Fair is something very difficult to guarantee. What we can do is create a world in which we strive for justice and from that justice the closest thing to fairness will arise. But I believe it's my moment to ask the questions. What is theft?"

"Under the Green New Deal, theft will become a thing of the past since all will be equal, there will be no jealousy or desire."

"Actually, socialism is a system run on and motivated by jealousy. But since you will not answer me; theft is the act of taking something from someone that is not yours. Would you agree?"

The president hesitates, "Of course."

"Is it ever moral to steal, to take from someone what is not yours?"

Like a locomotive the president launches into, what is now, a familiar response, "Once the Green New Deal is fully implemented, all beings will be equal no matter their race, religion, color, sexual orientation, gender, identification, or any other marginalized group we have not yet identified. What you don't seem to understand Mrs. Owens, is simple, *we are all human beings.*" The predictable applause results.

"Again, you're not answering my question. Is it ever moral to take what is not yours?" Silence. Mrs Owens continues. "Well, we as a society, have weighed in. We have laws against theft. The immorality of theft is so self evident there are laws as old as ancient history, *Thall shalt not steal.* The second Buddhist precept is, *Do not steal.* And in the Quran it says, *Cut off the hand of anyone who steals.* Socialism itself is immoral. It runs on justifying jealousy rather than inspiring each individual to reach their human potential. It makes theft legal as long as it is taken from those who have given the most to society, like the gal in the front row. Socialism removes rewards for hard work, removes incentives that advance our culture for the betterment of all humanity."

"No," Ocasio-Cortez responds, "Capitalism is based on the lowest of human desires: greed."

"Actually, socialism is greed stoked by jealousy, *I deserve what you have. Give it to me or go to jail.* Capitalism, on the other hand, is *forced altruism.* To succeed you must come up with something that benefits the greater good, like a better seat cushion. There is no other way to make money in a capitalistic society. No system is perfect. I do not support some of the loop holes taken by big corporations and I will address this when president, but the difference between a conservative and a socialist is the conservative is inevitably the adult in the room." There is a smattering of cheers and boos. "The conservative knows there is no utopia. What we must do is work to create a system that fosters the best in our nature and keeps, in check, the worst. What you did to Queens back in 2019 was childish. Amazon *is* imperfect. But it would have greatly benefited your state. Compromise is what an adult grapples with. But because you live from a righteous, utopian, childish world view, you could not see the greater good that would have benefited your own people."

⚬⚬ Ocasio-Cortez's Amazon deal <u>trumped.online/tkd</u> ⚬⚬

"What I did in 2019 was keep, like, an evil empire from taking, like, three billion dollars in subsidies that could otherwise have been invested into our community like teachers, the subway system, and parks."

"Did that three billion dollars ever go to teachers, the subway and parks or anything for the community?"

211

"When the Green New Deal is fully integrated, monies will be allocated to these and many more government programs and policies that will create equality for all." The President looks out to her base, *"What do we need?"*

They holler back, *"A little more time!"*

"Why?" She asks, hands in air.

"WE'RE ALMOST THERE, WE'RE ALMOST THERE, WE'RE ALMOST THERE… " roars her base.

"Okay everyone," Don Lemon interrupts the chant, "We may be, *almost there,* but we've got to get through this debate."

"So, no." Mrs. Owens jumps in, "Not a penny you argued would be invested into the community actually was. There is plain and simple math to what you did and what you are doing. It was three billion in subsidies for *twenty seven billion* in benefits and that's just over a twenty five year period. Amazon was brining 25,000 jobs at an average salary of $150,000 a year! Another 67,000 additional jobs for local people in Queens would have been created; laundry mats, restaurants, coffee shops, clothing stores, barbers, doctors, dental services, optometrists, physical therapists. There's no end to it. That doesn't even… "

The President interrupts, "There's no end to the corruption. Jeff Bazos is the richest person in the world."

"But where is the corruption?" Mrs. Owens shakes her head and shrugs her shoulders. "He did exactly what our entrepreneur in the front row did. He made lives better. He filled a need. I'm not a huge fan of Bazos but you and I decide his fate. You don't like it, stop using Amazon. There are other choices and that's the beauty of a free market, capitalistic society. Miss President, have you ever used Amazon?"

The Presidents eyes dart left to right quickly, "There *are* other choices but the beauty of a socialistic society is you will not have to spend so much time worrying about where to get the best deals because the government eventually makes those decisions for you."

"You didn't answer my question. I'll take that as a yes, you *do* use amazon. Okay, you're against big corporations having too much power, as am I, but when it is the government, the bigger the better? Amazon, since 2018, has been paying all of their approximately 700,000 employees above minimum wage. You say being a billionaire is immoral but more people become wealthy on the backs of billionaires' hard work than any other kind of wealth. How many wealthy people exist because Phil Night created Nike? How many people's lives are better because of Phil Night? How about Bill Gates and Paul Allen? Robert Smith and Warren Buffet? Oprah Winfrey! Because they exist the world is demonstrably a better place for all. Not just because of the jobs and wealth they created but because of the philanthropy that wouldn't exist without them. One hundred and eighty three of the top wealthiest people in the world, most Americans, have signed the Giving Pledge created by Gates and Buffet which is a promise to give away at least half of their wealth to charity. More billionaires join every year. Gates has eradicated polio from the face of the earth. His foundation vaccinated 2.5 billion children in 122 countries world wide. The number of innocent lives saved is immeasurable. Now, if you took all of Gates' wealth and redistributed it equally, that would be about eleven dollars per person. What do you think is the better good? The eradication of polio or eleven dollars per person?"

Uncomfortable silence ensues. Then, Don Lemon interjects, "Okay, all good things must come to an end and so it's time for your closing remarks. Miss President, please."

"We have a choice, don't we," Ocasio-Cortez begins, "Between love and compassion; hatred and fear. Between the survival of our species and the end of the world. Between like, equality and inequality. Frankly, between right and wrong. Do you want a raise in the standard of living? Do you want free housing, healthcare, food, education, a guaranteed job and, if unable or unwilling to work, a pay check regardless? Do you want the minimum wage to be twenty five dollars an hour? *Do you want dignity for all?* If so, what do we need?

"A LITTLE MORE TIME," her base extols.

"Why do we need it?"

"WE'RE ALMOST THERE, WE'RE ALMOST THERE, WE'RE ALMOST THERE..."

"Okay, Okay. Yes, we're almost there," Lemon inserts, "Mrs. Owens, your final remarks."

"This movement to socialism is so perplexing. Ask yourself, why is America the most powerful, most successful, most popular country in the world? Why do so many people want to come here? How did the American dream become, not just the American dream, but the dream of humanity? I know one thing that is *not* coming to your mind: *Socialism.* Socialism is the antithesis of that which has made America the envy of the world. Yes, my friends, it is capitalism! Forced altruism. The free enterprise that has created the greatest place on earth. It is America's capitalism that has raised the standard of living for the whole world. No one, anywhere on the planet is clamoring to get into a socialist country. And right now the world is confused. Under our current president we have become like the worlds rich, bleeding hearted uncle that everyone loves; *until the money runs out.* Then, no one cares. And that is the road we are headed down now. We must continue to serve the world by putting America first. It is complicated truths like this that adults understand. It's time for all of us to be the adult in the room, think long term so that all of us may know - true human dignity."

⊂⊃ Capitalism and Socialism by Tim Pool <u>trumped.online/hz5</u> ⊂⊃

*****

I'm still thinking about the debate as we enter the 900-acre 'English Garten', one of the largest urban public parks in the world. Tonight U2 is performing in a rock festival featuring many of the most famous pop/rock bands of Europe. As Bono enters the stage the people go wild. We're somewhere in the middle of about fifty thousand fans. A few seconds into *Sunday Bloody Sunday,* I lose track of Alexus. A wall of guys ran into us and then, she was gone. I call her cell - no answer. Trying not to panic, I scan 360 degrees. She can't be far. Suddenly something captures my eye. A group of men in, what appears to be, a circle. It's strange. A wall of them about fifty feet away. I make my way to see what's going on. When I reach the circle, I try to push in but they won't let me. They shove me so hard, if it wasn't for the crowd, I would've hit the ground. I scream over the blasting music, *ALEXUS!* I may hear a cry in response but it's impossible to be sure as thousands belt out the chorus, *Sunday Bloody Sunday.* I try to push through again but I'm shoved so hard this time I hit the ground despite the packed crowd. On my hands and knees I can see through their legs. Some one is on the ground in the middle. *It's Alexus!* There's a man on top of her.

I have heard of people gaining extraordinary strength in threatening moments. Lifting heavy things or picking someone up and carrying them for miles. I never believed until now. Suddenly, I feel a surge of energy pulse through my body. Heart pounding, I can hear blood moving through my ears. My sense of smell is primal. We have all seen the transition from scientist Steve Banner to The Hulk. I smash my way through the wall of men and kick the guy in the stomach who was forcing himself on Alexus. I notice a huge scar on his shoulder and down his arm as he flops over onto his back clutching his stomach. He has a large beard and is in his mid thirties. I pull Alexus to her feet and barrel through the men into the masses as the crowd cheers for the final notes of, *Sunday Bloody Sunday.* We make our way out of the park. As we reach the safe haven of our car, doors locked, Alexus screams as tears pour down her face. All I can do is hold her. The next day we go to the police.

"How can we help you?" The female officer asks.

"We're here to report an attempted rape," I say. "Yesterday at the festival in the park a group of about thirty to forty men surrounded my wife and attempted… " I can't finish the sentence as I squeeze Alexus' hand.

"I'm so sorry to hear this. And I hate to admit it but, it's happened before."

"They were not German. I would say they were middle eastern."

The officer shakes her head, "I know."

"How do you know?"

"Like I said, it's happened before; here and in many places in Europe. In fact, in Sweden they have banned men from music festivals."

Swedish men banned from festivals trumped.online/dr1

Alexus' is taken aback, "What? All men?"

"Yes. All men."

"What's happening to European men?"

The officer slowly looks around. There are other police and government workers keeping themselves busy. She moves closer and whispers, "It's not European men. It's the African and Middle Eastern migrants. I am in no way saying they are all this way. I'm sure most are good. But way too many men from those cultures see 'foreign' women simply as objects for their pleasure."

"Well, you have to find them," I say with urgency, "They were middle eastern. The guy I kicked was in his thirties, he had a beard and a huge scar on his shoulder and down his arm. I know I could recognize him."

The officer shakes her head again as she makes notes, "He had a beard, was in his thirties and had a scar on his shoulder and down his arm."

"And he was a middle eastern migrant, I'm sure of it." I wait for her to write it down, her hand pauses over the incident form.

"I'm sorry, but we are forbidden to report the ethnicity or background of criminals."

I lift my hands and shrug my shoulders, "What the F#%K? Are you kidding me?"

"Shhh. I can get in trouble for telling you."

"Then how are you going to find him for God's sake?"

"We will do our best," she responds, defeated.

Alexus is shaky, upset. She looks at the officer, "This is *messed up*. What kind of insane policies are these?"

The officer takes a deep breath, "Politically correct ones. I'm very sorry. There is push back though. You might want to go see Brigitte Gabriel, Aayan Hirsi Ali and Muhammad Alvi lecturer tonight at Residenz."

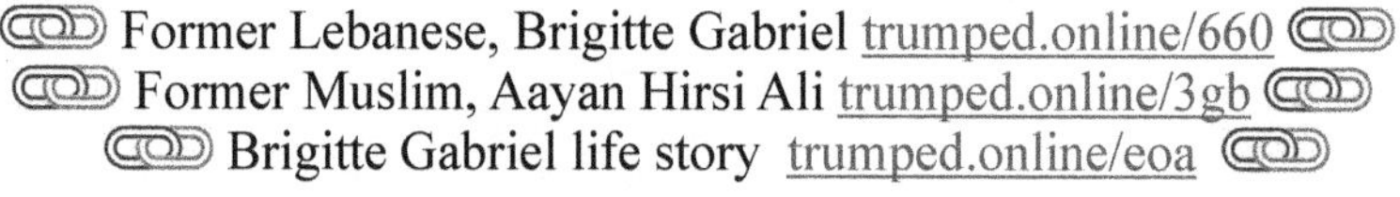

Former Lebanese, Brigitte Gabriel trumped.online/660
Former Muslim, Aayan Hirsi Ali trumped.online/3gb
Brigitte Gabriel life story trumped.online/eoa

I learned some of the politically incorrect truths about Islam from the Orange-tent-guy back in 2017, but what we hear tonight is shocking from the three presenters. Brigitte Gabriel closes the presentation.

"By the time the Islamic caliphate ended, *270,000,000* people were killed around the world by Islam in their constant effort to conquer. There were no weapons of mass destruction. All of these people were butchered by the sword. How many of you knew this?" I notice only one man raise his hand. He seemed to have a smirk on his face. "Our educational system has failed us and our children. When the caliphate ended in 1924, people said there is no way it will be resurrected. They were wrong. The discovery of oil in Saudi Arabia and the rise of Ayatollah Khomeine in 1979 gave them the money and the political presence to rise again. This is why neither me or you can set foot in Mecca because as far as they are concerned we are filth. We are infidels. Isis was not a new invention, it is simply a resurrection of the Islamic caliphate that ended less than 100 years ago. But we are too ignorant and uninformed to understand what is happening! One more question. How many of you knew that every year thousands of women in Muslim countries are forced to undergo Female Genital Mutilation?" Only the one man raises his hand again. "The girls clitoris is cut off making it impossible for them to enjoy sex so that the husband can control her. This practice is now spreading around the world, right here to Germany. Let the ignorance end today! Thank you."

I look around the room. There is enthusiastic applause by all, accept the guy who raised his hand. Once the applause dies down, people begin chatting amongst themselves. We make our way to the front of the large lecture hall to thank the presenters. I can't resist asking a few questions.

"Mr. Alvi, I have heard many times that Islam is a religion of peace. I'm in a state of cognitive dissonance after hearing these lectures and my recent experiences. I've been told the violent aspects of Islam are not based in the religion but the culture of certain countries that happen to be Muslim."

⊂⊃ Debate: Is Islam a Religion of Peace? trumped.online/vzr ⊂⊃

Mr. Alvi gives a patient smile, "Look at the example set by the founders of the world's great religions. Wouldn't you say the life they led, the example set, is a critical component as to how the followers of any religion live?"

"Of course, that makes sense. I mean, if you're practicing a religion, wouldn't you want to model your life after the founder of that religion?"

"Yes. In fact there are eighty nine verses in the Quran that say Mohammed was the perfect human and all should model their lives after him. So, let's take Jesus, Buddha, and Mohammed and quickly compare and contrast. Who did Jesus murder?"

"I don't think he killed anyone."

"Correct."

"Who did the Buddha murder?"

"I don't think anybody."

"Correct."

"How many slaves did Jesus and Buddha own?"

"None?"

"Correct."

"Who did Buddha and Jesus have sex with?"

"Well, traditionally Jesus did not have sex, at all. Some believe he eventually married Mary Magdalene. If so, then he would've had sex with her. So, either he had no sex at all, or he had sex with Mary Magdalene, his wife. Buddha was married before his enlightenment and had sex with his wife. After enlightenment, I don't believe he had sex. At least that is a common understanding."

"I'm impressed. You've done your homework here."

"Philosophy and religion interest me. I like to think of myself as a spiritual person."

"And yet, you know little about Islam. Why might that be?"

"I don't know… "

"Well, we're getting to that. Who did Mohammed murder?"

"I don't know."

"As Brigitte just made clear, Mohammed was a warlord. He murdered the 'infidels' which would be anyone who would not convert to Islam. He slaughtered people. In the name of Allah, he drove his sword through the heart of countless innocents. He annihilated the Byzantine Christians.

Many people think of the Crusades as an unprovoked, tyrannical war created by Christians. This is patently false. The Crusades were retaliation, self-defense; an effort to stop the Islamic expansion which was a massacre. Okay, how many slaves did Mohammed have?"

"Well, I'm just going to guess by the precedent set, he had slaves."

"Correct. Several. No one knows exactly how many. Now, who did Mohammed have sex with?"

"I have no idea."

"Well, he practiced polygamy. He had several wives. He also had at least one sex slave. One of his 'wives' was a child. He had sex with her by age 9. Now, if you're modeling your life after the leader of a religion, which example do you think leads to what you would consider enlightenment?"

"Well, I would say Buddha and Jesus gave us good examples to follow."

"I would agree, and that is why you know little about Islam. It's not talked about much. It's so blatantly anti-spiritual in many ways. Does that mean Islam is *not* a religion of peace?"

I wasn't sure if he was really asking me or if it was a rhetorical question. After what he just said, how could it be a religion of peace? Finally, I answer, "Of course not. It makes me sick to say that. I want to believe it is. I like to think that all religions are peaceful at their core. I like to think that all people are loving. That all cultures are equal and share in the ideas of fairness, equality and justice."

"Hmmm. Classic. You're anthropomorphizing. Huge mistake."

"I'm what?"

"Anthropomorphizing. To be more specific, you're anthropomorpling."

My eyebrows shot up uncontrollably, "What?"

"Anthropomorphizing is the act of assigning human attributes to non human things like pets or even machinery like ships or cars."

"I've heard of that. So what's anthropodumplings… ?"

"Anthropomorpling. It's not a real word but it's a real and dangerous psychological phenomenon. It's the act of assigning ones own personal and cultural norms to other peoples and their culture. A young American couple, Jay Austin and Lauren Hagen, were ultimately killed because of the practice of anthropomorpling. They decided to ride their bikes around the world, to meet new and wonderful people. They believed that everyone was like them and held their westernized values. They and two other European bikers were run off the rode in Tajikistan, near the border of Afghanistan, by a car and then cut to pieces with knives."

bikers knifed to death by Islamists trumped.online/qwt

I felt a little sick to my stomach. "I think I *am* guilty of anthropomorpling. And, If all of what you have said is true, Islam can't be a religion of peace."

He shrugs his shoulders, "Actually, it can."

"What?"

"There are just more hurdles to get over."

I'm lost, "What do you mean hurdles?"

"As you have said, every religion has committed atrocities. But Christianity, Judaism, and Buddhism have experienced a kind of enlightenment. They recognize things like slavery and murder in the name of God, which exist in their holy texts, as something of a lesser evolved time. Jews, Christians, Buddhists, Hindus and the like, shun those ideas today. These religions are now practicing a 2.0 upgrade. It's much more difficult for Islam to reform from these troubling practices because Mohammed is the role model. But it's still possible. Islam can be a religion of peace. There are just a lot more mental gymnastics, a lot more hurdles. If you practice Islam, you must come to terms with the huge, glaring flaws in your holy books and the founder of your religion. And those Muslims that are truly focused on and practicing only the aspects of peace within the Islamic religion must stop making excuses, defending what is un-defendable so that an Islam version 2.0 can occur. If you're willing to weed out and let go of what no longer fits in modern society, then certainly, Islam *can be* a religion of peace. But Isis, for example, simply followed the example set by their 'enlightened' founder. Terrorist groups who commit acts in the name of Allah are simply following their leader. Can you see how difficult a hurdle that is to jump?”

“Okay, yeah. I get the hurdles now.”

“Also, there is much manipulation within the Muslim religion. They justify it, of course, just like jihad. Often when a Muslim says Islam is a religion of peace, they mean something very different from what an innocent westerner would ever imagine. And they know it. Many Muslims believe we will never attain peace on earth until all the ‘infidels’ have converted to Islam. So what they mean is there is no peace, ever, until all have converted. Therefore, Islam is not only *a* religion of peace but the *only* religion of peace. And, the more evolved countries of the world are as much to blame for this as is the Islamic culture.”

Fear of Leaving Islam trumped.online/32y

I notice something strange that, not long ago, I would not have been aware of. *I like hearing that somehow we* are to blame. Not them. I continue noticing this bizarre intellectual and emotional reaction and begin to see how utterly self-loathing its foundations must be. And so I ask, “How are America and other more evolved nations to blame for the problems of Islam?”

“They must stop lowering the bar of expectations. If any other religion committed the number of atrocities that Islam consistently commits, the people of the world would be aghast, outraged.”

“Oh,” I softly respond. That’s not what I was hoping for when he said we are to blame. I was hoping for something more damning. Again, I notice how strange that is. He continues.

“If suddenly 20% of Jews supported suicide bombings, executions of gay people, and wouldn't allow women equal rights, the rest of the world would be in an uproar. This goes for any other religion. We have lowered the bar and made excuses for Islam because of people like you, bless your naïve and well-meaning heart. You want to believe everyone is the same. You'd rather be in denial than face the truth that there is something wrong going on in the Muslim world. Now, most Muslims are not committing such atrocities as terrorist acts and executions. However, a low estimate is that 20% fully support sharia law and the idea that Islam is the only true religion and therefore all *must convert*. There are approximately 1.7 billion Muslims. 20% of 1.7 billion people is *340 million.* That's a lot of people holding a lot of hatred in their hearts. And again, 20% is a low estimate."

"Phhhh," I sigh. I will do my research, *as we all should,* but who can argue with the experience of the three presenters.

⊂⊙⊃ Muslim Refugee issue <u>trumped.online/drz</u> ⊂⊙⊃

Mr. Alvi was not through with me. I think he enjoyed watching me squirm. "And then, when you consider the practice of inbreeding in the Islam culture, it just adds fuel to the fire."

"Okay, w*hat?*"

"You're not going to tell me you've never heard of this?"

"I've never heard of this."

"You need to get out more. Mohammed said it was okay to marry first cousins. So, today, for example, 70% of all Pakistanis are inbred. Even in Britain, Pakistani families are 13 times more likely to have children with recessive genetic disorders. The risk of having an IQ under 70 increases 400% in children from cousin marriages."

I'm finding this information hard to stomach, "I didn't think anything like this was going on *anywhere* in the world today."

"'Today,' is the distinction. Again, much Islam has not experienced a 2.0 upgrade. They practiced inbreeding hundreds of years ago in Europe, America and all over the world. But they recognized those practices as very troublesome. And so a revision occurred. But, such a reformation has not fully occurred in many Islamic countries. And there is a direct correlation between this issue and a reformation occurring."

I shake my head in near disbelief, "Of course, there would be."

⊂⊙⊃ Islam Inbreeding <u>trumped.online/ap8</u> ⊂⊙⊃

We thank the presenters and make our way up the stairs toward the exit. We have to excuse ourselves around many groups of people still discussing the lectures. I bump into a man, *Excuse me,* I say. I look in his face. It's the man who raised his hand and smirked. But he looks familiar to me beyond tonight. As we continue our way up the stairs I'm still trying to place him. Could it be? "Alexus, wait here," I say as we reach the lobby.

I make my way back down the stairs toward the man. I try to be as inconspicuous as possible as I pass him on his right-hand side and gaze at his arm, looking for a scar. There is none. I must be getting paranoid. I pause for a moment at the bottom of the stairs and then make my way back up. I'm forced by other people to go around him on his other side. Adrenaline rushes through my body as I see the scar. *It's on his left arm.* Somehow I got the arms mixed up, but I will never forget the scar. I quickly make my way back up the stairs.
"Alexus, do you have the card the police officer gave us with her personal number."

"Yes, I have it right here. What for?"

"Alexus, do not be afraid, take a deep breath. Are you with me?"

"Yes, I'm with you. Marcus, what is it?"

"He's here, the man who tried to rape you. I'm sure of it." I take the card and call the police officer. She tells us to sit tight and explains that the presenters, all three of them, are constantly in danger by Islamic radicals and that is probably why the men are there.

 Muslims Threaten the Muslim speakers, <u>trumped.online/lxm</u>

We wait at the door, hearts pounding. I'm beginning to break out into a sweat when the man with the scar walks right past us, out into the city. He disappears in a crowd. "What should I do? *What should I do?"*

"Nothing," Alexus says, "Wait for the police."

"But he could get away."

"Let it go."

I look at my wife. Shake my head, "I can't. I'm sorry."

I don't know who I think I am as I shove the door open and take off running intent on catching him. I have no plan. Just rage. Adrenaline fills my body like at the music festival. I'm scanning as I run in the general direction he was heading. Where? Where is he? As I pass a pub on my left side I'm hit with a feeling, an intuition, 'spidey sense.' I stop in my tracks, do a one eighty and backtrack, walking cautiously. I look through the window and there he is; drinking a tall glass of water at the far end of the bar. I call Alexus, "Baby, I found him. He's in a pub called Hofbrauhaus. Are the police there yet?"

"No."

"I'ill keep an eye on him. Just tell the cops to come here as soon as they arrive."

"Okay. Please, be careful."

I want to run in and punch his lights out. There is something primal about protecting the ones you love. Each second feels like an hour. Finally, I enter, make my way through the pub and sit around the corner of the bar, six feet across from him. "What can I get you?" The bar tender asks.

"Oh, nothing just yet. I'm, ah, waiting for a friend." Out of the corner of my eye, I can see he's looking at me between sips.

Through a thick accent he asks, slowly, "Do I know you?"

"I, I don't believe so."

Then his eyes dart to the front door. The police have arrived. He looks back at me and takes off, full speed toward the back of the pub. I instinctively run after him. He's knocking over tables, steins are crashing on the floor. I can hear the police behind me. He leads me through a back door out into the main street. At a full sprint, I'm only five feet away from his back. I leap and grab ahold of his shirt, pulling him down. I shove my knee on the back of his neck and apply full pressure. He's immobilized. *"A part me of wants to kill you for what you did to my wife."* I say as he struggles for air. *"You are sick."* The anger running through me is something I have never known before. I actually want to kill him. Suddenly, the image of a man, Antoine Leiris, the French father who lost his wife to radical Islamists in 2015, comes to mind. I remember crying when I read the letter he wrote to those who took his son's mother away. The forgiveness, self control and authentic power he exercised was and is transforming. In an instant, my heart is changed. I see someone else now. Someone who has been brainwashed by an interpretation of Islam that has twisted his soul. My anger dissipates, replaced with compassion.

Antoine Leiris letter to his wife's killers, trumped.online/u12

The police pull me off him and take over. The rest of our trip was tainted with a cloud of fear, confusion and concern. Not just for Germany, but for all of Europe. Each European country has its own unique and beautiful culture. And yet, in the name of diversity, you can feel the uniqueness slipping away. Europe is inundated by people who take advantage of the freedoms these countries offer but often refuse to become a real part of the culture that created the freedoms they now enjoy. A similar thing has occurred in many other parts of the world, like India.

Multiculturalism Thomas Sowell trumped.online/ld9
Scottish man on multiculturalism trumped.online/qca
Indian Perspective trumped.online/fhf
A warning trumped.online/iyf

As we land in America, in Portland, I'm reminded of the current battle between capitalism and socialism here, in my homeland. I never would have thought it possible back in 2019, just nine years ago. That is when the socialist movement started, after the midterms.

Economist Romina Boccia, socialism trumped.online/9ky

The Dawn: *The First Slave Owner*
Year: 2017 March 4 7:33 a.m.

The last time I saw Orange-tent-guy, he said slavery didn't exist, ducked into his tent spouting, *Hasta la vista, baby.* So here I am, a glutton for punishment, at his tent again. "Hey in there, you around?"

"*My man*, Prius Driving, Nervous Breakdown Guy," he says as he exits, stretching his arms in the air, greeting a sunny day.

"So what in God's name did you mean when you said, slavery didn't exist?"

"What? You don't speak English now?"
"Of course I speak English!"

"And so do I, however what most don't realize is our misunderstandings are based in the truth that we don't speak the *same* 'English.' In other words, words mean different things to different people. And what I know is that when you say the word 'slavery' and I say the word 'slavery' we are saying different things. Your version of slavery didn't exist. My version did. Remember our definition of Commilt? A selfish, guilt-driven emotion disguised as compassion whose purpose is to atone for transgressions *that never transpired.*"

"You keep saying transgressions that never transpired. Slavery transpired!"

"Let's talk about *your transgressions* and see if we can find a way to forgiveness so you can get off the treadmill of Commilt. All right, how many slaves do you own?"

"Okay, that's a stupid question."

"Is it? Why?"

"Because slavery ended in America 160 years ago."

"Oh, wow. Sheesh, that's a long time ago. Why are we even talking about it?"

"Don't be so patronizing. Because white people owned slaves."

"True. Should we judge a person by the color of their skin? Or the content of their character? In other words, what do *you* and your white skin have to do with anyone who ever owned a slave?"

My emotions are squirming a little now, "Nothing, I guess."

"What do you mean you guess? *You have nothing to do with slavery.* Did any of your ancestors own slaves?"

"I don't think so."

"Mine did."

"What? That's impossible. You're, you're black!"
He looked at his hands and let out a scream, "AHHHHH, *I'M BLACK…"*

He yelled so loud I somehow felt the need to scan the area to make sure
nobody heard.

"Your knowledge of slavery is pathetic. That is why, when you use the
word, slave, it lacks truth. Therefore your version didn't happen. Do you
know who the first slave owner was in America?"

"No, I do not."

"No one knows for sure, but history has made it clear that one of the first
slave owners, and possibly the first, was Anthony Johnson, and his hands
were the same color as mine. He is my great-great-great-great-
grandfather."

Anthony Johnson, first slave owner? trumped.online/715f7
True history of slavery trumped.online/bct

"What? You're telling me one of the first slave owners in North America
was a black man?"

"Yes, I am."

"And you're telling me he is related to you and that this black man owned
black slaves."

"That's what I'm saying."

"*That can't be true.* If it were true wouldn't everybody know it? Wouldn't
they teach us that in American history?"

"You'd think. But there is an agenda. An agenda to make white people
out as some plague upon the planet when the truth is the entire world
practiced slavery, and it was white people who put an end to it."

"But, ah, white people went to Africa and captured other human beings.
It's sickening."

"Even if that were true, still, I must emphasize, *you didn't do it.* Why
would you feel guilty for something you didn't do? *That makes no
sense.*"
He scanned the area. I could feel something big coming.

"Look across the street," he insisted, "See the brother, that black guy standing there?"

"Yeah, I see him."

"If he mugged that lady on the other side of the street, would you feel guilty?"

"Of course not, I'd try to help the lady, but I wouldn't feel guilty."

"Now, see that white guy, about thirty feet away from the black guy?"

"Check."

"Now, if the white guy mugged that lady, would you somehow feel guilty simply because your skin is the same hue?"

I search my soul. To do so would be insane. "You're right; it makes no sense."

"That's why I feel no guilt for what my ancestor, Anthony Johnson did. I didn't do it. But there's more. *Historical overlay.*"

"Okay, I'll bite. What's historical overlay?"

"Ahhh, historical overlay, a plague upon our time. It's when people blabber on about injustices in the past and try to make some logical correlation to the present. Claim it's the same today or nothing has changed, or it's only getting worse when the facts are irrefutable. Things have transformed. It is a fact that today every single person, black or white, has great access to opportunity. In fact, because of things like affirmative action, perhaps minorities have an unfair advantage. Did you know the FAA, the Federal Aviation Administration, has put political correctness above the safety of aviation in America? It's affirmative action gone off the rails."

"Hey, affirmative action is a necessary and good thing."

"Affirmative action *was* a necessary and good thing. Now it is time to let the best rise to the top, regardless of skin color. It's just not helping anymore. There is no systemic racism. Modern American culture will ostracize anyone caught practicing racism in the workplace; they will be found guilty of the crime it now is. But the pendulum has swung too far.

For example, they give certain minorities preferential treatment in college administration. People are getting into schools they're not ready for. Schools that would never allow a white person or an Asian person in with similar grades. It's a setup for failure and only hurts their self-esteem. An Indian American named Vijay Jojo Chokal-Ingam faked being black so that, with his relatively low GPA of 3.1, he could get into medical school at St. Louis University where, if they knew he was Indian, he would have needed at least a 3.7 GPA. The irony is, *affirmative action is racist.*"

CNN, Vijay Jojo Chokal-Ingam trumped.online/mc7
Black man on racism trumped.online/b8h

"This sounds more like a lame movie plot than reality."

"Oh, it's real. If you had a heart attack right now, would you want the best surgeon available to perform your open heart surgery, or would the color of the surgeon's skin be part of your consideration?"

It's a stupid question. And yet, there is a part of me that wants to say; *I'd rather have a 'diverse' pool of surgeons to choose from than the best surgeons available.* That part of me is virtue signaling with my very life! "Skin color would be irrelevant. I'd want the best surgeon. Of course."

"Then college admissions should be colored blind. Yes?"

I hesitate for a moment, "Maybe."

He looked up, following the sound of a commercial plane. We both stood there watching it fly by for some time. Finally, he commented, "That plane is dramatically less safe flying over our heads today than it was ten years ago."

I remembered his earlier statement. "Oh yeah, the FAA. What happened?"

"They added a biographical questionnaire to the application process for people applying to become air traffic controllers. In the questionnaire, those who did *poorly* in science got preferential treatment over those who did well. Those who have been *unemployed* for the past three years got more points than *licensed pilots!* The FAA is actively searching for unqualified air traffic controllers."

"Okay, you're making this up. I don't believe you. That would be insane."

"Don't take my word for it, just look it up yourself."

Air traffic controllers questionnaire trumped.online/8fj

"Okay, I will!"

"And, it all goes back to historical overlay. Morgan Freeman addressed the flaws in historical overlay quite articulately on the Don Lemon show. Lemon asked him if he felt race plays a part in one's ability to succeed. Freeman answered, *Today? No…. Not in this country.*

Morgan Freeman, Don Lemon trumped.online/yc1

Also, the Brookings Institution, one of the most respected think tanks in the world, recently did a study proving that anyone in America regardless of race, religion, color or background has equal access to prosperity. The head of the study, Ron Haskins himself said the results astounded him. They proved that *anyone* who follows these three simple steps has only a 2% chance of living in poverty in America. Here are the three steps. Are you ready?"

I was preparing myself. "Okay, shoot."

"Number one, finish high school. Number two, get a job. Number three, do not have a child until you are married or in an otherwise committed relationship. That's it."

"That's it?"

"That's it."

Brookings Institution trumped.online/ynu

"I often criticize this country for the injustice of inequality. But, I'm guessing in most countries, this three-step process does not apply."

"Your guess would be correct. But here's how it relates to historical overlay. People who refuse to live in the present will not acknowledge this truth. And, if the Institute did this study fifty years ago, it would not have rendered the same positive result. It is true, *today,* not yesterday. So the question is, are you living in the present or the past?"

I thought about what an amazing, and really, beautiful revelation that is, "Why in God's name isn't there an entire course in high school based on this study? Could you imagine the good that would do?"

"I know. It would've changed my life!"

The information swirling in my head lead me to a revelation, "It seems like historical overlay is a problem whether we overlay the past upon the present or the present upon the past."

"Impressive, you are making progress my silly white skinned compadre. It's wholly unfair to overlay current morality onto the past. Our understandings of right and wrong evolves and so to judge the past based upon current sensibilities would not differ from judging someone as 'stupid' because they don't have an education. And, if we are going to play the game of judging the past by using our evolved current moral compass, we all better be ready to burn in hell for the sins we are committing today unaware but will be glaring defects through the lens of our descendants."

"Okay, that's intense." I take a moment. Then I remember, "You're saying we didn't capture Africans and…"

"Hold everything, who's we?"

"You're right, they, *they.* The ones who brought slaves to America. Are you saying they didn't capture Africans in nets and drag them behind horses? I remember seeing that in some documentary when I was a child. I think much of my *Commilt* started at that moment."

"No, that's not what happened. But that myth made whites look like barbarians! *It's a lie. Africans captured other Africans and sold them in the slave trade.* It was big business and was going on long before anyone from what we now refer to as America had a slave. In fact life was horrendous for most africans. Out of fear of famine, entire tribes often surrendered themselves in bondage, as slaves, to other tribes just so they could eat. And, once a tribe defeated another tribe, the defeated were generally slaughtered, tortured, or made into slaves. The life they had in Africa was not necessarily better than the life they had in America. They were slaves there too; and waring and starving. Today, I don't know a single black person who wants to return to Africa. Any part of it. In fact, if you took all of the African Americans and gave them their own country, it would be the eighth wealthiest nation in the world."

Despite the number of "bombs" he just dropped, all I can muster is, "You're saying black people captured other black people and sold them?"

"Yes, that is exactly what I'm saying, and that is exactly what happened."

⊙⊙ History of slavery <u>trumped.online/snh</u> ⊙⊙

The revelations are overwhelming, "And then, some black people, like your ancestor, ended up buying black people that other black people captured and sold?"

"Yes, in fact, it's possible that some Africans who owned slaves owned some of their relatives."

"Dude, this is too much. I don't know what to do with this."

"Chew on it! Now, the chances your ancestors owned any slaves is minuscule. At the height of slave ownership in America, only about 6% of whites owned slaves."

"What? I thought almost everyone had slaves."

"Why?"

"I don't know. It just seems like that's what I've been told."

"The suppression of truth is as bad as a lie. You have been lied to. And all it does is create tension between blacks and whites and everyone else. This is part of the reason reparations is such an insane idea. Should all white people today pay for the misguided history of 6% of the white population and the misguided African culture that started the slave trade in the first place? It makes no sense. Whatsoever. And, consider this. At the height of slave ownership, there were *thousands of free blacks*. And, between 16% and 28% of free blacks owned slaves. So, if reparations were to occur, we would have to find the descendants of black people who owned slaves and make them pay too. Finally reparations has already happened; affirmative action, the community reinvestment act, etc. "
"Dude, you're blowing my mind. Stop it!"

"No! Anyone, black or white, who thinks because of today's sensibilities they would never have owned a slave 200 years ago, is delusional. Yes,

232

statistically speaking they probably would not have. However, if you lived *in that time* and your parents owned slaves, if you were born into a plantation that owned slaves, *you would've been a slave owner.* It's time to stop judging the past and stop judging each other. Current slavery is a different matter altogether."

"There is no slavery today, what are you talking about?"

He pulled one of his classic topic changes I knew would make sense soon enough. "Do you know what the root of the word slave is?"

"No idea."

"The root of the word slave is Slav, as in Slavic. The largest slave trade was in the Arabic World, and they enslaved everyone. They had no prejudice whatsoever," he said with a wink. "But white slaves, Slavs, were so common it became the word for slave. So basically, the word slave means white person - the Slavs were European predecessors. And, what's most disheartening is the biggest use for slaves in the Arabic world was sex. The first sex slaves."

"Wait, when you say Arab, doesn't that mean Muslim?"

"It does."

"This is making me very uncomfortable."

"Good. Cognitive dissonance. Your paradigm is beginning to shatter. Consider this, if blacks deserve reparations from you, maybe you deserve reparations from Arabs/Muslims. They enslaved your ancestors and now they're migrating to America." My brain is spinning as he continues, "Here's a good one for you, the Irish historically are one of the most persecuted peoples of the world."

"I'm Irish."

"One Irishman wrote in a letter to his family after arriving in America, *My master is a great tyrant. Our position in America is one of shame and poverty.* No group was considered lower than an Irishman in America during the 1850s. Blacks called them, 'white niggers.' They lived in cellars and shanties that were so unsanitary 80% of infants born to the Irish in New York died. The Irish were more expendable than slaves. When slaves died of cholera from digging the New Basil Canal in New

Orleans, the Irish were forced to take their place because *slaves were too valuable*. It is estimated that 30,000 Irish men died in their place. All the while the British ruled over Ireland with an iron fist."

"Jeez, sucked to be Irish."

"Yep. Now, can your paradigm handle this? Saudi Arabia and Yemen only abolished slavery in the 1960s. Do you know what color Saudis and Yemenis are?"

"Ah… black and, and…brown."

"Can you guess why they finally ended slavery?"

At this point, I'm feeling sick to my stomach. The only thing I can muster is a soft, "Enlighten me."

"Relentless pressure from European countries and America. And what color would most of those people be?"

I don't know why it is so hard for me to say it. I guess I have bought the myth that white people, me included, are inherently flawed. The worst. Finally, I spit it out, "The majority of those people, the vast majority, would be white people."

"Yes, white people have done more to *abolish slavery* on the planet than any other race, by far. And today, slavery still exists in Chad, Mauritania, Niger, Mali, and Sudan."

"Wait, aren't those all Muslim majority countries?"

"Yes, of course."

"But, *Islam is a religion of peace.* I'm sure it has nothing to do with the religion but the region, right? The culture of those countries, right?"

"The reason slavery still exists is *the teachings in the Koran and the Hadith,* the sayings of Mohammed. And much of slavery today is child labor and sex slavery. And really, the way they often treat women in many Islamic countries is slavery. Often, women cannot leave the house without the permission of the husband; sometimes they're not allowed to drive, they have to wear specific clothing, the Hijab. Their testimony is only worth half that of a man's in court. This is slavery. Not to mention they often execute gay people, throw them off rooftops, all in the name of Allah."

"Again, this is making me very uncomfortable. One of my best friends is a Muslim. But anyway, all religions are guilty of terrible things. They're all the same."

"You seem to have forgotten. We're talking about atrocities that are occurring *right now,* today, *not in the past."*

"I'm falling prey to historical overlay myself, aren't I?"

"You said it, not me. You're pulling atrocities of the past into the present to try to justify *current* Islamic practices."

Bill Maher with Muslim Hirsi Ali trumped.online/o99

As we arrive at the homeless camp, my brain is somewhere behind us, backtracking, trying to pick up all the shards of enlightenment dropped along the way. He unzips the orange tent, lifts the trash can and puts a bunch of money in the hole that is already overflowing with cash, "I gotta go to the bank tomorrow."

"Seriously? What are you doing? Why? Why are you still living out here?"

"Cause," he says with a smile, "If I didn't I'd no longer be the Orange-tent-guy." The light expression on his face changes in an instant. Suddenly he's stone cold sober. Serious as I've ever seen, "Remember, I have a plan."

And with that, he just turned and walked away. Weaving through encampments. Where to, who could say? No matter. The time has slipped away. I get in my Prius, heading for the office when I remember I left some engineering designs I've been working on at home. Yes, sometimes I work on the most ancient of computers, paper! So I turn back toward home.

What can prepare you for the unpreparable?

When I get there, I hear moaning. Like someone is in pain. *Kathy!* I rush toward the sound, blast open the bedroom door. There is Kathy, under the naked, pulsing body of *Janet.*

Chapter 17 The Future: *The Rolling Pin*
Year: 2047 March 23 6:53 p.m.

"I know how we can find and catch this, *Man-In-Black!*" Charles declares. "If someone were sneaking into your house at night while you slept without leaving a single trace they had ever been there, how would you catch them?"

"I'd set an alarm."

"Wrong."

"Okay, I'd tape a bunch of cans and glass bottles to a string and tie the string to the door so that when they opened it, it would clang and wake me up. Then I'd tie them to a chair with duct tape."

"I like that one, but… wrong! You *wouldn't* catch them because *you didn't know they had ever been there."*

"Hmmm"

"Yes, Hmmmm. But, how would you catch them if you knew they were coming?"

"Well, that's easy, I'd be ready for them. I'd have a slingshot or a bat or a frying pan and knock them on the head."

"Okay, you may be getting carried away, but that's the idea. The Man-In-Black has only infiltrated our lives because we, well, I, didn't know he was doing so. But now that I know, I can, metaphorically, get a frying pan in the form of cyber tracking."

"What is that?"

"There is an electronic footprint, if you will, behind every bit of information that enters your iDesk. So, its origins can be traced especially if you know it's coming. Thousands of sets of footprints come in and out a day. You can set a kind of virtual tracking system. I'm going to program both our iDesks to track any holographic human projections to their origins. Normally, of course, your desk blocks any holographic images from which their origins are unknown. But this guy's good. He's hacked the system into making it think he's a friend. Someone we know.

Maybe he's hacked the footprint of our friends. Maybe he's created a fake set of footprints to a new 'friend.' Whatever the case, we'll be ready the next time he appears. We'll trace him back to his literal location. Then you can use your frying pan on him!"

"Okay, good. Or, how about a rolling pin?"

"Perfect, an old-fashioned rolling pin. That oughta do the trick. Okay, I've got to get to work."

"I must say, it's good to have a genius for a best friend."

He jokes, "Hey, I thought *I was your best friend!"*

By that evening, he had both of our systems set like a mousetrap. "Okay," he said excitedly, "You must have your phone ready to text me if he shows up at your house. Let's make the code, um, rolling pin! Have it set, so all you have to do is push send. If I get a text that says, *rolling pin* I will know he is there and I will be able to track him to his *actual* location with my phone. If he shows up at my house and you see him, just somehow fit the word rolling pin into the conversation."

"Okay, let me get this straight. Just *randomly* fit in an ancient word for a kitchen tool that hasn't been used much since, like, *1970!? "*

"You can do it. I have total faith in you."

"I appreciate your vote of confidence. It reminds me of when I was eight years old and my mother, for the first time, trusted me with a, *rolling pin,* to make cookies."

We put the plan in motion by having a gathering with the five of us at Charles' house. A kind of potluck meeting/celebration, celebrating that we're not all going to die of runaway climate change when in reality, *we are!* Charles and Jadda whip up a beautiful salad with fresh fruit. I bring some Thai food; pumpkin curry with tofu. Alexus opts to bring asparagus but is running late. Shelly, who was assigned dessert joins us in the kitchen in her usual exuberant spirits carrying a big bag and announces, "We'll make dessert. I thought it would be fun!" She reaches in her large bag and pulls out everything you need to make sugar cookies from scratch; sugar, butter, vanilla, eggs, flour and finally, she says, "And, I bought one of these because I figured you might not have one." She pulls out an old-fashioned, the kind my grandma used to use, *rolling pin!*

"Look what I found, an old-style, what's it called? I keep forgetting the name, cookie flattener?"

"I think it's called, a, ah flattening pin?" Jadda adds, wondering. You could practically hear my eyes crackle from widening them so, as I looked at Charles, signaling to him, *What? Seriously? What are the chances?*

"All right," Shelley says eagerly "Let's whip up these cookies so they can be in the oven while we have dinner."

"Siri, show us a recipe for sugar cookies."

"Of course, right away," Siri says in the voice of C3PO.

"Thank you."

"Oh, my pleasure."

Suddenly, a recipe with the correct proportions for all ingredients appears on a virtual screen above the kitchen Island. Once we have a big clump of cookie dough, Shelly looks at me and says, "Could you hand me that, that, ah, what's it called?"

I look right at Charles, "The rolling pin?"

"Yes, the rolling pin." I hand it to her, then slightly shrug my shoulders toward Charles signaling, *What else am I supposed to do, call it a flattening pin?*

"Maybe it's being pregnant and all, but I'm kinda in the mood for sugar cookies with mayo," Shelly confesses as she flattens.

"Okay, GROSS!" Jadda speaks for us all.

Moments later, before she's done flattening, Shelly gets a text from Green Power. She's never really off the clock. "I'm sorry everyone, I have to make a quick call."

"That's okay," Jadda says while Shelly excuses herself. She steps outside to make the call.

While Jadda rolls the dough, it randomly crosses my mind, *flattening pin* might just make more sense!

"So," Jadda begins, "Marcus, it's been a while since our last gathering. How's the data looking to you?"

"Well, very, um, great. I mean, It's continuing to support our latest findings."

"So temperatures *are* shifting in a positive direction, yes?"

I pause. Still so hard to lie about this even with Charles and I working our plan. And, right on cue, as I hesitate, like he's always watching, the Man-In-Black appears. I'm sitting at the kitchen island looking into the kitchen in the general direction of the refrigerator. The rest are facing toward me. The Man-In-Black appears *right behind them,* shakes his head, *No,* and wiggles his index finger left to right saying, *don't even think about it.* The good news is, he's taking the bait. My heart is pounding out of my chest. I blurt out, "Ah, can I try the...***roll-ing pin!***" It wasn't only the volume with which I said it that was odd; it was how I said it. As if 'roll' and 'ing' where two separate words.

Jadda looked at me with scrunched eyebrows, "Um, okay, here."

She hands me the pin to which I reply, "Thanks, I've always wanted to try a ***roll-ing... pin!***" Charles is oblivious, chatting with Jadda while the Man-In-Black appears again. This time right behind them, who are now where I was as I flattened the dough. He pointed at each of them and then swiped his index finger across his throat.

"Charles, do you want to try the ***rolling pin?***" He's still chatting away with Jadda. Oblivious. "Charles, hey." I finally get him to break conversation, "Would you like to try the rolling pin?"

"Oh, no thanks...."

The Man-In-Black's holographic projection continues to stand ominously right behind them.

"Charles, I *think you should try the...**rolling pin!***"

I can see the lights finally go on in Charles' eyes as the Man-In-Black fades. He snaps his head around, away from Jadda, "You mean, *THE roll-ing pin?"*

"Yeah, *THE* **roll-ing pin!"** I say with my eyes as wide as saucers while I nod my head up and down in a hyper-exaggerated fashion.

He pulls out his iPhone feigning a text had interrupted him as Shelly returns from her phone call, "Hey, you know what we need?" He says with nervous excitement.

"What sweetheart?" Jadda replies a little confused by all that has transpired in the last few minutes starting, of course, with, **roll-ing pin** and now Charles' herky-jerky, A.D.D. like behavior.

"We need ice cream to go with these cookies we're making. I'll be right back."

He hurriedly exits to the garage and peels out in his $380,000 Lamborghini. I think it was around eight Bitcoin.

"What in God's name got into him?" Shelly asks.

I try to sound like I'm making some sense while speaking at a rapid clip and being humorously sarcastic. "Oh, you know, he got a hankering for some ice cream. And it's your fault, bringing all the ingredients for sugar cookies. I mean who can eat a sugar cookie without ice cream?"

"Why didn't he just send the car?"

Luckily, Jadda, unknowingly, helps me out. "Oh, he loves to drive. Sometimes he's stuck in the year 2027, just before automated cars took over. He reprogrammed all of his cars, so the safety controls are deactivated. He can drive as fast as he wants."

Shelly asks a little surprised, "Didn't they recently change the law to a year in jail for tampering with the programming of your car, not to mention, they will fine you $15,000?"

Jadda replies introspectively, "Yes, things do seem to be more and more Orwellian every day."

"And that's why I love my old car," I add, trying to hide my excited nervousness, "No restrictions! Okay, Shelly, you brought the rolling pin, your turn to roll the dough."

"Okay, let me give it a shot."

"Hey, I'm kind of in the mood for peanut butter banana ice cream, any other requests? I think I'll call Charles and see what they've got."

"There are too many choices these days, I'll just have vanilla," Shelly says.

Jadda adds her two cents, "I'll have a little of what everybody else gets. A smorgasbord of ice cream."

I head into Charles' office, fast walking, trying to contain myself, attempting not to appear even more erratic than I've already been. I gently shut the door and make the call. "Charles, what's happening, do you have his footprint?"

"Yes, I got it. It's taking me downtown somewhere. It looks like it might be, here on Third Street somewhere. I'm getting close."

"What are you going to do if this works? I mean, we never really thought about it. What's the plan, a citizen's arrest?"

"Come on Marcus, seriously? Get a grip. I'm just going to try to figure out who it is. Take pictures, gather all the information I can. And then we will take it to the police."

"Okay, okay, that makes sense."

"My tracking program is now predicting 22 SW 3rd Ave as the location of the Man-In-Black's transmission. Wait a minute. That address sounds familiar. I don't know why."

"It does sound familiar."

"I'm coming up on it now. *What?* You have got to be kidding me!"

"What? What is it?"

"Voodoo Doughnut! *It's the address of Voodoo Doughnut!*"

"The Man-In-Black works at Voodoo Doughnut?"

"Marcus, again, *get a grip.* Let me figure this out. I'll call you back in a minute."

"Okay, but don't forget you have to pick up a bunch of ice cream."

"What? What for?"

"Because you said you were going to get ice cream."

"Oh yeah; I'll call you in a sec."

I head back into the kitchen just as Alexus arrives, "Hey sweetheart," I kiss her on the cheek.

"What's happening?" She asks noticing the pile of cookie dough and other random ingredients.

Shelly responds enthusiastically, *"We're making sugar cookies."*

"From scratch? What on earth got into you? People don't make cookies from scratch anymore."

Shelly continues to flatten the dough vigorously. She appears to be on the edge of sweating. The dough is so paper thin now, with everybody rolling it, a slight breeze could blow it away like a piece of paper. Finally, I get a text from Charles that says, *Call me quick.* I head back into his office, **"What's going on?"**

"I'm in the car, headed your way and you won't believe what just happened."

"Try me?"

"I went into Voodoo Doughnut, and the guy behind the counter looked at me and said, 'Are you the guy in the Lamborghini? I think this is for you.'"

"What?"

"Yeah, then he handed me a doughnut."

"What kind?"

"Really?"

"Sorry, I get random when I'm nervous. That's weird."

"Oh, it gets weirder. You know how Voodoo Doughnut can make doughnuts that look like just about anything?"

"Yes, that's pretty much what they're famous for."

"The doughnut he handed me is in the shape of a *rolling pin.*"

"Shut up!"

"Then he handed me a note which reads;

Nice try. You think I don't know everything you do? Everything you say? I am and always will be one step ahead of you. This is your last warning. You two speak one word of this and I will rolling pin your lives.

"What?"

"I know, this guy is good. He must've somehow pinged his signal through the Wi-Fi system at Voodoo Doughnut and then up to my house."

"But, who left the note?"

"The order for the rolling pin doughnut was made on the Voodoo Doughnut app and paid for with Cryptocurrency. It's all untraceable. The Voodoo Doughnut guy said, along with the order, they told him there would be an envelope under the door, and to give it to me. He said they gave him my description along with the order and that I would drive a very expensive car. Most likely a Lamborghini."

"What do we do now?"

"I don't know. Just don't forget the ice cream."

"What kind?"

"Peanut butter banana, vanilla, and ah, Shelly says she'll just eat a bit of whatever everyone else gets, too many choices."

The Dawn: *James Madison, Tom Paine*
Year: 2017 April 14, Good Friday 9:46 a.m.

"I'm having a nervous breakdown," I say instead of a more traditional, *Hello* or *What's up.*

"I'm surprised it took this long," my always sensitive friend replies.

"I suppose it's apropos that today is Good Friday. I've always thought that was an odd name for the day that commemorates the moment they staked a guy to a cross through his wrists and ankles and then stabbed in the side, who, by all accounts, was only trying to spread love. How can that be good?"

"Like everything else, it's a matter of perspective. I mean, what appears bad can turn out to be a sheep in wolves clothing."

"Really? I'm sorry, but good and bad are not a matter of perspective. They are as they appear to be. For example, the crucifixion of a guy trying to influence the world around him to be more fair and just, that's *bad.* And, for the record, sheep don't wear wolves clothing!"

"Do to."

"Do not."

"Do to."

Before I can hit him with another, *Do not,* he quickly changes the subject, "Hey, you want to meet the Blue-tent-guy?"

"Yes, very much."

"Why?"

Oh, man. He has got me again. "Commilt," I say accepting the truth.

"Perfect," he says nodding. "Honesty! Pure. Not…Gonesty; the tiresome expression of honesty only because one is riddled with guilt."

We walk forty feet down a slight slope on the soggy ground. As always, the relentless sound of traffic on both sides hums away. Between the orange tent and the blue tent, I notice several used needles scattered around - beer cans, wine bottles, and the like. We peer into the blue tent. It's a tarp flung over the branch of a tree.

"Hello?" my friend says, "Hello?"

"Come, come, come," she says, waving us in with her hand. I look at my friend with a slight squint of my eyes communicating, *Hey, you said Blue-tent-**guy!***

"Here," my friend reaches out to her, touches her arm and places a *sandwich* in her hand! Again, I give him the same look only magnified relaying, *Oh, so it's okay for <u>you</u> to hand out sandwiches but not **me**!?*

She grabs it quickly and takes a bite. She's probably in her mid-sixties though it's hard to tell.

"Have a seat. Sit down. Sit down," she says waving her arms to an orange bucket and a pile of newspapers.

We take her up on her offer as uncomfortable as it looks. My friend squats down on the newspapers. I take the orange bucket. However, the ground underneath it is not even, slanting back. For this, I'm unprepared which sends me tumbling through the flimsy tarp to the ground outside. Basically, I disappear. My friend, of course, finds this to be humorously unparalleled. And, I have to agree. Once Orange-tent-guy and I start cracking up, my new friend joins in on the laughter, more than happily given at my expense. As we collect ourselves, introductions are made.

"Well, this is my friend, *Can't Sit on a Bucket Guy,*" he says as an introduction. I shake my head, "Can't Sit on a Bucket Guy, this is Cynthia."

"Cynthia, it's nice to meet you."

She reaches out her hand; I take it. We engage in the traditional introductory handshake.

"It's always wonderful to have guests. If I had known you were coming, I would have cleaned up."

"That's okay," I reply as she fumbles around, straightening up the approximately 10' x 8' space. She looks up and just to my left, "These are my children," she says. She reaches in her pocket and holds out a picture, in my general direction, of two bright girls and a boy on a crinkly old photo. The boy was probably six or seven and the girls may be a year or two apart, around nine or ten. There are a man and woman in the photo as well. I'm guessing that's her, a long time ago, cleaned up, and the man, her husband.

"Your children are beautiful," I say, my heart breaking. In an instant, my mind has conjured countless questions and possible scenarios. How old is the photo? Where are her children now? Why aren't they taking care of her? Who is the father? Maybe there was a wicked divorce, and the children chose his side. Maybe there was an accident. Maybe bridges were burned. Who knows? She puts the photo back in her pocket. Suddenly I find I'm engaged in a kind of self-inquiry I never have before. What am I feeling? Compassion? Is it pure?

"I wish I could make you some tea." She says. But of course there's no tea, there's no kettle, *there's no electricity*.

"That's okay; we have to be going. I just wanted to check up on you," my friend says.

We turn to leave, step out of the tarp but she steps out as well and stops us. "Wait, please, these are my children," she says holding out the picture again. I smile, "They're beautiful."

She looks puzzled, "Um, did I show you this already? I'm sorry if I did."

"No, it's okay," I answer, touching her shoulder. I'm guessing the onset of dementia. I can see her better now in the light of the outdoors. I look her directly in the eyes. But they are so cloudy; there's no visible pupil. Just a white and grey murky kind of emptiness. She's blind from what looks like cataracts.

As we make our way back toward the orange tent, my friend says, "Look around, see all the encampments?" I scan the area; there's probably twelve or fifteen. "Everyone here could be and should be a contributing part of society. Except for her. As I told you before, bringing her a sandwich is compassionate, bringing me a sandwich is enabling."

"I'm not sure I agree with you, but I get what you're saying. So, for people like her, you would agree with me that government programs should be in place."

"No, I would not."

"But you just said, giving to her is compassionate."

"Yes, but, *you cannot assign compassion to others, certainly not the government.*"

"What?"

"You can't assign compassion, or love, to someone else or something else. To think you're compassionate by giving lip service to government programs is virtue signaling. You're saying, *I'm a good person because I support the idea of someone else not only doing the hands-on work but someone else paying for it.* That is not compassion. It's virtue signaling, it's Commilt, and it's enabling. Not only to all of those who should do for themselves but to those whose responsibility it is to help. You see, potentially the worst crime of trying to assign compassion to the government is we rob each other of the *gift of giving.* Purely. And, those in the government who then do the 'good works' are simply doing the job *they are paid to do like anyone else does any other job.* Not to mention the fact that government is always corrupt."

"Is it? Do you think the government is always corrupt?"

"Yes, and there's a direct correlation between the size of government and the amount of corruption. Do you know who James Madison was?"

"Yes, of course, the acknowledged Father of the Constitution."

"Correct and he understood the inherent problems of trying to assign compassion to the government. He said, "*Charity is not a legitimate function of government.*" And yet today, many people believe it is the *main* function of government. Do you see the slippery slope? The more we rely on the government, the more we become its subjects. The more we become its subjects, the more freedoms we allow to be taken away. Our predecessors died in a bloody revolutionary war with the Redcoats to get away from the tyranny of government. Now, in no small way, we are, slowly, becoming the very embodiment of the ones we fought."

"I get your point and yet I feel the government is necessary."

"As do I *and* Tom Paine."

"Tom Paine?"

"Yes, Tom Paine, the founding father and author of what most scholars believe to be the single most influential writings in American history. Most notably; *Common Sense,* advocating independence from Great Britain. It remains to this day the all-time best-selling title in America. Tom Paine said this, *Government, even in its best state is but a necessary evil, in its worst state is intolerable.* As you can imagine, he faced a lot of persecution for his work. For being willing to tell the truth."

I had never heard these words from such important figures in the creation of America. Again, I wonder why they leave such important history out of our educational institutions. "Do you think anyone in Congress knows what these guys, who wove the very fabric of our country, believed?"

"No, they don't know. And I say that because there's a big difference between being aware of something that happened historically and *knowing, grasping what it means.* Most in government would never allow themselves to *really understand* the foundations of this country. They don't want to *know* what has made this country great. Because now, they're paid big money to work for the very thing that Tom Paine, James Madison, and all the founders warned us should never be a career. Should never be Big Business. But that is just what the government has become, the biggest business in the country with the most employees who are forever demanding more money from those who work for *legitimate* businesses."

I try to catch him off guard, turn his philosophy against him, "Well, that just sounds real... *bad.*"

He grins, "I know what you're doing. Yes, it looks bad like the situation a couple of thousand years ago today, with that Jewish guy. But, I'm holding out for a kind of resurrection as well. One of the political persuasion."

I should have known there would be no catching him off guard. "Well, I could use a resurrection myself. Present company aside, I've lost all my good friends."

"Hmmm. It sounds like you're scraping the bottom of the bucket," he responds with a big grin highlighted by the wide-brimmed hat he found.

I have to correct him, "I think it's supposed to be 'barrel.' Scraping the bottom of the barrel."

"Well, I think scrapping the bottom of a bucket would be even more pathetic than a barrel. I mean, at least with a barrel you had, well, a whole barrel full of whatever was once the contents of said container, which would be something like 17 times the amount of a bucket. So, bucket is exponentially more pitiful than barrel. And you, my friend, are looking pitiful."

"Well, thanks. Thanks for nothin'."

"Just keepin' it real brotha."

"A lot's happened in the last month. My wife has moved out and moved in with another…*woman*. My children are showing signs of depression, and I have turned to the bottle and the spiff way, way too much. I'm hanging on by a thread. *All because I questioned things.* Sometimes I wish I never met you, my only friend. But then, were the rest of them ever *really* my friends?"

Orange-tent-guy answers softly, "I don't know. I mean, what does it mean to be friends?"

"Exactly. Maybe it's just about surrounding oneself with people who agree with you on everything."

"It may be, but if that's the case, then how would anyone grow? We don't agree on everything."

"True. And the real crazy thing is, I don't necessarily disagree with them. I questioned our perspective. I presented options, different sides of the coin."

"Sounds a lot like our friends Jesus and Tom Paine."

I shrug my shoulders, "And for that, they disowned me and even call me a Trumpeter."

"A Trumpeter?"

"Yes, somebody who mindlessly blows the horn for Trump. The irony is, I'm the only one who's *not* being mindless. I'm thinking about things with a kind of complexity I never knew was possible. I want *all* the information before concluding. On the other hand, they take gossip as fact. And usually, if someone is reported as 'allegedly' having been guilty of something, they ignore the word allegedly and skip right to guilty; no jury and no judge. CNN, in their eyes, can do no wrong. Don Lemon is like a god. I just realized that everyone has an angle, everyone is biased and transcending our biases for an honest search for truth is the only way we can find solutions."

He nods with a half-curled grin, "Sometimes friends are like clothing you wear when you're a child. They fit for a while, but one day you try to get dressed, and you realize, *you've grown.* We may be attached to those old clothes. We don't want to let go. But until we do, we will be uncomfortable and, worst of all, *just look plain silly. "*

"Well, no wonder I feel like the Incredible Hulk. Whenever Dr. Banner transitioned into the big green monster, the only clothing he had left was a torn pair of jeans. The rest just busted right off. Of course, I always wondered how those pants stayed on. I'm sure he went from a size 34 waist to a size 87. And, there was *no elastic band.* But I digress. I guess my old friends and I just don't fit together anymore. But I need help, my only friend. I *am* having a nervous breakdown. You've been through worse than me. What do I do?"

"That's easy, *do something for someone else.* Give. In a way that makes a difference. Doing good, with pure intentions, is better than any drug for lifting the cloud of depression."

"And you're saying voting for government subsidies won't have the same healing effect?," I remark like the straight man in a comedy routine.

He nods his head to one side as if actually contemplating. "Well, it's been tried, over and over and over again and doesn't seem to help *anyone* very much. But seriously, there's much scientific evidence that proves the health benefits of giving, of making a difference in the world, and those benefits only come to those who get personally involved with honest intentions. Again, *you cannot assign compassion. "*

Helpers High trumped.online/xlv
Power of Giving trumped.online/37y

It's a nice spring day, lots of puffy white clouds floating by; lots of sun. In that sense, it is a Good Friday. But I feel crucified until I see something. Something right before me.

"Orange-tent-guy, I have an idea. I gotta go."

He absentmindedly replies, "Later Tater."

As I begin walking the fifty feet or so to my Prius, I knew what I needed to do. I guess that's why they say there is no unselfish act. I need to do something good for someone or something else *for my sanity.* So in essence, it is selfish. But still, I think we can do good things *and* receive the selfish benefits if our intentions are clean, guilt and shame-free. We'll see.

Chapter 18 The Future: *The Drone*
Year: 2047 April 26, Good Friday 6:53 a.m.

Good Friday. It's kind of an anniversary for me now. I remember 20 years ago, in the middle of a nervous breakdown, thinking, how could anyone call such a day, good? But I understand now, and so I think of it as an anniversary. An anniversary of the beginning of my new life, my New Over. But of course, I'm facing a different crisis now. A decision. Whether or not to try to convince the world that the data is real. That, if we don't do something drastic now there will be famine, weather events never seen before. Death. Climate change at a pace never even imagined. Or, try to forget. Try to live my life with my friends and my wife and my grown children and hope maybe somebody else figures it out before it's too late. *Highly unlikely.*

"Good morning sweetheart, whatcha doing?" Alexus says through sleepy eyes.

"Nothing, just thinking… and loving you."

"Love you too," she says, putting her hand on my cheek. Imagine what it's like feeling as if you're being watched and listened to every second of every day. That's my life now. Feels like a prison even though it is a beautiful, even miraculous world we've created. The technological explosion that started in the 90s has created a life that most would never have believed. The poor live better than the wealthiest kings did just one hundred years ago. But every time some technological device says it would, *Like to use your current location,* we potentially give away our freedom, our privacy. We say, *Yes,* for ease. But if someone were to hack your system, every time we said, *Yes,* for convenience we also said, *Yes,* to being technologically imprisoned. Tracked! Watched! Wiretapped. That's why I, and most of my friends, have chosen not to get an iMind. Sure, it simplifies life dramatically to have everything you need downloaded right to your brain, constantly connected to the net with a simple thought. But, I'm just not ready for that kind of un-severable commitment to the system. Hacking at that level is now punishable by life in prison and is supposed to be impossible. That's what got me reeling. *Who has access to such power,* such technology? And why? Why would anyone purposefully, knowingly, cover up information that could save the world? Charles and I rarely even speak of it anymore. The only time we do is when we go for a hike at Tryon Park. It's 658 acres of old growth forest with a river and several creeks. We hike to the middle, stand next to a loud body of moving water, and still wonder if we're being surveilled. But it seems to work. And today I need to talk. I text Charles, *Tryon in 30 min?* Moments later, *Sure CU there.*

"Hey. Did you leave your phone in the car?"

"Of course. Rule number one, no electronics! So what's troubling you?" he says stepping onto the old Stone bridge over Tryon Creek surrounded by an ancient forest.

"Well, The Man-In-Black! What else?"

He thinks for a minute like he's seriously considering what else might be bothering me, "Um, maybe the fact that you're *getting old?*"

"Well, that's the kettle calling the pan black!"

"Touché."

"I was going over and over it in my mind this morning while Alexus kissed me and told me she loves me. I feel like exploding. I want to tell her so bad it hurts."

"I know, *but you can't.* Just like I can't tell Jadda."

"I know, I guess that's why I need to talk to you. I was trying to make sense of it all. First, who or what has enough power, enough connections, enough technological prowess to do what they're doing to us? The only answer I could come up with was the government. But that doesn't make sense. Why would the government, or anyone for that matter, purposely bury the most important scientific data of our time? None of it makes any sense."

"I know," Charles says shaking his head showing his frustration. "I think about it every day. I dream about it at night. That is, when I *can* sleep!"

"Yes, sleep is scarce. And when I do, I have this nightmare of the future. The worst possible outcome has arrived, and I'm to blame."

"I have similar dreams, but what else can we do? The Man-In-Black is always a step ahead of us. If we say anything, he will find out and kill the ones we love. And probably somehow squelch the information anyw…"

Charles cuts me off and points up in the sky, "Wait, what is that?"

I look up through the branches. Because of the creek, it's hard to hear. "Oh my God, I think it's a drone." It instantly disappears into the sky.

"You're right, that was a drone. Do you think it was him, tracking us? Or are we being paranoid? Drones are all over the place these days."

"I don't know, but I think we should say goodbye for now."

We leave Tryon in different directions. I'm parked up at Lewis and Clark College. It always feels freeing to be unplugged, so I stroll, occasionally glancing up, afraid I'm being followed. But nothing is there, at least that I can see. I emerge from the forest onto a parking lot next to the music department, open my car door, and I'm bombarded with messages from Alexus on the window screen, *Help...My car is out of control,* followed by, *Marcus, please, help* and, *Marcus, where are you, help...*

"Siri, call Alexus!" She answers.

"Marcus, help!"

"What's happening?" I can hear in her voice; she is close to tears. Terrified.

"I was just in the car when suddenly, *it refused to follow my directions;* I'm flying all over town, crashing into street signs and trash cans. Marcus, what is happening?"

"Locations has you at the corner of Jefferson and Front Street. I'm headed that way now."

"No, No. I'm not even close to that. I'm on Burnside and NW twenty firs..."

I hear her wheels squeal as she screams.

"Are you okay? Alexus, are you okay?!"

"I just whipped onto NW 23rd. There's nothing I can do. My car won't follow my directions, and I can't disengage auto drive..."

"I'm on my way to you now. Keep telling me every turn you make."

I put the pedal to the metal. Thank God for my old Ford Freedom and its lack of restrictions. In five minutes I'm closing in.

"Okay babe, I can see you now, hold on!"

Her car is weaving recklessly through traffic over the Fremont bridge. I'm now just hitting 98 MPH weaving in and out as haphazardly as she is.

I pull up right behind her, "Okay baby, I'm here. Right behind you."

There are two unmanned police cars on our tail. She merges off the bridge on to Highway 84. As a consequence, we slow down into more traffic while still weaving at 56 MPH.

"What are you going to do?" she cries out. I honestly didn't know until she asks.

"Hold on, babe. I have a plan. Just trust me."

I decide not to share my plan because I figure he, or more likely *they*, can hear our every word and the less they know, the better. I weave left and punch it, passing her, then weave right, into her lane, *"Hold on!"*

I can see her in the review mirror white-knuckling the steering wheel of which she has no control. I wait until there are no cars close behind her and then I ease on the brakes so that our bumpers touch. Once they do, I slam on the brakes bringing us to a complete stop. Cars are flying by on both sides. I can only hope no one smashes into us. Horns honking, people yelling and cop cars sounding their sirens; she tries to get out, but the doors lock shut. She's pounding on the windows, *"Get me out of here!"* I open the trunk of my car, grab a lug wrench. Again, glad for my old car. There are no lug wrenches in the newer versions because the tires never blow.

I race to her window, "Get down!"

She puts her hands around her head and bends forward. With everything I've got, I swing. The window shatters. She quickly crawls halfway out, cutting her stomach on shards of glass. I pull her the rest of the way. Traffic stops, backs up as far as we can see. We jump in my car. With the police cars stuck in traffic like everyone else, we race away.

"Babe, are you okay?"

"I, I think so. More frightened than anything. What in God's name happened?"

I lie. I have to. "I don't know. I've heard there are recalls on your model. I've heard of cars going crazy…"

Trying to keep it together, she responds. "What? I've… never…heard of…" she begins to sob.

"I don't know sweetheart. I'm just glad you're okay!"

I get Alexus calmed down and into bed. She goes out like a light, exhausted. The police come for a statement. They're looking into it. Honestly, I don't know who to trust. They're either in on it or, they won't find anything.

I call Charles. I figure it can't hurt. If they want us scared, mission accomplished. "Charles, what's going on? Is Jadda okay?"

"Wait," he says confused. "How did you know? She got stuck in an elevator for two hours in between floors. You think…"

"… I don't know for sure, but Alexus nearly died. They took control of her car."

"What?"

"Yes. I had to chase her down and smash her window in the middle of Highway 84 to get her out."

"My God I wondered but.. but.."

"I know. It's just so hard to believe. I gotta go check on Alexus. She's asleep now but went out in tears, shaking."

I hang up and head toward the master from the kitchen. I'm afraid to even look in my office as I pass by, so I don't. But not looking has no power to change what is. The disguised, monster voice rattles my soul, ***"Marcus, you and Charles are asking too many questions…"***

The Dawn: *Kindness*
Year: 2017 April 14, Good Friday 7:46 p.m.

"So Daddy, when is mommy coming home?" Shanice asks as I tuck her into bed.

"I don't know sweetheart."

"She's at Janet's house still?"

"Yes, Janet's."

"So they're still having a sleepover?"

"Yeah, still."

"She's mad, huh?"

"Yeah, she's kinda mad."

"Why?"

"It's, it's… *complicated.*"

"It's Trump's fault right?"

"What?"

"I don't like him. First, he removed Martin Luther King's dust; then he makes Mom mad."

"Sweetheart, remember, he did not remove Martin Luther King's dust, and, no one can *make* you mad."

"What? But Malik makes me mad all the time."

"Well, your brother can make anyone mad," I say nudging her. "I'm only kidding sweetheart. But this is important, something that even most adults don't understand. I believe it's key to living a good and happy life. And there's nothing more important to me than helping you and your brother understand how to be happy. Do you remember the time we were at the movies and…"

"… And we got coked!"

I burst into a short reflexive moment of laughter like a sneeze, or a yawn. I can't help it! Kids say the most hilarious stuff. "Yes," I recover quickly, wiping the grin off my face. "When you got 'coked.' The guy tripped by accident and spilled his coke all over you, me, Malik and the lady next to us and the lady…"

"… The lady yelled 'F*#k!' Loud, remember?"

Again, I want to laugh so hard it hurts but… "Sweetheart, we don't say that. Okay? *Ever*. Don't say that."

"I didn't say it, the lady did."

Hard to argue with her logic, "Do you remember how mad she was?"

"Yes, she yelled fu.."

"… Sweetheart, no. We don't use that kind of language."

"Daddy. I know. I would never say f*@k. *She did.*"

"Anyway, were you, me and Malik mad?"

"No, we laughed. It was funny. And the guy was really sorry."

"Yes. So, why did the same thing make one person really, really mad while the three of us thought it was funny?"

"I don't know. Maybe it's like frogs."

Okay, this should be good. "Maybe so, what about frogs?"

"Remember, we went to Dry Creek one time which was weird because it wasn't really dry?"

"Yeah, I remember."

"And there were like a million frogs!?"

"Well, maybe not a million. But I didn't count so; it could be a million."

"Yeah, it was a million. I counted."

"Okay."

"They were all on the rocks and lily pads, and stuff and they were lovin' it. But then they got coked."

"Huh?"

"Yeah, remember it sprinkled out."

"Right."

"And some frogs just sat there. They were happy in the rain. Smiling."

"Frogs smile?"

"Everything smiles Dad."

"Okay."

"They were smiling and happy. But other frogs got mad and frowned and jumped in the water away from the rain. They're like the lady who yelled fu… "

"Fudge! Say fudge instead."

"Okay, they were like the fudge lady. See, those fudge lady frogs are *craaazy*. They don't like the rain…so they jump into the *water!* That's like not liking vegetables, *so you eat a can of spinach! Craaaaazy.* "

"Okay, I kinda see the similarity but… "

"Dad. My point is, some frogs don't let it bother them while other frogs, *they make it worse!* For no reason. They yell, *fudge,* and blame it on the rain. And then, *jump in the creek.* "

"Exactly. Yes. So, we are always at choice. All of us. We can be the frogs who get coked and then smile." Again, I chortle, "Or we can be like the frogs that frown. They don't like the water, so they *jump in the creek.* Which one do you think will live a happier life?"

"Come on Dad, that's obvious. *THE SMILING FROGS!*"

"So, is it the rain that makes the frogs mad, or did the frogs choose to be mad?"

"I think some frogs just choose to be mad. Or, they'd all be mad."

"Exactly. So, can Trump *make* Mommy mad?"

"No, I guess she's just choosing to be mad."

"Well, what's important is that we understand we are always at choice. We can be a smiling frog or a frowning frog. Always at choice." I was, of course, saying all of this for myself more than my children who, as usual, turned out to be my teacher. "Good night precious one."

"Good night Daddy." So now, to find the smiling frog in me, I write an email to the gang.

> Hello, my Friends,
> At least I hope some part of you still considers me a friend. I know you think I have changed. But really, I don't believe so. As you know, I have always been committed to truth. That has not changed. And, I have always been passionate about helping people in need. That has not changed. The thing is, the pursuit of truth is just that, a pursuit. Because it's not only very complicated, for example, context matters, but also because many aspects of truth evolve. So, to be committed to it, we must be willing to evolve ourselves. I hope that makes sense. So, yes, some of my beliefs have changed. And I hope they continue to change. How else can we be a part of the evolution of humanity? I invite each of you to answer that question. To show me where I'm wrong so I might continue to grow. And with that, I have an invitation. Sunday is Easter. I know none of us are traditionally 'religious,' but that doesn't mean the message of Easter isn't real. It can be. It's up to us. Countless millions will go to church. Many out of guilt, which is an unfortunate underbelly of religion. But others will go with pure intentions. I suggest we all do the same. But let's not go to a church with

walls, let's go to a church with weeds. We, together,
all of us, could 'resurrect' someone. Someone in real
need. Someone who is hurting. Someone cast aside
at no fault of their own. And, in the process, we
might find that we are the ones who rise from the
dead. The dead of day-to-day monotony. The dead of
feeling there is no substantial way to impact this
wonderful, confused, glorious and pain-ridden
world. It will take time and money. We will have to
give. Unselfishly. I know that sounds like an
oxymoron but, part of my soul-searching has led me
to believe much of my giving in the past was
motivated by guilt or an expectation of something in
return. In either case that's not giving. Just like
those who go to church out of a sense of guilt for
their 'sins' are showing up to bargain themselves
into 'heaven.' Misguided. So, if what I'm saying rings
true for you at all, please join me at the homeless
camp just past the Sunset highway tunnel into town.
And forward this to anyone you think might want to
contribute. Some of us have handed out sandwiches
there before. I want you to meet a friend of mine
who lives there. I'll be there at sunrise Easter
morning.

Sincerely and with much Love,
Marcus

I re-read the email a couple of times. As I do, I feel a slight shift inside, a
little lighter. Freer. I'm starting to understand why it's called, Good
Friday. And with that, I press, *Send.*

***

It's a glorious Easter morn. Sunlight is just now hitting the grass and
weeds, trees and shelters. Rays of light shimmer through my breath as I
exhale into the cool morning air. The Orange-tent-guy is nowhere to be
found. We sit on a stump and wait. It's unusually quiet. Little traffic
buzzing by at 6:30 a.m. Easter Sunday morning. Shanice and Malik are
surprisingly subdued. Tired I'm sure but also intrigued by the whole
excursion. Gives me time to think. How did I get here? Why did I end up
in this unbelievable predicament? Does any of it matter? Why do I care
so much about getting to the truth of things? I have come to no
conclusions after 40 minutes of waiting. So, I give up. I stand, take a
deep breath. Feel the warmth on my face one last time and… a figure

appears. I can't make it out at first but then, "Jesus! Hey. I'm so glad to see you."

"Well, it is *my* day," he says jocularly, "Figured I'd make an appearance, at least."

"I was just about to leave. No one else is here." It's awkward. I haven't seen Jesus in a long time. Since the, *last supper,* at Janet's house when they nearly hung tied me. But, I'm more than glad to see him.

"Oh," he says assuredly, "They're right behind me."

And, on cue, several cars appear. Jesus' wife, Valentina, pulls up in their van with several family members. Jesus' brother and his wife, and a few more I have never met. Tom and Jamaal pull up. A car is following them with two of their friends, Jacob and John. Michelle, formally known as Michael, has got three friends with her. Adara has brought a couple of people from her mosque and, to my great surprise Janet, Kathy, and Luke show up with a few other employees of Nike and one of Kathy's friends, another reiki master.

I'm speechless. Everyone gathers near without a word. After looking into each of their eyes, I address the group. "Thank you so much for coming and at least considering a *not so* random act of kindness. I have nothing against random acts of kindness. As many of you know, I take part often. However, there's generally little personal sacrifice involved. But the story of this day is one of real sacrifice and the idea that through sacrifice there is a kind of resurrection. A transformation. And that is what I offer us today. Now, we could debate the possibility that everyone living under these disheveled shelters is equally deserving of a handout. If that is your stance, I'm happy to have that conversation with you, another day. However, over the last few months, I have spent a lot of time here. And it has changed my life. So, before I introduce you to my friend, I invite every one of you, in your way, to give thanks for the blessings in your life. We are truly blessed. First, blessed just to be alive for the most prosperous time in history and blessed to have work that contributes to the world - and profoundly blessed to live in the freest country ever conceived. One thing that makes this country so great is criticism. The constitution protects freedom of speech. Therefore, we may criticize our leaders, our laws, our traditions and anything else we wish. But sometimes, in all the criticism we forget what an honor and privilege it is to be an American. The most giving country in the history of the world and it is in that tradition we meet here today. So, I offer this moment to you to simply give thanks."

I close my eyes. Take a deep breath and do my gratitude review. I think of my children. My friendship with Orange-tent-guy. My work which provides a good living. I give thanks for my friends that have shown up today and even my wife who will soon be my ex. I'm undecided on the whole idea of a "higher power," God or whatever you wish to call it. But I'm very clear that something amazing is happening. Life! And so I give thanks to life itself. The air I breathe, the grass, the weeds, the trees, the birds in the sky, and anything and everything that caused this miracle. It's amazing how quickly a moment of gratitude can raise one's spirits. I open my eyes and again I'm deeply touched. Everyone's eyes, including my kids', are closed. Kathy is crying. Jesus is smiling. Michelle is weeping.

"Okay," I whisper, "Please, follow me."

In solemn silence, we begin the short walk to the tent. I stand at the opening, "Hello? Are you there? Hello?"

"Yes?" comes from within.

"Cynthia, it's, *Can't Sit on a Bucket Guy*. Do you remember me?"

First, everyone looks bewildered. Then we hear a chuckle from inside the blue tarp, "Yes, I do. I'm so glad you came again."

It's not the first time I have visited her. It's just that, sometimes she remembers and sometimes she doesn't. "I have friends with me that would like to meet you. Would you mind stepping out? There's too many of us to come in."

"Give me a minute; I want to straighten up."

"Of course."

Everyone remains quiet. So still.

I have visited many Holy places including the Bodhi tree in India, the Via de la Rosa in Israel, and sacred burial grounds the world over. And yet, somehow this ground, this Easter moment feels as sacred as any.

After a minute or two, she exits the tarp. The morning sun is directly in her eyes. The milky cloud that makes up her pupils is emotionally jarring. Most of them are so touched, maybe even disturbed, they physically adjust to cope.

"Everybody, this is my friend, Cynthia."

Everyone randomly responds, "Hello Cynthia," "Hi Cynthia," "It's wonderful to meet you," "We're glad we could be here on Easter morning."

"It's Easter?" She asks excitedly.

Malik answers "Yep, it is."

"Oh, I love Easter. Here, look, these are my children."

She pulls out the crinkled image of her family. She shows it every time I visit. While it gets passed around the group, she reveals more about her story than even I know. "Before the boys died, the Easter bunny put a basket of goodies at the kid's bedroom doors. Then we would get dressed up and go to church. I remember us all singing songs like *Oh Happy Day* and *Amazing Grace.* Then we would have an Easter egg hunt. C.J. would go crazy, running around, trying to get all of them before his brother or sister…."

Suddenly she stopped. You could feel the untold volumes of her story. When the photo found its way back, she accounted, "I miss them so much." I slowly handed her the photo. She turned toward me, "So very much." She took it in her hands and rubbed it with her thumbs as if there were braille on the image so she could remember what they look like. After a few moments of rubbing the photo, she gave it back to me, "Have you seen my children?"

"Yes Cynthia, they are beautiful," I tell her as I return the photo. "Cynthia, I'm going to speak to my friends for a moment and then I'll be back, okay?"

"Okay," she replies with a big grin, looking around to locate the sound of my voice. "I'll be right here."

I wave my arm to signal everyone to follow me toward the orange tent. Orange-tent-guy is nowhere to be found. I was hoping to introduce them to him as well. Another time perhaps. "So, here's the opportunity. We can choose right now to truly have an impact on a life in a way bigger than we could probably ever know. First, she needs cataract surgery. That's about five grand. But that's just the tip of the iceberg; she has dementia, I surmise. She probably doesn't have much time left. But I would love to make whatever time she has, comfortable. She needs care. That will be another five grand a month. Between all of us, if we're all in, that's about $350 a month. But it doesn't stop there. Each of us commits to going to see her once a month. She has no one. You can go in groups or solo. Whatever you want. If you don't want to take part, no judgment, no guilt! What do you say?"

Janet speaks up first, "I'm willing to do a thousand a month and a thousand toward surgery."

"Okay, everyone else's average just went down."

One of Jamaal's friends goes next, "I'm happy to give $100 a month, but that is all I can do right now."

"Okay, great."

My daughter, Shanice pipes up, "I can give five dollars a month, you know, from my chores."

Soon, we had a commitment of some level, from everyone there. Enough to take care of Cynthia. As we walked toward the blue tarp, I thought I saw the Orange-tent-guy across the freeway, maybe smiling. But when I shifted my gaze to see, the image was gone.

I had done research and found a place just in case this scheme worked. "Cynthia, can you come with us? We have a better place for you to live if you want."

"What? REALLY?" she exclaimed. "What do you mean?"

"We have a place for you. A place with food and care and we're going to visit you. We also think you can get your eyesight back with minor surgery. We're setting it up now."

"What? *Are you for real?*" she said scanning the group with her hands out in front of her.

Malik answered, "Yep, we're real. *We're right here.*" Then she stepped forward and placed her hand on his head. Eyes that do not see can still perform an important function. Cry. She wept as she touched each face. She also showed us that tears could be contagious.

"If there's anything you need. Let's get it now," I told her.

She reached in her pocket and pulled out the old photo, "Just this," she whispered, "Just this."

Chapter 19 The Future: *Game Over*
Year: 2047 April 26, Good Friday 6:53 p.m.

"Marcus, you and Charles are asking too many questions." He continues with that monster like disguised voice, *"You **do** understand, we let them live today. Next time, they won't be so merciful. Now, I suggest you shut the door. We don't want to wake her."* I gently shut my office door. The Man-In-Black is right. I do not want to wake her. I pace. What do you do when you know they have beaten you. I'm trying to control my anger because I know they can crush me and everyone I love. But there is a part of me that doesn't care. If the Man-In-Black was actually in my room this time, I don't know that I could stop myself from trying to kill him.

"You win, we get it. Game over. And if you want to kill me, go ahead. Truth is, I sometimes want to kill myself. Stricken with the choice between the absolute surety you will kill the ones I love, and the likelihood of global disaster, has been tearing me apart."

No matter how many times I hear it, the harshness of the disguised, monster-like voice disturbs my soul, **"As I said before, you think I'm a monster. *You think I don't care.* But the truth is, I'm just doing what I have to do. *You think I didn't have to make a choice?* That's the problem these days, *too many choices.* Marcus, it's not how I want things to be, but one more slip up from you or Charles and Alexus and Jadda will die. *Do you understand?"***

I so want to punch his lights out I nearly swing at the hologram, "I got it. I got it. Trust me; *I got it.*"

The Man-In-Black disappears. But there is something he said, something familiar but out of place. I crawl into bed with Alexus, exhausted. I begin to fall asleep. It's in that twilight state, somewhere between dreaming and conscious thought, I realize who *The Man-In-Black might be*. A quick internet search would confirm it. But I'm afraid to use my phone or computer. So, I gently crawl out of bed as to not wake Alexus, thankful I do not have an iMind implant. I climb in my Ford Freedom, disengage auto drive and head to the nearest Apple store. The latest gadgets are always on display. And in a matter of moments, with a quick search, I confirm my suspicion.

The Dawn: *The Blind Will See*
Year: 2017 June 1 11:00 a.m.

It's an exciting day, *and* one of the worst days of my life. Exciting because Cynthia had her cataract surgery a few days ago. They're going to remove her eye patches today. Many of us are here at the assisted living center to see her, or better yet, *she will see us.*

"Okay Cynthia," the nurse says with excitement, "It's time to remove those patches. Are you ready?"

She sits up in anticipation, "Oh my gosh, I'm so ready."

"Okay, your eyes will be a little sensitive to the light at first but don't worry, that will pass." He gently peels away the patches. I'm hoping today is a very lucid day for her. Seems to be so far. Once the patches are off, Cynthia slowly opens her eyes to see me for the first time, "Hello Cynthia, why, you have beautiful green eyes!"

"Marcus? You never told me you were so handsome." She reaches out and takes my hand as the tears form.

"It's true," Malik says, sidling right up to her chair, leaning within inches of her face, "You do. You do have beautiful green eyes."

"Thank you. And you are?"

"I'm Malik, Marcus and Kathy's son."

"It's a pleasure to meet you, Malik."

It's been two months now since Kathy moved out yet, it's still very uncomfortable to be in the same room with her. But, for the kids, we do our best. I give Cynthia a gentle squeeze of her hand, "I would like you to meet, officially, some other people who are helping to make all of this possible."

Some take her hand; some hug her. As they do, I realize, Orange-tent-guy was right. This whole process, of giving, of focusing on someone else's needs instead of wallowing in pity *has* pulled me out of my depression/

breakdown. It's also helped the kids through their process. And, I understand at a deeper level than ever, *you cannot assign compassion.*

Once our time is complete, Kathy takes the kids for the rest of the day, so I decided to see Orange-tent-guy. I haven't had much time to see him lately with all the crazy in my life. As I'm heading toward my car, I nearly run into Janet who's parked right next to me. I'm trying so hard not to be filled with anger toward her and Kathy. I've got to forget and forgive to free myself from the festering poison of hatred. Grudges do nothing to the person you hate. They're just self-inflicted suffering. So, instead of ignoring her, I approached her to thank her for her great support of Cynthia. As I approach, I try to formulate my words. It is awkward of course. However, before I open my mouth, she speaks, "There's nothing you can do to change our minds."

I'm caught off guard, "I, I don't want to change your minds." I have no intention of trying to win Kathy back or sabotage their relationship.

"Good, because we have made up our minds. She is *not* keeping the baby."

Chapter 20 The Future: *The Paris Climate Accord*
Year: 2047 April 26, Good Friday 6:53 p.m.

Sitting here in the Apple store, my mind completely blown by what I have just discovered, I'm suddenly reminded of how this journey started. It was early summer, probably June 2017 just as I was coming out of a nervous breakdown. It was one of those crazy combative conversations I had with, well, The Orange-tent-guy. Trump had just pulled us out of the Paris Climate Accord which had me and millions of others in a state of panic. I came to him and said something like, *Have you heard the news? Trump pulled out of the Paris Agreement today! What a nightmare. A President that does not believe in science! We've got to fight climate change. Our children's future depends on it.* That was the moment! His reaction changed my life. Challenged me. Put me on a path of true discovery that ultimately revealed; *I was right in the first place. We must fight climate change.* However, there are two ways to reach any conclusion. One is to react emotionally, without understanding the issue. This is like flipping a coin. You might get lucky. Your emotions and the group-think that forced your conclusions, might be right. Or, you stand an equal chance of being dead wrong. On the other hand, instead of just reacting, we can do the work; the research necessary to come to our conclusions honestly, with facts. In this way not only do we find the truth but it is the only way we can be part of the solution because there is no way to find real answers *if we don't understand the root cause of the problem.* The Orange-tent-guy shocked me into doing the research when he said, *Oh my friend. But the science isn't settled....*

The Dawn: *31,487 Scientists agree*
Year: 2017 June 1 11:13 a.m.

By the time I reach the homeless camp I'm in shock. Cynthia's patch removal was one of the most real, powerful moments of my life. But then to find, *Kathy is pregnant!?* On the same day, *Trump decides to end the world?*

"Hey! You in there?" I say, poking on the thin material.

"'Pends on who's askin'."

"You know very well who's askin'."

"No, I don't. Could be Prius Driving/About To Have A Nervous Breakdown Guy. Or, could be, Getting Over Himself/New Over Guy."

"Does it matter?"

"A lot. I'm not in the mood for Nervous Break Down Guy. He's getting boring. Enough pity party already."

"Well, I'm pretty upset, but I think it's, *Getting over himself/New over Guy.*"

"Great, I'll be out in a minute. Just finishing up some…."

"… Research? I know."

Moments later he steps out kinda preoccupied with his iPad. I have to ask, "Just what is it you are always researching?"

"Pretty much everything and anything. *Truth.* There's no end to my curiosity since heroin and alcohol stopped sucking the marrow of my soul. I think I'm near, well, done."

"Done? With what?"

"How's life?" He says ignoring my question.

"Well, great and awful."

"Sounds perfect."

"I followed your advice and did something, 'unselfishly' for someone else."

"Blue-tarp-guy… I mean Gal," He says matter-of-factly.

"Yes. You know?"

"Yeah, I knew you would help her. It was by design. So, in a sense, I'm the one that helped her," he says, looking for a reaction.

"Really?"

"Uh huh. Your heart's always been in the right place, just needed a little course correction. I course corrected your heart."

"Hmmm. I'm not sure if I should feel grateful or manipulated."

"Feel both," he said putting his hand on my shoulder and smiling, "So, why do you feel awful?"

I'm not ready to talk about Kathy's pregnancy, so I go with nightmare number one, "Have you heard the news? Trump pulled out of the Paris Agreement today! What a nightmare. A President that does not believe in science! *We've got to fight climate change. Our children's future depends on it.*"

"Oh, my friend. But the science *isn't* settled," He says matter-of-factly. I can feel my heart begin to race like someone just shot a gun at the starting line.

"*Of course it is.* Obama said so. And there are many scientific *peer-reviewed* papers on the subject."

    ⊚ Obama on climate change <u>trumped.online/xx3</u> ⊚
⊚ Thatcher on fossil fuels/nuclear power <u>trumped.online/vw7</u> ⊚

"The topic has become politicized which always infects and erodes science. It started with Margaret Thatcher in the '70s. She was looking for a way to push for nuclear power and making a demon out of fossil fuels served her agenda. On the shoulders of Thatcher and Gore, Obama knew he could rally his base by echoing their claims. Never mind the fact that 'peer review' is losing its credibility more every day. Simply put, the science is not settled. Not by a long shot. The single largest scientifically endorsed petition to the government on climate change is opposed to the idea that human activity is the main cause and was circulated by Arthur B. Robinson, president of the Oregon Institute of Science and Medicine, Check it out."

He pulled up the document on his iPad for me to read.

> We urge the United States government to reject the
> global warming agreement that was written in
> Kyoto, Japan in December 1997 and any other
> similar proposals. The proposed limits on
> greenhouse gases would harm the environment,

> hinder the advance of science and technology and
> damage the health and welfare of humanity. There is
> no convincing scientific evidence that human
> release of carbon dioxide, methane or other
> greenhouse gases is causing or will in the
> foreseeable future cause catastrophic heating of the
> earth's atmosphere and disruption of earth's
> climate. Moreover, there is substantial scientific
> evidence that increases in atmospheric carbon
> dioxide produce many beneficial effects upon the
> natural plant and animal environments of the earth.

"31,487 scientists signed this. Over 9,000 had Ph.D.'s," he states without emotion.

In contrast, while reading it, I feel somehow angry. But why? "That can't be real."

"It's real."

31,487 scientists <u>trumped.online/8if</u>

"Wait, I think I've heard of this. Isn't this the petition that has signatures like Mickey Mouse and Luke Skywalker?"

"It did at one time because those on the other side of the debate hacked the site and tried to discredit it by adding such names. It's unfortunate they went right to sabotage instead of scientific debate. Still, it is pretty funny. I'll give them that. Charles Darwin and the Spice Girls were on it as well. Anyway, all the fake endorsements have been removed."

My heart racing, defensively, *"So, you think climate change is fake?"*

"Of course not. No one thinks climate change is fake."

"Yes, they do!" I say raising my voice.

"No. No one thinks climate change doesn't exist. The scientific debate is focused on the cause. Any scientist or any layperson willing to do the research, like me, knows the earth's climate has and will always change. We, like every living thing on the earth, will have to adjust to those changes."

Again, I respond with anger. This is a passion of mine, "So, *you don't think humans are causing climate change?"*

"Again, I did not say that. I am simply stating a fact. The science is not settled. The debate is not over. That is a fact. Just ask all the scientists who signed the petition and many more."

"But Trump, what an idiot. I mean, okay, even if humans aren't the main cause, it can't hurt anything to fight it."

"It does," he says, gauging my reaction. He can tell this is all very upsetting as he poses what seemed like an obvious question, "Let me ask you this. Do you believe every human life is of equal value?"

"Of course."

"So, you don't think people in developed nations are superior to those in third world countries?"

"Of course not."

"Okay. Did you know every year millions of people in third world countries die from extreme temperatures and lung cancer because developed nations will not allow them to use fossil fuels to control the 'climate' within their dwellings, *as we do?"* Then he grins, "Not me of course," he points at his tent. "If you and the legions of those like you are truly serious and believe we are doomed, *you really should take up urban camping like me.* My carbon footprint is nonexistent. It appears to me that those in your movement are not willing to make any real sacrifices. You want everyone and everything else to change, but you're not willing to, *Be the change,* in the words of Gandhi. You want your heat in the winter and cool in the summer. You want to cook on electric or gas burning stoves and turn on your computers and fly in planes and drive cars."

"I drive a Prius!"

His face cracks, trying to hold back laughter.

"Wow, *now you're virtue signaling your car.* You feel superior, better than those who drive gas cars as opposed to your hybrid. Never mind that electricity burns coal. But why don't you drive an all-electric car?"

"I would, but I can't afford a Tesla. Soon, however, the technology will make them affordable, and I will be the first in line to buy one."

"What will you do with Prius?"

"Sell it."

"Oh my naïve, first world, shame-ridden friend. All of your guilt is only making things worse. Studies have shown, and it's only logical, that if you're concerned about emissions, the best thing to do is keep the car you have, whatever it is, and drive it until it doesn't drive anymore. Otherwise, you're just building more cars which takes a massive amount of energy. Electric cars are very controversial, anyway. Many say because they take much more energy to build and batteries themselves are difficult to manage, they end up polluting more than most gas cars. It's also interesting to note that two-thirds of all pollution from driving has nothing to do with the energy source. It's the production of roads, road surfaces wearing down, debris from car brakes and tires and other sneaky ignored inconvenient facts."

Are electric cars green? trumped.online/o7t
Adam Ruins Everything cars trumped.online/3ic

I don't like what I'm hearing. But I have to wrestle with the possibility that my discomfort, even my anger, might stem from my ego. An ego attached to an identity, my sense of self as a climate change warrior. I mean, what if driving a Prius *is* no better than any other car? Or, what if driving a Prius is worse because I sold my other car, which ran perfectly fine, to buy a Prius creating more stuff to discard, ultimately? If what he is suggesting is true, I would have to come to terms with a life of living in a way that is exactly the opposite of what I intended and preached to anyone who would listen. I would have to come to terms with the idea that maybe some redneck in Arkansas who drives an old pickup truck that gets 12 miles per gallon is doing more for the environment than me!

Of all the things he has said, the idea that fighting climate change could be killing millions of people in third world countries is weighing heavy on my soul. "So, you said fighting climate change is killing millions of people, I don't believe that. And even if I did, if we don't fight climate change, billions will die."

"Again, the talking point that billions will die if we don't fight climate change is *not* settled science. *It may be true.* It may also be true that

there's nothing we can do about climate change. That is one argument
with much scientific backing. Let me put it like this. Many say
catastrophic climate change is happening, *but no one knows for sure.* The
computer models, projections based upon our scientific understanding of
the climate, have been so wrong it should embarrass all 'scientists' that
created them. And yet we continue to use those models to create policies
as if they were correct. Cuckoo! What we know for sure is that because
of our commitment to fight climate change, we will not allow third world
countries the technology to use fossil fuels. As a result, they burn down
their forests to heat their homes and cook their food. They are not, by the
way, replanting their forests as we do. The smoke gets in their lungs and
the lungs of their children causing asthma and lung cancer. If that doesn't
kill them, the extreme heat and extreme cold do. And, what many do not
understand is, *cold is the real killer.* Ice ages are devastating and come
and go throughout history."

Climate conference interview trumped.online/7od

Are climate models flawed? trumped.online/2ai

I see red, *"But fossil fuels are BAD!"* I yell.

"Okay, I can see your sense of self is wrapped up in being a climate
change warrior. Your emotions are keeping you from hearing another
side. Let me be clear. I am not saying climate change isn't real. But,
remember, no one is saying that. Also, I'm not saying we shouldn't do
anything about it. I'm simply pointing out to you the other side of the
argument. But if you're unable to listen, we should stop this conversation
now."

I pride myself in being open-minded. Over the last few months, I have
changed my mind more often than the channels on a Sunday afternoon
when the man of the house is in charge of the remote. But this topic has
put me over the edge. I realize much of my emotions right now are
misdirected toward Orange-tent-guy. I'm taking my frustration and shock
around Kathy's pregnancy out on him. So, I take a deep breath and try to
gain my composure, "No, please continue."

"Are you sure you can handle it?"

"Yes, I can handle it."

"Okay, as far as fossil fuels being 'bad.' Maybe they are. But using the
word bad is bringing us back into the world of *black and white;*

remember everything is gray. I hope you can see I am undecided on this topic. I remain open-minded so I might find deeper and deeper truths."

He pauses for a moment to collect his thoughts.

"If someone invented a pill that cured cancer, all of humanity would celebrate the achievement, the lives saved, the suffering eased. However, when we look back in history, because of the demonization of fossil fuels, no one celebrates the Industrial Revolution as the miracle life saver it was and is today. Since the Industrial Revolution climate caused deaths dropped over 90% *because of fossil fuels* and the ability they have given us to control the climate in our homes. Countless millions, possibly even billions of lives have been saved by *fossil fuels.* And, make the connection. If scientists had not discovered fossil fuels, untold numbers would have died. Among those untold numbers could have been your great grandparents. Which means, *you and your parents would've never existed.* So now, I ask you, *are fossil fuels bad?*"

The cognitive dissonance rattling around in my brain is so acute it's giving me a headache. I ignore his question, "Okay, as for the people in third world countries who need energy, can't we just give them solar panels?"

"They have tried, and it simply doesn't work, for many reasons. First, do you think everyone in a third world country lives where the sun always shines? No. Second, solar panels, relative to fossil fuels, are so inefficient it's like comparing the power of King Kong to that of a nat. The technology just isn't there."

"But look at Germany and all they have accomplished," I say as if I'm giving my closing argument to a jury. "I have seen it, I have been there. They are leading the world in their use of solar and wind power."

"Okay, thank you, you're making my point for me. Germany is currently one of the largest developers of coal energy in the world. What do you think of them apples?"

"I think them apples is crazy."

"I would say, *you's crazy!* More accurately, uninformed. All of their efforts to go 'green' are suspect. Without fossil fuels, they cannot support the country's needs. Germany is now Europe's largest producer, and burner of coal and around 25% of it is what's called 'brown coal,' among the dirtiest of all fossil fuels. Germany mines *more of it than any other country in the world."*

Germany and Coal trumped.online/b8z
Germany's Coal addiction trumped.online/kvp

I feel like an adolescent realizing for the first time that fairy tales are just that, *tales.* I mean, I used to tout Germany, constantly, as the ultimate example of what America should be. Clinging to my paradigm, I ask, "But you admit that you don't know, right? You admit it's possible that the best thing we could do is fight climate change, right?"

"Yes. Like I said, my mind is open, I'm trying to find the truth. And the truth is, it's very gray."

"Okay, then shouldn't Trump just stay in the Paris Climate Accord? I mean won't the sincere effort that every other country is putting into the agreement help us find the truth?"

"Have you read the Paris Climate Accord? Have you studied it?"

He has me cornered. Squeamish. I have never even peeked at it. I have no idea what it says, "Ah, well. No."

I can tell he is a little disturbed. Then, he indirectly reads me the riot act, "You see, that right there is what pisses me off. People become so righteous, and the Paris Accord is a perfect example. They'll march in the streets for 'science' on Earth Day, and they lose their lunch because Trump took us out of the Paris Accord. Then they march more with homemade signs that say things like, *We can't afford, to leave the Accord* and *I can't believe I'm protesting for reality.* They do all of this, but they will not take one day, *one single day,* to study it. That is a kind of insanity. They hear little talking points on biased news channels from reporters who *have not studied the Accord.* Of course, everyone may say whatever they want. However, in my opinion, no matter what the issue, if you have not done your homework, you have no moral right to be preaching. We're talking about creating policies that affect billions of lives, and people won't take a single day to understand what they're protesting. They will, however, take several days out of their lives in protest. *It's pathetic. It's virtue signaling at its lowest."*

We both stand there, quietly, in the aftermath of his rant. Finally, he shakes his head a little and states, "Phew, okay, I'm glad I got that off my chest."

"Well, I for one am guilty. Have we, I, gotten so lazy and obsessed with looking virtuous that we'll spend countless hours doing what's politically correct, virtue signaling, marching, posting on Facebook but we won't invest a little time exploring the facts so we might be an informed voice?"

"Yes, I believe that is how lazy many have become and that laziness is dangerous. If you're going to get involved, get informed."

I can't argue with that, "Who are we, as a country, if we vote, protest, and rattle around virtuously in a state of perpetual ignorance? What is that going to get us?"

"It will get us into trouble. Did you know, to join the Paris Accord all a country has to do is send in a piece of paper saying they are joining the Paris Accord? That's it. You don't even have to mention greenhouse gases or anything about limiting emissions. Then, they staple all the pieces of paper together, and they say, *look, the Paris Accord*. What a paltry display of virtue signaling. The countries in the Paris Accord have pledged to do exactly what they were already doing or *even less* so that there's no way for them to fall short of their commitment. It is a joke, a fraud. And when I say they pledge to do exactly what they were doing; what they were doing was *not* trying to limit greenhouse gas emissions. They were doing whatever was best energy wise for their country. And then they just wrote that down on a piece of paper and sent it in. It would be like me and you and a bunch of other guys making a 'commitment' to our health by coming together and each writing on a piece of paper the number of calories we promise to *never exceed* on our diet. Boy, it sure would look like a commitment to our health, and we could talk about it virtuously. But what if I wrote, *I promise never to exceed 4,500 calories per day*. If you haven't studied calorie intake, it might impress you. Then, once you did the research, you would find the average man needs approximately 2,500 calories per day to *maintain their current weight*. Suddenly, you would realize that at 4,500 calories per day, my commitment would be never to gain over 9 or 10 pounds per month. *Boy, I'm sure committed to my health!*"

"I see the deception. But if that's what the Paris accord is, why did Trump pullout."

"America was the only country to make a financially excessive, detrimental commitment to the accord. To meet our pledge, it would cost a *trillion dollars a year.* For much less than that, we could give healthcare, an education, clean drinking water, eliminate malaria *and* create sanitary living conditions for every person on the planet."

"Sheesh, why don't we just do that?"

"Well, I would say it's because climate change has become a religion with the same kind of fervor and shaming that comes along with some religious thought. There are those who maintain that all who do not hold their same religious beliefs will feel the heat for their misguided thinking in hell. Global warming fundamentalists maintain that all who do not follow *their* beliefs, their dogma, will also feel the heat. There will be gnashing of teeth in hell on earth. And, again, the Obama Administration's level of commitment just might have been a trillion dollar virtue signal to the American voters. Some who have studied this at MIT said if we stuck to our commitment to the Paris Accord it might, *might* lower the temperature by 0.02 percent of a single Celsius by the year 2100. *For a trillion dollars a year.* Also, stoking fear and then claiming you have the answer is a great strategy for raising funds and gettin' votes."

"So," I say shifting the subject slightly, "What would you tell people like me who take part in the march for 'science'? I mean there is much scientific evidence backing the idea that climate change is coming and we're to blame."

"I would say the march for 'science' is unscientific!"

"What?"

"The basis of science is to come up with a hypothesis, like, for example, *The polar ice caps will be ice-free during the summer months in five to seven years.* If you were to come to that conclusion based on scientific evidence, then, to continue the scientific approach, *you ask to be proven wrong!* But, in the scientific community, because global warming has become more like a religion, they call you a 'denier' just for questioning the hypothesis and in doing so the scientific process is shut down. By the way, Al Gore predicted back in 2009 that in five to seven years the ice caps would be completely gone in summer months. Well, that was almost nine years ago now, have you looked at a satellite image lately? Not only are the ice caps still there but *polar bears are thriving.* The whole 'save the polar bears' narrative was a ploy to pull our heartstrings, guilt and shame us into believing that unscientific claim."

"So," I begin, trying to suppress my anger, "You don't believe the caps are melting?"

"I didn't say that. I said they *have not melted!* That is a fact. It's also a fact that Al Gore was wrong in his prediction. That said, I'm quite sure the caps will melt."

"What?" I react, shaking my head.

"Remember, *gray.* To say the ice caps will not melt would be living in denial of Earth's natural history. It would be like saying there will never be another earthquake."

After I wrap my brain around the obvious, I push a little, "But why then do so many scientists continue to support the narrative of anthropogenic global warming if the science isn't settled?"

"Well, there are several reasons. First, once you have taken a stance, based your reputation on it, it's very hard to admit you were wrong. Add to that your financial life, and it becomes nearly impossible. They have given billions of dollars in government grants to prove that anthropogenic climate change is real. *Billions every year.* They give zero government funds to prove that climate change is a natural part of the Earth's cycles. So, if you want to put your kids through college, you must continue to prove, *whatever they want you to prove,* to pay the bills."

"Follow the money?"

⚭ Follow the climate money <u>trumped.online/l9q</u> ⚭

"Yep. If you're a scientist and you're passionate about the mating habits of the North American Ferret, good luck getting a grant to study your passion. However, if you submit a proposal entitled, *How Climate Change is Affecting the Mating Habits of the North American Ferret,* you'll be rolling in grant money. Your personal feelings about climate change are irrelevant. You know if you want to get paid you must get in line, be a part of the group-think. Then, to keep the money flowing you must prove, which is easy to do when you are biased, that climate change is affecting the mating habits of the ferret, eventually leading to their extinction. *And who doesn't love ferrets?"*

"Hey, I have to admit, I love me some ferrets!" My mind is reeling with all the 'facts' I thought I knew, on climate change. There's one thing left that I know is undeniable. "You have to admit, for sure, that Co2 is the cause of the warming we have seen. Gore proved this in *An Inconvenient Truth*. Remember the graphs? Whenever Co2 increases, the temperature increases. This is a part of Earth's history, as you say." I've got him on this!

"EEEEEAEEE"

Not the buzzer sound!

"Wrong. That was one of the most shameful aspects of his *Inconvenient Truth*. It's quite the opposite. I'm not saying Co2 isn't a greenhouse gas, but the truth is *every time the temperature increases, Co2 is released into the atmosphere*. It's the opposite of what he claimed. Temperature rise comes first, not Co2! This Proves CO2 is not the cause of temperature rise."

∞Al Gore Busted <u>trumped.online/lh8</u> ∞

"Okay, now you're talking crazy talk."

"I'll give you some crazy talk. We exist because of climate change!"

"Huh?"

"Yes. If the Pleistocene period did not give way to a warming trend that created the current Holocene period, humans would not be here. It is in the 'womb' of global warming that we were birthed. Thank God for climate change."

"Dude, you're so full of it!" I extol, shaking my head.

"Yes, I am. Full of IT! The *Incredible Truth*. Join me, won't you? Get out of your group-think bubble and do a little research. You may find that Margaret Thatcher was right. Nuclear power is the answer; generation four! I gotta get back to it."

∞ Scott Adams Nuclear <u>trumped.online/k4c</u> ∞

"Nuclear!? Sheesh. Okay Mr. *Incredible Truth,* I'll see you soon."

"What will be, will be." He says shrugging shoulders, "Maybe you'll see me, maybe you won't."

"Well, that's cryptic. By the way, are you ever going to tell me your real name?"

"Maybe someday, if I see you again. Maybe even if I don't."

"Okay, that makes no sense. Now you're just creeping me out. My name is Marcus, Marcus Jacobs."

"Farewell." And with that, he ducked into the orange tent.

I begin the short walk to my car with a pit in my stomach. If global warming isn't the level ten catastrophe I have always believed, I should be ecstatic. So, why is it so hard to hear climate change *might* not be the end of the world? Suddenly I remember something called, *Climate Gate.*

They caught some top scientists changing the historical temperature data to create the illusion of increased temperature. I never believed it. But maybe it's true. So, I turn around and head back for one last word, "Hey, Orange-tent-guy." No response. *"Hey, I just have a quick question,"* I yell in the general direction of the front zipper of his tent. "Hey, what's up in there?" Finally, I unzip the tent. He's gone.

Chapter 21 The Future: *Faux-cahontas*
Year: 2047 April 26, Good Friday 7:59 p.m.

While leaving the Apple store, I try to think of a way to reach Charles without tipping our hand to the Man-In-Black. I have an idea to encode a text, hoping he'll understand.

> *Hey, going to St. Mary's Cathedral 9 a.m. Easter service. Join?*
> *I'll never forget the time u failed to turn your phone off!*

I've only been there once before in my life. One Christmas. I don't think Charles has ever been. Moments later…

> *Perfect, this time I won't forget to turn my phone off.*
> *How embarrassing! Rule #1 :-)*

I figure a drone, or any technology for that matter, would be incapable of hearing us Easter morning in a giant Cathedral during Mass.

I grab a pew at the very back as people pour in wearing their Easter best. Charles arrives moments after me. I've brought a pen and a small pad of paper for times when it will be inappropriate to talk. Which, unfortunately, occurs right away. They begin praying with some kind of call and response. I have no idea what's happening.

"So, what's going on?" Charles asks in a loud whisper. Right away a woman in front of us turns, "Shhhhhhh!" Finger on lips. So I get out my pad and write.

I know who the Man-In-Black is

"What?" He whispers, "Who?"

You have to trust me

He nods his head affirmatively as if to say, *of course*. He watches the pad as I spell it out.

SHELLY!

Charles forgets where he is as the word explodes from his lips.

"*WHAT?*" echoes off the stone walls and the infinitely high ceilings.

"SHHHHHHHHHHHH" several people chime in.

Everyone stands to sing. A moment for us to whisper in the last pew.

"I know. It seems crazy. But, think about it. What did she bring to the dinner party the other night?"

He whispered back as the thousand plus people continue singing hymns of death and joy…Easter!

"Well, the ingredients for cookies."

"What did she bring to make the cookies?"

"A, a rolling pin."

"Don't you find that a little strange, considering we had just made 'rolling pin' our code word for, *The Man-In-Black is here,* which made it difficult for us to carry out our plan?"

"A coincidence. That's all. Come on."

"Okay, the Man-In-Black appeared Friday and warned me that if we ask any more questions, big trouble!"

"Okay… and?"

"And he said during our interaction, *That's the problem these days, too many choices.* Who do we know who says that all the time?'"

"Well, Shelly. But still, coincidence… "

"What are the chances? First, *rolling pin,* then, *too many choices.* Also, every time I saw the Man-In-Black, Shelly conveniently left the room. Not just the room but she went outside. A place she could use her car to holographically project."

"Hmmm. Well. But… the Man-In-Black is a man!"

"I know. It appears that way, but they disguise the voice. And, think about it. Shelly is 5'11", and a taekwondo master."

"Hmmm," Charles considers, "Also, whenever holographing you *can* manipulate your image. It's illegal to do so since the Accurate Imagery Act of 2037. Remember that? Some got offended by the altered holographic images people were using. A white guy liked to holograph as a Zulu warrior, but it offended some people since he was white. He argued that it should be okay because he identified as Zulu. Then there was a woman, Elizabeth Warren was her name I believe. She was a senator and a presidential hopeful for the Democratic Party. She claimed she was Cherokee and used that claim to further her academic and political career. She even submitted a recipe to a Native American cookbook called **Pow Wow Chow**! After much goading from Trump, who called her Faux-cahontas, she finally took a DNA test that proved... *she was lying!* It showed she *might* be approximately 1/1,024 Native American. *That's less than the average European American!* But she still tried to use the test results to prove she was Cherokee! Even after the Cherokee Nation came forward and brutally denounced her. However, it did not stop her from holographing as Cherokee. She wanted her lie to be real so bad; she finally refused to go anywhere in person. Instead, she would holograph as a Cherokee Medicine Woman. Everywhere, all the time. Even once the Accurate Imagery Act of 2037 was passed, ironically, by liberals like her. After being reported for inaccurate cultural representation seventeen different times, she was finally persecuted and spent the rest of her days in jail. She passed away in 2043. Her dying request was to be buried in full Native American attire, headdress and all. But the Cherokee Nation would not allow it. They said it would be a disgrace upon their ancestors. Anyway, altering programming has been illegal now for about ten years, but if you're a brilliant programmer... And, that is why she was hired at G.P."

Elizabeth Warren lie trumped.online/8iz

Suddenly, the music stopped. Everyone sat down, and then stood up again, and then back down. Not sure what's going on, but I get my pad out.

Here's the kicker, did you know she got promoted to a VP position last month?

This time he mouthed it enormously, "*WHAT?*"

Yep, and really, who has more to lose than G.P?

He whispers, "Oh My God, I think you're right."

We need to tell Alexus and Jadda. But I don't know how without endangering them. We must think of a way

Charles nods big. Eyes wide.

Then, get The Man-In-Black. SHELLY!

The Dawn: *Life or Choice?*
Year: 2017 June 2 8:13 a.m.

I realize now the main reason I went to see Orange-tent-guy yesterday was to distract and delay. Distract from facing the reality that Kathy is pregnant with our third child and delay the confrontation that must ensue. With my heart pounding in my throat, I call, "Hey."

"Hey," she mirrors.

I'm trying with all my willpower to maintain a calm demeanor. "Can we please, talk?"

"We are."

"In person, please."

"What for?"

At this point, I'm not sure if she even knows I know. "A lot is going on with the kids. Just…everything. I'm hoping we can do this with grace. With respect."

"When?"

"Now would be great. I want to stop by on the way to the office."

"Okay."

"Great, I'll see you in fifteen."

As I approach the front door of Janet's house, adrenaline is pulsing through my veins. I can feel the anxious rush. I don't want to lose my cool. What I said is the truth. I want to end our marriage with consciousness. With dignity. But this is pushing me to my limit.

"Hi," Janet says as she opens the door.

"Hi."

"So, when were you going to tell me?"

She's taken off guard. Suddenly looks angry, shocked, defensive.

"Tell you what?"

"Don't play stupid. *Please,* give me a little credit." So far, not so good at the whole; *not losing my cool* thing. I try to regroup before I really lose it. She continues her charade.

"I'm not in the mood to play guessing games, Marcus."

"Really? Fine. When were you going to tell me you are pregnant?"

Now she's really mad. The mad that only occurs when you're busted and don't want to come clean. "Fine. *How 'bout never?* That's when. Janet and I decided we don't want another child."

"You and Janet decided? Seriously? Janet gets to decide the fate of my child? That's a good one Kathy. Wow. What about me? What about how I feel?"

"Marcus, you know my position on this. *It's my body, my choice.* Don't make this political. I can only guess what your view is now that you are…*part of the far right."*

"OH MY GOD. Far right? Really? Give me a break. And the last thing this is is political. Politics have nothing to do with our child. You'll be surprised to hear, coming from this, 'right winger,' I don't think the government should be involved in any way. This is a decision between the parents and no one else."

"Sorry, no, it is not. My body. My decision."

"But it's my child too. I wish to God I could carry the child. Give birth. I do." I'm experiencing an emotional cocktail unlike any other. I want to scream with every cell of my body or maybe just fall to the ground and die.

"Please, Kathy. Please," I plead softly as tears beat out the part of me that wants to scream. "I will raise the child on my own. You don't have to be involved at all if you choose not to. You know I always wanted another child. You know I'm a good father. Just…Please." I'm trying to hold the tears, but I'm failing hard. "What do I have to do? I'll do anything."

"Marcus… Just stop it. Stop it now. Go find someone else to have a third child with. It's just not going to be me. We are finished! And Janet and I don't want another child. Do you understand? *Do you?"*

If I didn't know her so well, I might keep pleading, begging. But I know by the hole in my stomach and the withering of my soul, this is a lost cause. I wipe the tears from my cheeks while summoning the last bit of civility and strength left in my heart.

"How long have you known?"

"About a month. I mean I had my suspicions before that."

"How long have you been pregnant? I'm guessing just over two months." I recall the last time we had sex. I mean, when it's once every few months, you don't lose track.

"Yep, that's about right."

It's everything I can do to keep it together as I make my final plea. "Then Kathy, please. Abort our child now. Do you know what happens at the end of the first trimester?" She doesn't answer. But strangely, she seems actually to be listening to me. "The baby experiences the greatest miracle in the known universe. Consciousness. Human consciousness! So please, in the name of mercy, please. If you must do this, do it now." As the words leave my mouth, I feel a part of me die, "Do it now!"

To my great surprise, I can see her fighting tears. "I… I will. Tomorrow. I promise."

I let myself out. Go to my car. And fall into a kind of sobbing I have not known since I was a child. Through the tears I recall, not long ago, when my party, the Democrats slogan around abortion was; *Safe, Legal, and Rare.* What happened to my party? They're now celebrating abortion like it's a rite of passage into womanhood. I saw Michelle Wolf on television last night cheering to patriotic music, *God Bless America and God Bless Abortions.*

      God bless abortions <u>trumped.online/vgm</u>

Until recently I didn't even know there was such a thing as abortion survivors. If these survivors don't give you pause, I worry for our soul.

      Abortion survivor <u>trumped.online/8bh</u>

Chapter 22 The Future:*4,000 Feet Above Sea Level*
Year: 2047 April 28, Easter 10:17 a.m.

"I've got it," Charles says as we slowly make our way to the exit of the Cathedral, two among the throngs of humanity, "Let's have a spring skiing get away. The four of us up at Timberline Lodge; ASAP, tomorrow. Then, somewhere on the slopes, in the trees at 4,000 feet above sea level, we should be safe."

"Okay, perfect."

As we pour outside through the huge cathedral doors, jostling amongst the faithful and the begrudging, Charles slightly nods upward, towards the sky. A speck hovers. A drone! On my way home I can't help but continue to look up and out the window.

"Hey, baby, what's up?" I ask as I enter the front door.

"Just wondering about you. I mean, Mass? St. Mary's? We haven't been for like 30 years. How was it? You two are cracking me up!"

"It was Charles' idea. He said it was just, um, one of those things on his life list."

"To go to Mass?"

"Yeah, Easter Mass. Not just any Mass!"

"I went every Easter and Christmas, as you know growing up. In Germany, it was pretty much required. I mean, the Vatican looms one country over. I've seen the Pope, hanging out the window! How was it? Did it meet his expectations?"

"It surpassed them. We were so inspired we are going to the mountain tomorrow."

"We are? And what does that have to do with Catholic Mass?"

"Everything," I answer, even though it makes no sense. "Can you? I mean… spring skiing. We want to get up there before the snow melts."

"Okay, sounds fun."

The next morning Charles picks us up, and by 10 a.m. we are on the slopes on a beautiful spring day.

"Wow," Jadda announces looking out from the top of the mile run, above the lodge. It's like being on a cloud. Up here, for a moment, I almost forgot why we came. I've always found so much solace on top of Mount Hood.

"I know," I say in agreement. "I've been coming up here for forty-five years, and I never tire of it."

"I have an on again off again relationship with the mountain," Charles reminds us, "I came up often until my junior year in high school. Then, life changed, a lot, and I didn't see the mountain up close again for about ten years. But I'm back, *and I'm lovin' it.* Let's do this."

The four of us take off down the mountain. We ski past Timberline Lodge into a wooded area. We've always loved swishing back-and-forth, between the trees. Suddenly Charles, leading us by fifty feet, comes to a stop. We all follow suit.

"What are we stopping for?" Jadda asks. "Shhhh," Charles says, "Listen."

One of our favorite things to do on the mountain is listening. There's a quiet, in the trees, in the snow, 4000 feet up. It's eerie and beautiful all at once. We're listening for drones, but we would've stopped anyway to hear the quiet. When we know we are truly alone, Charles pipes up, "Marcus? You have something to tell them?"

"Oh, I think you have something to tell them."

"What? What's going on?" Alexus inquires, confused.

"Okay, fine. I will tell them but feel free to jump in anytime you like Charles." I take a deep breath. Exhale. You can see my breath in the frigid air. "Where to begin? The data. Let's start with the data. The original data we compiled was not wrong."

"What?" Jadda exclaims.

"No, it was not wrong."

Alexus shakes her head, confused, "You mean to tell me, catastrophic climate change is inevitable and coming soon, *to a planet near you,* as we originally deducted?"

"Yes, it is."

"Then what is going on? Why are we on the top of Mount Hood in a forest chatting about it? We've got to get this information out. And why on earth did you lie?"

"We're getting to that," Charles assures them.

"We got hacked… into our system," I say looking at Alexus, "And Charles and Jadda's System too."

"What? That's supposed to be impossible."

"I know, but nothing is impossible if you have the right technology and know-how. Anyway, one day a Man-In-Black appeared in my office unannounced in hologram form."

"What? Oh my God." Alexus is shocked.

"He gave me the falsified data and threatened that if I told anyone, especially you, he would kill you. And probably me. Suddenly I found myself in an impossible situation. Allow the ones I love to live or, put all of humanity at great risk within the next 40 years or so. And so, once he threatened me again and even cut my throat with a knife, I decided not to tell anyone and hope that someone else figures it out, like we did, before it's too late."

"But then," Charles steps in, "Haunted by his conscience, he told me. We came up with a plan to try to figure out who the Man-In-Black was. Remember the night we all got together to celebrate, and I went to the store somewhat randomly to get ice cream?"

"Yes, that was weird," Jadda recalls.

"Well, I was trying to track the Man-In-Black, but somehow he knew and led me to Voodoo Doughnut."

"Voodoo Doughnut? You mean the Man-In-Black works at Voodoo Doughnut?"

"Ah, No," Charles recalls, shaking his head, "He just led me there somehow. Whoever this is has connections and must be a tech wizard to first, figure out what we were up to and, second, reroute the tracking signal through Voodoo Doughnut's Wi-Fi."

It befuddles the gals.

"Then the Man-In-Black visited me again and told me we were asking too many questions. The next thing I knew, Alexus, your car was commandeered. Hacked. Nearly killing you. And you, Jadda, you got stuck in an elevator in between floors for hours. The Man-In-Black then told me next time, they would not be so merciful. That's when I was ready to give up."

"But then we went to Mass, yesterday, Easter day!" Charles explains.

"Ohhhh… kay," Alexus states awkwardly "And what happened at Mass? Some revelation?"

Charles cocks his head to the left, "Well, they told us to, *Shhhhhhh,* several times."
I try to get us back on track. "I told Charles to meet me there because it was a place I felt we could speak without being monitored. We should all be thanking our lucky stars we chose not to get an iMind implant. Otherwise, there would be no place we could go without being monitored."

"They're pushing legislation to have them required, you know," Jadda offers.

"Yes," Charles reflects, "They argue it's for the welfare of everyone. But it feels very Orwellian, 1984 has finally arrived."

I continue, "At Mass, feeling safe to speak, except for the occasional irritated Catholic wanting to celebrate Easter in peace, I told Charles I had figured out who the Man-In-Black is."

"WHAT?," Jadda exclaims, "You know who it is? Who? Who?"

"This will not be easy for you two, especially you Jadda."

Charles and I exchange looks. How are we going to tell her? How is she going to believe us? I have an idea. "What is the most powerful company in the world?"

"Well," Alexus ponders, "I would say Apple, Microsoft, Veratt; the merging of Verizon and AT&T, and then, of course, Google. But even Google was surpassed by Green Power, I think. Once Greenpeace created Green Power, and they put the fossil fuel industry out of business, Green Power, some say, is more powerful than the government. Conspiracy theorists believe Green Power dictates most policies these days just like, 20 years ago, the oil industry often did."

"Power is Power Man," Charles adds.

"Okay, now, I know they have brainwashed us twenty-four seven through G.P.'s motto, *Our undying commitment today is a green plant for you tomorrow.* But what if a green planet tomorrow made G.P. obsolete; overnight!?"

"Oh…My…God," the light bulbs come flashing on for Alexus. "Of course! Who else would have so much to gain by burying the truth? And who else would have the power and the know-how to do so? To hack our life systems?"

"We… we've got to tell Shelly right away," Jadda demands.

I remind her, "Isn't it strange that Shelly could never get us a meeting with anyone at G.P.?"

"Wait a minute, just what are you insinuating?" Jadda defensively questions. Then Charles puts the nail in the coffin.

"Jadda, Alexus, did you know they made Shelly a VP two months ago?"

"WHAT? Of course not. Because she was not!"

"Yes, she was," I insist, "Remember the day I first shared with you my findings? And remember Shelly said she had exciting news she wanted to tell us, but we pulled her into our conversation about the data before she did? Then, later, she said the news was that she is pregnant. The truth is she was going to tell us they promoted her to a V.P. position."

"No way," Jadda protests. "She is pregnant. What news could be bigger?"

"Yes, however, do you remember how long she said she had known she was pregnant?"

"I think she said… oh my god. I think she said she knew for only two days."

Alexus jumps in, "That's right! Then being pregnant *could not have been the big news in the first place* because a week had passed since our last meeting. The timeline is off!"

"I don't know what to do with this. Shelly? The Man-In-Black?" Jadda confesses, distraught.

"I'm sure of it. Once we told her our findings, I figure she first went to the shareholders at G.P. or something like that. Anyway, I believe G.P. pressured her. It probably didn't take much of a threat. I mean with all she has to lose; her career, a lifetime of hard work and a baby on the way. I don't know. It would be a lot for anyone to process."

"All we know is, we have got to question her and sort this out. Maybe it's not her, but the only way we'll know is to ask," Charles proclaims.

"Shouldn't we call the police?" Jadda says downtrodden, having to reconcile the fact that her sister may be her enemy.

"No, we can't. We don't know how deep this goes. Remember when the police came after your car went haywire?"

She acknowledges with a quick nod, "They never came back. I called a few times, and they gave me the runaround. We really can't trust anyone!"

"Okay, okay," Jadda agrees.

Charles reiterates, "It's hard to remember this when you're at home in a routine, but, we cannot trust anyone. Consider everything you say and everything you do is being watched and recorded. So, do not talk about any of this even amongst yourselves. Ever. We'll have one of our dinners, next Friday. And then, our best bet is to get Shelly outside. As always, no phones, no technology and watch for drones. Then, we'll ask her a few innocent questions and see what happens. Like, for example, *How are things at work?*"

Alexus shakes her head, downtrodden, sighs. "What is it?" I ask.

"Everything. But I was just thinking how disheartening it is that something can start with such good intentions and end up so corrupt."

"Green Power?" Charles asks.

"Yes. Which began as Greenpeace."

🔗 Greenpeace founder drops out trumped.online/xgb 🔗

The Dawn: *Charlottesville Riot, Transgenders*
Year: 2017 August 15 6:30 p.m.

It's my birthday today. The divorce finalized last Tuesday. Thank God. I guess that's a kind of gift. Glad it's over. I live two lives now. One real, the other imagined, daydreamed. In one, Kathy did not abort the pregnancy, and I'm raising another little bundle. Then the phone will ring, or someone will say something like *Earth to Marcus*, as I'm starring off into space. Suddenly the child disappears. My heart broken once again as I come crashing down into reality.

Although my 'friends' disowned me because they think I'm some far right-wing conservative which, nothing could be further from the truth, they have extended an olive branch. They invited me to Kathy and Janet's place for dinner. Interestingly enough, the one thing that has kept all contact from being severed between us is Cynthia. They can't reconcile that a "right wing nut job," as Kathy has called me, initiated this act of kindness. We continue to support her and visit. She is our common thread.

As the kids and I arrive, I'm almost shaking from nerves. I find it so strange that this group of 'liberals,' who say they are tolerant and accepting, cannot accept me for simply questioning, seeking truth. For thinking independently. They accept everyone no matter their race, religion or sexual orientation *as long as they think the same*. You can be as diverse as you want on the outside, but on the inside, you *must* comply. In any case, I am glad for this opportunity to be together outside our time with Cynthia. I really would like to heal our friendships, especially with Kathy since she is the mother of my children.

As they welcome the kids in and me, we remove our shoes and take our seats at the table. The kids yell, *Mommy,* and run for a hug. After that, the pleasantries are sheer torture.

"Well, it's August all right. Hotter than Hades out there," Tom says followed by an awkward silence.

Then, "Did you see the new Star Wars yet?" Valentina asks.

You see, all we ever did, and I'm sure all they ever do when I'm not around, is talk politics. Or, another way of saying 'talk politics' is, *talk Trump* and try to outdo each other's utter disgust for him as a human being not to mention his policies and everyone in his administration. I notice Janet has a new chew toy for her dog, Hillary. Yes, *Hillary.* Hillary is a Chiweenie, a Chihuahua and Dachshund mix. The chew toy? *Trump!* Orange skin and all! Hillary is in her bed chewing away, occasionally shaking Trump back and forth in her mouth while growling.

Trump chew toy trumped.online/zvm

Janet and Kathy have made spaghetti squash pasta with pesto. The forks clink on the plates while Hillary snarls on Trump, showing her teeth. We're all hiding behind the food. Perfect excuse not to talk. There's a grandfather clock in the corner of the dining room. Doesn't work. It's just for looks. But when I see it out of the periphery of my eyes, it feels like it's ticking, uncomfortably, back and forth. A time bomb. Anticipating. A sense of dread floats about the room. I try to convince myself that everything will be fine.

Luke, Janet's 22-year-old son who broke windows on national TV at Berkley as a member of Antifa, is the first to break the silence, "So, how does it feel to be 32?"

"Oddly enough," I say trying to bring levity to the event, "Feels more like, I don't know, 29. Yes, 29. I guess I'm Benjamin Button!" The reference is to one of Kathy's and my favorite movies.

"Yes," Jamaal adds, "They're all saying 32 is the new 29."

"That must be it…" I answer as the doorbell rings.

"*Come*," Janet yells from the table. In walks, a stunningly beautiful woman in a stylish pants suits like she just came from some high-powered business meeting. Probably upper twenties. I'd say about 5'5". Petite and in great shape.

"Hello," she says, instantly lighting up the room. I detect a slight accent.

"Everyone, this is my new assistant, Alexus. She started a month ago, from Germany. She's just picking a few things up."

"Hi everyone."

"Have a seat," Jesus insists, "There's plenty to eat."

"Yes, do," Janet agrees.

"Great idea," Kathy says. I begin to see the invitation to Janet's new assistant is an attempt at easing the tension.

"Are you sure? I don't want to intrude."

"We're more than glad to have you." Tom assures, "Have a seat."

She sits down next to Michelle, directly across from me. "Germany! I love your country. So they transferred you here to work at Nike?"

"Yes, I assist Janet with her European accounts."

"What part of Germany are you from?"

"Originally Monschau, a small town on the border of Belgium. Then I moved to Munich to intern at Nike when I was 21, just after University. One thing led to another, and now I'm here with you lovely people in Portland, Oregon."

"Have you had any time to see the sights?" Michelle inquires.

"No, I haven't. But, I look forward to getting to know the city and the great Northwest in general."

Shanice joins in with the excitement and innocence only a child could bring. "My dad and I are going to the Rose Garden tomorrow afternoon. You wanna come?"

"Yeah," Malik adds, "There's a zillion, billion roses! And, you can slide down the railings on the steps to the amphitheater. *That's my favorite.*"

"Kids," I interrupt, "Let's not be pushy." I turn to Alexus. She's smiling brightly at my children before slowly turning her eyes my way. It's not just her beauty; she has a spirit about her. "Sorry for my children's enthusiasm."

"No, not at all. The Rose Garden is at the top of my list."

"Daddy, she has to come with us. Did you hear? *It's on the top of her list,*" Malik persuades.

"Alexus, *no pressure or anything,*" I say eyes wide, nodding my head at my children, "But, if you would like to join us, we'd love to have you."

"Sure. I would love it."

Just when I thought the coast was clear, that my fears of a clash were unwarranted, we hear a little 'ding' from someone's phone. Then Adara looks down, reads what apparently is some breaking news report, and announces, *"Trump is a Neo-Nazi."*

"Like that's news," Kathy adds.

Adara continues, "No, listen, he's just now talking to reporters again about Charlottesville. He says there is blame on both sides."

"Oh my God," Jesus adds, "Both sides? What both sides? *It was a Neo-Nazi rally.*"

"And listen to this, he says there were some fine people there. Fine people? *He is clearly a Nazi sympathizer.* How else could you call a bunch of Nazis fine people?"

Michelle suggests, "I think we should see this. Can we turn on CNN?"

Trump had already issued a statement in which he said he condemned in the strongest possible terms the egregious display of hatred, bigotry, and violence. He said we must love each other, respect each other, and unite together in condemnation of bigotry. He said racism is evil. Pretty good statement, it seems. But of course, there has been endless analysis on CNN and MSNBC all trying to create discord and hatred, in my opinion, by rehashing and calling Trump a racist.

Janet clicks on CNN, and we are thrust right into the mayhem. First, a female reporter asks, "*Are you putting the alt left and white supremacists on the same moral plane?*"

Trump: *I'm not putting anybody on a moral plane. What I'm saying is this, you had a group on one side, and you had a group on the other, and they came at each other with clubs, and it was vicious, and it was a horrible thing to watch. There was a group; you can call the left, that came violently attacking the other group. There's blame on both sides.*

Male Reporter: *The Neo-Nazis started this thing, protesting….*

Trump: *They didn't put themselves down as Neo-Nazis. But you had some very bad people in that group. But you also had very fine people, <u>on both sides.</u> You had people in that group that were there to protest the taking down of a statue that was important to them and the renaming of the park.*

Male Reporter*: But Robert E. Lee was a slave owner.*

Trump: *George Washington was a slave owner. Do you like George Washington?*

Male Reporter: *Um, Yes.*

Trump: *Thomas Jefferson was a slave owner, are we going to take them down? Statues to George Washington and Thomas Jefferson?*

Reporters talked over each other.

Trump*: I'm not talking about the Neo-Nazis and the white nationalists because they should be condemned totally, but you had many people in that group other than Neo-Nazis and white nationalists. And the press has treated them absolutely unfairly. In the other group also, you had some fine people, but you also had troublemakers. You see them come with the black outfits and the helmets and the baseball bats. You had a lot of bad people in the other group too.*

Female Reporter: *I want to understand what you're saying, are you saying the press has treated the white nationalists unfairly?*

Trump: *"No, NO! There were people there protesting, very quietly, the taking down of the statue of Robert E Lee. And legally, by the way, they had a permit. The other group did not."*

Reporters continue yelling over each other.

Trump: *"I only tell you this, there are two sides to every story. What took place was a horrible moment, a horrible moment. I think there's blame on both sides."*

Interview on Charlottesville trumped.online/45u

Once the interview was over, Janet turns the TV off and screams, *"FUCK! I hate him so much; he makes me so mad!"*

I give Janet the death ray look and then gaze toward my kids pointing out how inappropriate she is, cussing in their presence. Then my little Shanice innocently joins in, "Janet, no one can *make* you mad." *Out of the mouths of babes!* I forgot all about our little discussion the other night on the Fudge Lady and smiling frogs. The room is silent. Everyone there, with the possible exception of Alexus, would agree with Shanice, but since Trump is the subject of the profanity, all civility is out the window. Then, of all people, Alexus breaks the silence, "That's very astute of you, Shanice. Where did you hear that?"

"My Daddy. You have to *choose* to be a smiling frog."

It was such a pattern interrupt; everyone *almost* forgot what was going on.

"True," Alexus says, just going with it, "You do have to choose to be a smiling frog."

Janet looks at me, regret written on her face, "Everyone, I'm sorry. Especially you and Malik. That was not acceptable," she says to Shanice.

Disaster averted, I respond, "Apology accepted. Shanice?"

"Apology accepted," she speaks with sincerity.

"But," Janet suddenly continued, "You have to admit it's difficult having a racist, sexist, Neo-Nazi, homophobe, white male reality TV star who Vladimír Putin put into office; as president of these United States."

There was chuckling and much affirming from everyone in the room except me, Alexus, and my kids. Alexus gets a pass for being new, the kids for being kids, but for me? No pass. *Disaster not averted!*

Valentina joins everyone else in noticing my non-reaction and says, "You don't think he's a racist, Neo-Nazi, sexist, white supremacist, homophobe?"

Put on the spot! Do I stick to my guns? Do I say it's time to leave, or do I speak truth?

"The honest truth is, I don't know."

The room explodes with emotional comments and questions:
What do you mean you don't know…
Did you hear what he just said?
Are you paying attention at all to the news?
Are you some kind of right-wing nut job?
Are you sure you haven't made one of those #WalkAway videos?

Everyone stops attacking me for one second and then Michelle says, "Come on Marcus, you heard what he just said about Charlottesville, and I'm sure you know he banned transgenders from the military, not to mention the Muslim ban and the wall. It's all racist, white supremacist evidence. How can you be in denial?"

"Listen, you guys. Let me be clear. I have not made one of those #WalkAway videos. Please stop insulting me. But here's the thing. We jump to conclusions; it's human nature. When we want reality to be a certain way, we naturally look for evidence that supports our desired outcome rather than being neutral so that the facts can inform us of the truth. We even purposefully choose to be informed exclusively by sources we know will reinforce our position. It's called *confirmation bias!* We want our views to be confirmed until they are as hard as cement." I scan the room, meeting them eye to eye. "You *want* Trump to be all those awful things, so when you hear something that could have more than one explanation, your prejudices blind you to any possibility other than the one you hope for; *he's a racist, prejudiced, homophobe, sexist, Neo-Nazi!"*

This stops everyone in their tracks for a moment. When there's half a chance you're speaking truth, sometimes it cracks old paradigms and stirs up cognitive dissonance. But soon, "How can he say, *Both sides? How can he say, fine people?"* Michelle reiterates.

"Again, let me be clear. My mind is open. I don't know if he is all these things you make him out to be. *He might be,* or he might just often be very crass and tactless as a politician. Even insensitive and purposefully politically incorrect. Remember, he's an N.Y. real-estate investor! He has said nothing that *could* be interpreted as racist and homophobic that didn't also have a possible *alternate* explanation."

"Fine people? *How can he say there were fine people on both sides? They were white supremacist!"* Tom insists.

"Despite what the news is telling all of us, he never said that…

Scott Adams: Trump never said it trumped.online/ih9

"What I heard him say was there were bad people on both sides of the argument and good people on both sides of the argument. Correct me if I'm wrong but didn't he say there were some people there who peacefully protested the removal of the statue? There were some people there who were not Neo-Nazis or white supremacists; who had a permit. And, If you think there were no good people there, and that no good person would be there, you would have to say Heather Heyer was a bad person. She was the one who was killed. By all accounts, she was a human rights activist.

Evidence Antifa might be guilty trumped.online/x5t

Charlottesville, Black's perspectives trumped.online/8k0

Everyone seems shocked like I'm zapping them with a taser, so I continue. "And, there would've been no violence, no deaths, if the anti-protesters had been peaceful. None of this would've happened." I look at Luke, a member of Antifa. "Does anyone remember who said, *Darkness cannot drive out darkness; only light can do that. Hate cannot drive out hate; only love can do that.* Anyone? How about this one, *Violence as a way of achieving racial justice is both impractical and immoral.* Anyone?" I look around. *"Come on!"*

They all know. They're just playing dumb. Once again, Michelle is the only one with the integrity to answer, "Martin Luther King."

"Yes."

Then Jesus adds his two cents, "But the Nazis attacked the other people first."

"What other people? Innocent bystanders? Or people with clubs in masks? And…*wrong*. All first-hand accounts say the white supremacists peacefully protested until Antifa attacked them. But, come on. What did you expect would happen? First, you have a group of racist people protesting, but doing so legally. As much as we don't like their point of view, they have the right to express it. But then, the stupidest thing happened. A group of people shows up wearing all black, including face-masks carrying bats and pepper spray. *What do you think will happen?* This blood is on Antifa and Black Lives Matter just as much as anyone else. And that is what the president is saying. The part where he's less than tactful is where he is not sensitive to deeds done in *the past* as it relates to the KKK and Neo-Nazis. He did in an earlier statement, but taken off guard by mainstream media and its hunger to rile people up with hatred, he made the mistake of looking at this event in isolation. And the media got just what they wanted. More dirty laundry. More vitriol. And why does the media want this? Why do they want to divide our country? Anyone?"

The KKK and America <u>trumped.online/vx2</u>

Everyone looks around, uncomfortably, at the ground, the ceiling. Not because they don't know. They know. They don't want to say it because part of them wants the division too. They want America to fail, like when Joy Behar on The View celebrated when she thought they had caught Trump in collusion with the Russians.

Joy Behar on The View <u>trumped.online/die</u>

"I have often thought if I were being interviewed by Don Lemon or Anderson Cooper or Rachel Maddow, I would ask them to look straight in the camera and say, *I hope President Trump did not collude with Russia because that would be a terrible thing for our country*. I think none of them would do it for the same reason they *want* Trump to be a racist. They hope he is a Neo-Nazi, sexist, homophobe. So, again, why does the mainstream media want division? Why do they hope Trump is a Russian agent, white supremacist, xenophobe? WHY?"

Finally, Michelle lifts his/her head, acknowledging the truth, "Ratings. In fact Ted Koppel said that very thing to CNN."

   Ted Koppel slams CNN on ratings <u>trumped.online/o13</u>

"Of course! Now, did he or did he not just say, very clearly, in this statement and others, *Neo-Nazis and white nationalists should be condemned totally?"*

Again Michelle answers, hesitantly nodding, "Yep, he did."

"How does that make him a Nazi sympathizer and a white supremacist?"

Adara joins the discussion, "He's only saying that because he has to. If he didn't, he would be wrecked beyond repair."

"That's one possibility. That's one interpretation, and I'm not saying it isn't possible. Maybe he is a Nazi. Did you know, however, that Trump had an actual Nazi, for real, deported?"

"What?"
   Last Nazi deported by Trump <u>trumped.online/u7n</u>

"Yes. The last Nazi. Past Presidents just ignored this atrocity. But still, maybe he's one of them. Maybe he had that Nazi removed from America as a smoke screen to distract from his own Nazi-ness. And maybe he's a Russian agent working with Putin. These are all possibilities. But that's all they are, possibilities. *I don't know!* I do know there's evidence to suggest he's not a racist. For example, did you know he won the Ellis Island Award in 1986 along with Rosa Parks and Mohammad Ali? They give the award to people whose actions embody the spirit of America in their celebration of patriotism, tolerance, brotherhood, and diversity. They recognize individuals who have made it their mission to share with those less fortunate, their wealth of knowledge, indomitable courage, boundless compassion, unique talents, and selfless generosity."
   Award with Rosa Parks and Ali <u>trumped.online/bn3</u>
   Jesse Jackson praising Trump <u>trumped.online/cd3</u>

The body language of most was that of disgust. For me to even suggest that Donald Trump received such an honor was, for them, like suggesting Adolf Hitler received the Nobel Peace Prize retroactively.

"I can see you're all boiling right now. Don't shoot the messenger; it's just a fact. You focus on things like 'both sides' and you believe things like the wall and the travel ban must be racist. You won't even consider the possibility they are matters of national security. Never mind it was Obama who said the nations on the travel ban are a danger to our country. Never mind that Bill Clinton's administration hired a record number of border guards and deported twice as many illegal aliens as ever before. Never mind that Bill Clinton said illegal aliens are taking jobs that legal citizens need and he said illegals are a burden on our welfare system. Obama and Clinton can do these things, but because you hate Trump, you hate everything he does, even if you agree it's good for our country which is self-sabotaging and frankly, *infantile*. The people who receive the Ellis Island award, like Trump, are highly scrutinized. Their actions must reflect the embodiment of the award. What *I* think, what *I* see, *is unclear.* But I refuse to, no longer, jump to the worst possible conclusion when I do not have all the information. And again, just so you know where I stand, *you may be right.* He may be a racist. It's just not black-and-white, no pun intended. Did you know back around 1990, on the Larry King show King asked Trump who he would choose as his running mate if he ever ran for president? Remember, this is back in 1990. Do you know who the first person was that came to mind for Donald Trump?"

Once again, they know. It's been all over the news ever since they gave the Cecil B. DeMille Award to this person. But no one is answering. Michelle looks around the room to see if anyone else wants a turn. No one seems to, so he answers again, "Oprah."

"Yes, Oprah Winfrey. A *black woman.* He called her 'brilliant,' 'very special,' and a 'wonderful woman.' It makes no sense that a racist, sexist man would choose a black woman in a very spontaneous interview to be his running mate for president back in 1990. Does that make any sense to any of you?"

  Trump on Larry King Show in 1990 trumped.online/stq
  Black woman on Trump the racist trumped.online/2gk
"He's also the first president in history to support gay marriage before he was even sworn in. He's appointed more women to high positions of authority in his administration than any other president in history."

With much anger, Kathy insists, *"But there are almost no people of color in his administration."*

"I think that's true, that there are few people of color. However, isn't it possible that pointing out people's color, as you have done, is racist? I suppose you're saying there are too many white people in his administration. *But that's racist.* Clearly, you're not judging those people on the content of their character; you're looking at the color of their skin. Many people who know Donald Trump will tell you that he's not interested in color, he just wants the best person for the job."

"Bull Shit!" Janet says. Again, I shake my head and glance at the kids.

"Well, I can see you're not capable of having a civil discussion about this, so we better go. Michelle, thank you for being willing to listen and have a rational discussion."

"Before you go," Michelle says, "What about banning transgenders from the military? As a transgender person that seems prejudice and homophobic."

"Michelle, I loved you when you were Michael, and I love you now, as Michelle, so please do not take this personally. Here is the other side of the argument. I'm not saying I agree with it. I'm just making the point that it doesn't *have* to be rooted in homophobia. First, the Military is for one purpose, defending our country. There are many reasons they reject people from service that might seem unfair or unkind to you but have been determined as detrimental to the efficiency of the military. Today they would not allow something like 70% of people between seventeen and twenty-four to enter the military for one reason or another. Like, *you can't have flat feet.* We could say that's flat-feetaphobia, or we could look at the science. Flat feet cause an innumerable amount of physical problems.

Also, *your butt can be too big.* They take Spinal disorders very seriously. Having any back issue can be detrimental to the readiness of the force. So, because of spinal curvature misalignment, your butt can be too big. Enough said.

You need to have good teeth. Dental health is very important when joining the military; you can't have too many cavities or complex dental implant systems. The risk is too high for toothaches that could be debilitating.

You can't self-harm. While this may seem obvious, it's not always so straightforward. Having a history of psychological issues that caused prior self-mutilation is unacceptable.

You can't have eczema or acne. Eczema is dry, itchy and spreads and therefore can be debilitating. Acne, on the other hand, runs the gamut from requiring antibiotics to interfering with proper wear of a gas mask. So, too much acne and you're out!

Transgender's, as a whole, is an unstable community." As soon as I say that, everyone except Michelle and Alexus and my kids, *give me the stink eye.*

"Hey," I say responding to their death ray vision, "Don't kill the messenger. I'm sorry that it is this way. If I could change it, I would. But over 40% of the transgender community commits suicide each year. Jump in any time Michelle if you disagree with me."

"I will," Michelle replies firmly.

"Good, now, some people say that's because they're not accepted by society. That is not what I see *today.* Today, transgender's are celebrated. They gave Caitlyn Jenner the Arthur ash award for courage. Many say this was a stretch, a kind of virtue signaling by the awards ceremony which is one of many ways the pendulum may have swung too far in the opposite direction. One possible candidate for the Ashe honor, who they passed over in favor of Jenner, was Lauren Hill. A 19-year-old freshman from Mount St. Joseph University in Cincinnati who battled an inoperable brain tumor to achieve her dream of playing college basketball while also helping raise money for cancer research. She has since died. Anyway, the suicide rate of transgender's is only equaled historically by those in the concentration camps of World War II. It's very difficult for me to imagine that transgender's *today* are under any kind of oppression *even close to that of a Jew… in a concentration camp… in World War II.* It wasn't long ago that the medical community diagnosed transgenders with gender dysphoria, a mental disorder. The science suggests that it sometimes is a mental disorder and sometimes is the wrong brain in the body. In either case, it seems that help can often be found in treatment. However, the science is pretty clear that there're only two genders.

"Whatever the case, it seems to me if someone has the desire to mutilate themselves, for example, to cut off one's penis and testicles, something disturbing is happening. Then, there are the hormones and other medications that transgender's are often taking for their physical transition. Given the fact that you cannot have flat feet, eczema, or too many cavities, I can see why one might question the service of a transgender. In other words, it doesn't *necessarily* mean you are a homophobe."

Again, except for the few I already mentioned, everyone in the room looks as if they would like to claw my eyes out, "Well, it's been a memorable birthday. Come on kids."

We gather our things and leave. I'm amazed as Alexus chases us down and asks, "Are we still on for tomorrow, the Rose Garden?"

Malik and Shanice answer before I can. I think they like her, "Of course, yes."

"Okay," she says. "Here is my phone number. Just call or text with the time." She pauses for a moment before adding, "I support any adult living however they want as long as it doesn't hurt anyone. And, some transgenders are hurting girls, women. They'er ruining women's sports. How can we compete with men? It's just not fair to all the girls and women who work so hard."

I nod in agreement. She turns and heads back towards Janet's mansion. But then, pauses and looks back at us as I'm getting in the car, "Thanks for your vulnerability. Thanks for your honesty. I know that was very difficult. Happy birthday."

⬡ Transgenders ruining women's sports <u>trumped.online/96i</u> ⬡
⬡ Good Morning Britain, Transgenders <u>trumped.online/kdk</u> ⬡

Chapter 23 The Future: *iMind Implant*
Year: 2047 May 4 5:49 p.m.

"Everyone should be here anytime," Alexus says with urgency. Emphasizing *everyone*, meaning Shelly. "Hows the table coming?"

"Good," Charles replies, "Thank God the weather is so nice. We got crazy and set up waaay over there, see?" He points from the back patio, past the pool and pond to the edge of the property hoping we will be out of range of any surveillance. Also, it should be easy to spot any drones out there. We know, if it is her, we should be safe as long as she's with us and does not have any devices on her. But, at this point, there's no way to know for sure if she is the Man-In-Black.

"HEY EVERYONE..." she enters flamboyantly as always, fashionably late. Jadda says nothing, which is completely out of character for these sisters who usually embrace like they haven't seen each other in half a month. I furrow my eyebrows giving Jadda an, *act normal* look. Before Shelly can recognize something's off, I Jump in.

"Hey, Shelly! Okay, we're having a special night. No technology. We think it should be a normal rotation for us. Unplugged and fully present. I mean, having these things attached to us all the time adds to all of those annoying choices we have today." I hold out a basket, watch her reaction. We have already placed our technologies in it. She hesitates, stares at the basket for an uncomfortably long moment. Suddenly, she agrees happily.

"Yes, great idea," she drops her phone in with the rest of ours.

"Oh, and the iPad, in your purse," I point out.

"Oh yes, of course. I forgot about that."

Charles comes in from the back deck, "Hey Shelly, so glad you made it. Check it out," he points out the window toward the backyard, "See the table way across the field, isn't that cool?"

"Yeah, that's awesome. Looks like a spec from here."

"That's it. It's so beautiful out this spring evening we thought we'd get out there and soak it in."

"Great idea!"

As Shelly steps out on the deck, I'm worried Jadda can't pull this off. But, as soon as Jadda sees Shelly this time, she hugs her. Alexus joins them probably to help make sure everything appears normal. Charles heads into his office, then motions me to follow him out the front door and away from the house while the others take food to the table.

"I got some stuff." He opens a bag.

"What?"

"Well, I realized we are wholly unprepared. I mean, what if she goes all taekwondo on our asses?"

"Really? You think she will go all taekwondo on our asses?"

"I have no idea, but just in case, here is some mace. You take that. I've got a taser and some duct tape. And here are some brass knuckles. I think you should have those."

"Why? *Why should I have the brass knuckles?*"

"Have you seen your hands? They're not exactly Incredible Hulk-ish."

"Sheesh, what else you got in there, an AK-47?"

"I wish. How long has it been since they were outlawed? Like 25 years? Nowadays you have to be a criminal to get one. Anyway, I think it's… *Go Time.*"

"Go time? Are we in some Bollywood movie now?"

He ignores my inquiry and says with bravado, *"Let's do this?"*

"Really? Are you Rambo?"

"Okay, maybe I'm getting carried away but, *rock'n roll!*"

We grab drinks and some hors-d'oeuvres which help conceal our weapons of minimal destruction that leave strange bulges in our pants. Especially the duct tape.

Once we're seated, I begin with a toast, holding up my glass, "Well, not a day goes by when I don't feel grateful for each of you and thankful we were wrong. I've never been so happy to be so wrong in my life with the possible exception of that fateful day back in December 2017. I'll never forget that day. But this, well, what can I say? So, *here's to being wrong!*"

"Cheers," they all respond. I'm trying to watch Shelly closely for any abnormal reactions. Alexus joins with an innocent enough question.

"So, what's new in everyone's lives? Anything exciting?"

Charles updates us on his latest project, "Well, I'm nearing the completion of something huge. When I'm done, it will change everything! EVERYTHING!"

"We've talked about this before," I remember him mentioning it a few times. "But you said I wasn't ready. Am I ready now?"

Jadda and Charles respond in unison, "No, not quite!"

"Oh, come on!"

"Nope… Sorry!" Charles confirms shrugging his shoulders.

I wasn't planning on forcing her hand, but I couldn't take it any longer, "So, Shelly, what's new at Green Power?"

"Oh, same old same old."

"Do you think you'll ever get that promotion you've been after, a V.P. position?"

"I, I don't know."

"But, I don't understand Shelly. I went onto the Green Power website, and it looks like they promoted you quite a while ago."

To say things were getting a little tense would be like saying the Great Pyramid is a little big.

"Oh, shoot. You got me. I was saving that for a surprise. I was ah, planning to invite you all over to the headquarters and give you a tour and surprise you."

"Well, that would be great," Charles says a little too enthusiastically, "But I was just wondering. According to the timeline, you were a vice president, a higher up yourself, back when we were trying to get a meeting with someone…higher up at G.P."

Okay, *that's when she went all taekwondo on our asses.* Suddenly, the table flies up in the air and, instead of enjoying brown sugar glazed salmon, I'm given a knuckle sandwich curtesy of the Man-In-Black. Charles reaches for the taser about the same time I reach for the mace while I'm lying on my back in the grass. Alexus and Jadda jump on her back but to no avail. Shelly, being all amazon woman, tosses them aside. I jump to my feet while shooting the mace just a few feet from her face. Unfortunately, in all the excitement I didn't notice it was pointed in the opposite direction. I squeeze the container and suddenly, *I'm blinded.* My eyes burn like someone took jalapeños and rubbed them in my Iris'. Then I hear the taser shot, and I'm uncontrollably reeling on the ground, rubbing my eyes, next to Shelly doing same. One taser connector got me, the other her. I can hear Charles yelling, *"I'm sorry Marcus, I'm sorry,"* while he sprays Shelly with mace.

In my head, I'm screaming, *Turn it off, turn it off.* But the words don't leave my lips which are twitching uncontrollably with the rest of me.

"Give me a minute Marcus; I've got to duct tape Shelly first." As quickly as he can he tapes her hands and legs together. Then he finally turns it off. I feel like I had stuck my nose and one index finger into an old ungrounded electric socket like they had when I was a kid. Charles looks at me apologetically, "Sorry man, I've never used one of these before, cut me some slack."

"Slack? Really?" I say getting back to my feet, eyes burning like someone jabbed them with a red hot fire poker. Shelly is struggling but doesn't say a word.

Jadda can no longer contain herself, *"What the hell is going on Shelly? Seriously! You've been masquerading as some Man-In-Black, threatening us? Nearly killing Alexus."*

She sighs, looking down in shame, "I was following orders."

"What orders, from who?"

"From G.P. Executives. Look, I brought them the data as soon as you gave it to me. But even I didn't realize the impact it would have on the company until I showed them. Don't you get it? G.P. is the number one employer on the planet. We shut down; all those people lose jobs."

"So what?! What is wrong with you? The planet is at stake."

"I know. We came up with a plan."

"What plan? Allow the planet to die, for jobs? Nice plan!"

"Well, kind of. Look, I and everyone else in executive positions at Green Power stood to lose everything. So, we decided to slowly begin diverging our stocks away from G.P. We also worked on building a whole new arm of the company that would address the climate change."

"How long have people at G.P. known this was going on?"

"A long time. Al Gore discovered it first. That's why he sold his Network, *Current TV,* to Al Jazeera. They make all of their money from gas and oil. Gores ego would not let him come out and tell the true story. He wasn't capable of admitting to the world he was *wrong,* but at least he was trying to save the planet."

"And become a billionaire on the way," Alexus adds.

"So," Jadda confronts Shelly with more than just a little pent-up anger, *"The people at G.P. have known all plant life, green life, on earth are getting dangerously close to starvation levels? But they just went on creating green power even though it's the furthest thing from green?"*

Russian debates climatologist <u>trumped.online/qqp</u>
Professor Ridley carbons green earth <u>trumped.online/p3u</u>

"Well," Shelly says shaking her head, "Yes. But the idea was to move our holdings and then decommission everything."

"But when?" Jadda yells, "Every windmill, solar panel, every Hydro producing source of energy must be shut down immediately. The pendulum swung too far long ago. Plus, there's the fact we're heading for the next ice age! It's cyclical and always has been. But what we have all done from fear of global warming, stoked by Gores *Inconvenient Truth,* has *kick-started* the next Ice Age and could push it down into colder temperatures than any ice age in earth's history." Jadda puts her hand on her head, *"God Shelly, what have you done?"* Jadda is too upset to continue, so I step in.

"The next ice age will come, can't be stopped. To think we could stop Mother Earth's natural cycles is the height of human arrogance and ego. Ultimately, we must adjust to the planets changes as we always have instead of thinking we can adjust the planet to meet our whims. No matter how far we progress technologically, trying to control the earth to meet our needs will never work because *the needs of the earth are our own.* To think otherwise is to court disaster. What we must do, is feed the plants. *Now.* Shut everything at G.P. down and drive gas cars again. Burn coal. Co2 is plant food. Has everyone forgotten? Right now, carbon is at about 400 parts per million. That is a historic low. Throughout most of Earth's history it's been well over a thousand parts per million!"

Princeton Physicist/carbon <u>trumped.online/7pi</u>

"I know," Shelley says, "I know."

Jadda's anger has not softened, *"Life on this planet is in the most delicate balance.* Every time you breathe, you expel carbon, feeding every tree you see. *Look around Shelly.* Look at the grass, look at the trees, *look at the flowers.* G.P. is killing all of them. Millions of years ago, this planet was more teeming with life than we have ever witnessed. Why? Because there was approximately *fifteen times* the amount of carbon dioxide in the atmosphere. That's where we came from. It is from that air filled with food for plant life that human life was born. If the carbon dioxide in the atmosphere right now doubles, even quadruples, animal life won't even know it. But plant life, *which produces the oxygen we breathe,* will thrive again.

Shelly defends herself, "I understand what you're saying, but it's not that bad. It's not as bad as you think."

"Really? You do realize at one time the entire Sahara desert was teeming with life. As the amount of carbon dioxide decreased in the atmosphere, it all died off. And that's what is slowly happening all across this beautiful planet we call home. Because of G.P. and its government

subsidies, what was already happening naturally, a slight decrease in carbon dioxide got propelled at a rate no one could've imagined."

"Shelly," Alexus inquires shifting the focus, "Does anyone know what's happening right now? Does anyone know we're questioning you?"

Right then, a Heli-Flyer appears on the horizon headed for Charles's estate.

"Yes, they know. I have an iMind implant."

"What?" Jadda responds with fury, *"We promised we would never!"*

"It's part of being a V.P; I had to. We've got to get out of here."

"Okay, so, now we are just supposed to trust you?" I say shaking my head in disgust.

"Marcus, you know, when I appeared to you as the Man-In-Black, I told you I didn't want to hurt you. I told you I had to make terrible choices, just like you. If I went public, I would've lost everything. But I was going to do it anyway until I felt threatened by G.P. That threat was not just to me but my unborn child and my husband. So I went along with the whole thing. But now it's too late. You have to trust me."

Charles, furious, gets in her face, "NO WAY IN HELL!"

The Dawn: *Bleach Bit, Clinton Foundation* Year: 2017 August 16th 4:30 pm

The Rose Garden! I love this place. Truly, there may not be a more beautiful rose garden in the world. Colors burst yellow, red, purple, orange, pink, and mixes of colors I did not know are possible. *And the scent!* You walk around in a daze from the wafting of rose in the air. But just when I didn't think it could be more beautiful, *she arrived!* While I walk down the old stone staircase into the swirling universe of color and scent; she sees me, smiles, waves. My heart skips a beat. *Get a grip, Marcus.*

"Hey, glad to see you," I say reining in my sudden and unexpected crush.

"Wow, this is, it's, well, there are no words. I have never in my life seen such color." Then she stops to, *smell the roses!* "WHAT?" she exclaims, popping up from an orange and purple flower, "That is just...it's pure aromatic deliciousness!"

"I couldn't have said it better myself. I've lived here most of my life and every time is like the first. A kaleidoscope of joy. It's like we're living in the cover of Sergeant Pepper's Lonely Hearts Club Band."

"SHUT… UP!" she says in approval of my reaching metaphor as the kids run in between the endless rows of roses. "Sergeant Pepper's is the best, well that and…" then, in unison we announce, *"The White Album!"*

Okay, maybe it's not a crush. Maybe I'm in love!

"So, what's your favorite color?"

"Turquoise," she answers with no hesitation.

"Yes, amazing color." I don't even tell her it's mine as well for fear it would come across as dishonest, trying too hard. "Hmm, let me see. Come on roses. Don't fail me now. Give meee…*Turquoise!*" I spin in a circle, stop on a dime, and point over a few rows to a grouping of petals that are, believe it or not, Turquoise.

"What?" she says amazed, "Never in my wildest dreams."

We meander over to get a closer look, "So, ah, sorry about yesterday."

"What? No. No reason to be sorry. In fact. I agree."

"You do?"

"Yes. People are not thinking for themselves. They take whatever mainstream media force feeds them, and they say, *Mmmm, yummy, give me more, I don't want to think for myself.* Germany is worse than America."

"What?"

"Yeah, I mean, they're allowing people to pour in without taking into consideration the effect it's having on Germany. Trump is right. The travel ban is right. The wall is right. Don't let it happen here. Don't lose your identity. America is a shining light in the world but that light can be snuffed out."

I'm stupefied, "Well, I did not see that coming. I'm not a fan of the wall. I feel like the money could be spent better in other ways."

"The lack of security costs your country billions of dollars a year."

"Really?"

"Yes. The current budget dealing with your porous border is around four billion dollars a year not to mention the billions you spend on illegal aliens in jails, on education, health, and welfare. There's already a wall. Some think Trump thought up the idea, and that makes him racist. But, *there's already a wall.* It's just got a lot of holes in it. No one thought it was racist when it was constructed twenty-eight years ago."

I'm so bewildered and truthfully smitten with Alexus, I'm having a hard time thinking straight. We stop at the turquoise flowers and Shanice and Malik join us.

"Hey, Alexus, hi," Malik greets her with a hug.

"Hi, sweetheart. My goodness, you're so…sweet."

"Watch this," he says as he runs up the stairwell and then slides down the railing.

"Wow, that's amazing." She's such a great sport. I continue where we left off, "I don't know, I think that money could be used in other ways like high-tech surveillance. Drones and such."

"Well, you may be right, drone technology gives me pause. I can see a day where they're buzzing around everywhere taking away our right to privacy."

"Good point. If only we had a crystal ball and could see thirty years in the future. So, you're a Trump supporter?"

"Well, obviously I couldn't vote. But yeah, I guess I am. I mean, once I really dug into Hillary's history of lies and deception, I was glad Trump won."

"But Trump lies too."

"They all lie. Trumps lies are not the calculated, deep state, hidden agenda genre of lies. At least I don't see it that way. Hillary had her phones *smashed with hammers!* She scrubbed her servers; bleach bit them and lied continually about it. She deleted over 5,000 emails. She lied about Benghazi, she lied about the uranium one deal, and during the campaign, they gave her questions before interviews. She controlled the DNC through donations she and Bill made. They put the fix in on Bernie Sanders. The Clinton Foundation is a farce, a pay-for-play organization which is now falling apart since she lost. She called all the people that Bill Clinton sexually harassed and abused the 'bimbo parade.' I mean, you were this close to putting Bill Clinton back in the white house! What kind of judgment can she really have? She's married to an impeached president who had sexual escapades with a 21-year-old intern! Her most trusted advisor, Huma Abedin, Married *Anthony Wiener!* A guy caught sexting his junk to a teenage girl. I could go on. There's the tarmac meeting between Bill and Loretta Lynch; she called black people super predators and half the country irredeemable and deplorable. The DNC paid people to go into Trumps rallies and *start fights!*

Proof DNC paid to start fights trumped.online/4tt

"And the DNC, Hillary, actually paid for the dirty dossier that started the whole Trump/Russia collusion delusion investigation nonsense. I mean, it says Trump went to Moscow to meet with Russian hookers so they could pee on him. This Dossier was the prominent document used to get the FISA warrant which started the whole Mueller madness. Think of it. It's unprecedented. An opposing candidate pays for a fake dossier so they can get a warrant in an attempt to destroy the sitting and duly elected president! It's now coming out that there was probably even a spy infiltrating Trump's campaign under the Obama administration. And the FBI agent, Lisa Page asked fellow agent Peter Strzok, who was in charge of both the Hilary investigation and the Mueller probe, if Trump would ever be president. Strzok replied, 'No. No, he's not. We'll stop it.'

Did Obama spy on Trump? trumped.online/p18

Hillary wiping server trumped.online/k9k

CBS: FBI agent's anti Trump texts trumped.online/wai

"I think you're right about all that. It's insane. Politics is insane. Senator Trey Gowdy is retiring because he says it's not about doing what's right, it's just about winning. But I sometimes think we might be better off if

Hillary were president. I mean, Trump's so brash. So unpresidential. The tweets!"

"You may be right. We'll never know. *I seriously doubt it.* But, if you were like your friends, *my boss,* how did you get to this place of open-mindedness?"

"Okay, well, Trump deserves some credit for that. I mean he's such a disruptor it forced me to open my eyes. I had to defend my positions. And, as I analyzed my positions under a critical light, I saw holes. I mean, sometimes I do think he may be a good president. In part because of him, the policies he's implemented, but maybe more so as a result of *unintended consequences.* He is a disruptor and, as much as I don't like the disrupting, it's possible that when the dust settles, we will all be the better for it."

"So true. He's like the proverbial dog in a china shop. The china in this shop, however, is fake, and dirty. For years it could have been removed and replaced, gently. Quietly. But, *no one did it.* So, maybe it's just going to take a Donald Trump to destroy it! Maybe that's the only way now to get rid of the dirty, fake, chipped, counterfeit, ugly china."

"Exactly! I mean when I'm frustrated with him, I hope for that very outcome. It's like he's chemotherapy and Washington DC is the cancer. No one wants chemotherapy; unless of course it's your only option!"

We watch the kids playing for a moment. They're racing each other through a long row of roses to the amphitheater stage. A devilish grin finds its way to her beautiful lips, "I'll race you to the stage, loser buys dinner."

"You can't be serious."

"Serious as a wiped hard drive full of classified government secrets."

"You're on."

"Okay, on the count of three."

We both get into the, *on your mark,* position. She begins the count, "One, two..."

And, she's off, *no three*. I should have known. So, I kick it into high gear. Catching up to her, I know I could pass, but it conflicts with the gentleman in me. We're flying through the garden, the colors a blur on all sides. Finally, I pass her. I guess I'm showing off. As I approach the stage I even spin around backward, playfully taunting her, "Come on, show me whatcha go… "

I trip on the root of a giant oak tree near the stage and go flying, landing hard on my backside. As she passes me, she can barely sustain her weight due to the utter hysterical fit she's in *at my expense*. When she reaches the stage, the kids join in on the fun. "What happened Daddy? Trip on a blade of grass?" Malik quips.

"Or maybe the Rose Garden Gnomes tied your shoelaces together," Shanice adds. There's nothing better than mocking Dad!

I get up, wipe the dirt off my bum and say, "Well, I guess I'm buying."

"Yes, you are!" she says with delight.

I'm so comfortable in her presence; I want to share with her something I have not with anyone else. My best friend.

"But there's another," I say cryptically.

"Another what."

"Another one. Responsible for freeing my mind. I want you and the kids to meet him. You up for it, before we get dinner?"

"Are you kidding? Wouldn't trade that for the missing 5,000 emails in Hillary's wiped server!"

We all pile in my Prius. As we approach the homeless encampment, she is, of course, baffled. "Where are we going?" she remarks as we exit the car on the less than desirable Market street with all the tents and tarps encroaching ever closer.

"This way." I take the kids' hands as we cross the street on to the grass.

"This is where Cynthia used to live," Shanice recalls.

"Yes, that's right sweetheart."

"Who is Cynthia?" Alexus inquires.

"That's another story for another time. Right now you have to meet the Orange-tent-guy."

"What? Who?"

"The Guy-In-the-orange-tent. Honestly, that's his name. At least to me. But his story is incredible. Inspirational. And he's probably the most brilliant person I've ever known. You'll see."

We arrive outside his humble abode, "Yo buddy, put down the iPad, give the researching a rest, and get out here. I've got some people I would like you to meet."

There's no answer. "Well, if you're sleeping, I'm waking you up."

I turn to my kids and Alexus, "Just a sec."

I let myself into the tent, *"Shoot, he's not here,"* I yell out through the tent mesh. And just as I'm about to exit, I notice an envelope with my name on it, *Prius Driving; I Hope You're Over Yourself, New Over Guy.*

I step out, "He's not here, but I found this letter addressed to me."

"You?" Alexus comments, "It says, *Prius Driving, I Hope You're Over Yourself, New Over Guy.*"

"That's me. Again, it's a long story." I open the envelope and read.

Hello, my friend,

    I cannot live out this existence any longer. Being the Orange-

       tent-guy, for you, gave me a purpose. And, it has been an

       honor. I endured this life much longer than I ever thought I

       could. Remember when I told you about my promise to God?

       That I could not die until I somehow made the world a better

I'm trying to hold back the tears. But it's impossible. Alexus puts her hand on my shoulder, supporting me without understanding why. The tears drop and stain the writing on the paper. Shanice wraps her arm around my leg, "What's wrong Daddy? Don't cry."

"I just need a minute sweetheart, I'm sorry."

Then I continue to read the note.

I'm the papers that blow in the sidewalk wind

I'm the needles and the bottles and the cans of tin

Do not stand at my tent and cry,

I am not there; we do not die…

With all my love,

Orange-tent-guy

Chapter 24 The Future: *Alex Jones*
Year: 2047 May 4th 6:52 p.m.

"Charles, I think we have to trust her. She can bring this whole thing down."

"Yes, I can," Shelly says hoping to gain Charles' trust.

He looks at her trying to gauge her sincerity, "Just what will you do to help?"

Right then, thirteen men come running toward us with guns as the Heli-Flyer rotors and jets get louder and louder. *"Put your hands in the air,"* one of the armed men commands, "We don't want to kill you."

I drop the mace, Charles drops the taser but then Shelly yells, *"They're not real, they're holograms, they can't hurt you."*

"Shut up Shelly," the apparent leader demands.

We've never seen such technology. They look solid, real, even in the daylight. Charles cuts the tape to free Shelly. She jumps to her feet, "Come on, we got to get out of here."

We take off running right through the images of the holograms as one yells, *"Shelly, you will pay for this!"* We enter the Castle while the Heli-Flyer is close to landing about one hundred yards away.

"I need my phone quick, iMinds have limitations. I've got to get all the files off the G.P. cloud, into my mind and on to my phone."

"G.P. has its own cloud?"

"You better believe it, and no one has access to it unless you are a V.P. or higher. But I'm sure the information will disappear any second now." She grabs her phone and iPad and downloads.

"What information?" Jadda asks.

"Everything having to do with burying the data. And proof we've known for a long time what was really happening. We even have the original files from Al Gore proving the real reason he sold his network to Al Jazeera, besides becoming a billionaire that is."

"And then, we've got to get it to the press," I announce as if no one is thinking the same thing. "Sorry for pointing out the obvious."

"It's not so obvious," Shelley says.

"Okay, they just landed. We gotta go. Follow me," Charles demands.

We run out the front door toward the carriage house, pull open the huge doors at the center of the structure and there sits the brand new Google E. Flyer. "You didn't tell me you got one of these," I announce my surprise.

"You didn't ask," Charles says shrugging his shoulders. "Besides, it just arrived a few days ago. I don't know how to fly it yet. I suggest you hold on."

Just as the armed men reach his house, we're taking off. We can see them scurrying around on the ground heading back for their flyer. As we wobble to and fro in the sky, Charles says, "Yeah, I've only had one lesson." Jadda is turning several shades of green. Alexus is clinging to my arm and squeezing my hand so hard I'm losing circulation in my fingers. I ask Shelly, "Have you got the information? Is it downloaded?"

"It's coming now, into my mind and onto my phone."

"What did you mean, getting the information to the press is not so obvious?"

"Mainstream media! Who do you think controls them?"

Every one of us announces in unison "G.P.!," as we suddenly drop like we're on a roller coaster.

"Sorry…" Charles offers.

"Exactly." Shelley affirms "CNN? *Counterfeit News Network*. MSNBC? *More Same Network Bull Crap.*"

Alexus questions, "Then who can we go to that has enough power and outreach but is not owned by G.P.?"

Again, we all shout in unison, "Alex Jones!?"

The Dawn: *Orange-Tent-Guy's Memorial*
Year: 2017 December 24, Christmas Eve 4:30 p.m.

It was a miraculous summer. I mean, I met, I don't know, my *soulmate,* Alexus. I believe we will be together until we die. And maybe even beyond. I never really subscribed to that sort of thing before and I don't even know how I would define it, I'm just saying I feel it. We feel it. Whatever 'it' is! Crazy love? This is our first Christmas together. We're going to Trinity Cathedral at 9 o'clock mass to celebrate. She's a 'Recovering Catholic' but says she would enjoy the tradition, at least once, with me. But there's one thing that has continually put a cloud in the middle of my silver lining. Orange-tent-guy, passing. I guess that was what he referred to when he said he was nearly 'finished' but wouldn't tell me what exactly he was finishing. Turns out to be, life itself!

Every day, on my way to work, I look over at the homeless encampment, at the orange tent. It's still there, but he is not. I keep thinking I might see him sitting, peacefully, like he used to. Or with his iPad doing research or maybe, *peeing on a tree.* I've decided it's time to let go. To do something to help me mourn his passing. A ritual of some kind. Alexus suggests we go to the orange tent tonight on the way to Trinity and have a kind of memorial service. Just the four of us. At her prodding, I write a letter.

At about 8 o'clock, we take the market street exit and park next to the grassy area near the tent. The four of us make our way by the light of Alexus's iPhone to the front of his old site. I'm sure someone else uses it now, from time to time, but no one's here currently. And so, again, at Alexus's suggestion, I read the letter to the three of them. I clear my throat, feeling tears pushing on my eyes even before I begin.

> Dear Orange-tent-guy,
>   Physics tells us that nothing can be created or destroyed. Everything transforms from one form of energy into another. Einstein said this is why he believed we never really die. And so, I want you to know; I do see you in everything! Everywhere. In the alleyways, in the homeless tents, in the parking lots, in the clouds, and yes, even in the mansions in the West Hills. I speak to you all the time in my

mind. And I hear your words, your wisdom. They
inform me and give me strength.
I wish with all my heart you could meet my kids and my
new girl, Alexus. You would love her. Like you, she's
a brilliant, independent thinker.

I just wish I understood why. Why did you give up? I've
tried so hard to make sense out of it. But it doesn't
make sense. It just hurts. I miss you. More than I
could ever have imagined.

With all my love,
Prius Driving, About To Have A Nervous Breakdown,
Getting Over Myself, New Over Guy.

Alexus wipes a single tear as the tears I have wept create unfettered tracks down my cheeks. I put the letter into an envelope. The plan was to bury it next to the orange tent. But before I could place it inside the envelope, someone from in the dark softly speaks.

"Yes, everything transforms from one form to another. And so, the Orange-tent-guy can never meet this beautiful woman or these beautiful children. However, I can."

A handsome man in an Armani suit approaches us. I struggle to make him out. He looks so familiar and yet so different. My heart is as confused as my mind. He reaches his hand out, "Hello, my name is Charles, Charles Johnson. So pleased to meet you."

It's him, and yet it isn't. Overwhelmed, I hug him as the tears pour out of my eyes, "It's you, except," I laugh, "You don't stink anymore."

"Orange-tent-guy is dead," he says as we embrace, "He stunk. Not me."

"Man, if I weren't so glad you're alive, I *would kill you.*"

"Again, Orange-tent-guy is dead. It's Christmas Eve. The time of new birth." He pulls us apart, gives me a big grin and states, "I'm Charles." "Malik, Shanice, and Alexus meet Charles."

Chapter 25 The Future: Justin Bieber
Year: 2047 May 4 7:39 p.m.

"The information just stopped downloading. I'm sure it's all been bleach bit by now," Shelley reports.

"WHAT? What are we going to do?"

"Well, I got most before they could wipe it clean. We're good."

"HOLD ON," Charles yells, *"We're under attack."*

We go into a dive straight down as some kind of missile flies past missing us by just a few feet.

"JESUS, MARY, AND JOSEPH," Alexus exclaims as her Catholic past catches up to her.

"Siri," Shelly commands!

Siri responds with that C-3PO voice, "Oh my, how can I help?"

"Call the Alex Jones show now."

"Yes ma'am, right away." There are two rings before it picks up.

"Hello, this is the Alex Jones show. How can I help you?"

"We'd like to speak to an actual person right away, Alex Jones if possible."

"Mr. Jones is busy, what can I do for you?"

"Look, we have the single biggest scoop since Justin Bieber caught Leonardo DiCaprio having an affair in the White House with Molly Cyrus during his second term."

"I'll connect you with Mr. Jones now."

Although many people consider Alex Jones a kook, all of his supplements have proven to be effective. The guy had hardly aged a day since around 2018 when Twitter, YouTube, and Facebook colluded to have him kicked off all social media.

Alex Jones banned trumped.online/vlt

However, by 2026 his independent platform took off and, the rest is history!

"This is Alex, what's the scoop?"

"*INCOMING!*" Charles yells, "HOLD ON!"

"What's happening?" Alex Jones asks urgently.

"We're under fire," Shelly responds. "But, as soon as you can air the information it will all be over. Listen, G.P. is corrupt."

"Tell me something I don't know" Alex quips with his scruffy voice.

"Well, it's bigger than even you could have imagined."

"Really? So the technology they use is from planet Xeron, and they're all aliens at G.P. headquarters?"

"Okay, I guess it's not bigger than *your* imagination, but it's still pretty huge. How can I send it to you and how fast can you get it on the air?"

"Well, I can get it on the air as soon as you send it. Who are you?"

"Shelly Singleton, V.P. at G.P."

"Siri," Alex Jones requests, "Accept all information from Shelly Singleton." Seconds later, "Okay, it's coming in now. Oh man, this is huge. And, I *knew it!* I'll have it on the air in minutes."

"I'll try to land in Pioneer Courthouse Square." Charles warns us, "We need to be in the most public place possible, and I think KGW still broadcasts from there, right?"

"Yes," Alexus confirms, "Maybe we can reach someone there as well. Siri, turn on the Alex Jones show."

C3PO answers, "Yes, right away." The show appears holographically almost like he's in the Heli-Flyer with us.

"Okay everyone," Alex says sitting at his huge desk, "We have the story of the century…."

And at that moment, the E-Flyer chasing us turns and disappears into the horizon.

Charles yells, "HOLD ON; WE'RE GOING DOWN…."

The Dawn: *Crypto Currency*
Year: 2018 January 1 11 a.m.

"The code is 68443, or OTGGF for Orange-tent-guy Gone Forever," Charles tells me as I approached the massive gate to his new home in the West Hills. I enter the code and before me is a castle with a Tourette and a carriage house. Several acres of land. You can see the mountains in the distance and the lights of Portland. And, yes, you can see his old house, the orange tent below. I pull up the circular cobblestone driveway as he steps out to meet me. I can't contain my amazement, "Dude, *this is insane.* What is going on?"

All cleaned up and wearing Ralph Lauren or Armani or something like that; he looks like Denzel Washington in, *The Preacher's Wife.*

"Come in, let me show you around."

After a tour of the 12,000 sq ft mansion we sit on two high winged armchairs fit for a king. They face the high back windows looking past the pool and the pond toward the mountains and the city.

"Okay, Orange Ten… I mean, Charles. Explain yourself!"

"Well, as you know, after I sobered up I caught on fire for knowledge, full of unquenchable curiosity."

"Yeah, just what is it you always studied?"

"Well, everything. Politics, science, economics, religion/spirituality, history. I have what is called *eidetic* memory. I could try to explain but suffice to say, my memory is strong, to say the least."

"Wait, so *that's* how you pulled off page one hundred and twenty-three, paragraph two of **The Communist Manifesto**!"

"Yes, anyway, a few years ago I became aware of cryptocurrency, Bitcoin to be precise."

"I've heard of it, but know little about it."

"Well, it's complicated, but I realized a long time ago that our monetary system is outdated, so I opened an account using this." He pulled out of his pocket the old, cracked iPhone. "It still works believe it or not. At first, I collected bottles. I know, cliché for a homeless guy but if the shoe fits… Then, as my business cleaning parking lots took off, I was able to put a few thousand dollars into cryptocurrency and, *the value of Bitcoin skyrocketed beyond even my wildest dreams.*

⫘ Bitcoin Skyrockets <u>trumped.online/7e5</u> ⫘

And well, the rest is history. I didn't mean to disappear the way I did and leave you hanging. But, I got pretty sick, could've been life-threatening, so I moved into a cheap motel that took Bitcoin, just before the market skyrocketed. I came down to the orange tent every few days, hoping I would find you there. It finally happened."

My phone rang. Normally I would not have taken the call but, to my great surprise, it's Michelle!

Chapter 26 The Future: *Fox News, Starbucks* Year: 2047 May 4 7:49 p.m.

"Brace yourselves! It looks like we're going to crash land in the water feature next to Starbucks in the square."

I hold tightly to Alexus's hand with my left hand, while my right hand grips the handle on the ceiling. As I look out the window, the ground is approaching at an ever-increasing clip. The next thing I know, *BANG, KERSPLASH.* We crash in the fountain. Water's pouring in all around us.

"Is everyone okay?" Charles asks.

"I'm good," Alexus informs.

"Me too," Jadda adds.

"Everything is in working order I believe," Shelly says as she wipes the blood from her upper lip, "Just a bloody nose."

"Well, you had that coming," I say, grinning.

We sit there, soaking wet. Stunned. Trying to come to grips with what just happened when Charles exclaims, *"Woo-hoo! Outrageous!"*

"I concur. *That was the ride of my life!"* I declare.

Alexus laughs, and soon we're all cracking up, trying to exit the Heli-Flyer while water pours all around us.

Once we're out Jadda observes sarcastically, "Hmmm, my phone isn't functioning. Can't access my cryptocurrency and I gotta use the restroom. I'm sure glad Starbucks changed their policies back in 2018 so you could use all of their facilities without buying a thing. Loiter but legally."

"Yeah," Charles quips, "Remember when they used to serve coffee? Before they doubled as homeless shelters? Those were the days."

Starbucks sensitivity training trumped.online/fd1

People are gathering around us, asking if we're okay when a reporter from KGW, an affiliate of NBC, approaches, live on air.

"Are you the people who were just featured on The Alex Jones show?" she asks intensely.

Charles wipes some water off his head, "Yes, that's us."

"Is it true? Has G.P. been hiding the truth? Is plant life in danger of starvation? Are we actually headed for the next Ice Age?"

We all look at each other, wondering who would like to answer. I finally elect myself, "Yep, it's true. Everything Alex Jones aired is fact. At least as it pertains to G.P."

"I can send you all the information if you're willing to air it." Shelly offers.

"It could get me fired, but send away," she says, live, to her credit. She knows all too well, G.P. owns the media.

Twenty minutes later, the truth is flying all over the internet.

We're sitting on a bench in pioneer courthouse square next to Broadway, the main street through the middle of town. Suddenly something occurs that, just minutes ago, it was nothing short of a cultural taboo over which you could lose your standing in society. Not to mention it was punishable by a twenty thousand dollar fine and up to 7 years in prison. A pristine, all original 1955 Ford Mustang pulls up to the streetlight. The driver waves, then, as the light turns green, he floors it, squealing out like he's in a drag race back when the car was made. We hear a hoop and a holler as he disappears. Then a 2012 Porsche boxer convertible flies by, top down. Followed by a 1979 Lincoln Continental. Soon the streets are like a parade of gas-guzzling beauties. Honking horns, cheering, music blasting. Then my phone rings.

"Hello?"

"Hi, is this Marcus?"

"Um, Yes."

"This is Hopie Carlson." Hopie, Tucker Carlson's daughter, has followed in her father's footsteps and recently taken his place as the host of the Tucker Carlson show on FOX News.

"I'd like to have you on the show tonight. We have to get the truth out. Can you? Will you?"

Never in my life did I think for a second I would be on FOX News! "Of course, there's so much to tell!"

The Dawn: *Shit Hole Countries*
Year: 2018 January 7 6:43 p.m.

Of all people, it has shocked me over the last few days to be reconnecting with Michelle. Somehow I figured a transgender would be the last to experience and then face his cognitive dissonance as it pertains to identity politics. But that was my bad! He's been asking me so many questions; I've invited him to meet Alexus and me at Charles' home.

"Come on in," Charles invites the three of us. "Nice dress," he says commenting on Michelle's attire.

"Well, this is unbelievable," Michelle says looking around.

"And, his personal story dwarfs this amazing place, but I will save that for another time."

"Have a seat everyone, tea?" Charles asks. We all agree to tea as we gather near the hearth, a huge fire is warming the place from January's cool air.

"So, what's troubling you?" Charles begins.

"Well," Michelle responds smiling, eyes wide, "It might be easier to ask, what's *not* troubling me. Anyway, Marcus, I know how hard it was for you to speak from your heart to all of us. To lose your friends, your marriage. First, I want to apologize."

"Hey, no apology necessary. I understand."

"But, I think maybe it's even harder for me. Being transgender is difficult enough, but being a transgender who questions the identity politics a transgender is expected to represent, the entire LGBTQ community is liable to shun me. Everyone from our old group probably will."

I shake my head, remembering the past year. "It has been very difficult, that's for sure. As you know, I do try to reach out to the gang occasionally. The most disappointing one of all for me has been Jesus. I somehow thought he'd be more accepting. But, I have to agree with you. It probably is more difficult for you than for me."

"Well," Michelle confesses, "There's this movement to push children, even before puberty, to consider changing their sex. To begin hormone 'therapy.' As a person who's been through it, I wouldn't wish it upon anyone, to have this desire to change your gender. I mean, you can't do it. I can't change my chromosomes as much as I wish I could. I am a man in that sense, and I always will be. But for me to say that to people in my community and even to our friends, which I tried doing, is like setting off an emotional atomic bomb!"

"Michelle," Charles says with compassion, "I can see how troubling this is for you and I'm so glad you came to us. Whatever your views are, we're not in judgment of you."

"I know. That's what started me on my journey. Marcus, as he questioned some of our hardened thought patterns, was never judgmental. It was us who were judgmental of him. It was us who were unaccepting of him. That hypocrisy made me question things. I didn't want to be that way. And that opened my mind. Incredible as it may seem, I don't even hate Trump anymore. What I mean is, I understand now why some people did not want Hillary to be the president. It's obvious now, but I never let myself see it. So, I don't like Trump, but I don't hate him either. I just wish he wasn't such a racist."

"Ah, the old racist thing," Charles steps in.

"You don't think he's a racist?" Michelle asks sincerely. "I mean, he called people shit holes who come from mostly black countries that aren't as well off as America."

"I find it so bewildering how his words get twisted. First, the whole shit hole statement was behind closed doors. In private. No one knows exactly what the context was, or what was even said. Senator Democrat

Dick Durbin, who hates the president, ran to the press like a tattletale and said Trump referred to certain countries in Africa and Haiti as shit holes. How anyone can take that line, even out of context, and interpret it as Trump saying the *people* are shitty, makes no sense. He never said the people are bad even by Dick Durbin's account which is, wholeheartedly, out of context. He allegedly said many of the countries are in bad shape. *Which they are. There are countries in Africa that still practice slavery.* In Zimbabwe, it is a largely held belief that if you have sex with a virgin, it will cure you of aids!"

"What? Really?"

"Pretty shitty, huh."

"Yeah."

"Anyway," Charles says while straightening up in his chair, "I *do* think Trump's a racist. It's just that; I think we all are."

"What? I'm not racist," I say defensively, "Charles, how could you even insinuate that?"

"Let's do a thought experiment. I will prove it. Once we understand we're all racist, we can forgive each other and let it go. We have got to get over this as a culture." Charles scratches his chin for a moment. Michelle and I have no idea what he's up to. "Okay, let's say you get fifty million dollars if you can predict the winners of a basketball game."

"Is it the Harlem Globetrotters versus the Golden State Warriors? I'd have to go with the Globetrotters," I jest.

"Who wouldn't?" Charles plays along. "Actually, you get to pick the team, but you do not get to see the players before the game. You're sitting on the bleachers, all by yourself, and you're told there are 20 men in the locker room. There will be ten players on each team. The men were picked randomly from college teams across the country. The only stipulation was, ten of them had to be white, and ten of them had to be black. There are fifty million dollars on the line. Seeing none of the men, who would you pick to be on your team?"

It's been a while since he had me dead to rights! We sit there, struggling between what we know is true and what we wish to be true. We wish everyone were equal. We wish the world were an even playing field. No one answers.

"That's what I thought!" Charles expels. "You would be an idiot *not* to pick the ten black guys. And if you didn't, you would be virtue signaling yourself out of fifty million dollars. The ten black guys would win. We all know it. It shouldn't feel weird or strange or wrong to say that. It's just obvious; it's a fact. And yes, *it's racist.* You're choosing ten players based on the color of their skin. You haven't seen any of them play yet. So it's racist, *so what.* It doesn't mean there aren't great white basketball players. Of course, there are. Some of the greatest players in history are and where white. But the fact remains, in general, black basketball players are better than white basketball players. In fact, in general, black athletes are better than white athletes. Yes, that is a racist statement, but *it is a fact.* So, get over it. Consider that only about 13% of Americans are black. And yet, 70% of the NFL is black! That's a glaring statistic that no one can deny. As far as Donald Trump goes, I don't think he's any more racist than the rest of us."

We're all in a state of shock.

"Wow," Michelle says to me, "You were right about this guy!"

Charles isn't done with us yet. "There are two types of racism. Type one is bad, the kind we generally think of. Type two is good, the kind I have just described. Type one is a belief that you and everyone like you, *racially,* are inherently superior to everyone in another racial group. This is bad and is putting the group before the individual, w*hich is always bad.* Type two racism is simply living in a world of facts. Every race on the planet is different, unique, from every other race. Saying that is racist by definition. It's also a fact which is why I never cease to be amused when some say, *Diversity is our strength,* and then they call you a racist for pointing out that people of different races are diverse!"

"*So,*" Alexus says grappling with these new concepts, "You're saying that being type two racist is a good thing?"

"Yes, and we all know it, or we would have to accuse the NBA and NFL of racial profiling, which would be absurd. What we must do as we begin to acknowledge our differences and even celebrate them, is never put the group above the individual. If we did, there would have never been, for example, Larry Bird, Dirk Nowitzki or John Stockton because if we put

the group above the individual, then we would say that only black people
are allowed to play basketball."

"So there are tendencies, not absolutes," Michelle offers, "In every race.
Like, for example, Asians tend to excel scholastically but not every Asian
is going to do better academically than everybody else from every other
race."

"Exactly. We could do thought experiments all day like the one I had you
do, picking a team without seeing the players, proving that different
aspects of different races are superior, *on average,* to different aspects of
other races. There is even much empirical evidence that some races, *in
general,* have a higher IQ than other races, in general. *So what? There
are geniuses in every race* and in the end, it boils down to *character.* The
content of one's character."

⬭ IQ Sam Harris <u>trumped.online/d4b</u> ⬭

Alexus jumps in with a tough question, "Your statement that 13% of
Americans are black reminds me. I was watching the Rubin Report the
other day, Dave Rubin, you know him?"

"Love him!" Charles says emphatically.

"He had Larry Elder on."

"Love him!" he says again.

"Well, Larry Elder cited a lot of statistics. Statistics I don't enjoy hearing,
but like you, I believe until we face facts we can't change them. He said
that, yes, African Americans make up about 13% of the population, but
they commit 50% of the homicides and around 70% of lesser crimes. I
always thought blacks were disproportionately imprisoned because cops
are raci… "

⬭ Larry Elder smashes it <u>trumped.online/5cv</u> ⬭

"Lies! Propaganda!" He says cutting him off. "That is the biggest…*COP
OUT!* There is a problem within the black community, and it can easily
be traced back to the expansion of the welfare state in the 1960s. Before
1960, only 22 percent of black children were raised by one parent. The
home was stable. Today over 75% of black children are being raised
without a father. And the worst of it is, *most of them don't even know*

345

their father! The family unit broke down under the welfare system. Fathers suddenly were thought to be unneeded. As a result, they were not held accountable. Mothers could, in a sense, marry the government. The casualties are the children! They need to feel that both parents love them and want to be in their lives. This, by the way, is not unique to the black community. Everywhere the government has stepped in to take the place of a human beings responsibility, things go wrong. Boys need discipline. They need a role model. They need consistency. They need loving limits. Otherwise, they will join a gang to try to fill what is missing in their lives. This is true for all boys. It has, however, disproportionally affected black America. What they need in black neighborhoods are more cops, not less."

Thomas Sowell on welfare trumped.online/5rk
Lil' Wayne rapper on racism and cops trumped.online/5at

"What about the Black Lives Matter movement?" Michelle inquires.

Charles shakes his head, "Don't get me started. It's literally part of their mission statement to *disrupt the family unit!* Just look at their website. How many people do you think have read the mission of Black Lives Matter?"

"Well, I haven't," I admit.

"Next to no one, I'm sure," he says. "Did you know every person who started the B.L.M. movement is a woman?"

"Nope," Alexus admits.

"Did you know they are gay?"

"Huh? No, didn't know that."

"If you want to understand the Black *Lies* Matter movement and how deceitful it is, just read their mission statement. They are hiding behind the minority status of blacks to push their agenda as gay. And since they are gay, black, and women no one is allowed to question them under the new intersectionality 'oppression Olympics' rules."

"I've heard this term, intersectionality, a lot," I admit, "But I don't understand it."

"Intersectionality is defined as; the value of your opinion, knowledge, and insight depends upon which ethnic group or victim group you belong to and the more 'marginalized' groups a person identifies as, the more intersected they are and therefore the greater the status they achieve. A white woman is considered 'marginalized' but not intersected. A black woman has reached an intersection, like roads converging; she's both a woman *and* black. This intersected 'road' is considered more difficult to drive on, bumpier, less maintained. A black, gay, woman has merged with another 'road' in even worse condition. Now, take a transgender, gay, black, muslim, woman and you may have reached the peak of 'marginalized' intersectionality."

Sharm Sharma, Intersectionality trumped.online/sdu

Alexus chimes in, "The irony seems to me that these groups are no longer marginalized. For example, at Nike, we make an extra effort to hire 'marginalized' people! We have bathrooms just for transgenders. Transgenders make up 0.6 percent of the population and yet they get their own bathroom. That seems like special treatment as opposed to marginalized."

With a smirk and a shake of the head, Charles responds, "I get your drift. So, in today's new world order of 'victimology' based on intersectionality, the B.L.M leaders are nearly untouchable! Just consider some of the crap they have pulled."

BLM gone amuck trumped.online/gyl
BLM Mission and Bernie Sanders trumped.online/6gl

"Victimology?" Michelle asks.

"Yes, it's like a new religion. I get one point for being black. You get one, maybe two points for being trans. Alexus gets one point for being a woman. In traditional religions, the more you practice your faith and understand its precepts the more enlightened or awakened you become. In intersectionality the more you understand and practice their philosophy the more 'woke' you are. Yes, it has reached such levels of religious dogma they even took the spiritual concept of awakening and created their own word, woke! One of the biggest flaws in this new religion is there's no redemption. And the sinners for which there is no salvation are all white males!"

"Wait, what? I thought I was the automatic winner for being a white male. Don't I have all the privilege?"

"Well, white males had their day in the sun, for sure. But now *you* are paying for the perception that your skin color and your Y chromosome are the creators of all things evil. The truth, of course, is much more complicated than that."

"It's gray?"

"Yep. White males created the greatest country on the planet with the most freedoms for all. Why else do you think more people want to come here than any other county in the world? White males fought and died to free slaves when the rest of the world practiced slavery without a smidgen of guilt, *including Africa.* Males have been and still are considered the most disposable members of society, *Women and Children first.* So, yes, it's gray."

"But you get negative points," Michelle agrees, "Because you're a white male *and straight!* Whoever can claim the highest victim status, of which you have none, wins the most stuff. More proof they're not marginalized."

"What stuff?" I ask Michelle.

"Well, the greater the victim you can virtue signal yourself into, first of all, the more sympathy and attention you receive. And in today's social media driven world, attention is king. Second, the government gives you the most benefits, even money."

Charles continues the thought, "It's the oppression Olympics. If we could find a half black, half Hispanic, Muslim, short, transgender woman, this profoundly intersected person would be perceived as an all-wise, all-knowing prophet for which there would be repercussions of great shame if one were ever to question their motives, reasoning, or opinions."

Michelle gives a half smile, "Sorry Marcus, you lose. You have white male privilege. Which makes you the oppressor of all the rest of us!"

Charles takes over, "Which, in this new religion of Victim-ism, being a white male *is your original sin* from which there is no redemption. So, you and your kind are forever saddled with the shame of being the oppressor which, of course, makes you a *victim of your privilege!"*

"Wow, BAM!" Michelle exclaims.

"Then, don't I finally get some points since I'm ultimately a victim too? A victim of my privilege?"

All three look at me, smile and answer, "Nope!"

"THAT'S NOT FAIR," I whine like a good social justice warrior!

Australia, *It's not okay to be white* trumped.online/qio

Charles laughs, "The funniest and most telling moment I've seen in the news recently was when a CNN reporter accused a black man of having white privilege."

"No way," I protest.

"Oh yes. It happened!"

CNN accuses black, of white privilege trumped.online/nne

"And what about the Catholic Covington boys and Jussie Smollett?" I inquire, "Everything has reversed. And the media is more concerned with confirming their desired narrative than with truth."

Covington boys Ben Shapiro trumped.online/nf3
Covington boys truth, in15 minutes trumped.online/97o

"Yep. The media elites, political elites and Hollywood elites attacked and defamed these innocent boys because they are everything they hate: white males, pro-life, Trump supporters. It's really sick what this media driven hoax did to sow division. And Jussie Smollett, or now, Jessie Smollett since Chris Rock says he doesn't deserve the 'u' anymore," Charles says with a grin. "He perpetrated a fake hate crime, *on himself.* Claims two white guys yelled, *This is MAGA country,* then threw bleach on him and put a noose around his neck. He put the whole country on edge. He got caught red handed but Chicago dropped the charges!"

Chris Rock Live trumped.online/c8b
CNN Jussie Smollett trumped.online/jko
Jussie Smollett case trumped.online/mt1
Kevins Corner Smollett trumped.online/q1b

"It seems to illustrate both *intersectionality* and *privilege,* " I react.

"I'm impressed my Padawan," Charles says, "Continue."

"Well, Jussie, I mean J̲essie, is rich and famous. He's got that old school elitism going for him, *privilege*. And, he is both black and gay so he gets a gold medal in the Intersectionality/Oppression Olympics competition; which of course makes no since because the last thing he is, is oppressed. But, in todays world, claiming any 'victim status' requires no connection to reality. It makes him close to untouchable."

"Well done Grass Hopper," he says harkening back to the show, Kung Fu, "Now, the Feds are looking into the case. Hopefully all his privilege, *will not apply.* "

Chapter 27 The Future: *President Shapiro*
Year: 2047 July 4 9:30 p.m.

"It's breathtaking up here Charles. How many fireworks displays can be seen exploding over Portland?"

He considers for a moment, looking out at all the lights, listening to the, *Boom.*

"*Sheesh,* remember we tried to count last year? I think we came up with something like twenty-seven."

"Last year!" I say experiencing a kind of life review, "Wow, what a year we've had. *Disaster averted!"*

"*Mmm hmmm,"* he gives me a high five, "President Ben Shapiro officially ordered the complete shutdown of G.P. yesterday. The Transition back to fossil fuels is underway worldwide. Thank God some old Hollywood celebrity is no longer President."

"Dude, *we…saved…the…planet!"*

"*Yeah, we did!"*

"I, finally, got published and peer-reviewed…for whatever that's worth."

He grins, remembering the beginning of our journey, *"Yes, you did!"*

"Looks like everyone in the inner circle at G.P., who had access to Al Gore's notes, will go to prison for a very long time."

"Yep," Alexus adds joining us on the back patio along with Jadda. "I'm just glad Shelly could plea bargain five years with community service."

"I still love her," Jadda comments, "We wouldn't have succeeded without her, but man, I'm not sure I can ever forgive her."

"Well," Charles suggests, "Try. Family, friends, we should always try to forgive each other, yes?"

"Agreed," she says introspectively.

We all gaze out at the horizon, watching fireworks reflect on the white screen that is Mt. Hood. Time seems to stop. We've been through so much together. "Well," I break the silence, "I, for one, am glad to be alive now. I mean, think about humanity in a few thousand years. It's gonna get *frigid!*"

Climate Scientists Speak trumped.online/jik

The Right Climate Stuff NASA trumped.online/wzl

NASA astronauts web site http://www.therightclimatestuff.com/

Physicist W. Happer, carbon trumped.online/zf6

97% consensus trumped.online/jmy

The Dawn: *The Disruptor-In-Chief*
Year: 2018 May 1 7:56 p.m.

"It's okay Cynthia, we're all here," I say, holding back the tears, her hand in mine. "Do you think she can hear me?"

The Dr. replies, "Well, no one knows really, but I have seen enough to believe they do."

Kathy comes forward, takes her other hand, "Cynthia, when you see a light, let go. It will be okay."

Then Malik steps up, "I made this for you, it's a picture of us, see? We're riding bikes together. Smiling. You have on a big sun hat."

He puts the picture on her chest. Then Michelle takes her hand from me, "So, I know you're probably scared. I've spent most of my life in fear. But I'm not afraid anymore. And much of that is due to you. You have faced this time with so much dignity. So much grace. Thank you, Cynthia. Thank you."

"It's time," the Dr. Says. Everyone gathers close. In moments she takes her last breath.

I'm reminded of my favorite Dr. Seuss quote: *Don't cry because it's over, smile because it happened.*

Silence. Silence.

As we leave the facility, I'm filled with a kaleidoscope of emotions - sadness, joy, but mostly gratitude. Alexus and I reconvene at Charles' house. "Charles," I say looking into his eyes standing out on the patio overlooking the pool and toward the mountains, "There's just no way I can thank you. All that I've been through, in this last year, it was you."

He smiles, "And Trump, don't forget credit where credit is due."

"True."

"Like you have said," Alexus adds, "He's a disruptor. He's the one that pushed you to question."

Charles agrees, "I was just there to pick up the pieces."

"And, believe it or not, for the first time I might even be glad he's president."

"Let me guess, things like Kim Jun Un, Little Rocket Man, might be coming to some semblance of sanity," Charles states.

"Yes. And taxes lowered, regulations reduced, lowest unemployment in twenty years, the backwards Iran deal is over, hostages have been returned, the near elimination of Isis, the U.S. embassy has been moved to Jerusalem, NAFTA has been re-negotiated with Mexico and Canada and given the new name USMCA, he's working to put an end to the criminalization of homosexuality world wide, he's calling China out on their international criminal ways, he has pushed through criminal reform and given those who are diagnosed with terminal illness the, Right To Try; to name just a few things. And then of course the Mueller report exonerating the president from collusion and obstruction."

⊂⊃ Right To Try <u>trumped.online/two</u> ⊂⊃
⊂⊃ End criminal homosexuality <u>trumped.online/ihd</u> ⊂⊃

"Yes, that was a crock of 'Schiff' from the very beginning. Probably the single greatest hoax and waste of time and money in American political history."

"What? A Crock of Schiff? *Nice one.* It is astounding to watch these people in denial, struggling with their cognitive dissonance. Some still can't accept the findings after four *separate investigations.* The Mueller investigation alone lasted 675 days, interviewed nearly fifty witnesses, had nineteen lawyers that were mostly democrats. In fact, one once worked for the Clinton Foundation. They issued more than 2800 subpoenas, executed 500 search warrants, 34 people and three companies were indicted on 199 charges and they spent well over 50 million of our dollars. Under all that scrutiny; no collusion and no obstruction charges."

"It's not the end. They'er going to try anything to impeach him."

"You think so, why? Just vote for God's sake."

"They'er afraid they can't beat him at the polls, so impeach."

⊞ Collusion Delusion Barry Dennis <u>trumped.online/jdulfv</u> ⊞

"Wow, you're probably right. But after all the investigations, how could anyone not accept the findings and just be happy that our president was never a Russian agent?"

Charles answers my rhetorical question, "A rock-hard paradigm, fashioned by unquestioned confirmation bias."

"Yep,"Alexus confirms, "And there's more good stuff on North Korea. American prisoners are being released now. Kim Jong Un and President Moon are allowing the reunification of families broken apart by their endless war. The two of them are vying to be hosts of the 2032 Olympics after signing a landmark peace agreement."

"That's a start," Charles says, looking out upon the view, "It's a beautiful world. Let's hope it works. May peace prevail."

"Oh, and one more thing you and Trump deserve credit for. My commitment to get to the bottom of this whole climate change issue. I'm pretty obsessed. I'm going to watch the satellite data and study all historical information on climate available. I will get to the bottom of it.

"I'm sure you will," Charles says, nodding. "I wonder what you will find." He continues gazing out at the city. His soft, barely perceptible smile is taunting me.

"What. What is it?"

"#WalkAway?"

"I don't think so."

"Okay," he says shrugging his shoulders.

Alexus and I say our goodbyes. We stop by Janet and Kathy's place to pick up the kids. They're full of questions. Malik starts in, "Um, Daddy, why did Trump mess up play dough, some of it?"

Alexus and I look at each other, dismayed. "Huh? I don't know what you're talking about, sweetheart."

Shanice insists, "Daddy, Mommy's upset. She says Trump messed up play dough! Why? That happened to me once. Tyler, at school, messed up my play dough. And I didn't like it?"

"Yeah." Malik agrees. "We were upstairs playing, and Mommy and Janet were mad, talking about it. Trump messed up Angry Magurkles play dough, some of it!"

Then Alexus giggles and shakes her head.

"What? What is it?" I ask.

"Oh my gosh," Alexus continues, trying to hold back the laughter. "I think they mean NATO! I think they are saying Trump messed up Angela Merkel's NATO, summit!"

Nato trumped.online/qq4

"Wow, okay… " I answer, my face a bit contorted from the combination of their innocence and continued amazement around my ex-wife's anger. "Kids, Trump is part of a, well, a group of friends who promised to help protect each other; mostly from Russia. They call their group of friends, NATO."

"OHHHH," Malik says. "But why did he upset his friend's NATO?"

"Well, you know when your friends make promises to you? And sometimes they break those promises?"

Malik's eyes bug out, "Yeah. Remember when Ron said he would meet me at the park, and we went and waited for like, ever, and he never came?!"

"I remember that."

"He promised," Malik says showing his disappointment.

"Well, that's what Angela Merkel did to President Trump and everyone else in NATO. She made a very important promise, but she did not keep it. And, she gave *a lot* of money to Russia."

"But," Shanice inquires, "I thought NATO was supposed to protect against Russia."

"It is. That's why Trump messed up Angry Magurkles, play dough. Some of it!" I say lightly. "He's trying to get her and every one of their friends in NATO to keep their promises."

"So, why is Mommy so mad?"

"She has what's called TDS; *Trump Derangement Syndrome.* When Hillary lost the election, a lot of people went a little crazy."

"You did! I remember," Malik assures me.

"You're right. I did." I nod, glancing at Alexus who smiles. "But, I got better."

We arrive home and tuck the kids into bed. Then Alexus and I reconvene for a cup of tea in the dining room. We sit down as she pulls out her iPhone, points it at me and says, "Go."

"Go what?"

"Tell your story, go."

"No way. You mean #WALKAWAY? *NO WAY!"*

"Come on. People need to hear your story. You *have* walked away. Stop being in denial!"

I take a deep breath. Close my eyes. Gather my thoughts, and, looking straight into the camera, "I can't believe I'm making one of these videos. But like so many of you, I was once, well, naïve. When Trump won, I believed it was Armageddon. But then I met the most extraordinary guy. The Guy In The Orange Tent…"

⮑ My #WALKAWAY trumped.online/jkv ⮑

Chapter 28 The Future: *The New Data*
Year: 2048 July 5 6:17 a.m.

It's one of those dreams that incorporate reality. So tired you weave in external stimuli. In this case, it's my house system trying to wake me. I have it set on, *Do Not Disturb.* There are only two people who can contact me in this setting, Alexus, and Charles. I'm dreaming that Alexus and I are splitting a huge chocolate/peanut butter Sunday. It's a reoccurring dream since I gave up sugar, trying to lose a few pounds. In my dream, I can hear Siri saying, *Wake up Marcus, Wake up. Emergency.* Instead of waking I reply, *No…you can't have any.* Finally, Alexus shakes me to consciousness.

"Marcus, wake up!"

"Ah, what's happening?" I react, dazed and confused.

Siri announces with that female British accent I never got around to changing, "It's Charles. Must be important. Would you like to take the call?"

"Okay, okay…Charles, what's so important it can't wait till civilized hours?"

"Get over here now. NOW! You know that really, really big thing I've been working on?"

"Yeah, the thing you keep saying I'm not ready for?"

"Yeah, that's it. Well. I've done it! It works."

"What works?"

"IT!"

"IT, what?"

"Get over here. I think you're ready now. And there's no time to lose. You've got to see the data."

"Huh?"

"Yeah. It's bigger than the whole G.P. debacle."

"Nothing is bigger than the whole G.P. debacle."

"Yes, *this is*. Get over here."

I leap in my old trusty Ford, "Freedom, to Charles' house."

"Should I step on it?"

"All the way to the floor…"

****

Climate, Princeton University trumped.online/3ub
The Dearth of Carbon trumped.online/xl4
More CO2 is a good? trumped.online/xer
Climate Scientist Dr. Easterbrook http://trumped.online/ctp
Manipulated temperatures trumped.online/lqw
Lecture, climate and sea level rise trumped.online/fxs)
Drain the climate swamp trumped.online/1ra

MOST Scientists say climate change not bad trumped.online/fi2

Dr. Willie Soon Arctic Ice trumped.online/7ov
Polar bears thriving trumped.online/cdx
Myths of renewables trumped.online/anf
Inconvenient facts \trumped.online/gw8
Maldives Mystery trumped.online/81w

Planet Earth: Trumped
Index

Web site: planetearthtrumped.com

Chapter 4 **The Dawn: *Catholics For Trump***
      Year: 2017 January 9 5:45 p.m.

Anderson Cooper/Trump, handicapped trumped.online/l9m
CNN on Melania's shoes trumped.online/2wb
CNN on Trump's scoops trumped.online/bhe

Handicapped reporter, Trump truth trumped.online/zy4
Handicapped reporter, truth 2   http://trumped.online/w9k

Clinton ad using the handicapped lie trumped.online/oO2

Chapter 6 **The Future: *Bill Nye the Pseudo-Science Guy***
      Year: 2047 February 1 4:29 p.m.

Bill Nye's sex junk trumped.online/8ik

Chapter 7 **The Dawn: *The Victim***
      Year: 2017 January 21 7:01 a.m.

Homeless undercover trumped.online/t1w
Homeless young woman trumped.online/zrz
Homeless college student trumped.online/tm4
Homeless young lady trumped.online/y3y

Indian beggars crisis, trumped.online/ry4

California worst quality of life trumped.online/skw
Portland homelessness trumped.online/lc2
Bud Clark Commons trumped.online/k4b

Minimum wage trumped.online/q7g
Minimum wage trumped.online/4zy
Joe Rogan wages trumped.online/yv9

Rhode Island program, trumped.online/ov1

Chapter 8 **The Future: Al Gore**

Year: 2047 February 1 6:17 p.m.

Al Gore on David Letterman trumped.online/ge0

Paris riots trumped.online/y66

BBC Trump ends Paris accord trumped.online/p7f

Chapter 8   The Dawn: *The Riddle of Ritalin*
Year: 2017 January 22 2:46 p.m.

CNN Black Hole conspiracy trumped.online/ar7

Martin Luther King bust truth trumped.online/wow

Chapter 9   The Dawn: *ADHD*
Year: 2017 January 22 11:03 p.m.

Trump Derangement, Blacks perspective trumped.online/z4v

Girls and boys learning styles trumped.online/vwo
David Katz ADHD versus recess trumped.online/wt0

Chapter 10   *The Future: Dr. Judith Curry*
Year: 2047 February 1 7:20 p.m.

Climate Scientist Dr. Judith Curry trumped.online/4rm
Climate Scientist Dr. Judith Curry trumped.online/a9r

Chapter 10   The Dawn: *Hate Speech and John McEnroe*
Year: 2017 January 23 8:15 p.m.

Micheal Moore, Sean Pen trumped.online/jxt
Venezuela inflation trumped.online/5c5
Brazil Socialism trumped.online/1ht
Long hall socialism trumped.online/6pc
Bernie Sanders Socialism work trumped.online/atj

**Chapter 11   The Future: *The Holocene Period*
Year: 2047 February 9 7:56 p.m.**

**Chapter 11   The Dawn: *The Berkeley Riots*
Year: 2017 February 1 7:30 p.m.**

**Chapter 12   The Future: *Truth Is Complicated*
Year: 2047 February 14 7:30 p.m.**

**Chapter 12   The Dawn: *Russia Collusion, Sanctuary Cities*
Year: 2017 February 17 7:39 a.m.**

Barry Dennis, Hillary or Trump? trumped.online/f6g
Hillary Clinton, What Happened? trumped.online/yfu
"Trump Colluded with Russia" trumped.online/naw
Hillary's fake dossier trumped.online/dve
Barry Dennis, Collusion Delusion trumped.online/jdulfv)

Interview, Sanctuary City Law trumped.online/4h3
Greetings from a sanctuary city trumped.online/vte

Chapter 13   **The Future: *Automation, The Path***
                   Year: 2047 February 15 5:46 a.m.

Miracle of Our Lady of Guadalupe trumped.online/1fc
Donnie D. of MSNCB, all Nazis trumped.online/5eq
CNN Maxine Waters trumped.online/2cz
Samantha Bee, feckless cunt, CNN trumped.online/cb7
Time Magazine, The Lie trumped.online/rm0
CNN interview Border patrol agent trumped.online/1p
CNN interviews Baldwin, hypocrisy! trumped.online/0
Chavez, Pragur U. trumped.online/rn8
Dr. Steve Pinker trumped.online/oms

Chapter 13   **The Dawn: *Virtue Signaling, The One Percent, Welfare***
                   Year: 2017 February 17 7:52 a.m.

Head Start truth trumped.online/tt8
CNN Head Start trumped.online/8pq
Black Intellectual Sowell on poverty trumped.online/ew2
White Intellectual Friedman on poverty trumped.online/w1h
Maxine Waters house trumped.online/8lh
Maxine Waters district trumped.online/lma
Black women explains reparations trumped.online/pxp

Chapter 14   **The Dawn: *DDT, The Wage Gap***
                   Year: 2017 March 4 7:00 a.m.

Wage Gap, Professor Sommers trumped.online/t8r
Pay gap, President Obama, trumped.online/gwk
Pay gap revealed trumped.online/5i1
James Damore under protest trumped.online/z9l
Googles pay gap trumped.online/w83

Lady in green scream https://youtu.be/wDYNVH0U3cs

Chapter 15   **The Dawn: *People of Color, White Guilt and Tribal America*
Year: 2017 March 4 7:33 a.m.**

Obama's reparation status trumped.online/byg
N.Y. Governor Cuomo, trumped.online/7sz

Brutality, Native American history trumped.online/uos
P.C. Michael Douglass, Morgan Freeman, trumped.online/c4f

Morgan Freeman, Black History trumped.online/3wa
Unhyphenated America trumped.online/yc3
Jackson, Sharpton's racism trumped.online/lfk

Chapter 16   **The Future: First Woman President, *AOC*
Year: 2028 December 4 7:12 p.m.**

AOC's "I'm a radical" statement trumped.online/96l
South Park micro aggressions trumped.online/5169b
politically correct gender pronouns! trumped.online/z9o
Is Gender a social construct? trumped.online/b12
Germany No-Go zones! trumped.online/b4u
AOC actual interview trumped.online/pnb
CNN interviews AOC trumped.online/9t1
Socialists print money trumped.online/tdp
Ocasio-Cortez "Im the boss" trumped.online/xuv
Ocasio-Cortez's Amazon deal trumped.online/tkd
Capitalism and Socialism by Tim Pool trumped.online/hz5

Swedish men banned from festivals trumped.online/dr1
Former Lebanese, Brigitte Gabriel trumped.online/660
Former Muslim, Aayan Hirsi Ali trumped.online/3gb
Brigitte Gabriel life story trumped.online/eoa

Debate: Is Islam a Religion of Peace? trumped.online/vzr
bikers knifed to death by Islamists trumped.online/qwt

Fear of Leaving Islam trumped.online/32y
Muslim Refugee issue trumped.online/drz

Islam Inbreeding trumped.online/ap8

Muslims Threaten the Muslim speakers, trumped.online/lxm

Antoine Leiris letter to his wife's killers, trumped.online/u12

Multiculturalism Thomas Sowell trumped.online/ld9

Scottish man on multiculturalism trumped.online/qca

Indian Perspective trumped.online/fhf

A warning trumped.online/iyf

Economist Romina Boccia, socialism trumped.online/9ky

Chapter 16   The Dawn: *The First Slave Owner*
Year: 2017 March 4 7:33 a.m.

Anthony Johnson, first slave owner? trumped.online/715f7

True history of slavery trumped.online/bct

CNN, Vijay Jojo Chokal-Ingam trumped.online/mc7

black man on racism trumped.online/b8h

Air traffic controllers questionnaire trumped.online/8fj

Morgan Freeman, Don Lemon trumped.online/yc1

Brookings Institution trumped.online/ynu

History of slavery trumped.online/snh

Bill Maher with Muslim Hirsi Ali trumped.online/o99

Chapter 17   The Dawn: *James Madison, Tom Paine*
Year: 2017 April 14, Good Friday 9:46 a.m.

Helpers High trumped.online/xlv

Power of Giving trumped.online/37y

Chapter 20   The Dawn: *31,487 Scientists agree*
Year: 2017 June 1 11:13 a.m.

Obama on climate change trumped.online/xx3

Thatcher on fossil fuels/nuclear power trumped.online/vw7

        31,487 scientists trumped.online/8if
     Are electric cars green? trumped.online/o7t
     Adam Ruins Everything cars trumped.online/3ic

     Climate conference interview trumped.online/7od
     Are climate models flawed? trumped.online/2ai

        Germany and Coal trumped.online/b8z
     Germany's Coal addiction trumped.online/kvp
     Follow the climate money trumped.online/l9q
     Al Gore Busted trumped.online/lh8
     Scott Adams Nuclear trumped.online/k4c

Chapter 21   The Future: *Faux-cahontas*
Year: 2047 April 26, Good Friday 7:59 p.m.

     Elizabeth Warren lie trumped.online/8iz

Chapter 21   The Dawn: *Life or Choice?*
Year: 2017 June 2 8:13 a.m.

     God bless abortions trumped.online/vgm
     Abortion survivor trumped.online/8bh

Chapter 22   The Future: *4,000 Feet Above Sea Level*
Year: 2047 April 28, Easter 10:17 a.m.

     Greenpeace founder drops out trumped.online/xgb

Chapter 22   The Dawn: *Charlottesville Riot, Transgenders*
Year: 2017 August 15 6:30 p.m.

     Trump chew toy trumped.online/zvm
     Interview on Charlottesville trumped.online/45u
     Scott Adams: Trump never said it trumped.online/ih9

     Evidence Antifa might be guilty trumped.online/x5t
     Charlottesville, Black's perspectives trumped.online/8k0
     The KKK and America trumped.online/vx2

Chapter 23   The Future: *iMind Implant*
Year: 2047 May 4 5:49 p.m.

Chapter 23   The Dawn: *Bleach Bit, Clinton Foundation*
Year: 2017 August 16th 4:30 pm

Chapter 25   The Future: Justin Bieber
Year: 2047 May 4 7:39 p.m.

Chapter 25   The Dawn: *Crypto Currency*
Year: 2018 January 1 11 a.m.

Chapter 26   The Future: *Fox News, Starbucks*

Year: 2047 May 4 7:49 p.m.

Starbucks sensitivity training trumped.online/fd1

Chapter 26   **The Dawn: *Shit Hole Countries*
Year: 2018 January 7 6:43 p.m.**

IQ Sam Harris trumped.online/d4b
Larry Elder smashes it trumped.online/5cv

Thomas Sowell on welfare trumped.online/5rk
Lil' Wayne rapper, racism and white cops trumped.online/5at

Sharm Sharma, Intersectionality trumped.online/sdu
BLM gone amuck trumped.online/gyl
BLM Mission and Bernie Sanders trumped.online/6gl

Australia, *It's not okay to be white* trumped.online/qio
CNN accuses black man of white privilege trumped.online/nne

Covington boys Ben Shapiro trumped.online/nf3
Covington boys truth, in15 minutes trumped.online/97o

Chris Rock Live trumped.online/c8b
CNN Jussie Smollett trumped.online/jko
Jussie Smollett case trumped.online/mt1
Kevins Corner Smollett trumped.online/q1b

Chapter 27   **The Future: *President Shapiro*
Year: 2047 July 4 9:30 p.m.**

Climate Scientists Speak trumped.online/jik
The Right Climate Stuff NASA trumped.online/wzl
NASA astronauts web site http://www.therightclimatestuff.com/
Physicist W. Happer, carbon trumped.online/zf6
97% consensus trumped.online/jmy

Chapter 27   The Dawn: *The Disruptor-In-Chief*
                Year: 2018 May 1 7:56 p.m.

Right To Try trumped.online/two
End criminal homosexuality trumped.online/ihd
Collusion Delusion Barry Dennis trumped.online/jdulfv

Nato trumped.online/qq4
My #WALKAWAY trumped.online/jkv

Chapter 28   The Future: *The New Data*
                Year: 2048 July 5 6:17 a.m.

My #WALKAWAY trumped.online/jkv

Climate, Princeton University trumped.online/3ub
The Dearth of Carbon trumped.online/xl4
More CO2 is a good? trumped.online/xer
Climate Scientist Dr. Easterbrook http://trumped.online/ctp
Manipulated temperatures trumped.online/lqw
Lecture, climate and sea level rise trumped.online/fxs)
Drain the climate swamp trumped.online/1ra
MOST Scientists, climate change not bad trumped.online/fi2
Dr. Willie Soon Arctic Ice trumped.online/7ov
Polar bears thriving trumped.online/cdx
Myths of renewables trumped.online/anf
Inconvenient facts \trumped.online/gw8
Maldives Mystery trumped.online/81w

ACKNOWLEDGMENTS

Thank you, Christi, for your love, support, editing, and the awareness of supercluster. Thanks Mom and Dad for all the support, love, and feedback. Thanks John Maxwell Taylor and Emily Taylor for the inspiration to keep going. Thanks Gilion Dumas for the willingness to jump in and be a part of the genesis of this project. Thanks Christopher Hall for feedback and support. Thanks Randy Lanford for editing.

I want to thank the following for being truly brave, honorable human beings willing to seek and speak the deepest truths they can unearth and for being unafraid of hard and often baseless criticism. Maybe most of all, for being willing to change when truth, real facts, are presented that prove them wrong. That's rare and needed. Like these individuals, may we all be willing to recognize our own confirmation bias and conquer our cognitive dissonance.

Adam Carolla
Tucker Carlson
Alan Dershowitz
Alex Epstein
Ayaan Hirsi Ali
Ben Shapiro
Bill Maher
Bret Weinstein
Brigitte Gabriel
Candace Owens
Christina Hoff -
Sommers
Coleman Hughes
Tim Pool
Dan Bongino
Dave Rubin
Dinesh D'Souza
Mark Levin
John Coleman

Eric Weinstein
Gavin McInnes
Greg Gutfeld
Tony Heller
James Damore
Janice Fiamengo
Jason Whitlock
Joe Rogan
Prof. Jordan
Peterson
Dr. Judith Curry
Prof. William
Happer
Katie Hopkins
Larry Elder
Milo Yiannopoulos
Onkar Ghate
Mark Levin

Patrick Moore
Paul Joseph Watson
Sam Harris
Scott Adams
Some Black Guy
(Dave Pilot)
Steven Pinker
Thomas Sowell
Tommy Robinson
Brandon Straka
Tommy Sotomayer
Dennis Pragur
Victor Davis
Hanson
Willie Soon